Candlestickmaker

By
Reid Matthias

ISBN paperback: 978-0-6450472-4-0
　　　　ebook: 978-0-6450472-5-7

This edition first published by A 13 in November 2021

Typesetting by Ben Morton

Publication assistance from Immortalise

Front cover Photo by Thomas Lipke on Unsplash

Back cover Photo by Moodywalk on Unsplash

For my wife Christine. Life is infinitely more beautiful because you are in it.

And for my daughters, Elsa, Josephine and Greta – no greater gift to a father. Thank you for your support, your laughter and creativity.

Acknowledgements

Candlestickmaker, like its predecessors, *Butcher* and *Baker*, is a work of fiction. Some of the place names are real, but Amicable is not. Although its geography and layout may seem familiar, at least to many who live in small Iowa towns, Amicable is a figment of my memory. It is situated nowhere near the Boondocks and not even close to Gravity. All characters are composites and generous exaggerations of my imagination, but any bearing more than a passing resemblance to real life people is unintentional, albeit welcomed. I have borrowed surnames and Christian names from people I have encountered throughout my travels - good and lovely people - and I hope that you who read these pages can connect with them as I have.

Some have asked why the Amicable Circle books are so different in theme and mood. My only answer is this: Each chapter of life is different than the last. To explore all emotions, all thoughts and feelings and 'what if's' is to categorically give meaning to all of life's joys and sorrows. For Amicableans everywhere, we resonate with the things that most disturb us (both positively and negatively).

A special thanks to my incredible wife Christine who continues to amaze me with the generosity of her joy at reading these books. As she has read and reread the Amicable Circle, her editing skills and eye for details have been extraordinary. To Elsa, Josephine and Greta, my daughters and constant source of love and amusement, thank you for pushing these Amicableans onto the page. Thanks, also, to Debbie Gortowski who highlighted the technical aspects in the medical field.

Prologue

My Dearest Reader,

Two years have passed.

It's hard to explain the misgivings I feel as time, the emperor of illusions, rushes past me, smiling and waving. There is nothing I can do to stop it, much less slow it down. It is a resource that feels... how shall I write it? Endless?... yet it is not. No, not in the least.

It is much more fun to write of frivolous things. Frivolity, though, is an expensive gift because it costs time. Grief's price is greater. More than just time; it requires a mortgage on our souls. When we lose someone, especially someone close to us, we draw near to the trembling line of spiritual foreclosure.

I am nearing bankruptcy.

I should say we, we Amicableans, have lost someone dear to us, and now it often feels like we are lost. Sometimes at night we, John and I, walk down Amicable's Main Street and nothing appears to have changed, yet everything has. The lights are dimmer, the trees are less green, the sun has lost some of its warmth. This is natural with loss, but I don't like it at all.

At the end of every walk, we stop by the cemetery. Across the graves, decorating headstones, are flowers and mementos. They are painful reminders of what used to be. John and I stop at the memorial. We pause and breathe in silence. I know that as we stand there, his hand in mine, a simple symbol of life's brevity, we remember. The memorial is losing its shape, but the memory is painful. What is harder for John and me – and for Amicable – is that the fading pain represents the struggle that life must go on. We don't always want to go on.

As life moves forward, regret plays a significant and (sometimes) helpful role. It shapes how we look at the river ahead of us. Regret plots a course that hopefully brings us to the precipice of the falls with a sense of magnificent wonder. Regret allows us to enter the mystery of life and death; as we look back, we recognize that we do have some control over some things.

We can choose how we want to live.

1

Candlestickmaker

This will be the hardest story yet. Together we have come far, you and I, from laughter to rage, adultery to adoration. Perhaps you have shed tears because of these people who are indelibly imprinted on my life. But, we have a few more tears to cry. As I write this missive, musings on the river of time, I realize the brevity and how few breaths we are actually given.

When you finish reading all that has been written, close the book, turn off your computer, dump the remnants of your coffee into the sink and find every person that you love and hug them. Remind them that they are what makes your life meaningful.

This is our only defense against mortality.

Chapter 1.

Life is funny.

On a warm summer's afternoon, 12:59 to be exact, seven women arrived outside an exercise studio at the northern end of Amicable's Main Street. Normally, at least two, maybe three of the women, depending on their need to finish *The Bold and the Beautiful*, would be late, but not today. No way, not today. Each of them had received a personal invitation that Carley's X-Er-Size studio would look quite different.

When Leona arrived, she caught Linda looking through the plate glass window in the front. Her hands were cupped on the darkened glass. Jeannie stood beside Linda copying her, but it appeared as if their inquisitiveness had been blocked.

"What's going on?" Leona asked.

Linda backed away from the window. "I'll tell you what's going on." She pointed inside the building. "I got this phone call from Carley, something about the newest fad – a craze – sweeping all the big towns." She frowned. "Supposedly even Clancy."

"What is it?"

"That's just it: we can't see. She's put up dividers between the window and whatever the crazy fad is."

Linda turned back to find the other women, Anne Johnson included (her walker was pushed to the side), all now standing with their foreheads pressed against the glass.

"Ladies," Linda stamped her foot, "I need your attention."

Five faces turned towards Linda whose hands were like stanchions on her hips. "What?" Angela Chandler responded.

"Does anybody know what's going on?"

Penny's forehead had a red mark in the middle from where she had pushed it against the window. "No, no more than you."

None of the women liked to be kept in the dark about anything. Peevishly, Linda checked her watch and stamped her foot again. "Well, I hope she opens the door soon so we can get this show on the…"

At that moment, the door to X-Er-Size was thrown open and a round, jolly face, bright with happiness, appeared. Carley stepped out and closed the door behind her, then clapped her hands daintily.

"Oooh, I'm so glad you could come. So excited!"

"All right, Carley, what's this all about?"

Carley held up her hands in front of her. "Okay, so, as we have our session today, I want all of you to keep an open mind. This may be uncomfortable for some of you."

"Jeepers, Carley," Anne had sat down on her walker's seat, "we're not going to do any of that fancy yoga stuff, are we? I can barely get out of bed the way it is."

"Pilates," Jeannie said, but pronounced it like *pirates*.

"What?"

"It's pi-lah-tees, Jeannie," Leona corrected.

"Par doh de nem wua," Jeannie tossed her hair.

"Now," Carley began again, "if you'll all follow me." She opened the door and allowed the women to file in behind her. Bouncing with happiness, she guided them around the makeshift barriers to the main exercise area. Dimmed lights illuminated a stage which held can-do-it posters and shelving for towels. On the stage though…

"What are those?" Donna asked.

Carley curled her fingers in front of her mouth and giggled happily. "Poles!"

"What for?"

"Dancing. Lots of dancing."

Leona approached the parquet floor. "These are stripper poles, aren't they?"

Carley's eyebrows raised and she held up her hands. "Like I said outside, keep an open mind."

"We're going to practice being strippers?" Anne Johnson stated. Her almost ninety-year-old body was unsure of how stripper poles were going to help her fitness.

"It's the latest thing. Women all over the world are learning how to twirl and spin." Carley demonstrated, almost falling over on the second revolution. "Empowerment, ladies!" Breathing heavily, Carley unsteadily came to rest in front of them.

"What's wrong with what we were doing before?" Connie touched one of the poles as if it were electrified.

"Nothing! Nothing! But these," Carley tapped it, "will build our upper body and core strength. In months, we'll be fit and fighting ready."

"For stripping?" Jeannie asked.

"No, sillies, for life." Carley brought Donna to one of the poles. "Now watch. Put your hands like so," one above the other two feet apart, "and then lift your body off the ground." Carley exerted herself, grunting with effort. With a short jump, she left the floor and then landed again. Turning towards the women, she smiled. "See, it's easy."

"You don't really know what you're doing, do you?" Angela asked with arms crossed.

Sheepishly, Carly shrugged. "Just have to build some core strength first."

"I can't believe I missed the last ten minutes of B & B so I can practice learning how to be a stripper for my husband in the nursing home." Anne shook her head.

"He might like the new spice," Leona waggled her eyebrows.

"Oh for Pete's…"

"Well," Linda said, "we might as well give it a try while we're here."

Carley smiled. "Now, let's do some stretching."

For the next thirty minutes, the Monday morning X-Er-Size crew did five-second planks, pseudo crunches, a series of sit ups and stationary bikes. At the end of it, sweating and tired, the women gathered together on stools, water bottles in hand, sipping furiously. This was the hardest they'd worked in years.

"Good job, ladies!" Carley encouraged, while chugging water.

Linda dried her brow and neck. "Speaking of a good job, did you hear what happened at Lake Ikmakota this weekend?"

Donna's eyes lit up. "Do tell."

"Well," Linda stretched out the word, "supposedly there was a bachelorette party on one side of the lake while on the other, the boys got together."

"Is this Derek and Tracy's parties?"

"Yup." Linda's 'p' popped loudly.

"And?" Penny asked.

Linda looked at Connie. "Your daughter was there. Did she mention any details?"

Connie shook her head. "No, but according to Carrie Ann, there was some midnight swimming involved."

The ladies tittered. "And," Connie continued, "even Reverend Deakins was there."

"Oooh…"

"I'm sure he was there only to chaperone the twins," Penny said.

"I'm sure," Linda responded, unsurely.

"According to Carrie Ann, the boys drove a boat over just after midnight and they were thrashing around in the water, naked as jaybirds."

"When is that wedding again?" Donna asked.

"Next year sometime," Connie said. "Gee, probably next October."

"That's a long time before the wedding."

Connie shrugged. "You know kids these days. Any reason for a party."

"It seems like Butcher and Rhonda and Reverend Deakins and Leslie are a little mature for these kinds of things."

"Oh, come on, ladies, you're never too old for a good bachelorette party."

They glanced around the room. Their faces reflected in the mirrors on the wall. "That's crazy talk, Connie," Penny said.

Connie smiled. "It's not the only wedding coming up."

All eyes focussed on Connie Redman, whose Cheshire Cat-like smile appeared from nowhere.

Butcher sat in his office chair staring over the head of his patient. Unconsciously, he clicked the pen, *click, unclick, click, unclick*, until David Larson turned to him. "Do you mind, Butcher? I'm tryin' to tell my story."

Apologizing, Butcher motioned with his hands for David to continue. Butcher, of course, could read David's entire story of his weekend; the well-intentioned thoughts of helping around the house, taking his kids fishing, but time devolved into sloth. While David blathered his way through his bad choices, Butcher thought back to the bachelor party. At midnight, John Deakins, at the request of the groom-to-be, loaded the men into the boat to make the trip across Lake Ikmakota. As they rode, the moonlight glittered over the water and the scented breeze blew through their hair. Derek, Nash and Stedman were all tipsy and happy, while John and Butcher, as the 'mature' statesmen of the party, remained semi-sober.

When they arrived at the girls' cabin, the women were already in the water. For some reason, Naida had decided a midnight swim was a good idea.

After disembarking from the boat, the girls called out to the boys. Stedman was the only one without a partner: Summer, his girlfriend, had scheduled a trip to Sioux City for the weekend. The girls motioned for the boys to enter the water. Butcher shook his head as Rhonda used her finger to motion him into the water.

She emerged like a Siren. Her swimsuit hugged her curves. Although she'd given birth twice, her body was still tall and lithe. Butcher smiled and shook his head again. "No way. There is absolutely no desire in any cell of my body that wants to get into that frigid water."

Before he could finish the sentence, Rhonda tugged his arm. Lifting his shirt over his head, Rhonda slapped his stomach, which caused him to *ooof,* and then she unbuckled his pants. As his pants dropped around his knees, he tripped and fell to the ground. Rhonda laughed and jumped on top of him. Her freezing body hit him like a bucket of ice and he shouted.

Once freed from his clothes, Butcher sat up. "Do you really think this is a good idea?"

"Of course not," she smirked, "but now that we're parents, we let too many bad ideas pass us by." She tapped his chest. "Come on, let's get this over with." She pulled him forcefully into the water. On the way in, Butcher noticed Stedman's eyes flick over his wife's body.

Butcher hoped he was imagining it.

As he allowed himself to be dragged under the water, his skin felt as if it was being pricked by a thousand needles taking his breath away. Stifling a curse, he waited for his body's thermostat to level out. Rhonda pulled him deeper into the swimming area. Butcher cringed as the lake's muddy bottom squished between his toes. "That's disgusting."

Rhonda squeezed his hand. "People pay good money to wipe that stuff on their faces."

Because the Jensen's were taller than everyone else, they found a place to stand at a distance. Rhonda floated next to him and then moved in behind him. The sensuality of the moment caused Butcher to shiver. As the small waves splashed over his neck, he felt a sense of euphoria. While the Jensens' enjoyed closeness, the rest of the revellers splashed in the shallows.

Like a tetherball circling a pole, Rhonda swam in diminishing circles closer and closer to her husband. When she had exhausted her treading abilities, she latched onto him from behind. She pressed into his back; he could feel the length of her encircle his waist and her voice whispered into his ear. "When was the last time we did this?"

"What, you mean a midnight swim with yahoos?" he pointed at the rest of them.

"No, silly, just to be in the water together."

Butcher was struggling to put a sentence together. "I... well, probably at least a couple of years."

Rhonda's shivering body pulled him in closer still. "Why do we wait so long to do extraordinary things?"

"I don't know, hon. Maybe we just get used to living and then one day we wake up and all the spontaneity is gone."

Rhonda laughed and bit his ear playfully. "Not anymore."

Unfortunately, Butcher's ear was dripping with algae. Rhonda began to spit out the putrid tasting mixture. Laughing, she pushed herself from Butcher.

"To be continued?" he asked.

"After the weekend," she shouted over her shoulder as she swam back to shore.

Butcher rolled his eyes and squished through the mud following her. After he dried off, he wondered how long it would take for feeling to come back to his toes.

Chapter 2.

They had met the first day of college. From the beginning, they had been roommates. Demetrius wasn't sure whether it was because they had similar interests or attributes, and by attributes, he meant that they were the same skin color. After the first days of classes, Demetrius was aware that most young African Americans did not attend small colleges in Iowa. Mid-America University seemed to be a natural progression for Demetrius, though. From small town to small college, not too far away from Amicable. For some, this seemed to be the far side of the moon.

This was how it was for his roommate, Olaudah Equiano. Mid-America had been Olaudah's last choice. He had wanted to play football for a Division I school; his size and athletic ability were perfect, but his abilities to stay out of trouble, well…

On that first day of their freshman year, Demetrius pushed the door open to his dorm room. Olaudah sat at his desk chair in his shorts and nothing else. Angela, Demetrius' mother, had blushed and excused herself quickly, while Demetrius stood outside the door looking at the number to make sure he was in the right room.

"Holy crap," Ola said at their first meeting, "you're a big sucker."

"You're not so small yourself." Demetrius remained in the hallway.

"You might as well come in. This will be your home too." Ola smiled.

"Thanks." Demetrius ducked his head to enter the room and neared his roommate. "Demetrius Chandler."

"Olaudah Equiano."

"That's a cool name," Demetrius said.

Ola flashed a million dollar smile. "I'll tell you all about it later."

Demetrius' father cleared his throat.

"Oh, this is my dad, and my mom…," he looked out the door again to see his mother pretending to look out the hallway window. "She's a little bit

10

shy, it seems."

Olaudah had flexed his pectoral muscles back and forth and smirked.

When Demetrius' parents had left, which included multiple hugs and tears from Angela, who crushed her enormous son in her arms and explained multiple times how much she (they) would miss him, and not to worry about the chickens because they'd hire a local kid to take care of the chores, and she would text him every night to see if he needed anything, Demetrius smiled at Ola.

"So..."

"Dude, you got white parents? How did that happen?"

Demetrius grinned. "I'm adopted."

"Ya think?" Olaudah reached down for his t-shirt with a large bulldog emblazoned on the front. "Come on. Let me show you around and you can tell me your story."

As they approached the cafeteria, they stopped in the courtyard to appraise the physical closeness of Mid-America. "It's meant to project a certain 'community' feeling - like we're all in this place as one big happy family." He looked over and up at Demetrius and shaded his eyes with his hand. "You might be used to it, Meat, but I'm not used to the lily-white sheen across the campus."

"What do you mean by that?"

"Well, you grew up with white people and their... tightness... and their exuberance to make us black people feel comfortable, like they really want us to feel cared for, but what they're really about is not getting sued for racial discrimination."

"Huh?"

"White people, at least the ones with power, which is most of 'em, they shake your hand and they clear their throats and they call you by name, and they smile, yes sir, they smile through those perfectly polished teeth, not because they think you are anything special, but because they want to keep you in your place. They don't want to argue with you because that would mean you're on equal ground. No, they want to lift you up a little, make you feel all

comfortable so that you never poke your head up and make a fuss. Because..."
he paused his diatribe to lift a finger towards Demetrius, "... if we make a
fuss, the entire world knows about it."

"*Huh.*"

"*Take me, for instance. My real name isn't Olaudah Equiano.*"

"*It's not?*" *Demetrius' eyes raised.*

"*Nope. Not even close. My real name is Ronald Eastmann.*"

Demetrius' eyes widened even farther. "*So what's with Olaudah?*"

"*Shoot, Meat, 'Ronald Eastmann' is not a black man's name. It's a*
white guy, computer nerd kind of name. Nah, when I got here, I wanted a
black man name, one people will remember." *He looked around at the student*
population, which had stopped whatever they were doing to stare at the two
very large black men in the middle of the courtyard. When Olaudah caught
their eyes, he smiled as they tried to avert their eyes.

"*Olaudah Equiano.*" *He looked at Demetrius.* "*Has a nice ring to*
it, don't you think?"

"*Sure,*" *Demetrius agreed,* "*but why would you do that?*"

"*Haven't you been listening? I want people to remember me.*"

"*And they'll call you that because they're afraid of a discrimination*
lawsuit?"

Ola had clapped him on his shoulder. "*Now you got it. Besides, most*
of them don't even know who Olaudah Equiano was."

"*Who was he?*"

"*Come on, Meat. Am I going to have to tell you everything about our*
culture? You've been rotting in small town Iowa too long."

"*No, really, who was Olaudah?*"

"*He was an abolitionist from Africa - way back in the 1700's*
around the time of the Revolutionary War. He lived in England for a while,
but he wanted to help the cause of our people."

"*So you're majoring African American studies?*"

Ola screwed up his face. "*Hell no. I came here to play football.*"

"*What's your major then?*"

Ola smirked. "*Art.*"

Chapter 2.

Demetrius' eyes expressed excitement. "Me too!"

Frowning, Ola paused to look at his new roommate. "But you're not playing football? Art is for athletes. Draw a few pictures and make sure you can memorize the names of white-people art."

"No, no, no. I really am interested in art."

"Uh... okay," Ola said rolling his eyes. He hadn't known that Demetrius had come to Mid-America on a full ride scholarship.

Demetrius started walking again. "I still don't understand why you think people won't remember your name. If you succeed, won't they automatically remember it?"

Ola shook his head. "You've got so much to learn."

As they continued, he noticed pockets of students, some walking around with their parents, mothers hanging onto their children's arms pointing at all the things they remembered from their own college experience.

"Do you want to get something to eat?" Ola asked Demetrius.

"Yeah, okay," Demetrius responded.

After entering the cafeteria and filling their trays with plates of food, they pulled up chairs at a table in the middle. Ola began stuffing food into his mouth. "Are you stressed out?" Demetrius asked.

Ola made a psshing noise as the fork was halfway to his mouth. "You got to be joking. That's a white person disease."

Demetrius snorted. "What do you mean?"

Leaning in, Ola gestured to the tables around them. "You see all these white folk in here?" Demetrius had looked around the room at young men and women with books and phones stretched out in front of them. "In about two weeks, they'll finish eating their lunch, go back to their rooms by themselves and sit on a nice, comfortable cushy sofa that mommy and daddy gave them. They'll cuddle up into their cushy cushions and hold onto their stuffed teddy bears and hug them all gushy gushy tight because mommy and daddy aren't here to give them a little squeeze to tell them, 'It's okay, Lil' Muffin,' mommy and daddy will protect you from the big old nasty wasty world. Did your professor tell you that you had to work hard for the grade?

Those bad professors. I'll call them and tell them that they're making you feel all stressed out inside your little bitty minds.'"

"Do you ever feel sorry for them?"

Ola took a playful swipe at his new friend who ducked out of the way. "I don't ever want to hear those words come out of your mouth again." *He lowered his voice. "We never feel sorry for them. Never. They are children of privilege who will become adults of privilege. Mark my words - those same anxious kids will be carried through life. By the time they're thirty, they'll be on their second marriage, anxious and depressed because life is not a fairy tale and they are neither Prince nor Princess Charming." Ola sat back and folded his arms. "If I say this once, I say this a thousand times. White people don't deserve our pity. They deserve our contempt."*

Demetrius shook his head. "All the white people in Amicable that I know are not like that."

"You don't know white people like I know white people. You know farmers and small townspeople who probably couldn't name on one hand the names of five non-white people." He held up his hands as Demetrius was about to protest. "I know, I know. Your parents are nothing like that."

"I still think we can feel sorry for them." Demetrius chewed morosely.

"I'm just trying to save you grief, Meat." Ola had taken a deep breath and refocused on his meal.

Two years later, Demetrius and Ola were sharing another cafeteria meal; one in the long line of shared meals over the years.

"Hey Meat! How's that new sculpture going?" Ola inquired.

"It's going well." During the first two years of his college experience, two of his sculptures, three of his paintings and one of his drawings had been purchased by regional galleries. The income had been useful and his parents were incredibly proud of him.

Now, in his third year, his newest piece, a sculpture, incorporated the fluid lines of water while contrasting them with the solidness of stone and wood. Roughly four feet in height, his art professor was already touting it a fiscal certainty.

Demetrius looked over Ola's head at a young woman who had entered with a group of girls. Although Demetrius had spoken to Kelly McMurtry multiple times, he had never expressed his feelings. Kelly was African American also - a member of the choir and a competitor on the track and field team. Long and broad, she was muscular and extraordinarily attractive.

Ola looked over his shoulder, smiled and turned back to his roommate. "All right, boy." He pronounced 'boy' as 'boieeey.' "Somebody's got a candy crush on little miss yummy."

"Shut up, Ola."

"I certainly will not," he tapped Demetrius on the arm. "You should go talk to her, maybe show her some of your artwork. You could 'Ghost' it." Ola laughed at the thought of Demetrius sitting behind Kelly as the pottery wheel spun in front of them.

"Very funny."

"I'm serious. Go talk to her."

Demetrius shook his head and grabbed his tray. As he stood, he tripped over the leg of his chair and lost the contents of his tray onto the table next to him.

Olaudah Equiano held onto his sides as if splitting with laughter. Demetrius apologized one last time, picked some food from the hair of a co-ed and moved towards the exit. Demetrius caught Kelly's eyes. She smiled and waved.

Demetrius inwardly cursed and walked to the counter to indecorously deposit his messy tray.

Without looking back, he left the building to attend to his artwork.

As she bent over her shoe, Rhonda checked her watch. 5:30 a.m. This was her favorite time of day. It was her alone time. It gave her a chance to clear her head.

Quietly pulling the door shut behind her, Rhonda stepped out into the brisk morning air. It was early September. Even though it was technically still summer, autumn was charging across the plains from the north; the cool mornings were pushed by the shifting axis of the earth and Amicable was about to prepare for another brawl with winter.

Adjusting her grey stocking cap, she stepped lightly down the porch stairs and moved out into the empty street where her quiet footsteps transformed into the gentle pound of jogging. Starting slow, she moved northwards out of town on the asphalt. The only people who would be out and about this early in the morning were restless farmers anticipating the crop about to be harvested.

As her body loosened, Rhonda's thoughts shifted to Butcher. This, their eighth year of marriage, would be just like the last. The kids had already begun school - J.T. was in first grade now. As she dressed him for the first day of school, she remembered the first time he had excitedly donned a backpack and almost tumbled down the steps to toddle the two hundred yards across the playground to the front doors of the school.

A mile down the road she checked her watch and smiled happily. Rhonda had taken up running the year before and had an idea to run in a half marathon the next summer. Although she had been an athlete in high school, running had never really been her thing. But now as she aged, 'Use it or lose it' was a daily mantra. Butcher had remarked that she would eventually give it up, but she wanted to prove him wrong.

As she ran, a set of questions skipped in her mind like a scratched record: Is life in Amicable everything that I dreamed of? What do I like? *Well, there's the serenity of the nights, warm summer breezes and fireflies, the screaming of cicadas and the laughter of beloved people.* Rhonda enjoyed the bowling alley and the nights of shooting the breeze with neighbors and friends. She loved white Christmases, decorated trees, carols and church services. She enjoyed everything, but…

What would I change?

Her footsteps fell quicker and her breath came faster. Sweat gathered under her stocking cap so she took it off. The cool air felt good on her brow. As she turned the corner for the last half mile home, she increased her pace consciously wondering if the effort would make a difference. The last two hundred yards she began to sprint. Her heart felt as if it was going to explode. Her lungs stretched and strained. One hundred. Fifty. Twenty. With a groan she hit the imaginary finish line in front of their house and immediately slowed. Heaving deeply, she put her hands on top of her head and walked westwards. She passed George's house, it would always be his house, even though it had been sold.

As she walked down the western side of the school, she looked up at the aged bricks cratered by time and weather. Over a hundred years of education had occurred in the building; a myriad of teachers, countless students and an ocean of ghostly memories remained. Now, the class sizes were twenty-ish; the teaching style leaned technological. Even last year in Kindergarten, J.T. said that they watched a lot of movies.

I sound like an old lady.

Turning the last corner to circle the school, she looked to her right where cars were beginning to chug towards Main Street. Checking her watch, she noted that Human Beans would now be serving coffee. The thought of coffee stirred Rhonda and she quickened her pace back home. The sun was now above the trees and streaking towards its zenith. Rhonda finished her cool down and stepped up onto the porch to prepare for her day.

It seemed like Groundhog Day every day.

Chapter 3.

Linda Harmsen had not been feeling well - not well at all. At first, she had chalked it up to undercooked chicken, or maybe a bad Jell-O salad, but then, after the ache had hung around for a week, she wondered if she hadn't caught one of those dreaded late summer colds. Lord, she hated those things, the sniffing, sneezing, coughing, achy, stuffy-head kind of thing, which were only cured by chicken soup, not for the soul, mind you, but by some crushed garlic in milk. Her mother and grandmother swore by the stuff. When Linda heard that all the new fancy dancy homeopathic hippies were prescribing garlic for colds, Linda nodded at the TV, pointed and said to her husband Dick: *See? See? What did I tell you? Now who's laughing?*

But this didn't really feel like a cold either. It was deeper than that, somewhere in her bones. Linda knew that the pain could be from her work. She'd been dressing hair for years and it was difficult, arduous work. There were times when her feet hurt, her hands ached and her ears were just plain full of stories from those who sat in the chair. Not that she minded the stories. They made such delicious gossip salads that could be passed around on Friday night smorgasbords with the ladies. But it seemed like her back hurt all the time. And now, her hips were starting to play up. Recently, when Linda looked into the mirror, she wondered if the size of her breasts had been the reason for her pain. She'd read in a Women's Day magazine that big boobs were often a cause of back pain.

Just to be sure, Linda decided that she would go to the doctor to get it checked out. She was quite happy that she'd lost five or so pounds in the last weeks, but if she did have the flu, she wanted to take a little more than garlic to get over it quicker.

Linda called up Jeannie and Leona who came over to ride with her to the doctor. The three of them packed into the car to go to Clancy for the day, hit the doctor's office, then Target (which Linda liked to pronounce 'Tar-zhay') and then stop at Dairy Queen for a Blizzard. It was still summer and ice cream sounded good, even if the thought of it made Linda feel nauseous.

Leona stopped outside Linda's house and honked the horn. Within seconds, Linda had closed the house door behind her and walked slowly to the vehicle where Jeannie was sitting in the back seat.

Leona put the car in drive. There was a little early morning school traffic, 'rush quarter hour' as Jeannie proclaimed, which caused them to pause a little longer than normal at stop signs.

"So, you're not feeling so good?" Jeannie's head was positioned between the two women at the front of the minivan.

Linda shrugged. "I just can't quite get over this ache. It's in my hips."

They settled into a comfortable silence. Leona turned on a country music station. Like every other ride they took on every other day, they chatted amiably about the weather, the school and other people in town.

Leona turned right and finished the last miles to the Clancy hospital. Once reaching the clinic, Leona parked her minivan in one of the open bays. Linda winced as she stepped onto the pavement and limped towards the door of the clinic. Leona and Jeannie watched her walk and shared a concerned look behind her.

At the front desk, the nurse looked up from her computer. "Good morning, can I help you?"

Linda tried to hold back the discomfort she was feeling. "I have an appointment with Dr. Neale."

"Name, please."

"Linda Harmsen."

Nurse Simpson typed the name into her computer and found Linda's appointment. "Dr. Neale will be with you in a moment. Please take a seat."

Each of the women picked up a different magazine and, while waiting for the doctor, they leafed through the information pointing out to each other snippets of articles that made them laugh. Linda's eyes lingered on a young woman with thin hips, a summer dress billowing around her as she danced among a field full of daisies. As Linda looked into her eyes, it seemed as if nothing could touch her or her happiness. Without knowing why, Linda ground her teeth and turned the page.

The door opened in front of them. "Ms. Harmsen?"

The nurse who called her name looked surprisingly similar to the young woman whose page she'd just turned. Sandy brown hair pulled back into a ponytail behind her head; her arms, devoid of the cellulite-filled flabs of middle age, were loose inside the sleeves of her light blue shirt.

"It's 'Mrs. Harmsen,'" Linda responded and stood. Jeannie and Leona rose also, but Linda told them to sit back down as she would only be a few minutes.

The nurse held the door open for Linda who limped towards the doctor's office. Smiling, the nurse pointed to the third room on the right and then closed the door behind her. After they entered the room, the nurse took Linda's measurements. Why they needed to know Linda's height was strange, but she was shocked to see that she had somehow shrunk an inch since the last time she had been to the doctor's office. She was even more surprised to see that she had lost almost ten pounds, not the five that her scale told her. This was strange because Linda had not really changed her exercise routine other than the pole dancing. Linda had noticed, though, that her appetite had diminished, but that was surely the result of the summer cold.

"Okay," the nurse said pertly, "Dr. Neale will be in soon."

Chapter 3.

Linda nodded and sat on the cushioned chair. Perusing the room, she noticed various medical pictures, a cross section of the ear, another for various and disgusting forms of skin cancer and another, the stages of pregnancy. Linda was thankful that she was beyond the stages of pregnancy. Her three children had not been easy births and each one had left her with months of pain. Breastfeeding had been a real chore.

There was a rap on the door and a figure emerged. Dr. Neale.

"Good morning, Mrs. Harmsen." Dr. Neale was in her forties with thick, dark hair. Her wide eyes were full of good humor and her smile revealed divots in both cheeks.

Dr. Neale sat down across from Linda on a black covered stool. "Now, Linda… do you mind if I call you Linda? I'm Antonia."

"No, of course, please."

"Okay, Linda. Tell me what's going on."

Linda looked into the doctor's eyes, took a deep breath and exhaled. "I think I've got a summer cold, or even the flu. I've been feeling a little… different lately. I've lost some weight - which is a good thing, mind you, but I'm tired all the time. My back aches, probably from the cold, and my hips hurt." She swallowed. "Any idea what it might be?"

Antonia typed the symptoms into Linda's chart. "You say that you've lost some weight? How much do you think? Ballpark."

Linda shrugged. "Maybe five or ten pounds. Do you think that's important?"

"Just being thorough. Were you trying to lose weight?"

"No. Just happened." A stab of worry pierced Linda.

"How long have you had the tiredness? Any fever, vomiting or diarrhea?"

Scrunching up a cheek, Linda thought before answering. "I suppose a few weeks, maybe a month. No puking or diarrhea.

Can't remember having a fever."

Antonia smiled and typed her responses into the computer. "We'll take some blood tests to see how your liver, kidneys and other organs are working. How does that sound?"

Nodding, Linda looked at the computer screen in hopes that she could see what the doctor was typing, but the font was too small.

"Okay," Dr. Neale said. "Just head down the hallway and the nurse will take blood samples."

"When will I know the results?" Linda asked.

Antonia smiled. "It shouldn't take too long."

Dr. Neale opened the door for Linda who rose, checked the room to see if she'd forgotten anything, and took one last glance at the picture on the wall. For some reason the bisected head displaying the inner ear, throat and air passages disturbed her.

"Thank you, Doctor," Linda said as she limped down the hallway.

Chapter 4.

Connie Redman fidgeted nervously in the living room chair. There were things that needed to be discussed, and her early rising provided time to think; and worry. Previous forays into reality-based relationships had been a constant source of anxiety and stress for her. Marriage had not been good to her. Her first husband had treated her abysmally. But now...

While Butcher and Rhonda had been carousing at Lake Ikmakota, Connie had done the exciting and unthinkable; she had invited a man over to their house. Although she was watching J.T. and Georgie, Carl arrived at 9:00 after the kids had been tucked into bed. Georgie had asked why she was so dressed up, but Connie had pooh-poohed the question saying she just felt like wearing a dress and putting her hair up for the night.

Carl had knocked lightly, cautious of Connie's warning not to wake the children. After Connie opened the door, Carl looked towards the street and entered. His brown eyes twinkled as he stared down at the 'younger' woman. Carl, a widower of four years, aged sixty-seven, was tall and thickset. He worked hard; his time at the foundry, when he was younger, had molded his muscles, but now that he had retired, his body had 'loosened,' as he said. Carl's lips were full and perpetually smiling. Anika, his beloved wife, had always wanted him to take care of himself in his old age, but her departure had ripped the need from his life. Now that he and Connie had been seeing each other for about six months, Carl had found a new lease on life.

Connie thought back to the beginning of their relationship. As she had sifted through the online profiles of so many different local men, she had finally chosen Carl. She found his picture to be simple and beautiful; his thinning white hair had been carefully parted to the side. He was not wearing a shirt and tie, but a simple button-down like he wore last night.

Smiling, Connie wrung her hands and then realized that her fingers were catching on something.

A diamond ring.

When Connie heard Rhonda leave for her morning routine, she began to rehearse the words that she would speak to her daughter and son-in-law. She blushed remembering what had happened the night before.

"Hi," Connie said, welcoming his brief peck on the lips.

"Hi, back."

Taking his hand, she led him into the living room where the television was on. A program from the Hallmark Channel - Connie's favorite. As they sat on the sofa, she realized that his hand was sweaty.

"What's going on?" She rubbed the sweat onto the upholstery.

He smiled nervously. "Nothing. Nothing. I've just never been to your house before. We're always meeting in restaurants or at my place."

"Don't worry," Connie said, "Leo and Rhonda won't be back until Sunday. Let's just enjoy the time we have tonight." She noticed that his forehead was damp. "Are you warm? Can I get you a cold glass of something, a beer?"

"A beer would be nice." Carl took a seat in front of the TV, but instead of watching the program, he looked around at the pictures on the wall. "So this is the family?"

"Yes, that's Rhonda and beside her, Butcher, er… I mean, Leo."

"Why do you call him Butcher?"

She popped the top of a beer can. "Well, when he first moved to Amicable, he was a butcher, but the longer he stayed, the name stuck. He's an amazing man."

Carl nodded. "It's good to have solid family members." Carl had two children, two boys, now grown men with families of their own, who no longer lived in Iowa. When Anika had died, they had come back for the funeral and

Chapter 4.

fussed over their dad for a few weeks, but neither father nor sons wanted to spend any more time grieving.

Connie brought Carl his beer and was pleased that he rose from the seat to receive it rather than waiting for the service. So different than her first husband.

"So anyway," Carl said, as he lifted his beer in Connie's direction. She did not drink alcohol, but it did not bother her that Carl drank beer. "How are you?"

Connie frowned. "For jeepers Pete, Carl, we just talked half an hour ago on the phone. You're not going to dump me, are you?"

Carl almost aspirated his beer. "Heck no! What would give you that idea?"

"You can barely sit still. It's like you've got ants in your overalls."

He laughed. "No, I'm not trying to dump you. Quite the opposite, actually."

Connie's heart leapt.

"I...um...I...have been doing some deep thinking." His hand trembled slightly as he took another sip of beer. "The last few years have been difficult. Anika's death was devastating for me, and at the age I was, I never thought that I would find someone else to..." he gulped, "...share time with."

"Okay..." Connie said slowly.

"But now that we've been... interacting, I feel like my time of grief is over."

"That's good," Connie said, and leaned towards him elbows resting on her thighs.

He took a deep breath. "Connie, I think... well, I know that I can be a stubborn mule sometimes and you're just getting to know me, I know that, and there are times when I can be..."

Connie interrupted him and placed a hand on his arm. "Carl, I love you too."

Carl glanced up sharply at her and he sucked in a breath. "That's not what I was going to say."

25

Connie recoiled. "Oh, Carl, I'm so sorry…" she covered her mouth. "I hope I haven't ruined everything."

"No! NO! Connie, that's not what I meant. I'm making a mess of this." He took a deep breath. "I mean, I love you too, but what I wanted to say was this: since I've met you, I've found that I can breathe again. A weight has been lifted off my chest. When I wake up in the morning, my first thought is of you." Connie's face reddened with pleasure. "And then, when I go to bed at night, you're the last thing I think of."

"Oh, Carl, that's…"

Now it was Carl's turn to be embarrassed. "I mean, that's not… okay, Jeez, I'm really flushing this down the crapper."

"Keep going, Carl," Connie encouraged, "I'm loving this!"

Carl sighed gratefully. "What I'm trying to say is that I have a reason to live, and it's you. I know I'm in my late-sixties and I should be far beyond the feeling of puppy love, but the fact of the matter is, I'm smitten."

Connie laughed. "I don't remember the last time I've heard the word 'smitten.'"

"I don't know why I said that, but it's true. And now that we're sitting in your house, surrounded by your history and I feel like I want…well, I want to make a future with you."

She gasped.

He began to reach into his pocket, but then realized with great embarrassment that there was nothing there. "Oh, shit," he said.

"Are you looking for what I think you're looking for?"

He nodded.

"Oh, Carl! Oh, Carl! How exciting!"

"So…? Will you?"

Connie toyed with him. "Will I what? Do you want to go to Branson? Is that what you're going to ask me?"

Carl threw his head back and laughed. "That's so funny, and so appropriate."

"You have to get down on a knee and ask me, Mr. Jacobsen."

Shaking his head, Carl stood. "There's no way I'm going to get up if I get down, so I'll do this the only way I know how. Connie Redman, I love you. I'm a fool for it. Will you marry me?"

Connie nodded and began to cry with delirious joy. "Of course, Carl." She pulled his neck down and kissed him. Then, after they had finished, she pushed his chest. "Now, go find my ring."

He grinned and found it on the passenger seat of his car.

Connie's fingers played over the full carat diamond. It had been such a long time since she had worn an expensive item of jewelry. Restlessly, she had tossed and turned during the night just to check that it was still on her finger. While she was studying the rock, the front door opened and Rhonda appeared. Rhonda looked shocked to see her mother.

"Mom," Rhonda exclaimed still breathing hard, "what are you doing up at this time?"

Connie smiled through her nervousness. "I… I have something to tell you."

"What have you ladies been doing…?"

Putting up her hands in surrender, Connie laughed. "Nothing! Nothing, really. This has nothing to do with X-Er-Size."

Rhonda let the words soak in. "You haven't been talking to my father, have you?"

"No, no, no, nothing like that."

"Well, what is it?" Rhonda moved to the refrigerator door, opened it and took out a cold bottle of water.

"I need you to sit down."

Rhonda froze. The cold water paused on the way to her mouth. "Are you sick? Has something happened to the kids? What is it?"

"Now, Rhonda, it's nothing like that. Good news, actually."

"Okay, tell me."

Connie raised her left hand. The diamond sparkled in the early morning light. It took a few seconds for the non-verbal response to register in Rhonda's mind. This was the last thing she had been expecting. Connie was beaming.

"Oh, heavens. Mother, what have you done?"

The smile turned to a frown. "What's that supposed to mean?"

"You're engaged? When did this happen? Who is it? Why have we not met him before? Where did you meet him?"

"Hold on. I want to tell you the whole story, but you need to sit down."

Rhonda moved to the kitchen table where she stood. "Does anyone else know about this?"

"No. No one."

Connie proceeded to tell her adult daughter about Carl Jacobsen who turned out to be the one true love of her life. Five minutes into the narrative, Rhonda sat down. Connie's face was animated with happiness. Rhonda pondered what her mother was telling her, recognizing that an incredible transformation had taken place - joy. Rhonda had never seen her mother like this.

"So," Connie concluded, "two nights ago, Carl came over while you guys were at Lake Ikmakota - don't be mad, please…"

Rhonda's eyes narrowed.

"…and now you've got a sixty-plus-year-old mother who is going to be a blushing bride."

Rhonda forced a smile. "Well, congratulations, Mom. I hope you know what you're doing."

In the tentative silence, Connie's frustration appeared. "Don't start with me, young lady. Why is it that you are the only one who gets to be happy?"

"That's not what I'm saying, Mom. It's just…well, you know how your time with my father didn't turn out so well. I'm just trying to take care of you."

"I can take care of myself, thank you very much." Connie sighed deeply and put her head down. "Now, I just want you to be happy *for* me. Carl is a great guy and I'd like you to meet him."

Rhonda nodded. "Sure. When would you like that to happen?"

"How about tonight?"

Rhonda hesitated. "It's a weeknight."

"Yes…?"

"Well, the kids…"

"Will be fine," Connie finished the sentence.

"I'll talk to Butcher."

Coincidentally, Butcher emerged from the hallway yawning. As he entered the kitchen, he looked at Rhonda, and then at his mother-in-law, and immediately knew what had happened. For the last six months, he had read it on Connie's face that she had been seeing someone.

"Did you know about this, Butcher?" Rhonda asked.

He moved towards the kitchen and pulled a box of cereal from the cupboard. "Know about what?"

"Oh, please, Butcher. You knew, didn't you?"

Butcher shrugged, not looking at either of the women behind him. As he pulled the cereal out, it slipped from his grasp and crashed into the sink. The tingling in his left hand had not stopped and his toes were still numb from the weekend. Soon, he would have to visit the doctor to get it checked out.

"Are you all right?"

"Yeah," he responded, as he picked up the box and squeezed it a little more tightly.

"Okay, then. Answer my question. Did you know about Mom?"

Butcher was tempted to fib, but Rhonda would have seen right through it. Even though he could no longer read her, it seemed that she could read him.

"All right, yes, I guessed that she was seeing someone."

Connie reddened. "How did you know? I mean, I know how you knew, but what was it that gave it away?"

Butcher continued to fill his bowl with cereal and milk and then pulled a chair out and sat down with them. "Lots of things. You were withdrawn, which means that you're trying to hide something, and then when you did talk to me, your eyes kept dilating which means that you had been thinking about someone else." He took another bite. "And then, as I'm doing the laundry, there were dresses that I had never seen before. Things that you don't wear around here." They listened intently, but impatiently. "Okay, I'm beating around the bush. He's probably four or five years older than you - a widower? He's from nearby guessing by the fact that you want him to come over soon. I noticed some dust on the floor last night and a large footprint - not mine, though - foundry dust. Retirees never completely shave off their previous life."

"You are amazing," Connie said. "Exactly right."

"Butcher," Rhonda said, "why didn't you tell me?"

He shrugged and pointed with his spoon at his mother-in-law. "Same reason she didn't tell you. You'd overreact."

Rhonda gasped. "Do I really make such a mess of things?"

"No, no, dear," Connie said, "you are wonderful. It's just that... well, sometimes you think you can control the future but," Connie laughed as she clapped her hands, "I love surprises. You never know how long you're going to get them."

Butcher nodded. "Ain't that the truth?" He munched contentedly on his cereal.

At 8:00, Butcher approached Peterson Butchery. Pushing the door open, Butcher heard the bell tinkle above his head, and he looked towards the counter. Nash was standing patiently, with arms crossed, helping a patron decide between pork chops and chicken breasts.

Butcher nodded at Nash who smiled and motioned towards the back cutting room.

"Thank you, Mrs. Collins," Nash said to the older woman, as he pulled out a pork chop and placed it in a plastic bag to weigh on the scale.

After she paid, Nash walked back and found Butcher with an apron tied tightly around his waist. Butcher was surveying the cold room.

"How are you feeling, old man?" Nash asked.

"All right." Butcher didn't really feel all right, but he didn't want to explain. "Just tired. Not as tired as you look, though. Where's Derek?"

Nash laughed. "He's taking a sick day."

"Too much bachelor party, huh?"

"You got that right."

Butcher walked into the cooler and hefted some meat onto his shoulder. Stumbling, he cursed and caught himself. Nash smirked but didn't help.

"You guys all right?"

Nash's eyes dropped. "Yeah, it's just weird, you know? He's my little brother and it's just strange thinking of him being married."

Butcher laughed, as he picked up his knife and started honing it. The blade flashed and ticked quickly, metal against metal. Flash... tick... flash... tick. "You know, he is only five minutes younger than you."

"Those five minutes count."

"Sure they do." Flash... tick... flash...tick. Butcher checked the sharpness with his thumb.

Nash watched his star employee work. As always, Butcher's skill was unparalleled. In minutes, the meat would be trimmed, cuts

31

stacked and lined up. "I think he should be fine by tomorrow."

"What about you? Do you feel like life is changing before your very eyes? How is Shania?"

Nash smirked and when Butcher looked up…

He stopped cutting. "Holy crap, Nash! Are you kidding?" *Pregnant.*

"Bun in the oven, Amigo. Knocked up. With child. You name it, we got it!" His smile was broad.

"But what about the bachelorette party? Didn't she drink? It seemed like they were all having a pretty wild time."

Nash's grin widened. "She had lots of champagne in her glass, but when no one was looking, she kept pouring it into Naida's. That's why she was so drunk." He laughed. "We didn't really want anyone to know, but it's not like I could have hid it from you."

"How far along is she?"

"You tell me, Butcher."

"She's not here for me to read." Butcher studied Nash's face and already knew. *Ten weeks.*

"Try anyway."

"Fifteen weeks?" Butcher lied, and picked up his knife again and began to cut.

"Way off," Nash responded. "Ten weeks." He moved back to the counter where a customer was leaning over the display. "You're slipping, Dude." The sound stopped and Butcher gasped. Nash turned just in time to see the tall man holding his left hand in front of his face. Blood was streaming down his arm.

Butcher's left index finger was hanging by a thread.

Chapter 5.

Rhonda and the town council were being led around Amicable High School when her phone rang. Disengaging herself from the group, she frowned to see Nash's name come up. It was unfortunate timing that Nash call her. So many good things were happening at the high school: students were busily working on their projects, whether mathematics or chemical engineering, home economics or diesel mechanics. During the last two years, after the elevator explosion, Amicable had been blessedly inundated with outside aid and assistance. The grain elevator was slowly being rebuilt and the town was reaping the benefits. The council continued its supervisory capacity, but the council was in the midst of its own restructure. In three months, Amicable would elect a new mayor. It was widely presumed that Tracey Thomas would take the position. In the last two years, Tracey had been headhunted by various corporations throughout the United States, but she had steadfastly refused to break her vow to help Amicable rebuild. That, and she was getting married to Derek Peterson.

Rhonda pushed the green button.

"Hello?"

Tracey Thomas heard Rhonda exclaim, *Oh my God, no...* and watched her cover her mouth with one hand.

When she disconnected the phone, Tracey moved towards her. "What is it, Rhonda?"

"There's been an accident. Butcher..."

Tracey gasped. "Is he okay? Was it a car accident?"

"No, it was at the locker. He's cut himself, but he's on the way to the hospital. Nash is taking him."

"How bad is it?"

Rhonda's eyes locked on Tracey's.

Bad.

33

Twenty minutes later, Rhonda nervously parked her car in the emergency parking at Clancy Municipal Hospital. Hurrying to the automatic doors, they shushed open, and Rhonda entered. Nash and Stedman greeted her with worried faces. Stedman must have come as soon as he heard. She rushed over to them.

"Where is he? How is he?"

Nash placed his hands on Rhonda's arms. "He's with the doctor right now."

"What happened?"

"I don't really know. One minute we're talking and the next second I turn around and he's holding up his hand. He didn't scream or shout or anything. It was like he was in shock."

"What kind of damage is it?"

"Oh, man, Rhonda, I don't know. He cut his finger pretty bad."

Rhonda began to cry. Stedman reached out to put his arm around her waist. Gratefully, she smiled then stood in stunned silence. Rhonda pulled away from Stedman and moved to the reception desk.

"Can I see my husband? Butcher... I mean, Leo Jensen."

She checked the computer. "Yes, but I'm not sure...well, it's not pretty..." Her voice trailed off.

"It doesn't matter. I can handle it."

The nurse buzzed the door. "Room 6," she said. "I just want you to be prepared. Even though his hand is wrapped, there is quite a bit of blood."

Rhonda took a deep breath and opened the door.

There was indeed a good deal of blood involved.

She began to cry as soon as she entered the room. Butcher looked up at her - dazed.

"Oh, Sweetie," she said, and rushed towards him to give him a hug.

"I don't know what happened," he whispered. "One minute I'm cutting up meat and the next..." he held up his wrapped hand.

"How bad is it?" She questioned hesitatingly.

Butcher looked into his wife's eyes. "Almost through the entire finger below the first knuckle."

Rhonda winced. "What did the doctor say?"

His lower lip quivered. "Amputation, possibly. Because I cut into bone and the knife, of course, had raw meat on it, they don't want an infection..."

"Oh Butcher," Rhonda moaned, "I'm so sorry."

"Me too." He looked down. "Me too. This has never happened to me before. Never. I've had a few nicks, but in the last week or so, it's felt like my fingers have had a life of their own, like I can't control them. I should have said something."

"Why didn't you?" She asked.

"Because I didn't want to worry you." He pondered the wrapped hand. "Four fingered man..."

She hugged him again. As his face was pressed against her chest, Butcher could feel the rapid rhythm of Rhonda's heart.

And his finger, or lack of finger, was beginning to throb. Still, he listened to the sound of his wife's heart.

Thump bump, thump bump, thump bump...

Behind them, the door opened and Dr. Ditmore appeared. He was short, balding and bearded.

"Hello, I'm Tim."

"Yes, Dr. Ditmore, we've met before. A friend of ours came in here a few years ago, bald and smelling like feces."

"Oh yes! I remember him! That was odd. What happened to him?" It was as if Dr. Ditmore had completely forgotten the patient.

"He's in the waiting area, but that's a long story, Dr. Ditmore," Rhonda said. "Back to Leo."

"Yes, yes, of course," Tim said as he sat down beside the two of them. "Well, we've taken x-rays…" He paused. "You've done a good job of it, Mr. Jensen. We've got two options, really. We'll pump you full of antibiotics and reattach the finger as best we can, but to be brutally honest, there's little chance of having full use of that finger again anyway. The better option, but harder emotionally, is to amputate under the second knuckle reducing the chance of infection."

Butcher lowered his head.

"I'm sorry Mr. and Mrs. Jensen. It's really up to you how to proceed. Do you want a moment?"

They nodded and Dr. Ditmore left the room. Rhonda stroked his face. "What do you want to do?"

"What do I want to do?" Butcher snorted. "I want to rewind this morning and start over." He took a deep breath. "I'd like to try and keep it if I can. Is that okay with you?"

Rhonda nodded. "Of course it's okay. I'll support you in whatever, but I don't want to risk your health. Okay?"

They both stared at the blood-stained wraps. "Let's do this."

Later that night, a hand specialist drove from Omaha to do the surgery. He reattached Butcher's finger and prescribed a heavy dosage of antibiotics and painkillers. Driven home by Rhonda, Butcher was helped into the house.

Worried, Connie met them at the door. "And?"

Butcher's eyes were glazed with painkillers. Rhonda responded for him. "So far so good. It's going to be a few weeks before we'll know anything for sure."

"What happened?"

"That's the question of the day, isn't it?"

Connie stood in front of Butcher. "Can I get you anything? A cup of coffee or something to eat?"

He shook his head slowly.

"I think we'll just get him into bed." Rhonda held his arm as they walked towards the hallway. "What did you tell the kids?"

"Nothing, yet. I figured it best if the news came from you."

Rhonda smiled at her mother. "Thanks, Mom. I really appreciate it."

Ten minutes later, after Rhonda had tucked Butcher into bed, she came back out to the kitchen where Connie had brewed two steaming cups of coffee. The cups, chipped memories of vacations long past, 'Life's a Beach,' and 'Coffee keeps me going until it's time for wine,' were set in front of them.

"How are you feeling?" Connie asked.

"Shaken."

"Is he okay?"

Rhonda shrugged. "Not yet. Maybe not ever. This would put an end to his butchering." Although the thought had already crossed her mind, she hadn't vocalized it. Things weren't real until spoken.

Connie moved behind her daughter and wrapped her arms around her. Rhonda smiled through her tears and grabbed her mother's forearm. It had been a few years since they had truly shared in sorrow, not since George had died, perhaps.

Rhonda tapped her mother's arm, wiped her tears and thanked her. She felt tired. It had been a long day and tomorrow would be just as difficult. Taking a deep breath, Rhonda stood and stretched her long limbs towards the ceiling and looked at the clock. Sleep was calling and she really wanted to be with her husband tonight.

After one more hug, Rhonda left the light of the kitchen and entered the darkness.

Chapter 6.

Water slapped against the sides of the boat echoing through the seats and soul. Aware that he was lying down, Butcher tried to move but found that his muscles would not respond. Although the darkness seemed to have a certain weight, he sensed the boatman also; he could see his strong muscles pulling the pole against the water. The man's face was impassive. He had made this journey countless times. Lifting his head, Butcher peered over the side of the boat to see. He and the powerful boatman were alone. It appeared that they were on an underground river; a strong current pulled them inexorably into the yawning mouth of the darkness.

Along the shore, he saw figures who seemed so familiar, memories of a time long past - There! His mother? She looked so young and vibrant! With leaping heart, he reveled that these memories reminded him of his youth. This trip down memory river, dark though it was, was pleasant. The boat driver dug his pole into water and they turned suddenly. The scenery changed. Lighting, torches and fires on the shore, cast dancing, eerie shadows on the walls of the cave. The great artery seemed to throb with something more sinister.

"Where are we going?" He croaked.

The boat driver did not respond.

He repeated the question.

"You have to see..." the boat driver said.

"I have to see what?"

The boat driver's face gazed pityingly at him. "It's what they all have to see in order to finish the journey."

"I don't know what you are talking about."

"No one does, but knowledge does not help. Until you experience it, you cannot find peace."

For the first time, he felt a gripping fear and a weight on his chest. His torso and legs were wrapped tightly in some kind of fabric. It was inelastic; and the harder he tried to sit up, the tighter it held him.

Chapter 6.

"Please," the boatman said sadly, "don't struggle against it. That will only make it worse."

Butcher leaned his head back and stared at the ceiling of the cave. Stalactites were closing in on them but the boat driver cared not. The cave was swallowing them.

Now, he was very afraid.

"What do I have to see? How can we stop this?" Panic set in. Fighting against his restraints, Butcher felt the cords in his neck stand out.

The driver shook his head.

"We need to stop! I need to go home!"

Pieces of stalactites began to fall crumbling onto his face. To his great horror, Butcher suddenly realized he was not breathing. He could neither hear his heart nor feel the pulse in his veins. Struggling, pushing, the boat seemed to be lower in the water and now he pushed his head up as far as it would go and noticed that the boat was indeed sinking. Water was rushing in through a hole in the floor and soon, if he couldn't escape, the water would reach his back, then his sides, his chest and eventually his face.

"Help me! Help me! I'm not breathing."

The boatman pushed his oar into the water causing it to brake, and even though the current was strong, the boat came to a stop. Extending an arm, the oarsman stretched out a bony hand and finger towards the farthest shore.

"You must look. Before we can go on, you must see."

"What is it?"

The boatman shook his head and his chin dropped to his chest in sorrow.

His head inches from the pointed stalactites, Butcher looked to the shore where the figures of all the people he loved were huddled on shore around a large box. Rhonda's hand covered her mouth; her shoulders were shaking. A sob issued between her fingers. J.T. and Georgie, seemingly older, far too old, clung to their mother; neither looked directly into the casket. Then he saw a body inside the coffin.

The casket held his physical body, but what he traveled in now was the coffin holding his immortal soul. Horrified, he struggled against his restraints, but Butcher could not move. He wanted to yell out to them, scream, tell them that he was right behind them, but no matter what words he tried to produce, they couldn't hear him.

Then, he saw a figure arrive - a shadow, something sinister hovering behind his wife and children. He wanted to warn them, but he couldn't.

"What is that?" he screamed.

"Only you know." The boat driver's head remained on his chest.

"But how can I warn them! The shadow..."

"Yes, the shadow that all of us must face or else we pass it on to our loved ones."

"I don't understand! That doesn't make sense!" His body tensed. A scream erupted from his mouth.

"Then the shadow will find them..." The boat driver shook his head and pulled the oar from the water. The boat jumped in the current. At the same time, the ceiling retracted and he could move his arms again. Reaching out for Rhonda and the children, he stretched his hand towards the edge of the craft in an effort to throw himself from the boat.

The boatman's face morphed into a mask of fury. His mouth snarled, teeth like fangs. He bent over, inches from Butcher's face. "You cannot," his gravelly voice intoned echoing of the ancient dead, full of the grave and dark things. And then he brought the oar down on Butcher's hand.

Butcher screamed with agony and woke up. As his eyes adjusted to the pain and the darkness, he saw Rhonda's face hovering over his.

"Butcher! Are you okay? You're finger..."

Looking down at his throbbing hand, he realized that his finger must have bumped against the bed frame. As the waves of torturous pain washed over him, he felt nauseous and close to passing out. Breathing deeply, he steadied himself and swallowed. At that point, he recognized his body was caught in a cocoon of blankets, which explained the constricted feeling in his dream's boat.

"I'm okay," Butcher responded breathlessly, "I just hit my finger…"

Rhonda stroked his forehead with her hand. "You were screaming in your sleep. You were having a nightmare."

He blew out his cheeks. "Yeah, yeah, I think so."

"What was it about?"

Instead of looking at Rhonda, Butcher closed his eyes and the subterranean scene of Stygian darkness returned. He shook his head. "It doesn't matter. The nightmare is over."

"Okay," Rhonda said uncertainly. Laying her head on his chest, she snuggled into the place of certainness and security. "Sleep well."

For Linda Harmsen, her night had been as disturbing as Butcher's. The pain in her hips and back had increased. Rather than a stabbing pain, it was a dull ache, a constant pressure. At two o'clock in the morning, Linda got up and stretched her back. She was sure it was just a pinched nerve.

Turning on the hallway light, she moved into the living room where she settled into her recliner. Wincing, she readjusted her hips and reached for the television remote. As the Hallmark Channel came on, Linda picked up her half-finished cross-stitch.

After staring blankly at the frame, Linda shook her head and tried to focus.

Linda wondered how she got so lucky. Even though she and Dick did not spend that much time together anymore, they had a love/love relationship and a beautiful sense of personal space and perspective. Dick did not intrude into Linda's business, neither professional nor private, and Linda did not take offense to his perpetual need to be out with the boys playing golf and remembering the good ol' days of the 80's.

Linda winced as a crab seemed to pinch her spine. A flare of worry sparkled momentarily. Sighing deeply, she put her cross-stitch on the lampstand, hit the off-button on the TV and pulled herself from the cushiony chair. It took three attempts to extricate herself, but even as she got to her feet, a spasm of pain stabbed her and she almost cried out to Dick.

Sucking in lungfuls of air, she put her hands on her hips and waited for the pain to pass. Ten minutes later, after taking two painkillers, she nestled in next to her now-snoring husband.

Connie put on her bathrobe and went into the kitchen and was surprised to find a note from Rhonda:

> *Dear Mom,*
>
> *I've gone for my morning run and before you think me heartless leaving Butcher all alone in his pain, he woke up and told me that I should go. If you could wake the kids at 7:00 and get them their breakfast, I would appreciate it.*
>
> *Thanks,*
>
> *R.*

After thinking her daughter heartless anyway, Connie sighed and turned towards the coffee machine and flipped the switch. As the pot gurgled, Connie went to the front porch to retrieve the morning newspaper, which had been tossed in the near vicinity of the house. Little Tim Olson was an avid bicyclist, but not such a good pitcher. If she was up early enough, she would see him wavering attempting to pull the next newspaper from his bag and then, after approaching the house, he would rear back to toss it. Occasionally, (very occasionally) the morning news ended up on the porch. He never stopped to put it where it belonged.

Once inside, Connie impatiently placed her coffee cup under the drip where it filled. After filling her mug, she moved the pot back and sat at the table. The Omaha Herald proclaimed the same old news just with different photographs. The President was having difficulty with partisanship; gas prices were skyrocketing due to religious strife in the Middle East; virtue wars continued as the battle for supremacy between right and left wing waged incessantly. Finally, as she always did, Connie read the obituaries. She was moved by their biographies and what the families thought important to write about. All of them were good, caring and supportive people who died early (or late) and left behind grieving families who would soldier on without them. Of course, the reality was somewhat different. They were, just like everyone else, humans simply trying to make it through life with as little pain as possible.

Three-quarters of the obituaries were elderly people. The next group, Connie's age bracket, 50-74, were cancer contractors or some other terminal disease. Lastly, the young ones, the Unfortunates, those in the wrong place at the wrong time doing the wrong thing with the wrong people. It made Connie's heart hurt to see these young one's waste their lives on instants - moments of tragic excitement ending in crushed metal or drug overdoses. And the last, at least one per week which was unfortunately increasing, were the suicides. It wasn't just a teenage thing. How did the world get to this place?

Connie hoped she'd die in her sleep.

Sipping her way through her first cup of coffee, the caffeine slowly taking affect, Connie turned the page to the sports page where she scanned the baseball scores. She jumped as the front door opened and was surprised to see two faces.

Derek and Nash bumbled into the living room. "Hello, Ms. Redman," they said simultaneously.

"For goodness sake. Stop calling me Ms. Redman. My name is Connie."

Derek looked at Nash. He still struggled to erase from his memory the crazy Ms. Redman from years ago. "Uh, okay." He smiled. "Can Butcher come out and play?"

Connie's jaw dropped. "Are you serious? Have you even looked what time it is? And do you have even the foggiest idea of how he's feeling this morning?"

Derek's grinned stayed. "Yes. Yes. Yes."

Nash pushed in front of his brother. "We're very sorry Ms. Red... er... Connie about the early morning interruption, but we wanted to see the patient before we went to work. Is his... um... is his.... you know... still attached?"

Connie frowned testily at the twins. "He's still sleeping. He's in a lot of pain and fortunately for your business' sake, his finger is attached."

The twins looked relieved. "Then can we go see him?"

Connie's frown deepened. "What part of 'He's still sleeping' is confusing you boys?"

Derek moved forward to push past her. "The sleeping part." The boys sidestepped Connie and quickly moved down the hallway.

"Don't go down there!" Connie hissed. "You'll wake up the children."

"We'll be quiet," Nash said as they hustled towards the bedroom. Without knocking, they stepped into Butcher and Rhonda's room and flipped on the light.

Butcher flinched and squinted into the light. "What the..."

Derek held his hands out in front of him. "Don't say anything you'll regret later, Butcher. There are children in the house."

"Boys," Butcher groaned and rolled over. He put a forearm over his eyes. "What are you doing here?"

"We wanted to see if you're coming in to work today. We need a day off because we took care of you. We'll probably have to dock your pay, but you're loaded, right?" Derek laughed.

"Are you guys complete morons?" Butcher asked as the pain in his finger began to throb.

"Nah," Nash said. "I'm about a third, but Derek is close to seventy percent."

"Get out of here!" Butcher shouted. "Rhonda!"

"She's not here, Butcher. We saw her out jogging. We stopped her, which I think annoyed her. She got this crinkly look on her face, like…" Nash screwed up his face. "She said you were resting."

"And…?"

"Well," Derek plopped down on the edge of the bed causing it to shake. This jarred Butcher's hand and caused him to grit his teeth. "We thought that there was no better way to improve your spirits than to bring you some presents."

"This couldn't have waited until later?"

Nash closed the door to give them privacy from Connie's ears and eyes. "No. Some people like us have to work. You're going to play hooky for at least a couple of days, right?"

"Just give me the dang presents and get out of here." Even through the pain, he couldn't quite mask the love he felt for the younger men. These were his brothers, some of his closest friends.

"You don't have to get snippy," Nash said and then opened his bag.

"Me first," Derek said and reached into the bag. "We went to the grocery store yesterday afternoon, and although some of these presents may seem *slightly* insensitive…"

"We don't think you'll care," Nash finished. "But it's probably best if you don't show them to Rhonda."

Butcher snorted.

"Okay, first gift - Spicy Cheddar Witch Fingers. They're delicious." Derek laughed and held the bag out for Butcher to inspect. He lifted an eyebrow and smiled. "Do you mind if we try them?"

"Go ahead, Derek. You must be hungry. It's almost seven o'clock in the morning."

"Next," Nash announced, "we found some penne pasta tubes and we've decorated them." Nash withdrew a tube. They had glued a shell pasta on the tube and painted it red to look like a fingernail. It had been broken at the base.

Butcher shook his head and smiled.

"Lastly," Derek said proudly, "we got these from our own shop and thought that if the finger reattachment doesn't work, we can use these." He produced two duck legs, which had the webbing trimmed from them.

Butcher laughed and then winced. "Those are great, really."

"Yeah," Nash said, "we know. But seriously, if there is anything that we can get for you, just let us know. Maybe we can come over later and drink your beer."

At seven o'clock, Connie hurried down the hallway past the closed door. The children needed to be roused for school. She raised a fist to Rhonda and Butcher's room and pushed her way into J.T.'s room.

Meanwhile, at 7:01, the front door opened quietly. Rhonda, sweaty and invigorated, smelled the coffee and thanked God for her mother. Although she was only a minute or two late, it would take ten or fifteen minutes to take a shower, look after Butcher and get the kids ready for school.

Pulling off her shoes, she dropped them at the front and then, as was her routine, she pulled off her sweatshirt, shirt and sweatpants and dropped them in a pile by the laundry door. Reaching under her arms, she pulled her sports bra up and over her head. The sweat was already beginning to dry as she moved towards the hallway and to their bedroom.

She heard Connie with the children and smiled. Taking a deep breath, she prepared for her time with Butcher.

Pushing open the door, she was not prepared to see the Peterson twins look up at her, down at her breasts, and back up at her face. For the first time in his life, even Derek Peterson was speechless.

"Holy Shackleton!" Nash said.

Rhonda screamed and ran from the room.

Connie screamed. "What's happening?"

Derek screamed. "Butcher, I saw Rhonda's boobs!"

Incredibly, Butcher laughed through his pain.

Chapter 7.

A late summer thunderstorm was building in the northwest. The signs were obvious: increased humidity, birds chattering excitedly, warm blustery wind pushing the heat across the acres of restless leaves of corn. The rustling sounded like an endless stream shushing down the beaten track of a riverbed. Clouds banked on the western horizon. Light grey changing to metallic blue closer to the ground. From miles away, the casual storm watcher could see that this would be a doozie.

Liam Wilson paused from his work on a 2014 Chevy Suburban to glance outside his service station. Small pieces of gravel flicked against the siding. As he stood in the door, socket wrench in hand, he pushed his grease-smeared hat back onto his head. His striped, grey shirt, tattooed with grime and grease, billowed in the breeze. Shaking his head, Liam cleared his throat, spat on the ground and moved back inside to finish the automobile surgery.

Across town, Reverend John Deakins pulled open the screen door of Adeline Larson's ranch style house. He'd had a wonderful visit - they both thought that. Adeline was confident that in her advanced age, 'eighty-three years and a bit' as she said, she should not look too far into the future. After they spoke of life in Amicable, she loaded Reverend Deakins up with German mudcake - which John Deakins ate both guiltily and pleasurably. As he licked his fingers, they both noticed the shadows filling the room from clouds passing over the western sun. Adeline told John that she was 'feeling it in her bones. A storm was coming.' John nodded even though he was quite sure that Adeline's sense of meteorology came more from her perpetual Weather Channel addiction than her osteo issues.

As the door was yanked from his hand, John leaned back into the entryway and told Adeline that she was right about the storm. Holding his hair with one hand, he pushed the door shut behind him. Unfortunately, John had walked to Adeline's house. He gritted his teeth, squinted and put his head down into the bluster. When he approached 1st Street West, he looked to his right two blocks past the Amicable High School building and snuck a look at the faraway Jensen house. If the weather would have been better, John would have made another trip to visit Butcher, his best friend, but it was already five o'clock. Leslie would be ready for him to take the kids off her hands for a little while.

Gabrielle and Michelle heard the front door open and streaked for their father who, after placing his keys on the key rack, bent down to scoop the giggling girls into his arms. Alternating kisses, the girls smooched his cheeks happy to have him home. John looked over their heads at Leslie who leaned against the door frame, arms crossed, looking both amused and exhausted by the girls' energy.

"How are you?" John set the girls down. Carefully, he maneuvered his way between the building blocks scattered across the floor.

Leslie shrugged. "Worried."

"What is it?"

Waiting for him to finish crossing the room, Leslie held out her arms to him. He leaned down to kiss her. Leslie turned back to the kitchen and pulled him with her.

"I had a conversation with Rhonda this afternoon. The doctor, I can't remember his name…"

"Ditmore, I think," John reached his hand out to the cookie jar, but Leslie smacked it away.

"No treats for you."

"Why not?"

"Because you've still got some of Adeline's German cake on your upper lip."

Unconsciously, John reached up to swipe at his lip and guiltily smiled at the smear.

"So anyway, Rhonda said that Doctor Ditmore wanted to see them, notice I said *them* on Monday."

"Maybe it's good news?"

"Yeah, right." Leslie's brown eyes were worried.

"So," John crossed his arms and leaned on the counter, "Ditmore does the worst thing possible and calls them on Friday to let them worry about it for the weekend."

"Mmm hmmm." Leslie turned her back on her husband and began to wash her hands in the sink.

"Well, we've got something to pray about this weekend."

"That's not the only thing," Leslie said as she moved to the towel rack and dried her hands. "Leona called me today and said we should pray for Linda also."

"What's wrong with her? Too much coffee?" He smirked but Leslie turned sharply to him.

"It doesn't sound right, John. I've never actually heard any of them talk like that before. Yes, I know, they can be a little bit..." she searched for the right word, "...dramatic, but this is something different."

"Anything else I should know?" John pushed away from the counter and began to help with dinner prep.

Finally, Leslie smiled. "I thought you'd already know, but there's going to be another wedding in town."

John glanced at her sideways, puzzled. "Who?"

"For sure, I thought they'd have called you first to ask about having the big day at St. Clements."

"Who?" He responded with exasperation.

"Connie. Connie Redman."

"You're joking. Really?"

50

"Really. She met some guy on an online dating website and now they're getting hitched."

John blew out his cheeks. "What do Butcher and Rhonda think?"

"Well, it's a little quick but she says Connie is happy."

"Have they met the guy yet?"

"Not yet." Leslie pulled out a cutting board and began to chop potatoes. "Supposedly the guy is coming over sometime soon."

"Even while Butcher is laid up?"

"That's what I said, but Rhonda and Connie thought it would be a good diversion for him. He's retired, late sixties or something like that. It's not the worst thing in the world if Connie gets back on the horse."

"As long as it's not a rodeo."

Leslie snorted. "You got that right."

"I wonder why they didn't say something to me about it yesterday?" John mused.

"I guess we'll just need to pray for the best."

"I guess so."

Linda Harmsen felt the onrushing storm hit the house. Before the wind, she saw the lightning and heard the rumble of thunder. She looked up at the kitchen clock, a tractor with a child standing in front of it waving to the farmer. It was just after five o'clock. Dick would be home in an hour, his golf game cancelled by impending weather. He would be frustrated, but it would be good to have him home. Golf and lightning weren't great dance partners.

Sighing, Linda moved to the bathroom for a shower. The warm water would feel good, and even though the storm continued to brew outside (she knew she shouldn't take a shower while the lightning was flashing) the water's relief would be helpful.

Linda stepped out of her clothes and removed her blue jeans. Suddenly, a knife jabbed into her back and she buckled. The pain almost caused her to pass out. *What in the world...* Once the pain subsided, she pulled herself upright and stared into the mirror. Face wrinkled and pinched, she frowned and leaned on the white porcelain. After a few seconds, she tested pulling herself upright.

Relieved that she could now move, Linda carefully pulled off her favorite t-shirt and bra. Just as she was about to turn to the shower, she noticed something odd. Whether it was simply the light above or a shadow below, she moved closer to the mirror and lifted her left breast. Frowning, she noticed a small bump near her left nipple. She had heard stories about breast cancer, and fortunately no one in her family (none that she knew of, anyway) had contracted the horrific disease, but still... that didn't seem good.

It had been a while since she had manually checked her breasts - maybe a year or so, and even though the commercials kept telling her that she should get a yearly mammogram, she despised them. So painful. It had been at least two years.

Checking the skin, she was horrified when her fingers felt another small lump underneath her left breast. Why she had never noticed it before, she was unsure, but now that the nodule had raised the surface of her skin, her fingers flicked back and forth over it.

She knew.

She knew what the doctor was going to tell her on Monday. Now that she had two days to ponder and worry and be anxious, Linda was certain that she would not be sleeping for the entire weekend. Whatever the back issue was, it most definitely could not be of the same magnitude as the intrusive lump. Linda continued to move her fingers and was horrified to find that not only were there bumps under the breast, but all the way along the side to her armpit. For an eternity, she stopped her ministrations, still holding her breast, and stared at her reflection in the mirror. She had gone pale. Claws of fear scratched her.

What am I going to do? How are Dick and the kids going to live without me?

Once again, she forced herself to breathe and dropped her breast. It made a slapping sound as it hit her rib cage. Linda checked the other breast and was relieved to find no lumps on that side. Maybe this was just a case of infected lymph nodes or mammary ducts. Maybe hot water would move them on. Linda smiled at herself in the mirror, encouraging her reflection and giving it the mental thumbs up.

Linda opened the shower door and reached across for the handle. Starting the stream of warm water, Linda waited until it suited her skin and then stepped in.

Seconds into her shower, a spasm of pain caused Linda's sight to pinpoint. Without knowing why, she collapsed into the blackness.

And the storm rolled across the forlorn landscape crushing it under its mighty weight.

Just after six o'clock, Rhonda heard the ambulance screaming from one side of the town to the other. Butcher was sitting on the sofa watching the evening news while Georgie and John Thomas were playing quietly on the floor with Barbie Dolls and army men.

"That doesn't sound good," Rhonda spoke over the television.

"What's that?" Butcher said. He cleared his throat, his voice slightly gravelly.

"The ambulance. Didn't you hear it?"

"I'm watching the news." He didn't turn to look at her.

Rhonda craned her neck and saw the ambulance moving towards the house then turning left. "I wonder who it could be?"

"Maybe it's going out to the nursing home?" Butcher asked.

"Why would they turn on their lights and sirens then? It's probably a farm accident. Maybe someone rolled a tractor."

Butcher *mmmmed* and continued to watch the news.

"Do you have a cold, Hon?" Rhonda set the table for dinner.

"I don't think so. Just a husky voice. Maybe too much dry air."

"All right, everyone. Come and eat." The smell of a pot roast, vegetables and mashed potatoes permeated the room. The children, hearing the call to eat, quickly dropped their plastic dolls and army men and rushed to the table where they pulled their chairs out.

Butcher moved slowly from the sofa. Careful not to upset his finger, he curled it into his chest taking his time. In slow motion, Butcher shuffled five steps to the table and pulled out the chair to sit down. The exertion taxed him. Rhonda sliced the children's meat into manageable portions and made sure that they would eat their vegetables also. J.T. created a mountain of mashed potatoes which he called his 'Devil's Tower.' Once, J.T. had surreptitiously snuck out of bed to watch *Close Encounters of the Third Kind* from behind the wall of the hallway before he was caught by Grandma Connie who chased him, tapped his butt and hustled him back to bed, Rhonda filled the 'Tower' with gravy before moving on to Georgie who was waiting patiently. She clapped her hands happily.

Finally, Rhonda pulled out her own chair. Just as she was about to sit down, an extraordinarily loud clap of thunder shook the house and the lights went out. J.T., who was just about to take a bite of Devil's Tower, dropped the dollop of mashed potatoes directly onto his lap. All four were startled, and all four reacted in different ways: Rhonda uttered a short profanity. Georgie, scared, began to cry and called for Rhonda who came to her quickly. J.T. was more interested in scraping the mashed potatoes off his pants and stuffing them into his mouth, while at the same time, repeating the profanity that had escaped Rhonda's lips.

"John Thomas Jensen," she scolded, "you don't say that."

"But you did, Mommy," he pouted, as he licked the potatoes from his fingers.

"Yes, but..." she stopped short when she saw Butcher's silhouette. Even in the dim light she knew that something was wrong. "Leo, what is it? Are you okay?"

As Rhonda moved to him, she placed her hands on his cheeks. His mouth, agape, a darker hole of agony, stoppered the voice caught somewhere within him.

"Butcher," Rhonda said forcefully, "what's wrong? What happened?"

Snapping his mouth shut, he leaned forward pulling from Rhonda's grasp and cradling his hand in front of him.

"RRRRRRGGGGH!" Rocking back and forth, he seemed like a man in a religious trance.

"What can I do, Sweetheart? What can I do?" Rhonda's rising hysteria seemed to frighten the children who stared into the darkness at their father. He seemed like a shadow rather than their father. The sound he emitted was dreadful.

At last, Butcher stopped rocking and panted. In and out. In and out. Finally, he was able to speak. With superhuman effort, he sat up.

The absence of light was eerie. Slowly, Butcher lifted his left hand. J.T. immediately saw what happened. His face registered no emotion, but he was staring at Butcher's hand.

This is not good at all.
Butcher's finger was no longer attached.

Leslie Deakins could barely hear her phone ringing. Not only was the storm raging, howling like a caged beast clawing at its constraints, but the children were frightened and crying loudly. Windows shook and rattled in the wind. Once the electricity went off, it seemed as if the world was swallowed in a whirlpool of fear. John took the girls into the living room where he made a game of trying to find candles, and once he had lit them, they carried them around the house.

Frustrated, Leslie searched for her phone. Now that the electricity was out, she wouldn't be able to finish the potatoes. Wiping her hands on her apron, Leslie located her phone and touched the screen to accept the call from Rhonda.

"Hello neighbor. How's ev…"

Leslie's eyes widened and her face drained of color. "Of course. Of course. Bring them over. I'll wait for you on the porch."

John poked his head around the corner and peered into the darkness to see his wife's face ghostly illuminated by the screen of her phone. "What's going on?"

"There's been an accident. Rhonda is dropping the kids off."

"In this storm?"

"Can you just hold the girls in the living room while I wait for Rhonda?"

John nodded. "But what happened?"

"I don't know all of it yet, but Butcher made a wrong move. They've got to head to the emergency room."

"What a miserable night to be out. Where is Connie? Why isn't she watching the kids?"

"Rhonda didn't say. She must be with her boyfriend."

"Oh."

Minutes later, as Leslie peered outside the octagonal window in their front door, she saw approaching headlights. Putting on her rain jacket, Leslie opened the door, but the blast of the storm pushed her back inside. Struggling out onto the porch, she held onto the railing as she descended the steps. The rain stung her cheeks. Rhonda opened the door and pulled the kids out. They weren't wearing any rain gear. Leslie took off her rain jacket and like a mother hen, she wrapped it around both of them.

"Call us when you know something!" She shouted over the wind.

"I will," Rhonda yelled.

Briefly, Leslie checked the passenger window streaked with raindrops. Butcher's head leaned against the glass and for a moment, it looked as if he was dead. "Will you be all right?"

"Just get the kids inside!" Rhonda yelled, as she ran back around the car to the driver's side, "I'll..." the rest of her statement was swallowed by the fury of the storm.

Now soaking wet, Leslie gently but quickly guided the children up the steps and into the house. J.T. and Georgie looked like soaked rats.

John gathered the Jensen kids in his arms. Moving them down the hallway, he grabbed some towels and dried them off.

Slowly, Georgie's cries ceased. J.T. allowed John to buff him dry, but as soon as the blood began flowing back into his limbs, he proclaimed that he was good enough to finish the rest of the job by himself. After they were dry, they moved like blind people back down the hallway into the living room where the candles were glowing. Leslie produced extra plates at the formal dining table so that the six of them could eat together. The meal seemed to lack flavor.

"My daddy's finger is yucky," Georgie stated.

"What do you mean?" Leslie asked.

"It was…off."

John and Leslie shared a look. "You mean, it didn't look right?"

Georgie shook her head and J.T. responded gravely. "No, Unca John, his finger is actually off. He hit it and it fell off."

Leslie gasped and covered her mouth.

It was then that the lights came back on.

Linda vaguely remembered the fall. The pain, a lightning bolt shooting through her spine, had taken her legs out from under her. When her foot slipped on the wet floor, she distinctly remembered crumpling. Then, nothing until Dick found her almost an hour later.

After arriving at the Clancy Municipal Hospital, Dick began to make phone calls to their kids and then, with a sigh, to Leona who would pass on the information to everyone she knew (and probably everyone she didn't know).

After turning off his phone, Dick moved to Linda's side. She'd been speaking oddly, strange things, indecent things, ramblings about bumps and breasts. Dick knew that Linda's back had been hurting her, but this rant was new. And it frightened him.

An hour later, a young doctor, perhaps in her forties, pushed aside the curtain. Her rosy cheeks glowed with good humor and her smile, comforting but… tense, led the conversation.

"You must be Mr. Harmsen. My name is Dr. Neale. Please, have a seat." She motioned to the chair near the bed.

"That's all right," Dick stammered, "I'd rather stand next to Linda."

"How is she?" Dr. Neale asked.

"I was hoping you could tell us that. She seems kind of out of it."

"Yes, well..." Dr. Neale looked down at the chart. "The good news is, she's alive. But..."

"But... what?"

"There are some complications with Linda's health."

"What does that mean?

"Mr. Harmsen. I'm afraid I have some bad news."

Dick's heart raced. "What... what is it?"

"Linda has cancer."

"I don't understand." Dick's mind stuttered, unable to grasp what Dr. Neale was telling him. "Linda doesn't have cancer. She has a bad back."

"I'm very sorry to tell you this, Mr. Harmsen, but Linda has an advanced stage of breast cancer."

Dick attempted to process the horror of the doctor's words. "But... but... how is this possible? She's healthy! This is... no... you must have the wrong chart!" Dick looked like a trapped animal. His eyes were drawn to the window where the passing storm was still lighting up the sky to the east.

Holding the chart to her chest, Dr. Neale held Dick's eyes. "Dick, Linda is going to need all of your strength, all of your love and all of your hope in the next months."

"Is she going to die?" Dick's pleading voice echoed in the room. Dr. Neale's eyes shifted.

"One step at a time, Mr. Harmsen." She read from the chart. "When Linda came to the clinic, she complained of back problems. We did some blood tests and they came back positive for breast cancer. Unfortunately, the back problems stem from the fact that because the cancer has metastasized; there is a tumor sitting on her spine and it's impinging her spinal cord."

Dick began to get angry. "What are all these bullshit words? Metastasized? What is impinging? Just tell me in English and none of this bullshit doctor lingo!"

"Mr. Harmsen," Dr. Neale said calmly and slowly, "the breast cancer has spread through various parts of her body. Some of those original breast cancer cells have broken away and are growing near her spinal cord and pinching it."

"So what are you telling me? That she's going to be paralyzed?"

Dr. Neale responded soberly. "Once again, let's not jump to conclusions. We'll work through treatments when she's ready to talk about it."

"But for how long? How long does she have?" Dick's voice broke.

"Step by step, Mr. Harmsen. That's really the only way that we can do this."

Dick looked down at his wife. He'd never seen her so frail. Throughout their marriage, she had been the linchpin, the strongest link, the person who kept the entire family together, but now…

Dick did not even notice when Dr. Neale left the room. He had simply knelt beside Linda's hospital bed and buried his face in the back of her hand. For one of the first times in his life, Dick prayed a prayer of exchange. *God, this is not fair. If you're going to take someone, let it be me.* Then, as he looked up at his wife who was attempting to open an eye, the first sob started. As he wailed, a nurse came down the hallway to look in. With sorrowful eyes, she softly closed the door.

Rhonda heard the keening down the hospital corridor. It was much more than a moan. Someone was far beyond physical pain. The sound reverberated deep within her and Rhonda wished that she could unhear it. It was frightening and it felt like a bad omen. To some extent, this sound was riding shotgun on her own emotions and if she truly let it go, she might begin to understand the depths of whatever that other person was feeling. At this point, though, Butcher's main struggle would be waking up permanently short one finger on his left hand.

As it was, the ER doctor told them that he would be back to look at the bandages. What was left of Leopold Jensen's finger would be trimmed down to the palm and covered with the flap of skin.

"We can make up a bed next to him if you'd like, Mrs. Jensen," the doctor said.

"No," Rhonda said, "we've got two small children. I'll stay with them during the night and bring them back with me tomorrow."

The doctor nodded. "Okay. We'll keep him comfortable." His eyes strayed automatically to the chart and then flashed back to her.

What is he hiding?

As the doctor left, her phone rang. Assuming that it was John or Leslie, she answered without checking the screen.

"Hello?"

"Are you okay?" Rhonda was nonplussed. She couldn't place the voice.

"Who is this?"

"It's me, Stedman."

Rhonda felt relief. "Hi Stedman."

"What happened?"

Rhonda robotically relayed the events of the evening.

"Oh, man, that's awful," Stedman said.

"How did you find out that we were here?"

"Do you want the convoluted version, or the basic?" Stedman asked.

"How about the basic?"

Stedman took a deep breath. "John called Nash, who immediately called Derek. Derek, of course, let Tracey know which led to Summer and then to me…" His voice trailed off. "Is there anything that they can do for his finger?"

"Look, Stedman, at this point we don't really know. The first doctor seems to think that it can't be saved. We could get a second opinion, but it's been off for a while."

Stedman shivered with revulsion.

"Is there anything that we can do? Any of us in Amicable?"

"No, Stedman, not yet. We'll be all right. I'm coming home tonight to pick up the kids and we'll be back in Clancy tomorrow. It's a Saturday, so there won't be any hurry."

"Oh." Stedman sounded disappointed, as if he'd been rejected.

"But thank you. We'll definitely let you know." Rhonda looked at Butcher who was beginning to stir. "I've got to go. Thanks for calling."

She pushed the disconnect button and turned to her husband.

"How are you feeling, Butcher?"

He groaned and tried to maneuver his body so he could see her better, but the effort was too much. "I… what's going on?"

"Just rest," she was awash with guilt. Her first thoughts were of all the extra things that she would have to do around the house that he normally did: the washing, the laundry, the cooking and cleaning.

Rhonda reached out to touch him. His stubbly cheeks seemed strange against her palm.

"That feels nice," he mumbled.

"I'm glad you can feel something good," she responded. Her hands ran across his forehead and touched his temples. She noticed the grey hair that had appeared in the last couple of years.

He was going to be a very handsome old man. "How does your finger feel?"

Butcher smiled and winced. "You mean my lack of finger?"

She snorted. "I'm glad you still have a sense of humor."

"I won't ever lose that," he said, "no matter how many fingers I lose."

"I would prefer it if you stuck to just this one. I want to be able to hold your hand, not just your palm."

Butcher smiled groggily. "I'll stick to just this one. Far too messy."

"Leo," Rhonda's face began to break. "I'm so sorry. So, so sorry. I wish I could take this pain away from you."

"My little bedbug... We've always shared everything, haven't we? For better or for worse. I think we've done them all now. Richer, poorer, sickness, health..."

"I think we'll wait a while for death," Rhonda responded, and leaned over to kiss his forehead.

"Good idea," he smiled and closed his eyes. "I don't really want to live without you. The odds are you're going to die first," he joked.

A few tears leaked. "I love you," she whispered into his ear.

He was already asleep.

Taking a deep breath, Rhonda retreated and looked around at the emergency room suite. A few machines stood as beeping sentinels behind him. A pulse monitor had been placed over his right (and only remaining) index finger. His cheeks were gaunt, especially with the four-day growth of salt and pepper beard stubbling his cheeks.

Grabbing her handbag, Rhonda opened the door and stepped into the corridor. There, she was surprised to see Richard Harmsen.

J.T. wasn't quite sure what was going on, but when he looked up at Leslie and John, he was pretty certain that there was something seriously wrong with his dad.

He could read people really well.

His dad's finger wasn't going to be put back on, and because of this fact, J.T. flexed his own finger multiple times in preparation. It was almost as if he was preparing to be his dad's surrogate pointer finger.

Holding his hand up in front of his face, he noticed the small little lines. The imperfections, even in his young and supple skin, were apparent to his finely tuned eyes. J.T. noticed everything. If someone were to ask him to name all the objects in a room, he could close his eyes and point to them. If someone asked him to repeat an entire story, he could do it. No one ever asked him to test this ability yet, although sometimes he did it himself.

For J.T., it wasn't just about remembering where things were, it was knowing where they should be. He had the ability to order and re-order; he could see patterns that others couldn't. Inconsistencies frustrated him, like a field of flowers where two of them did not have the same number of leaves, or when a builder got lazy and didn't put the same number of nails in one post as another.

"J.T.," Leslie knelt down in front of him, "how are you doing, Little Buddy?"

Pursing his lips and crossing his arms, J.T. took in all of Leslie's non-verbal signals simultaneously. The crease between her eyes had three lines. Not good. Her left hand kept fidgeting with the hem of her jeans. She was agitated. "Okay," he said shortly.

"Your mom texted me and said she'd be here to pick you and Georgie up pretty soon."

From the back play area, Georgie, in her blissful naivety, was laughing with delirious joy as she played with the twin Deakins girls. J.T. frowned. She was still a baby.

"That will be good," he responded as he stood in the center of the dining room. Behind him the clock was ticking. Tick tock. Tick tock. J.T. didn't like ticking clocks. They annoyed him.

"Would you like something to eat? Or, do you want to draw a picture?"

This was definitely not what he wanted to do; only little kids drew pictures.

"No, thank you. I'll be fine."

Leslie crouched for a few more seconds, just long enough for J.T. to register her emotions. Sighing, J.T. wrapped his arms around her neck and squeezed. Leslie thought that he was doing this for his sake. Hugging him tightly, Leslie kissed the side of his head and pulled him back.

"Everything is going to be okay, Little Buddy." She stood and straightened her shirt once more.

"Sure." He remained unconvinced.

Leslie's phone chimed and she moved towards the kitchen to answer it. J.T. looked out the dark windowpane. He could see his reflection in it. The storm had diminished, but there was still a lurking fury, a snarling tiger waiting for them right outside the window.

Rhonda's heart was still caught in her throat. Pulsing, it pounded against her skin. She could feel it in her head, behind her eyes, in her wrists and especially her chest. Dread suffused every part of her being. What traumatically began as a trip to the emergency room for Butcher had turned into a nightmare for one of Amicableans most recognizable citizens. Linda Harmsen lived and breathed the town. Linda didn't deserve this. Her thoughts, unbidden, strayed to a basket of deplorables that certainly merited punishment - pedophiles, rapists, murderers and the like - and she wished to transfer Linda's illness to them. It was totally unfair that a down-to-earth, normal, good person like Linda should have her life cut short.

Dick had been beside himself. Although she didn't know him very well, only in a casual, Amicablean way where surface information was necessary, Rhonda knew enough to know that he had been a hardworking, productive member of the community who did and said the right things. And, he had married his high school sweetheart. Dick's presence in the hospital was a shock, yes, but the revelation was beyond comprehension. An advanced stage of cancer was never a good sign.

What had most frightened Rhonda was the wild, rabid look in his eyes. Dick's eyes switched from the clock on the wall at the nurses' station quickly to his wristwatch, then to his phone. This rapid management of time, checking time pieces to control time itself, was almost subconscious. If he could somehow turn back the minute hand, he would wake up and realize that this was all just a very, very bad dream.

"I'm sure she's going to be all right," he said unconvincingly. "She's a tough lady and we've got the best medical personnel in the world helping her."

"Yes, of course," she responded. "Is there anything we can do?"

Dick spotted a young nurse who leisurely typed into a keyboard behind a high-fronted desk. She had the appearance of a person unconnected to the tragedy that surrounded her in the ward. Dick wanted to shout at her, to remind her that PEOPLE ARE DYING HERE! SHOW A LITTLE RESPECT! but it wasn't her fault. This was just her job.

He sighed. "No, no, we'll manage. I'll call the kids and see what we can do. I just… well, it's such a shock and Linda's in there…" his hand motioned towards the ER room, "… and… and… lying there, full of needles and medicine and canc…" Dick couldn't finish the word before his resolve broke. His face, which had been frantic, suddenly melted into a pool of his greatest fears. He seemed like a little boy floating on a small raft in the middle of the ocean.

"Oh, Dick," Rhonda moved forward to embrace him. As she wrapped an arm around him, he covered his face and began to sob. His voice was muted, but his great shoulders shook. Rhonda's thoughts for Butcher were momentarily set aside.

For a while they remained in that position. A few other night denizens of the emergency room walked by, but they took a wide birth around the two grieving people in the middle of the room.

While comforting Dick Harmsen, she worried about her husband and his future. And her own. Would she have to go back to work? Would Butcher be a stay-at-home dad? Could he handle that change? How would Georgie deal with it?

As she drove back to Amicable, Rhonda's mind eventually moved back to her husband's missing finger which would be a perpetual reminder that he could never again do what he was best at; it would be like a piano player missing a thumb or an artist suddenly going colorblind - yes, it could be done, but never in the same way.

Leslie opened the front door. Her face, pinched with worry, was illuminated by the dim porch light. Rhonda stepped beyond her much shorter friend and into the alcove where she wiped her feet on the rug. Georgie, hearing the door open, caught sight of her mother and raced as fast as her little legs could carry her. Rhonda bent down to collect the little girl and embraced her. Georgie buried her face in Rhonda's shoulder.

"What did you do, Georgie?" Rhonda asked softly.

Georgie pulled back from her mother's face and smiled. "We pwayed bwocks."

"That's good," Rhonda responded and looked over Georgie's curly hair into the living room where J.T. was standing stock-still, hands hanging loosely at his sides. His expression was blank. It was as if he was gazing through her, or at least around her. It was this expression, or lack thereof, which worried her sometimes. It was her fear (she didn't know why she was afraid) that he was autistic. Rhonda had heard horror stories about the struggles of autistic kids and she wasn't sure she could deal with that, but the doctors said that he didn't exhibit any other signs.

"Hi, Kiddo."

"Hi, Mom," he responded quietly. His eyes didn't meet hers.

"Are you okay?"

J.T. wrestled with his frustratingly limited vocabulary. Because he'd been hanging around with Uncle Derek, he'd picked up a few words, some helpful, others tantalizingly just out of reach for his six (almost seven)-year-old brain. What he wanted to tell her, of course, was that he was frightened. His restiveness, which was internal rather than external, was not due to boredom, obviously, but of an inability to understand the things that he was thinking, seeing and hearing. His father, always a bastion of strength in the family, was not with them and he had seen something...

"J.T.?"

"Okay, Mom. Can we go home now?"

Rhonda nodded and reached out for him who moved zombie-like across the room. As he neared his mother, it was only then that he sensed the maternal care and worry. Finally, he broke through the flimsy walls of his lack of understanding, ran to her legs and hugged her.

With her free left hand, she held him and thanked Leslie over the heads of her children. "I really appreciate this so much, Leslie." John appeared and she smiled at him also.

"Of course," Leslie responded, as they turned to leave. "You'll let us know what happened at the hospital, won't you?"

"After I get the kids to bed, I'll fill you in." Dick Harmsen's face arose unbidden in her mind.

"Okay." Leslie opened the door and allowed the Jensen's to depart back into the windstorm. Fortunately, the downpour had stopped and only a gentle mist fell. Rhonda hurried the children to the car while Leslie shut the door behind them.

A little while later, after Rhonda had skilfully pajamafyed her children, brushed their teeth and tucked them into bed, she flopped onto the sofa exhausted. Georgie fell asleep immediately.

After J.T. had been tucked into bed, their prayers said, a special one for his dad, he stared up at his mother with his blue eyes wide. She was scared of something – very, very scared – but she wasn't willing to share it with him. *Why did he notice everything? Why was he able to see that his mother's fingers seemed to have smudges of ink on them? What was this from? Her right ear still carried the red imprint of her phone. Who had she been talking to? Why was her pulse rate so high? Was it just because of his dad?* He didn't think so.

"Just go to sleep, John Thomas," his mother said as she flipped the light switch throwing the room into darkness.

"I will, Mom," he lied.

When the lights went out in J.T.'s room, everything seemed to come alive.

John Thomas Jensen's visual acuity was miraculously good. From even great distances, J.T. could focus on the smallest details much the same as a hawk can look into a grass field and notice a mouse from a great height. Strangely, J.T.'s night vision was equally acute; not only could he still see shapes in the dark, he could also see color. He had never asked if other people could do the same thing; he just assumed that they could. The act of turning off the lights at night seemed to suggest a pattern of behavior to him rather than a practical application for sleep. Just as his mother turned off the light every night, he simply assumed that this was the signal that he should close his eyes.

But, he could still see everything.

As the fading lightning flashed through his window illuminating lines and forms both moving and inert, he watched them, followed them. This was his routine – usually he followed the casual meanderings of spiders or bugs in the room; he could watch a lone mosquito circle lazily in mid-air floating on the minute currents in the room endlessly waiting for its prey to fall asleep. Sometimes he made a game out of the hunt; J.T. would lie very still watching as the mosquito honed in on his body. Just when it hovered above his skin, he would snap it in his fingers like a Venus flytrap. As he rubbed the remains of the insect between his fingers, he noticed the striations, even its sharp snout. J.T. felt sorry for the little creature, but he still was glad that it would not be sucking his blood.

If other eyes watched him at night, they would have wondered if he was having a bad dream or even sleep talking. What they couldn't possibly have known was that while they were standing in the dark, J.T. was sitting in the brightness of the dark. There was no difference to him.

J.T. focussed on the corner of the room near his closet. Far up in the corner, a daddy longlegs spider was absentmindedly flicking two of its legs. It was like a cat licking its paw and cleaning an ear. While he watched, J.T.'s mind refocused on the events of the night and specifically of his father's missing digit. He only had a brief look, *but in the blood...*

His door opened again. It was his mother. She noticed his eyes were still open.

"I thought I said you should go to sleep?" Her voice was not frustrated but worried.

"Okay, Mom."

She moved into the bedroom, one step farther. As her eyes adjusted to the lack of light, she saw him sitting rigidly in the middle of the bed. His erect posture made it seem as if he was a little Buddha.

"What are you doing?"

At last he pulled his gaze away from the spider and turned his full attention to her face. There were seven lines poking from the corner of her right eye and five from the other. "I was looking."

"At what?"

He pointed to the corner. "At the spider."

Rhonda shook her head and sat on the edge of the bed. She grabbed his face in her hands. "Are you having a nightmare already? Don't worry, it's too dark in here to see any spiders." She laid him down again and pulled the covers up to his chin. "They won't get you."

J.T. turned his eyes onto his mother and she was shocked to see how dilated they were, but he was not squinting into the light at all. "I'm not worried."

Rhonda paused and tapped his chest. "Good. Now go to sleep."

Turning away, J.T. looked back to the corner to notice that the spider had moved. Then, to satisfy his mother, he closed his eyes. He was tired.

Rhonda kissed him one last time and exited the room.

She was still worried about him.

Chapter 8.

At 5:38 am, Butcher believed he had reached the nadir of his existence.

Butcher's first thought was to lift his left hand to see if this whole thing had indeed been a long, intense nightmare, but the reality was worse than the nightmare. Sighing deeply, he pushed his head back into the pillow and stared up at the ceiling. Although the morning glow would increase in intensity in the next hour, the dimness seemed comforting. In those dim moments, he reflected nostalgically, to a different time.

When he was twenty-nine, Butcher met a woman. Unexpectedly, she had materialized like an angel of mercy, mercifully breaking the tedium of his days in the butchery. Leo, as he was known at SaveMore Grocery in Walden Woods, Massachusetts, had been slaving away for a particularly boorish fellow named Jannick Stern, a 'lapsed Jew,' as he called himself, who thought about nothing else than making money. Mr. Stern, as Leo was supposed to call him (and he did, completely aware that the name was ironically befitting for the shop owner), was insistent that Leo do everything by the book. This included only the tried-and-true ways of cutting meat, selling meat, wrapping meat and eating meat. Leo's smile faded when Mr. Stern, preceded by his voluminous beer gut, weekly inspected the deli. Mr. Stern would lean close to the glass and with his finger near his face point out the cuts, counting them, checking them for the correct thickness and marbling. If there were perceived imperfections, Mr. Stern would pull his tiny, circular lensed glasses down to the tip of his nose and frown. Tepeeing his hands under his nose and in front of his mouth, Mr. Stern would expound (with a great, dramatic sigh) how the thickness of the loin chops needed to be just this much *smaller. This annoyed Leo very much and he wanted to shove* just this much *of his tenderizing mallet up Mr. Stern's nose.*

Chapter 8.

One day, as Mr. Stern stopped Leo to lecture him on the correct amount of spices in the Polish sausage, the front door opened. Mr. Stern stopped his tirade. His mouth, hanging slightly ajar as a young woman entered, paused mid-lecture. Butcher, almost a foot taller than the lapsed Jew, stared over his head at the customer.

She was tiny, a smidgeon over five feet tall, with wavy, auburn hair. Her slender waist was accentuated by the strange assortment of clothes she was wearing. The dress, with its circus of color, geometric shapes of orange, brown and yellow, stopped at her knees revealing wiry, yet muscular (and clearly unshaven) legs. A small yellow purse with brass clasps draped over her right arm. She nodded a polite good morning to the staring men.

With all the charm he could muster, (which wasn't much at all, but as most middle-aged men believe that they have not lost it whether they ever had it or not), Mr. Stern smiled and opened his arms in welcome.

"Alo haver!" Mr. Stern didn't actually speak Hebrew or Yiddish, though he remembered a few phrases from his childhood religious instruction.

"Hello."

"Welcome to my store! I am Jannick Stern, owner and proprietor. How may I serve you today?"

Butcher rolled his eyes. Mr. Stern hadn't served anyone in his store for years. The young woman noticed his expression and smirked. Stern quickly looked behind him at Leo who shrugged.

"I need pork chops and bacon."

Leo tried to cover his laughter with a cough. Even though Mr. Stern was a 'lapsed Jew,' he had never entirely embraced the necessity for having pork products in his store. The common *mensch enjoyed pork, so he stocked it.*

Mr. Stern frowned at Butcher and turned back to the young woman. "Oh, my young, beautiful woman. You don't understand what pork does to a fine person like yourself. Why not choose some wonderful steaks, or even fresh chicken breasts."

She stepped back. "No, thank you." Pushing past the flustered shop owner, she placed her hands on the glass. "Good afternoon," she said to Leo. "Maybe you can help me? I'd like some pork chops and bacon."

"Whatever you would like, ma'am." Butcher noticed that Mr. Stern's face had turned a bright scarlet. *"How many would you like?"*

"It depends."

"What does it depend upon?"

The young woman's face glowed with an impish grin. *"It depends on how many I'm cooking for."*

Butcher crossed his arms and leaned towards her on the other side of the counter. *"And...? How many are you cooking for?"*

She cupped her chin in her hand and stared up into the eyes of the tall butcher. *"That too depends."*

Butcher laughed. *"I'm intrigued. Okay, I'll ask. What does* that depend on?"

The young woman paused and spun around. *"Excuse me,"* she said to the ruffled storeowner, *"don't you have someone else who might need your expertise? I would prefer if you weren't listening to my conversation with the nice butcher here."*

Mr. Stern's face turned a brighter shade of red. Without a word, he pivoted and walked quickly away blustering towards the checkout counter to let off some steam.

"Now, as I was saying," the woman said, *"it depends on* you." She pointed at the befuddled butcher.

"I'm not following."

"I've heard rumors about you. I know you've only been in Walden for a little while, it's been a couple of months, is that right?"

Butcher frowned and nodded.

"A few of my friends said that you have a unique talent."

Butcher put his head down. *"Oh."* How disappointing.

She laughed. *"They said you're really good at making the perfect chops."*

Thankfully, she was just toying with him. He smiled. *"That's right, Ma'am. I'm here to serve you pork scampi, pork gumbo, pork jambalaya, pork kebabs..."* playing off Forrest Gump he pointed to the different kinds of meat.

"Do you think you could stuff some breasts for me?" the young woman said suggestively.

Leo's face froze and he read her quickly. She was being serious. She definitely wanted chicken breasts but she was also asking for something else…

"I'll… I… let me…um, see what I can do…"

Brought back to the present, Butcher smiled at the thought of Jennifer. All those years ago. He hadn't thought of her in a long time.

Leaning over to the bedside table, Butcher reached out for his phone. Whether the drugs, the pain or simply exhaustion, he was having difficulties texting. Oddly, his fingers were still a little numb.

Hello Swetheart, Up I'm waake. Just give call em when you have chance.

Weird, he thought as he looked the message. *What was I thinking? Man, I must really be out of it?*

Rhonda's phone dinged. It was very early and she was just on her way out the door. Her mother had come home late last night, almost midnight. There would be no purpose in lecturing her about a pseudo-curfew imposed by her daughter. Her mother looked very happy which was strangely annoying; she should be wallowing in pain with her and the children, not galivanting around like some teenage schoolgirl sneaking out of the house to make out in the back seat of the station wagon on a Saturday night.

Rhonda had been up for her normal run, a little earlier, in fact, because she wanted to get to the hospital at a decent time so that the kids could see their father, and then be back for the second half of the school day. When she saw that it was Butcher, she felt a stab of guilt. There were so very few things in life that were just *hers*.

She puzzled over the message. Obviously, the drugs were still affecting him. Rhonda checked her running watch. If she just ran for half an hour, she could be back to call him. Guiltily, she overruled the loving thing to do and went with what she needed most. Putting her phone back down on the table, she ran away.

While Rhonda Jensen cruised through her second mile of vigorous jogging and Butcher waited somewhat impatiently for his jogging wife to respond to his text message, Linda Harmsen completed her own breast exam. She was acutely aware that they were betraying her. Linda had not slept during the night. Minute after minute, she chastised herself for not noticing the strange small lumps. Then, she chastised Dick for not noticing. *Certainly, he should have felt them, right?*

Around three o'clock in the morning, her thoughts moved from accusation to planning. The doctor had warned her not to go searching online for prognoses or life-expectations, but she couldn't help it. Knowing at least *something* about the disease seemed like it would be more beneficial than worrying irrationally. At the end of the hour of surfing, she was almost quivering with fear, especially the stage of cancer she had. She should have followed Dr. Neale's advice.

Linda felt one of the bumps on the side of her left breast and cursed the little thing. *How could something this small be so... so... deadly? Why couldn't the smartest brains in the world figure out how to kill something as tiny as cancer cells?*

For the first time she felt the unfairness and the indecency of the disease. Although she only knew what she read (and could reasonably understand), she knew that she was up against a heavyweight champion. Breast cancer at her advanced stage seemed hopeless, and yet... and yet! when she saw the odds, there was still hope.

At 6:34 a.m., Linda was as exhausted as she had ever been in her life. Her mind skipped like a scratched record. Every last minute of inactivity was an extra minute for the cancer cells to rub their greedy little hands together and plan their attack on another organ.

Slowly, Linda pulled back the covers and edged her feet over the side of the bed. For the first time, she noticed the age spots on her white legs. They were beginning to look *old*. Linda was acutely aware that not only did she not want to *look* old, she also did not want to *be* old.

Sliding slowly off the bed, she placed her feet into the flimsy hospital slippers and pulled herself erect. Her hips reminded her that she was in the hospital for a reason, but she wanted to fight already. Against *it*. She wanted to find Dr. Neale and see if she could get some answers.

Linda grasped the movable stand which held the bags of intravenous fluids and walked tentatively to the door. Surprised by its weight, it took most of her strength to open it. Feeling lightheaded, Linda paused in the doorway unsure whether to cross the threshold or go back to bed. *I need some reassurance.*

The thought caused her to grit her teeth and move past her fear.

"Hello?" she called out into the hallway. "Is anyone out there?"

Linda moved farther out into the corridor and turned right. Before continuing, she looked back over her shoulder for her room number, and then kept walking. The nurse's station was in the center of the ward, but it seemed a thousand miles away. In her current condition, she wondered if she was going to make it.

Cutting the distances into pieces, Linda paused at the door of each room on the ward. As she approached the second to last room on the left, she called out one more time hoping that a nurse might hear. "Hello? Anyone? Can anyone hear me?"

After a beat, a male voice answered her. "I can."

"Where are you?"

"I don't know what room I'm in, but it sounds like not too far from you."

Room 13. She took two steps towards it. "Are you in here?" she asked through the crack in the doorway.

"Yes," the voice said.

"Can I come in and sit down?" Linda's legs were beginning to quiver. Soon, she was going to collapse.

"Sure. Don't mind the mess."

Linda scrunched up her face. She knew that voice, or at least it sounded incredibly familiar. It wasn't until she saw Butcher's face that she put it all together.

"Oh! Butcher!" She shuffled quickly to the chair in the corner of the room. The pain was intense.

"Linda? What are you doing here?"

She held up a hand as if in catching her breath. He waited patiently. "Okay, wow. That was interesting."

"So anyway, fancy meeting you here." Linda sank into the chair and readjusted her hips. She glanced at the saline bag noticing that it was already half-empty. She was being sucked dry, just like the bag.

"Yes, fancy."

"What happened to you?" she asked.

He held up his tightly wrapped left hand. "A mishap."

"I heard about that," Linda said. "An accident at work, wasn't it?"

He waggled his right hand. "The first one, yes, but the second time, just bad luck." He lifted his left hand a little higher. "It looks like I'm going to be the nine fingered man."

"Oh, that's terrible, Butcher. I'm so sorry."

"They still need to do surgery to clean it up so it doesn't get infected."

She shook her head. "Sounds like the week for amputation."

Butcher frowned but then opened his eyes and read it in her. *Breast cancer.* "Oh no, Linda. Mastectomy?"

For the first time the word had been spoken. Involuntarily, she touched her breasts with her hands, almost in reassurance that they weren't gone yet.

Linda began to realize that grief was not a linear process. Not only did it not travel in a straight line from exposure, to shock, to sadness, anger and acceptance, but it also didn't take into account the verticality of the emotions. No one could explain to the sufferer the heights and depths of whatever end was coming. To make matters worse, suffering does not allow one to actually see what that end is: whether restoration, perpetual pain or, ultimately, death.

In the dim stillness of the hospital room, Butcher averted his eyes out of respect for the suffering woman sitting in the chair at the foot of his bed. As he pondered what was occurring in his room, he marvelled that when Linda had entered, he hadn't thought about his own pain. This revelation caused him to wonder if he had stumbled upon something quite useful.

Now that the sun was yawning and stretching its arm-like rays above the trees, the light changed from a rosy pink to delicate white. The empty seat next to Linda seemed symbolic, a space that could be filled by only one, impermanent person. A small end table was littered with various magazines detailing various ways to enhance one's love life. The window was inset into the wall and a cushioned space for an extra visitor, a child, perhaps, could sit on the similarly colored green pad and read books while waiting for healing.

"How did you know?" Linda asked. "I mean, I know that you have special powers, but how..." Her voice trailed off.

"I…well, you know, I can't explain it. When you came in and said… There was something in your demeanor, something tragic. I just saw it."

"What do you mean?"

Butcher re-adjusted himself in bed and cradled his left hand close to his chest. "When I looked at you, you were holding your hands across your breasts. Our hands always touch the things that are most precious to us – they protect them. That's why we touch our faces five hundred times a day."

"But Butcher, the cancer isn't just in my breasts. It's everywhere!" Terror widened her eyes. "It's like… I can feel it eating away at my insides, even now. It's like I've got bugs crawling around under my skin and I can't kill them."

"I'm sorry, Linda."

"Why couldn't you have told me sooner? How could you not have known?" Linda projected her anger onto Butcher.

"It doesn't work like that, my friend."

She sniffed and put a hand on the IV stand. "I probably should get going."

Butcher scratched his head. "Don't go, Linda. Not yet."

She didn't take her hand off the stand but didn't move either. "What do you want to talk about?"

"Anything. Nothing. Something besides pain."

Linda smiled. "How about the weather?"

"That sounds wonderful." Butcher relaxed into his pillow.

For the next half an hour, the two Amicableans wandered through traditional topics of distraction, alighting like butterflies on the petals of comforting topics, beloved people and beloved times in Amicable. Linda spoke about her family and then about her closest friendships and what they meant to her. Linda wasn't sure how everyone would react – well, she was: they would be frightened and saddened and smother her with attentive kindness

Chapter 8.

– but she wasn't sure she was prepared for that yet. Her friends, her exercise ladies...

Butcher, too, opened up about his life before Amicable. Butcher's mysterious past had been hung carefully in the closet, but he shared about his time in Massachusetts. This was only because he had gone there already this morning.

"Her name was Jennifer." Butcher's face faded back to that time again. "She... she had this way about her, this... I don't know how to explain it other than she had a total disdain for anything normal." Butcher attempted to make quotations marks with his fingers, but forgot that he could only complete one side of them. He winced at the pain.

"She came into the Butcher's shop and asked for stuffed chicken breasts, and when she left, she was carrying not only a package but my phone number also."

Linda, blessedly forgetting her own cares, leaned forward into the story.

"She was short with mousy auburn hair and hazel eyes, and she always wanted me to call her 'Nif,' because 'Jenny' or 'Jen' was too common. Her wardrobe drove me crazy. There was nothing out of bounds for her. It didn't matter if she wore polka dots and striped pants, an orange top with pink slacks and then purple lipstick to complete the outfit." He laughed at the memory.

"My favorite was when she came to meet me at the Butcher's shop and she had shaved off all her hair, right down to the skin. She looked like a Hari Krishna. She wore a suit and tie that day because, according to her, 'it just seemed right.'"

"She's sounds fit for Amicable," Linda coughed a laugh into her hand.

"You thought Stedman was bad..."

"So," Linda interjected, "you loved her?"

Butcher shrugged. "I think so. I mean, I loved things *about* her, but I don't know if I actually loved *her*. She was a genuinely beautiful distraction and she made me laugh. But she didn't talk about her feelings. Nif could go on endlessly about the horrors of the whaling industry, or the indifference of American public on the Gulf War, but ask her about her parents and she shut up tighter than a submarine door at twenty thousand leagues under the sea."

"What happened?"

"I guess we both got tired of faking it."

"Faking what?"

Butcher took a deep breath. "That life doesn't really mean anything."

Linda looked up sharply. "What do you mean?"

"We spent too much time honing our skills of remaining unaffected by everything. Even if moved by causes or desires, we never did anything but talk about it. Eventually, we found out that our relationship was just full of air. We never actually engaged in the pain of life itself."

"Wow."

"Yeah," Butcher responded bemusedly, "it took me a long time to get over Nif, not just because breaking up is hard, but it took a long time to get her indifference out of my system."

Linda smiled. "Well, you certainly care for people now. Everyone seems to need your presence."

A shadow passed in front of Butcher's face. "Yes, well, we'll see."

At just that moment, his phone buzzed. Rhonda. She and the kids were on their way to the hospital. "The true love of my life..."

Linda smiled. "Does Rhonda know about Nif?"

He shook his head. "There are some things about the past that your loved ones don't need to know."

Chapter 8.

Rhonda was frustrated as she pulled into the parking lot of the Clancy hospital. She hadn't properly diagnosed exactly what was eating away at her, whether stress or worry or even selfishness, so when she pulled open the sliding door on their silver minivan, Georgie complained that Rhonda was tugging too hard on the seatbelt.

"I'm doing my best by myself," Rhonda replied testily.

"But it hurts," Georgie started to cry. Her small upper lip quivered. This annoyed Rhonda.

"Time to tough it out, Georgie," Rhonda said as she grunted her from the seat and set her on the pavement. J.T. had undone his own seatbelt (he was quite proud of the fact that he was big enough to get out of the car without help) and was crawling in front of Georgie's chair to get out. He didn't want his mother to help him down because he wasn't a baby anymore. As he jumped from the car onto the pavement, he overbalanced and ended up sprawled on the ground. At his age, his height was very much a danger.

"Careful!" Rhonda groused.

J.T. brushed his hands off and even though they stung, he didn't care. It was fun to fly even just for a moment.

Rhonda slid the door shut behind him and shouldered her purse. Taking a small hand in each one of hers, she walked them through the parking lot briskly, much too fast for their tiny legs. Georgie complained again, which only increased Rhonda's annoyance. Not for the last time that day she wished that her mother would have come along to entertain the children while she and Butcher figured out what they were going to do.

Because her mother (she didn't call her *Mom* when she was frustrated with her) had been sleeping right up until they were leaving, Rhonda popped her head into her bedroom. Connie apologized with a smile, which grated on Rhonda's nerves.

83

Just as the trio was about to enter the automatic doors of the hospital, J.T. looked to his left. A car, about fifteen blocks away, was hurrying up the street towards them. Focussing his eyes on the driver, he recognized her but did not know her name. He stopped suddenly to get a better fix on who the lady was, but Rhonda pulled on his arm again.

"But Mom, it's one of the ladies."

"What are you talking about?"

He pointed back over his shoulder. "In that car. The ladies."

Rhonda looked in the direction of his finger and frowned. "J.T. that car is far too far away. Now, let's go see your father."

J.T. struggled in his mother's grasp. His eyes fastened on Jeannie Simpson's stern and worried face. Her mouth was pinched, her hair unkept and she hadn't applied makeup this morning. The car was driving well over the speed limit.

Moments later, Rhonda and the children made their way down the corridor smelling of noxious cleaning agents. As they paused outside of Butcher's room, Rhonda took a deep breath. She needed to collect herself for the trial ahead. After checking her watch, she noticed that it was not quite eight o'clock. She rapped lightly on the door and pushed it open.

She was surprised to see Linda Harmsen resting in one of the hospital chairs. Her right hand was on the IV rack beside her.

"Oh!" Rhonda exclaimed. "Linda! I wasn't expecting to see you here."

Linda unconsciously covered her chest in surprise. "Oh, Rhonda! I'm sorry I startled you. I was just out for a morning walk..."

Rhonda released her children's hands who rushed to their dad. Butcher raised his four-fingered hand above his head to protect it. Embracing a duo of kids, who giggled at the sight of him and his long legs sticking over the edge of the bed, Butcher closed his eyes and enjoyed the sound and fury.

"I suppose I should be going," Linda said

"You don't have to," Rhonda said.

Linda attempted to stand, but she couldn't quite make it. Rhonda's compassionate nature won out. Putting a hand in her armpit, Rhonda lifted gently. Surprised by the fleshiness of Linda's arm, Rhonda's free hand moved to her back. Looking down into Linda's face, Rhonda saw the pain showing.

"Are you okay?" Rhonda asked.

Linda's voice was pinched. Helplessness was much more frustrating than pain. "I'll be fine."

"I'm going to walk you back to your room, okay, Linda?"

Linda nodded appreciatively. Rhonda glanced over at Butcher who was watching the women stagger from the room. He nodded.

When they left, J.T. looked up at his dad from the floor. "Dad, she really needs help, doesn't she?"

"Yes, J.T., she certainly does."

"I don't like the bumps. They scare me." J.T. was looking absentmindedly out the window.

"What bumps are you talking about, Champ?"

J.T. scratched his head. "The ones under her arm."

"J.T.," Butcher said, "how could you possibly see the bumps under her arms?"

He shrugged. "And it looked like they were… moving. Like bugs."

Unfortunately, for J.T., he was unable to describe his miraculous vision. He could practically see the cancer cells moving. It took a huge amount of effort to focus that hard, but he could do it. They scared him, though.

For the first time, Butcher felt a chill of something supernatural in his son. Although he had at various times

85

wondered if either of his children would have the same innate gifts as he did, it wasn't until that moment that he guessed. "J.T.," he said, "can you tell me what letters are on the wall?" Butcher pointed to his left where a print proclaimed the words, *Faith, Hope and Love.*

"Yes, Dad."

"Tell me what they are."

"M...c...m...a..." He read slowly.

Butcher smiled and shook his head both relieved and disappointed that his son did not have the same gift.

"Thanks, Chief," Butcher said, "you did a good job."

J.T. smiled and moved towards where his sister sat in the padded seat of the windowsill. He knew that he did a good job. He liked reading out his letters, but at the same time, he wondered why his dad wanted the letters read out from the room across the hall where Ted McManus was staying in room 14. J.T. had read the name on the manila folder in twelve-point font from twenty-five feet away.

Meanwhile, in the hallway, Rhonda helped Linda shuffle back to her room. About halfway there, the doors at the end of the corridor opened, and a whirlwind of commotion broke through. Leona, Jeannie and Carley snowplowed to get to Linda's room. Linda, seeing them first, smiled. Even though her pain was increasing, she was quite happy to see her best friends. Jeannie noticed Linda and Rhonda first, and pointed them out. The race was on. Jeannie, likely because she was smaller than Carley and younger than Leona, outpaced the other two and arrived in front of Linda.

"Oh, Linda," she cried. "How... how did this happen?"

Linda continued to push forward. "We'll talk about it in my room, but to be honest, I need to get to my bed."

In the next seconds, Leona and Carley came up behind Jeannie. "We'll take it from here, Rhonda. You probably have to get back to Butcher." As soon as they had gently, but forcibly, taken control of their Linda, they turned their backs on Rhonda.

"Thank you," Linda called weakly over her shoulder.

"You're welcome."

Rhonda returned to her husband's room.

Dick's stomach had roiled all night. Although Dick and Linda didn't touch when they slept (they both needed that extra space for a good night's rest), he definitely wasn't accustomed to *not* having her nearby. Her breathing calmed him. The threat of… well, he was not going to think about that.

After groggily pulling himself from his side of the bed, he looked dejectedly at the vacant spot on the other side and turned away. After he had showered and shaved, he drove to Clancy.

Dick turned the radio on in an attempt to negotiate the turbid waters of his imagination. He quickly switched the station to something a little more appropriate when one of the country singers began to wail about his wife leaving him. Fortunately, the morning was clear, and as he drove to the west, he was thankful that he was not driving in the storm like the night before.

As he entered the hospital, the first sound that greeted him was one that made his heart sink. Women's voices, and voices he had heard many, many times over the last thirty years of his marriage. Although he had called them the night before, he hadn't really wanted to. Now that they had shown up unbidden and unannounced, he knew he would have to withstand the tsunami of noise.

His pace slowed and he swallowed. Just as he was about to turn into his wife's hospital room, a small face peeked out from the doorway a few rooms down. It was the Jensen boy; a cute kid, but serious. He didn't know the boy's name, but he waved to him. The

87

boy stared. No movement, just a vacant gaze. Feeling uncomfortable, Dick turned into Linda's room.

"So anyway," Jeannie was halfway through a story. Dick couldn't quite stop the thought that first entered his mind: *You'd think they hadn't seen each other for years...* "Eldon Workman, you know, Denise Workman's husband, they live over on 485th Avenue across from the old Childer's place, you know the one with the big white barn that is kind of listing to the side. They have three kids – odd one's if you ask me, but you don't have to ask me..." Jeannie's running commentary stopped mid-sentence. Even though she could have continued for a good twenty minutes trying to connect the multitude of dots in Midwestern stories to locate the characters back two generations so that everyone was on the same page, she pointed at the door.

"Dick! Hello, Dick! Look everyone, Dick's here? Linda, your husband, Dick."

Linda shook her head. "Thank you, Jeannie. I know who he is. You don't have to say his name over and over."

Four pairs of eyes watched him enter. Carley pushed herself next to Leona into one of the green hospital chairs while Jeannie remained daintily on the edge of the bed.

"Hello," Dick said softly. "Good morning."

"Yes, yes," Leona stated too loudly, "it is a good morning. The sun is shining and the birds are singing..."

Jeannie frowned. "Leona..." she warned.

"It's okay, Jeannie," Linda said, "it is a good morning somewhere – just not, well, here."

"Good morning to you, Sweetheart," Linda said, turning a tired smile to him. "I missed you."

For Dick, on any other day, these words would have elicited a grunt and, if she was lucky, a quick glance up from the sports section of the paper, but on this day, Dick's face began to crumble one section at a time. A tear formed in the corner of his right eye, a perfect diadem of sadness, and he quickly wiped it away. Then, as he gazed at his wife, who seemed to have both aged and weakened overnight, his left eye followed suit. His upper lip quivered and for a moment, he was unsure whether he'd be able to stop. He did not want the women to see him cry. In that instant, Dick was frozen and could do nothing about his emotions.

"Oh dear," Carley said as she began to fan herself with one hand, her own emotions showing quickly. Leona, who saw Dick and then heard Carley, was caught in the crossfire and soon started to weep. Jeannie couldn't help it either. She waved a hand in front her face. The only person in the room who wasn't crying was Linda, but she had spent most of her tears in Butcher's room early that morning.

Dick sat on the bed next to Linda. "I appreciate the fact that you all believe that Linda's spirits need lifting." Dick reached out to hold Linda's hand. "At this moment, we just need to be honest and talk about the tough battle ahead."

"Okay," Leona said slowly, "what do we need to talk about?"

"Right now," Linda continued, "I have cancer in my right breast, some of my lymph nodes and there is a tumor near my spine which," she added with a wry smile, "is why I've been having problems with my hips."

"Oh dear," Carley repeated and fanned herself again.

"So," Linda looked down at her hands, "when Dr. Neale gets here, we have to figure out where to go next."

"But... you're so healthy. I mean, when, er... how did this happen? Are there other women in your family who have had it?" Jeannie asked.

Interrupting the discussion was a sharp knock on the door and Dr. Neale poked her head through. "Do you want me to come back?"

"Heavens, no!" Linda responded and waved her in. "My friends are just here to support me."

"That's wonderful," Dr. Neale walked into the room and stood on the outer fringe of the group. "Now, how are you feeling this morning?"

"Tired, and in some pain. I've tried not to push the pain button too often. I don't want to get addicted."

Dr. Neale shook her head. "I should have explained that to you a little bit better. The pain meds only come in certain doses – you can't really overdose or become addicted. It's just to take the edge off. So, push away. It's actually better for you if you do, so that your body can relax."

Dick patted Linda's hand. "Now, Linda, do you want your friends to wait outside while we talk?"

Linda looked at the pleading looks of her friends, and then the clenched jaw of her husband. She was aware that her friends were dying to know (if she could put it so crassly) the exact details of her infirmity, but Dick seemed to need just the two of them. "Yes," she said finally, "I think it's best if Dick and I were alone." Linda apologised. "I'm sorry, ladies. I'll let you know the details later. If you want, Butcher is down the hall. I'm sure he'd enjoy some company." Linda was quite sure of the opposite, actually, but she needed to get them out of the room. When she looked back at Dick, he seemed relieved.

As the women picked up their belongings, Linda stopped them. "Just come back in about half an hour and then we can talk."

They left their personal items and exited the room.

"Now, Doctor Neale," Linda said, still squeezing her husband's hand, "give it to us straight."

Dr. Neale, although a seasoned professional, hated these moments. How many times had she looked into the same, pleading eyes, desperate for a sliver of hope, delivering the news that what was growing inside of them was waging a war of shock and awe, and their bodies had no natural defense against it.

"Okay," Dr. Neale sat on the opposite side of the bed from Dick, "we're taking you for more tests today, but I think they will reveal what we've feared all along." She opened up a piece of paper and described the malignant process of cancer's growth and timeline. Because the cancer had spread, the odds for long life had decreased greatly.

Linda watched Dr. Neale's eyes. She was glad that the doctor wasn't sugar-coating anything. "So, how do we treat it?"

Dr. Neale gave a quick shake of her head. "Before we talk treatment, let's get a good look at the results of the tests, okay?"

Linda and Dick looked at each other and nodded. "Okay."

In the cushioned seat of the alcove window, Georgie perched herself like a majestic princess as she soaked in the early morning sun. She pulled a colorful women's magazine up onto her lap with the headline 'Seven New Tips for Pleasing Him When He Is Down in the Dumps.' Georgie studiously gave a rambling commentary in her four-year-old voice about various celebrities. On the other hand, J.T. had assumed a position on the other side of the cushion where his attention was captured by a small spider web clinging precariously to the high left-hand corner of the window. A flap of the web had broken off in the updraft and fluttered tenuously. From his perch below, J.T. could focus his eyes on the web, the gossamer string so delicate, yet incredibly strong. J.T. scoured the window in search of the spider itself and soon found her curled up away from the riotous draft. She looked scared and confused. The spider's eyes wide and unblinking. J.T. desperately wanted to reach out to her and console her, to tell her everything was going to be all right, but he knew his parents would think he was talking to himself, or 'baby-talking.' And the last thing he wanted to be called was a baby. That was Georgie. He was a little man, or so his dad called him.

J.T. turned his gaze to his mother whose wrinkles around her eyes looked quite similar to the web in the corner of the window. J.T. wondered if his mom was very much like that crouching spider in the corner of the window, fear causing her to pull into herself in order to ride out the storm.

"What are you thinking about, J.T.?" Rhonda asked with a forced smile.

J.T. paused and then pointed to the corner. "A spider."

Both Rhonda and Butcher looked to where their son was pointing and squinted. Butcher smiled and absentmindedly nodded his head.

Turning her green eyes to her husband, Rhonda studied his haggard face. He had slept poorly, and if they were in any other place than the hospital, she might have tousled his unruly hair.

Butcher broke the silence. "How are you feeling?"

She smiled. "Okay. Tired. Worried… about you, about everything, really." She touched his arm. "And you?"

Butcher's eyes looked haunted, like an animal caged; his thoughts paced back and forth inside his head. He didn't want to tell either Rhonda or the doctors about the curious tingling in the tips of his fingers and toes.

"A little worried about what the future is going to look like."

"What did you come up with?"

"Butchering, driving… buttoning up my pants," he laughed, hoping that she would smile, but she didn't. "All the important things," he mumbled.

"Sweetheart, this surgery will be a big change for all of us." She glanced toward the window where the children continued to amuse themselves although J.T. was listening intently. "We'll be okay. I can go back to waitressing. Rodrigo said that I could come back to work for him at any time. My job is always available."

Butcher frowned. "You have so much more talent than just being a waitress."

"What is that supposed to mean?" she asked testily. "Is waitressing beneath us?"

"You should know me better than that. I'm trying to give you a compliment. You're an extraordinarily talented woman who…"

"I know what you *think* you meant," she interjected, "but I am quite content being a waitress."

"I'm sorry," he repeated, with gritting teeth.

Shaking her head, Rhonda touched his arm. "No, I'm sorry. I'm edgy."

He shrugged and looked down at his hand. "We'll have to take it one step at a time."

Rhonda moved her hand to his leg and stroked it. "Can we bring you something? Anything to eat?"

"A steak, if you can find one without a finger in it."

"Very funny," Ronda replied sardonically.

Butcher sighed. "Tell me what's going on with your mom."

Rhonda gazed at the blue sky outside the window. Her eyes were drawn to a shifting of the light as a cloud passed in front of the sun.

"She's glowing. She's bouncing around like a giddy schoolgirl, humming like a princess."

At that moment, Georgie, hearing her mother pronounce the word 'princess' began singing a Disney princess song about letting things go. Both Butcher and Rhonda smiled which caused Georgie to giggle. She covered her mouth with her hand. "Elsa is a princess," she said sagely.

"Yes, she is," Rhonda said. "And now your grandma is also."

"She is?" Georgie's face showed astonishment. "That is awesome." At the age of four, everything seemed to be awesome.

Rhonda turned back to Butcher. "I wish that we knew this Carl better. She needs to bring him around for dinner so we can hear his story and see if he's right for her."

"You sound like you've switched roles. It's a good thing that she's a grown woman and can take care of her own social life."

"But it is hard," Rhonda pressed. "She's still so... so vulnerable. It seems like yesterday that she was suffering from depression trying to get rid of *you*."

"That was a while ago," he responded, shifting his body in the bed. "Our baby has grown up a lot since then."

Rhonda rolled her eyes. "A lot has changed."

There was a rap on the door. Dr. Ditmore. "Good morning, Jensen family. How did you sleep?"

Shrugging, Butcher waggled his hand. "I've had better nights."

"Pain?"

"Yes. But manageable."

Dr. Ditmore read the chart. "Are we all right to talk now?"

"About the surgery?" Butcher's eyes scanned the doctor. He was worried. *Not just the finger? What...?*

Ditmore hesitated. "Yes, we can start there. Surgery is tomorrow morning here in Clancy, thankfully."

"Okay," Butcher said slowly, "you said we could *start* there. Where are we going to finish up?"

The doctor pulled the chart in next to his chest. "Mr. Jensen, have you been experiencing anything different, strange sensations in your fingers or toes, maybe even stumbling over things?"

Butcher's eyes narrowed. "Why do you ask?"

"It was just something you said when you first came in. I've written it down here. I just wanted to talk about it." He perused the notes. "You said, 'I don't know what happened. It was like my fingers were tripping over each other.' I said, 'What do you mean by that?' and you said, 'It was just like my foot has been doing lately – kind of dragging. That's what my fingers felt like.'" Dr. Ditmore looked up from his notes. "Tell me about the foot dragging."

"It's nothing. I'm just tired, on my feet too much. My legs feel *heavy*, you know, like there are weights attached to my toes."

"But you said 'foot' not 'feet.'"

"Does that make a difference? Is there something else wrong?"

Before Dr. Ditmore could respond with the typical doctoral *let's not jump to any conclusions,* J.T. spoke. "Yes, Dad, there is."

A spooky silence ensued as the adults turned towards the boy who was now standing with his arms hanging loosely at his sides. There was no expression on his face, but his voice trembled slightly.

"What are you talking about?" Butcher asked J.T.

"I can see it. Your finger." He pointed at Butcher's hand just as he had the spider. "There's something wrong."

"Yes," Butcher said testily, "I know that there is something wrong with my finger, but Doctor Ditmore is implying something else."

J.T.'s eyes searched his father's. "Okay, Daddy."

But Butcher could certainly read what was going on in his son's mind.

And it wasn't good.

Connie Redman whistled while she worked.

According to the lingo of her own generation, she and Carl had shacked up last night. Connie could not remember the last time she had sex. Certainly, she had been taking care of Rhonda all these years, but now that Rhonda had Butcher and children, Connie recognized her own deep need to share time with someone else. Carl filled that emptiness nicely.

Carl had been gentle, something she had never experienced before, and now that they were a 'thing,' as kids were wont to say, she noticed an unambiguous sense of happiness.

Before their conjugal connection the night before, Connie and Carl had decided on a date for the wedding. Because of their age, neither wanted to wait long. If they wanted to reach their silver anniversary (as both of them were already talking about), there was no better time than the present. They had settled on a post-Christmas wedding.

Her cell phone rang and Connie laughed as she danced across the living room to retrieve it from the coffee table.

"Yello."

"Hi, Mom, we're on our way home."

"Hi, Honey. How's Butcher?"

"Sore. His surgery is scheduled for tomorrow. We've spent a couple hours with him and now the kids are getting antsy. Would you mind watching them while I run some errands?"

"Sure, sure, that would be fine." Connie crossed her free arm over her ribcage while her phone was pressed against her cheek. "What are you going to be doing?"

Rhonda hesitated. "I'm heading out to ask Rodrigo for a job."

"Oh," Connie responded, "things are changing drastically…"

"Yes. Yes, they are." Silence. "Look, Mom, I'm just going to drop the kids off outside the house. If you can collect them and feed them lunch that would be great."

"Of course. Say, do you want to hear my news?" Connie's face radiated happiness.

"What is it?"

"Carl and I have set a date."

More silence.

"Are you still there?" Connie asked into the phone.

"Yes."

"We're getting married on December 27th. Isn't that wonderful? I'm so excited!"

A measured response from the phone. "I'm very happy for you, Mom. Maybe we can talk about it tonight, okay? I just have a lot of things on my mind with regards to Butcher."

"Sure, of course. So I'll see you in a few minutes."

Rhonda disconnected the call without saying goodbye. Connie shook her head, but didn't lose any of her happiness.

Chapter 9.

At the convergence of cancer, suffering and wedding plans, Amicable was changing.

For those two months from September to November, Labor Day to Thanksgiving, the community watched and whispered with breathless activity wondering what would happen with three of Amicable's most prominent citizens. Linda Harmsen's mastectomy went without a hitch, but her spirits sagged. During the long hours of chemotherapy, as her hair fell out, her weight fell off, she rued the removal of her curves. Although she had opted for 'falsies,' Linda was not prepared for the lack of sensation. The surgeon had assured her that for most women, some feeling would return. But what was more disconcerting for Linda was the fact that her boobs did not move the way they used to.

Through it all, Linda Harmsen lived in hope: hope in modern medicine, hope in her faith, hope for a new day. In spite of the chemotherapy, which was far and away the worst thing she had ever endured, she ground on. She lost her hair. She felt like vomiting. She felt exhausted and cranky. She waited with dread for a possible back surgery which, worst case scenario, lead to paralysis. One little slip...

Dick had been a real trooper. After the first rounds of vomiting, he had grown used to rubbing her back and holding back her hair (until it started to come out in his hands). By November, he was a puking pro. When she told him it was coming, he expertly arranged the bathroom and turned on the shower. Dick had been transformed into a dedicated and adoring husband, the likes of which Linda had always desired. She only wished it wouldn't have been cancer that brought it out of him.

Chapter 9.

When Thanksgiving arrived, Linda felt tears come to her eyes as her true to life angels, X-Er-Size friends, invited her to the old Traveler's Choice Restaurant. Even though it had been gutted and reconditioned as a conference center (though never used as a 'conference center'), it created a space for card clubs, Bingo nights and eventually a youth area with pool tables and video game consoles.

The Thanksgiving party given in Linda's honor was a potluck, of course. Linda and Dick did not need to bring anything. Dick seemed particularly pleased that he had organized it himself, although ninety-seven percent of the work (Leona's figures) had been done by the fitness ladies. Angela Chandler had cooked the turkeys, two home grown, monstrous birds. Leona had crafted her Thanksgiving specialty, an odd concoction of orange Jell-O on a bed of canned mandarin oranges, infused with a layer of carrot shavings and covered with marshmallows. Jeannie brought a gigantic mound of mashed potatoes with sour cream, chives and cheese. Carley, instead of bringing food, brought her sound system and music and set up a playlist of Christmas. Thanksgiving was the gate for Christmas music.

As they gathered around seven tables set end to end, Linda and Dick took up the spot of honor in the middle table. When the turkey finally made its way to the other end of the table into Carley's hands, she promptly licked her lips, grabbed the metal tongs and announced to everyone, 'I can't wait to get some breast into my mouth.' Ed Simpson almost snorted some of his Snickers salad out his nose while everyone held their breath. Linda stared at Carley with an unreadable look until a tear formed in her eye. The party went quiet, save for Perry Como. Carley was frozen with tongs in mid-air aware of her verbal faux pas. Linda's face quivered and then suddenly, she took a deep breath and an explosive laughter burst from her mouth.

"Oh, good Lord, Carley," she exclaimed between laughs, "That's the funniest thing I've heard in two months." Linda covered her mouth and waited for the laughter to abate. It was painful but necessary.

Carley giggled, shrugged and piled her plate high with turkey and potatoes. "Wait till you see what I do with the eclairs!"

As the afternoon wore on, the meal settled into a comfortable, restful day of giving thanks. The talk centered around Linda's prognosis. It didn't take long for Linda to want to move on from her health and boobs, thank-you-very-much. At the two-hour mark, Penny walked into the old kitchen and pulled out two pumpkin pies, and then went back for the tub of Cool Whip. Carley rubbed her hands again. She motioned with her hands to bring the pies to her first. Giddy with delight, she licked her lips as she casually scanned both pie tins for the largest piece and then proceeded to place it on her dinner plate. To top it all off, she heaped four Cool Whip dollops on top.

After the last smear of creamy pumpkin had been wiped from the plates with index fingers, the men adjourned to the kitchen to wash the dishes. They cleared the tables of dishes, leftover food, drinks and trash, and grabbed an ice-cold bottle of Busch Light on the way to their domestic duties. The men, although acquaintances, did not know much about each other, but the activity provided them an opportunity.

As the dishes and plates clattered in the sink, the dulcimer tones of Andy Williams rang out from the speakers, the women leaned back in their own chairs to settle in for post meal gossip.

"Has anyone heard from Connie lately?" Donna asked.

"I invited her today along with her 'beau,'" Leona responded with quote fingers, "but she said that she and Carl were going to have Thanksgiving dinner with Rhonda, Butcher and the kids."

"That's such a weird situation, don't you think?" Jeannie asked. "I mean, her 'beau...'" Jeannie repeated the gesture, "has got to be, what, seventy years old? That's kind of..." she pretended to shiver, and then looked up at Anne who was frowning. "No offense, Anne."

"Some taken," Anne said grumpily. "For your information, Gordon is still a wild animal in bed."

Carley laughed and covered her mouth. "I guess it depends on whether he is a mountain lion or a sloth..."

Anne cracked a smile. "Let's just say he's more like a big cat."

"Getting back to Connie..." Linda leaned forward. "Do you all have jobs at the wedding?"

Leona raised her hand. "Communications."

"What does that mean?" Carley asked.

"She asked me to help with all the invitations and the decorations and stuff like that."

"I've got catering," Angela announced.

"I'm the DJ," Carley looked pleased.

"Where is the reception again?" Donna raised an eyebrow.

"Here," Jeannie said, "or at least that's what I heard from Rhonda."

"How is Butcher doing?" Linda asked, changing the subject.

They all looked at each other. Although this kind of information was their specialty, it seemed that no one had actually heard anything.

"The amputation was successful," Leona said, as she cleared her throat and ran a hand through her hair. "But I heard that he is sinking into the depths of depression. A nine fingered Butcher is probably not a good sign."

"Where did you hear that?" Jeannie asked.

Caught, but unwilling to admit it, Leona casually waved a hand in the air. "I… can't remember, probably one of the Peterson twins."

"That doesn't sound like them. Usually they are so positive."

"And positively avoiding us," Linda said.

"Well," Leona replied testily, "I guess none of us can imagine what it's like to have something amputated."

Linda sighed. "I can."

"I'm so sorry, Linda," Leona apologised.

"No, it's okay," she said with a wry smile. "We have to talk about these things. I don't want to walk on eggshells for the next months or years just because people feel sensitive about not wanting to hurt my feelings."

"But…" Leona started, but Linda interrupted her.

"Imagine Donna had something in her hair, or her teeth, and instead of telling her about it, we avoided her. I mean, we'd do it with the best intentions: we don't want her to be embarrassed or have her feelings hurt. Instead, she starts to wonder if she's done something wrong." Linda looked at Donna who had unconsciously touched her hair and checked her teeth to make sure that nothing was there. "Imagine how she'd feel. The confusion. The anxiety. The loneliness."

"You haven't done that to me, thank God, but listen, you're not going to hurt my feelings. I realize that there may be times when I can't control my tears, but it will have nothing to do with what you say; it's just the way it is. Right now, the prognosis is surprisingly good. My oncologist says that the cancer is responding in the right way. I'm in the five percent. I have hope."

"Well," Carley said, louder than appropriate, "let's hope for more good times today. Anyone want some wine? I brought a box!"

Chapter 9.

At the thought of boxed wine, the ladies clapped their hands.

Later, after the dishes had been carefully repositioned in the appropriate drawers, the leftover food into Tupperware containers and the drinks refilled at least thrice more, the men moved to the pool tables and the women cackled in a circle. The time for giving thanks turned into nostalgia; the men spoke of high school sporting conquests while the women reminisced about moments of delight, especially revelling in the downfall of Baker Insurance. As they enjoyed the retelling of the story, their eyes were drawn to the west where the setting sun illuminated the shiny new elevator constructed by the community, for the community. Things were looking up in Amicable; businesses were recovering, families were moving in and Amicable had become a surprising tourist hotspot for grey-haired nomadic couples crossing the country in their gigantic motorhomes.

"Hey Ed," Jeannie said loudly to her husband, who was preparing for a pool shot, and clanked the cue when startled.

"Jeepers, Jeannie! Don't do that while I'm shooting!"

She ignored him and pointed out the window towards the car. "Whose car is that?"

He turned to inspect the car and then shrugged. "Never seen it before."

"Doesn't Donnie Davids have a car like that?"

Ed shook his head and ignored her as Dick moved in to take his shot.

"Well," Jeannie intoned, "we might have a visitor in town." All the women turned to follow the late model Buick of indeterminate color slowly move towards Main Street and take a right.

Chapter 10.

In the lowering darkness, Jennifer Adams peered at the quaint buildings lining the old-fashioned Main Street. On the left side stood a red brick bank with a tall electronic sign stating that the 'State Bank of Amicable was closed for the Thanksgiving weekend.'

A hardware store sat next door with the smiling face of Hardware Hank, a happy, helpful handyman who could service all your home renovation needs. On the next corner, Jennifer stopped and got out. *The Chop Shop-In the business of helping you mind yours.* The signage on the siding said the proprietor was a counselor named Leopold 'Butcher' Jensen.

Jennifer swallowed.

Leo, she thought. *Are you still the same?*

A few months had passed since Jennifer had read the article in a nationally syndicated newspaper about the Amicable elevator explosion and subsequent rebuilding. She was awed by the way the community banded together.

Car locked, she approached the Chop Shop and stared at her reflection in the window. There was no way that Leo would ever recognize her. When he had last seen her, she was a pixie-esque, rebellious little girl with a mountain-sized chip on her shoulder. At his last sighting, she had brilliant pink hair in two ponytails with yellow ribbons.

But now, as she perused her two-decades-later appearance, there was very little that resembled the attention-seeking young woman she had been. Brownish hair had been cut shoulder length, some of it poked up from the middle of her scalp. Wide-rimmed glasses, brown, not fluorescent green as she would have chosen in the past, circled captivating hazel eyes. Her dress, casual and comfortable, was decidedly different than her 90's army fatigues.

Chapter 10.

Her figure had softened. Jennifer was neither thick nor thin, but a shapely middle ground. She was still fit, but not hardened. Her legs, though, were muscular from daily walking.

She smiled at her reflection but unsure of why she did it. Perhaps it was to see what she looked like when she was happy.

She tried to remember.

"You're very beautiful," Leo said towering over her running his hands down her cheeks.

"I'm not concerned whether I'm beautiful or not, Leo," Jennifer replied testily. She had been preparing for a coordinated attack on the fur industry. It was her life to protest: against the meat industry, against the oil industry, against the cigarette industry. She loved it when people were angry with her. Often, she dressed up in outrageous outfits. The television cameras loved her because of her smallness – the newspapers called her the Protest Princess. Jennifer did not like this at all.

"I know," Leo pulled back from her. Jennifer was wearing flesh-colored nylons, a tiny beige tank top and a fake-fur stole wrapped around her neck. Nothing was left to the imagination. "I just think it's interesting *that instead of drawing attention to the fur around your neck, a lot of eyes will be drawn to your... um..." his eyes strayed to her backside.*

"That's a sexist thing to say." She moved away from the bathroom mirror and into the bedroom where she grabbed her mass transit card.

Leo rolled his eyes. "You know, if you really wanted to make a change, have you ever thought about debate rather than spectacle?"

She turned on him. "Look, Leo, I can understand that you don't *understand. If you think this is about getting attention, well, you're wrong! I'm fighting for the rights of animals."*

"This is not about me understanding, but no one can take you seriously! You prance around like some kind of anti-chameleon. You don't try to fit in. You don't try to connect. Ironically, you are afraid of rejection, so you reject everyone else first."

"Nice, Leo, thanks for psychoanalysis."

"*I'm just saying...*"

"*I know the ins and outs of the fur industry, Leo!*" *She adjusted the fake fur around her throat.*

Leo snorted. He hadn't meant to turn it into a fight, but this was the way it always went. Leo and Jennifer had a love/disgust relationship. He loved her; she was charming and witty, pretty and athletic; her love of causes was part of the attraction – kind of. The sheer irony that he was a butcher and she 'the protector of fur' had only been touched on once or twice, but somehow they had co-habited for almost a year. Without asking, Jennifer had shown up on his doorstep in the middle of the night dressed in an 'outfit' created from plastic wrappers of various food products. When he opened the door to see who could possibly be pulling him from his sleep at three o'clock in the morning (on a Wednesday! for crying out loud), he peered down at the diminutive social castoff in her Snickers and bread bag clothing. With just a smile, she walked through the door into his apartment, and proceeded to remove (without any self-consciousness, mind you) the wrappers one by one until she stood stark naked by the coffee table. She asked him if she could take a shower – plastic made her sweat – to which he opened his hands and told her to make herself at home.

Which she did.

"*Which cause is it going to be next week, Nif?*"

"*Careful, Leo. We've already walked down this road before.*"

"*I'm being careful! I'm considering you and your ability, or lack thereof, to grow up and be a productive member of society! When is all this going to stop? When are you going to get a job, or care about other people? When are you going to pay rent? Maybe take care of yourself?*"

"*That's rich!*" *Jennifer said as she stormed out of the bedroom.* "*You who go to work, judge people, push everyone else away because you can 'read' them!*" *Her face was flushed with anger.* "*We walk around the park and you point at young and old people alike and think you are so much better than they are because you see things.*"

Leo ground his teeth. "*I see you.*"

"Oh yeah? Come on, Leo, give it to me. What do you see? What do you really think of me?"

Leo could have responded and ripped her to shreds, but he kept silent.

"That's what I thought. You're a coward. Always running away from a fight."

Those were their last words. When she returned home from her protest, which the media proclaimed as her finest yet, Leo had packed a bag and left his key under the pot at the front door with a note telling her of his decision to move on.

"Figures." Even though it was their apartment (she had been added to the lease even though she wasn't paying anything for it), it was now hers. A twinge of guilt and pain tugged at her heart, but she pushed past it, opened the door and shed the fake fur and threw it into the trash.

It was time to move on to a new cause.

Jennifer smirked and her eyes moved back to the name plaque on the wall. *Leopold Jensen*, she mused.

"Most people don't window shop in the dark," a voice said next to her.

Startled, she jumped. "Oh, I didn't see you!"

The very tall man held up his hands, stepped back and smiled. "Sorry. I didn't mean to scare you. It's just that most people don't look for a counselor at night. You know…" His voice trailed off as the tiny woman peered up at him with an open-mouthed stare.

For a moment, Butcher was nonplussed, but quickly, he regained his composure. She looked so familiar. Scanning his memory, the eyes and the size, the voice. *Oh, wow.*

"Nif?"

The woman's jaw dropped even further. Her voice dropped to a whisper. "You still remember me? Even after all the years and all the… changes?" She self-consciously touched her hair.

Butcher shook his head. "This is…"

Jennifer laughed. "Amazing?"

He smiled. "I was going to say disconcerting, but that's not the right word. More like… well, unbelievable. What are you doing here? How are you? What…? I don't really know where to start."

Jennifer's face reddened with embarrassment. It was something that Butcher had never seen before. "Those are a lot of questions, but I can start with the easiest ones first. And you know, I didn't actually think you'd remember me."

"How could I forget you?" It was Butcher's turn to be embarrassed. "I mean, we were together for a while."

"I just thought since my look is so different…" She spread her hands so that he could take her in.

"Yeah, I know. You look so…"

"Normal?"

"That, yes, but…" He reached up to his hair and his hand shook. Jennifer noticed. "I was going to say *peaceful*. Like you've found yourself."

Jennifer smirked. "You're reading me, aren't you?"

He glanced to the side and then back down at her. She was almost a foot and a half shorter than he. "Umm… I'm sorry about that. Old habit."

"It's okay. Give it a shot."

"I'd rather you tell me what you've been up to. It's much better."

Jennifer looked around at the dead street. "Is there anywhere we can get a cup of coffee or something? It feels kind of weird to be standing out here in the dark."

"Of course. Of course." He felt his pockets. "Everything else is shut in town for Thanksgiving, but I've got a coffee pot in the shop if that works for you."

She nodded. "Sure. But shouldn't you be at home with a family or something?"

Chapter 10.

A key appeared in his hand and he opened the door for her. "Yes. I've got a family. A wife and two children, in-laws and everything."

Jennifer was surprisingly disappointed at the news, but not entirely shocked. He was still a good looking man. Suddenly, her eyes noticed the missing digit.

"What happened to your finger?"

He paused his coffee making to lift the stump. "Butcher's tattoo."

"What?"

"Butcher's tattoo. It's an inside term meaning a scar, or amputation, caused in the line of duty." He turned on the tap and filled the carafe with water. "Carving up meat, I carved off a finger."

"I'm sorry."

He shrugged. "I lasted much longer than most. A lot of guys lose them in the saws, but..." He stood and looked at her. "How do you have yours?"

"Just black," she said.

He smirked. "I thought you'd have it with all the fancy names like frappicelli or whatever. That used to be you, I guess."

"Those days are long past." Jennifer stood awkwardly for a moment under his gaze. "So, your family? Thanksgiving?"

"My wife, Rhonda, has gotten into a fitness kick. She likes to keep toned, I think." His eyes shifted slightly. There was something going on that Jennifer noticed also. "The kids are relaxing with Connie, my mother-in-law, and her fiancé, Carl. I needed some fresh air, so I went for a walk. I saw someone standing outside the office, so I thought I'd see who it was. I would never have imagined it would have been you."

"Yes, well, I never would have expected to be here either, but I had to come and check out the world-famous Amicable, Iowa, population two hundred, or something like that."

"Almost fifteen hundred now." Butcher poured a steaming cup of coffee into a mug that read, *Research is the leading cause of death in mice.*

"That's incredible. What? Is Amicable a boomtown now? Found gold in them thar hills?" She accepted the cup and smelled it.

"No, just a really nice place to live."

Jennifer sipped. "I think it's great that you have settled out here in the country, on the plains, where the deer and the antelope play."

Butcher frowned. "Hmm. A predictable assessment, this incredible assumption that because there isn't a megamall or a twenty-screen cinema, multiple cafes on the same streets or even a chain supermarket, that people who live in it are suffering."

"I didn't mean to offend you," she said.

"Not offended, really. I'm used to it. People on the outside don't understand what it's like to live contentedly simple lives. But," he raised a finger, "they aren't simple people. They might be the most complex I've ever been around, and that's saying something. They would even give your former self a run for her money."

Jennifer's smile lit up the room. "That's very funny."

"So are you really different?"

Looking over her mug, she peered up at him. "You tell me."

For five seconds, Butcher studied her. He saw that she was wearing a floral dress, an utter taboo in earlier days. Her brown hair swept upwards; her glasses perched on the bridge of her nose. Everything about her bespoke normalness. Perplexed, Butcher read her face, her hands and the littlest things. Her pulse was racing – as was his – but it was not just because she was nervous. There was something she wasn't tell him, and then he saw it.

"Oh, that's funny..."

"What did you find out about me?"

"You've done a counseling degree, haven't you?"

Jennifer smiled and her eyes widened. "I can't believe that you can still do it." She nodded. "Yes, that's what happened. I went out and got respectable. Maybe you changed me."

"Should I apologize?"

She shook her head. "I needed to change, grow up, mature – you know, the things that you said to me the last time we met."

He watched her eyes. "So you never got married, but got your counseling degree?"

"Marriage was never my thing – too normal, you know? The thought of floating through life lost its sheen once I hit my late twenties. All my friends were having children and settling into a routine, and as much as I fought it, the thought of having something of my own sounded positively... nice."

Butcher laughed. He knew that she always hated the word 'nice.' It was a word that didn't mean anything, a throw in word so as not to offend anyone. It was the same word that Amicableans accepted with openhearted glee. To be nice was to be boring. "And you never met anyone. Never had kids?"

Jennifer held his gaze. "No. No, I never met anyone else and certainly never had the courage to open up to a man to have a child. I guess I was destined to be a wanderer."

Butcher thought ruefully about his own journey and those same ideas which had run through his mind before he found Amicable. She obviously had hit some hard times and bounced back. If she was anything, she was determined, but now there was something very different about her personality. There was a wistfulness, a desire, for something fulfilling.

"I read about Amicable in the New York Times. At first, they did exactly as you talked about and described the citizens of the town like they were some kind of mindless cattle. But you know what really got me about Amicable by the end of the article?

There was this picture of a semi-truck driver standing on the top step of his rig, grinning out over a large gathering of people. He had his hat cocked back on his head. He was overlooking the crowd and smiling." Jennifer smiled at the memory. "There was something really touching and beautiful about the picture that moved me."

"That still doesn't tell me why you're here…"

She put her cup on the table, stood up and crossed her arms. "In the background was a man who was a head taller than everyone else in the crowd. I enlarged the picture and I saw that it was you. I honestly couldn't believe it. What a coincidence."

Butcher smiled.

"I looked around my apartment, various pictures of me, by myself, wandering around lonely areas of the world, the back woods, the mountains, seascapes, deserts, trying to find myself. After I saw the picture, I wondered if I just needed to be around people again. Good, honest, hardworking people like you told me about all those years ago."

"Quaint, isn't it?"

She nodded.

"Do you think that's the way it really is? It's probably not quite so simple to describe."

Leaning forward to take in a picture of Leo's family, she spoke towards the photo frame. "But what about culture? Movies? Plays? Sports? Don't you ever miss that?"

Butcher paused, and then looked towards the bookcase. "How about we step into my office and sit for a little bit. Do you feel comfortable doing that?"

Jennifer smiled to herself. This was the kind of question she was used to asking every day of her life. When she told her partners at the practice that she was going on sabbatical, (*for how long?* they asked with pleading eyes, to which she replied, *indefinitely*) she felt a sense of peace that she didn't need to ask other people if they were comfortable.

She nodded, and Butcher held out his hand towards the office door.

In the office, furnished with dark wood furniture, were mementos of country life. A pair of golf clubs were criss-crossed on the far wall. A stuffed ring-necked pheasant was locked in mid-flight on top of the bookshelf. Butcher did not hunt (just as he did not play golf), but the bird was a present from one of his clients and he thought it best to display it for community relation's sake. The bookshelf was full of books that Butcher had never (and probably would never) read.

"Interesting décor," Jennifer said as she perused the surroundings. "I really like the dead bird on the wall."

"You would," Butcher responded with a grin. "Still on the protest trail?"

"No, I gave it up a dozen years ago. My voice was getting tired." She grinned and looked at the pictures on the wall. Her eyes fell on the family photo; the smiling Jensen family from a few years before in a very staged, pastoral scene. Butcher and his wife sat in autumn leaves while their children rested obediently in their laps. The girl smiled while the boy was stern. "The family?"

"Yes."

"Your wife is beautiful."

"Yes."

"And your children? Tell me about them."

Butcher's eyes moved from the picture to the diminutive woman beside him. She was so small that when they were together, he had the incessant urge to either protect her or pick her up. Both of these things displeased her equally. Emotions stirred, Butcher concentrated back on the picture in front of them.

"It sounds like we're settling in for a counseling session," he grinned good-naturedly and crossed his arms. "Georgie is almost five years old, a true gem of a young lady. Very much like her mother. Strong willed, resourceful, impatient and loving."

"She sounds wonderful."

Butcher wasn't sure which lady Jennifer was talking about.

"And the little man there is J.T. His real name is John Thomas, named after my best friend who, and you'll laugh at this, happens to be a clergyman."

Jennifer raised an eyebrow and looked up at him. "That is interesting. Found Jesus, did you?"

"Nah," Butcher responded without thinking. "Probably the other way around, I guess."

Jennifer moved from the picture and took a seat on one of the cushioned chairs in the center of the room. Butcher followed her. "You've got yourself staked out nicely in rural America."

"Other than a missing digit, this has been a real oasis for me. I've finally found a place to sit still."

Jennifer studied the backs of her hands to give her time to digest the conversation. "You were going to talk about missing the culture – movies, sports, entertainment, plays and such."

She felt herself being drawn into his soft, brown eyes. An odd sensation swirled in her stomach, but she attempted to hide it.

Butcher saw what was going on inside of her. It also gave him a warm feeling, a feeling he hadn't encountered for a long time. "Interesting that your idea of culture has to do with diversion rather than the beauty of the community mind. We have those things, but the collective is always at the center of who Amicable is."

"Fascinating," Jennifer responded.

"You talk of entertainment, like movies or plays or surfing the internet, but have you ever seen a community play?" She shook her head. "Despite its amateurishness, the town embraces the play and encourages the actors. As we sit together and watch the drama, we are transported to another world, another stage ringed with the dying light of the plains watching the fireflies twinkle like mad stars hurtling towards the earth. The freshly mown grass smells of newness and rebirth, and, after the performance, as we pull ourselves from creaking camping chairs, we stretch and tell our neighbors, 'That's the best one yet,' not because it was, but because we watched it together. There's something incredibly special about that."

"It sounds heavenly."

"I wouldn't go that far, but it is Iowa." Butcher leaned forward in his chair. "Tell me about you. What have I missed in the last couple of decades?"

She fingered the edge of the chair. "You missed everything, actually."

Butcher smiled and reddened.

"I don't say that to make you feel guilty, but somewhere after you left your key in the garden pot in front of the apartment, I had my own coming-to-grips with trying to be an adult." Jennifer hadn't planned for any of this to happen. She had only mapped out that she would find Amicable, catch a glimpse of Butcher and leave. Every person has a daydream of running down an old flame, just for a few minutes, to spy from afar and see if they made the right choice.

"I reconnected with my family who, after a few hours of wondering if I was there to berate them for driving SUV's or eating steaks for dinner, recognized that something serious was happening with me – a mid-life crisis twenty years before mid-life."

"Is your second mid-life happening right now?"

Shrugging, she shyly smoothed her dress against her legs. Unconsciously, she wanted the tall man to look there, to follow her hands and be reminded. "Maybe."

"What happened next? With your parents?"

"I told them I wanted to go to college. They laughed, of course, and said that I had never finished anything in life. I only wanted to be difficult. I only wanted to stir up trouble. I sat there and took it. At the end of the diatribe, my father, with this stern look on his face and his moustache twitching, said that he was hopeful…" she attempted to mimic his voice and mannerism, "… and if I minded my p's and q's and kept my nose clean, he'd think about funding some education for me."

"What did you say?"

"I said, 'You bet, Dad. I'm ready for the challenge. Show me where the p's and q's are and tell me how to mind them. While I mind them, I'll blow my nose every once in a while." Jennifer laughed.

"And what did he do?"

"At first he thought I was reverting back to the old Jennifer and giving him lip, but I wasn't. I went to night classes in the city and I got my psychology degree six years later. To my father's astonishment, I worked my way through college and only relied on them minimally for support. Interestingly, my father is proud of me and often, when others come to his house, he points to the former Protest Princess, who turned psychologist?"

"Good for you, Nif."

"You're the only person who ever called me that."

"That's interesting."

"No, really, Counselor. No one else."

"I guess we all have our little idiosyncrasies," Butcher said.

"None as big as yours," Jennifer responded, referring to his gift.

"None as big as mine."

Rhonda's pace quickened. She had lapped Winslow Park four times. Although she'd been jogging for over an hour and the sweat was soaking through her clothing, Rhonda did not really feel like going home.

Butcher had been quiet. Something was eating at him. As she was leaving, she noticed that he, too, had put on his tennis shoes and coat and told Connie and Carl that he was going to work off some of the excess Thanksgiving dinner weight. Rhonda had noticed that Butcher's hands shook slightly as he was dissecting the bird; perhaps he was still nervous about the accident.

As she ran, Rhonda reflected on her children also. J.T. was unusually inactive, especially after a day inside. Normally on holidays, he would be aching to get out into the fresh air, but today, he sat morosely on the couch watching Georgie, Connie and Carl play a board game. She asked him if anything was wrong. He said he was reading, which was odd because he didn't have a book in his hand.

For the last month, Rhonda had daily conversations with herself about the present and future. Although she was engaged in the family, it was passive, like going through the motions. Each day was a carbon copy of the day before: wake up early, jog, prepare the kids for school, domestic duties, ensure that Butcher was comfortable, shopping, pick up the kids, then nightly activities before falling into bed next to a man who seemed to be turning into a ghost. Rhonda didn't, or couldn't tell Butcher about her feelings, feeling trapped, discontented. Where was the happiness in marriage and family life? Excitement? Romance? Mystery? I was all swirling down the drain in a whirlpool of domestic redundancy. As she jogged towards Main Street, Rhonda subconsciously understood that she was slowing down, not because she was tired, but because she didn't want to go back to real life.

As she approached Amicable's main 'thoroughfare,' she noticed a light on inside of Butcher's office. Even though he had been back to work for a few weeks, she didn't expect that he would be there on Thanksgiving Eve. A wave of fear washed over her and Rhonda's first thought was to call the police. As she neared the shop, though, she wondered if Butcher had just left the light on.

117

Pausing at the door, she opened it quietly and found it open. Just before entering, she saw him sitting in his 'shrink' chair, a reupholstered antique. His hands rested on the arms and his right leg was crossed over the other. Butcher was smiling; he seemed eager to be relaxed. *When was the last time he smiled at me like that?*

"Hello?" she called, from just outside the office.

Butcher jumped, startled. His eyes searched the doorway, but then noticed Rhonda. Looking guilty, he popped up from the chair. His first step was too slow, and he stumbled, almost falling, into the door. Going to a knee, he looked down at his feet.

Rhonda pushed open the door and helped him to his feet. "You okay?"

"Yeah, yeah. My foot must be asleep. I must have had my legs crossed too long."

"What are you doing here at night? It's Thanksgiving."

"I'm talking." His eyes moved towards Jennifer, who was primly sitting in the other chair.

Rhonda's surprise was palpable. She was like a beautiful little doll. Her feet barely touched the floor and her floral dress was so... she couldn't think of the word, but wanted to say, girlish. Rhonda raised an eyebrow.

Brushing his hands as if there was something on them, some dirt or grime, he paused, to think of the right thing to say.

"Rhonda, this is Jennifer."

"Hello," Rhonda responded stiffly.

Jennifer smiled brightly. "How do you do?"

'How do you do?' What is this, the 19th century England? "I am doing fine." Rhonda's eyes went back to Butcher.

"Uh, Jennifer, is a psychologist from the east. She's come to Amicable to... um..." he looked at Jennifer for help.

"I read about Amicable in the newspaper. I thought that maybe I could help out."

The woman's words seemed acceptable, but Butcher appeared to be hiding something. Her eyes narrowed. "That's very kind of you. Are you going to be setting up shop somewhere?"

"I was actually going to ask your husband for a job."

Butcher glanced sharply at Jennifer who betrayed nothing.

"When September 11th happened, I remembered New York's struggle to move on. People couldn't seem to grasp happiness because the memories kept coming back. I did my PhD on how communities band together after trauma and I thought I could use some of my findings to help people here. That is, if Leo doesn't mind a little 'competition.'" Her smile was bright.

"I...uh...well, I suppose that's something we'll have to talk about." He responded as if it was a question to both women.

An uncomfortable silence ensued until Rhonda took a deep breath and flashed a grimacing smile. "So anyway... I guess I'll be running home. We'll see you in a few minutes." Her words were more a threat than expectation.

"Of course," he said.

"Nice to meet you," Rhonda said half-heartedly.

"Likewise," Jennifer responded, never moving from her position in the chair.

Rhonda moved towards Butcher and kissed him on the cheek – something she never did, but it seemed an appropriate thing to do, to mark her territory against predators. Jennifer politely stared at the wall.

Once Rhonda left, Butcher returned to his chair.

"She seems lovely," Jennifer said.

"The best."

"Is everything about her the complete opposite of me?" Jennifer's eyes gleamed.

"I don't know what you mean." Shifting uncomfortably, he was aware of what Jennifer was now trying to do. She was toying with him. Psychologists were the best at it. Butcher read in her playfulness, but also something deeper than that, pinched eyes, fidgeting fingers. It wasn't revenge…

Jealousy.

Whoa. Butcher's heart sped up and he felt lightheaded.

Sitting higher in her chair, pushing her breasts out slightly, head tilted to the side revealing the slightest flash of neck, Jennifer smirked coquettishly. "She's like a Greek goddess. Tall, attractive and those eyes… green, like emeralds. No wonder you married her. I didn't know they grew them like that in Iowa."

Clearing his throat, Butcher paused. "Let's get back to the 'I'm looking for a job' part. What was that all about?"

Jennifer leaned forward. "I'm serious. I really am writing a journal on communal grief and how people deal with trauma." She leaned back again. "I wasn't *just* interested in seeing you again."

But she did want to see me again…

"Well, I suppose we could look into something, considering your background. Do you have any paperwork for your qualifications so that I could at least give some notice to my fellow Amicableans?"

"Ami-what-eans?"

Butcher held up his hands in apology. "Sorry. It's what we call ourselves."

"Ourselves," she mused. "You have really become one."

"Yes, Jennifer, one doesn't become part of Amicable without letting the town grow on them."

"Whether a fungus or a flower remains to be seen," she responded with a glint.

Chapter 11.

Ola stood in the center of the dorm room exercising with free weights. He was shirtless, not because he was warm, but because the girls across the courtyard were watching him. His biceps, large, chocolate brown bowling balls, flexed and released, flexed and released. His pectoral muscles, although not completely engaged, were popping just for show. Ola pretended not to notice the girls ogling him; he enjoyed it. Demetrius, on the other hand, did not. When Ola took up center stage in their room, it left little space for actual study.

"Do you have to do that in here? There is an entire multimillion dollar exercise facility not one hundred yards from here, and you choose to stink up the room."

"Yo, Meat, this is my room too. I can't help it that I'm so sexy it causes you to squirm." Ola's sentence took fifteen seconds to spit out because he broke up every third word with a curl and a grunt.

"Ola, I'm trying to work."

Ola set the curling bar down and grinned. "There is a multimillion dollar reading facility called the 'library' not one hundred yards from here…"

"Look, you may have come to Mid-America to play football, but I came for an education. I've got far too much riding on my studies to be distracted."

"Dude, you got to lighten up. There's so much more to college life than your education. I mean, think about the education you get from interacting with the ladies." Ola glanced across the courtyard to the four girls, who were pressed near the window watching them.

"*Dude*," Demetrius emphasized, "it's a mix. I've got to study and the rest…"

Ola snorted. "McMurtry. Yeah, Boieee."

Demetrius' relationship with Kelly had blossomed into something beautiful in the last months.

"Yes, Ola, Kelly also, but I really need to have some quiet to finish this drawing."

Ola walked past Demetrius to see what he was working on. "What is this, anyway?"

"It's the beginning of a sculpture. A candlestick."

"A what? Candlestick? Why are you wasting your time on something like that? People don't even use candles anymore."

"Look, Ola, art doesn't have to be useful – in fact, most of it isn't. You don't use a painting to cover your bed and you don't use a statue as a doorjamb. This candlestick is about symbolism and meaning. Light coming out of darkness."

"You lost me, Meat."

Demetrius pointed at the drawing. "In my hometown, there is this woman who has cancer – she's a friend of the family." He traced the drawing with his finger. "She is here, the center of the candlestick."

"Bent over?"

"Pain, sadness, anger, sickness."

"And what are these other things surrounding her? They look like people without faces."

Demetrius nodded. "This is the rest of the community. They don't have faces because they could be anyone, and see how they surround her? Notice that they are the ones who will be holding the candle."

"They're holding the light for the cancer lady."

"Her name is Linda."

Ola ignored him. "And what's this thing at the bottom? At her feet?"

"It's a crab."

"That's kind of weird. Why a crab?"

"Cancer," Demetrius said. "The astrological sign for cancer is the crab."

"That's cool," Ola responded. "And what about this person off to the side. It looks like they're about to plant a stake in the crab. Is that the doctor, then?"

Demetrius playfully pushed Ola. "Now you're getting the hang of it. That's the doctor holding a caduceus."

"A catawhat?"

"It's the icon that symbolizes medicine. It's a serpent on a pole."

"Damn, Meat, you are a philosopher as well as an artist." Ola pronounced it *arteest*. "So what are you going to make this candlestick out of?"

"Right now," Demetrius shrugged and picked up the curling bar, "I just needed to get the drawing done. When I figure out the medium, I'll let you know." Demetrius did ten curls effortlessly and put the bar back down.

A knock reverberated in the room and both young men looked at each other as to who was going to open the door. Demetrius opened it.

Kelly.

"Remember," Ola said over his shoulder while putting on his shirt. "Priorities. Education. Focus." He continued laughing as Demetrius walked out the door.

Chapter 12.

In the three weeks after Jennifer's arrival, the change in Amicable was palpable. Although the community had long trusted the Butcher's services, Jennifer Adams provided something that Butcher was never able to give: an unreadable future. Although Butcher promised confidentiality, Amicableans always reserved the deepest secrets because Butcher was a permanent member of the community. When Dr. Adams hung her shingle next to Butcher's plaque outside the Chop Shop, the curious came calling. Those who met her immediately felt at home, comfortable. Dr. Adams seemed like such a *nice* person. A true Amicablean

After the first tentativeness, many of the women in Amicable made appointments. "It was so good," they said, "talking to a woman who knows how women feel. No offense, Butcher." Thus, Jennifer Adams became a receptacle of secrets.

It had been a long, drawn out conversation with Rhonda to make the work situation, well, work. Butcher wasn't quite sure why he didn't tell Rhonda that they had dated in the past. He knew that it would not sit well with his wife when she found out. It never registered with him, though, that Amicable might be used as a psychological guinea pig; he simply enjoyed Jennifer's presence and how easy it was for him to come to work now.

After staying a night in a seedy motel in Clancy, Butcher found her accommodation in a nostalgic place: 184 Peppertree Lane. As Liam Wilson introduced her to her new digs, Butcher reminisced about his first thoughts when he arrived in Amicable.

The day was cold. Liam raised a hand and then blew warm air on it again. "Howdy, folks."

Butcher shortened his stride to match Jennifer's. To the untrained eye, Butcher's leg seemed to be dragging slightly, just a hitch in his giddyup, or so the locals would say.

Chapter 12.

"Hey Liam, this is Dr. Adams. She's going to be staying with us for a while."

"Okay," Liam said slowly. The mechanic was always mistrustful about the word 'doctor.' Some travelers had stopped in Amicable to have their Lincoln's or Cadillacs or Mercedes repaired and introduced themselves as 'Dr. So and So.' When he asked them what kind of doctor they were, it seemed to always be something weird like *Doctor of Philosophy,* or the weirdest one was *Doctor of Packaging.* When Liam asked if the guy was pulling his leg, he looked offended and began to give his dissertation about how he was improving the lives of American citizens by improving the packaging of foods and other products. Liam had tried not to roll his eyes.

"Please, call me 'Jennifer.'"

Receiving her friendly smile, Liam extended his grease-stained hand. She shook it hard – not what he was expecting. *I bet she's a Doctor of Feminism.*

She read his expression. "I'm a psychologist, Liam," she said as she passed under his arm and entered the house.

"I didn't ask," Liam bemusedly glanced up at Butcher who towered over him.

Jennifer quickly went from room to room; the living room was tidy, but dusty. The furniture was three or four years old. Earth tones were the dominant colors: ecru rug, brown matching recliners, green sofa. To Liam and Butcher, it seemed homey. To Jennifer, it felt dreary.

"Do you mind if I spruce it up a little bit? Some flowers or even some paintings?"

"As long as you don't put any nail holes in the walls." Liam was quite sure that this woman's idea of decorating would be womanpower – lots of anti-pink. She was friendly enough, but you couldn't trust a woman who shook hands like a man.

125

"Thank you." They kept moving and wandered to the bedroom, where the queen bed with brass header and footer sat resolutely in the middle of the room. A cheap, antique boudoir with mirror and washing basin took up a corner. She ran her finger along it. More dust.

"That was my grandmother's," Liam interjected. "She died."

Looking back at him, she smiled. "I'm sorry for your loss."

Butcher looked at Liam and frowned. Then, he mouthed the words, *What are you doing?*

Liam's eyes widened. *What?*

As they moved to the bathroom, Jennifer paused and sniffed. "Has the septic tank backed up?"

Butcher and Liam froze.

"Uh, that's a long story. You'll have to have Butcher tell you that episode." He moved back out of the bathroom. "So, what do you think?"

"Let's go to the kitchen first."

The contrast between the kitchen and the living room was stark. Bright colors, yellows and blues covered the walls.

Liam stepped forward. "My girlfriend told me that this room need a more feminine touch. I told her that was offensive. Women don't belong in the kitchen."

Jennifer stopped and turned to him. "What do you mean by that?"

"Umm, what I meant is, that I don't believe it's just the woman's job to be in the kitchen and that making it feminine was like so last century." Liam's face froze into a strange grimace.

Butcher laughed. "I think what he means in his very clumsy way is that Liam thinks that there is a partnership in cooking. Isn't that right, Liam?"

Liam sighed audibly and swallowed. He didn't want to suffer the wrath of a violent feminist. She might use big psychological words on him and then make him talk about his mother or something.

"Okay," Jennifer said, "I'll take it."

For the next five minutes they haggled over the price until eventually Liam gave in. His fear of her perceived radical nature cost him fifty dollars per month.

Ten minutes later, Liam gratefully departed. Butcher and Jennifer were left standing in the middle of the empty house. It was quiet; the only sound was the ticking of a plastic kitchen clock above the sink.

"What do you think?" he asked.

"It's quaint," she replied noncommittally.

This was her opinion of almost the entire town of Amicable.

In those first weeks of her time in Amicable, Jennifer made notes in her large black and red ledger book which she secured with a rubber band each night. As time wore on, Jennifer began to notice that a 'trapped-ness' was a common motif among those who visited with her. It would be an interesting exercise to scan her notes in six months to see if anything changed.

Even Anne Johnson availed herself of Jennifer's talents once. She was curious about 'psycho-babble stuff' and made it immediately known to Jennifer that she wasn't sure about this 'hooey.' But, Jennifer's winsome smile and amenable manner made Anne feel comfortable to share about her eighty plus years of life and sixty years of marriage to Gordon. When she finished offloading, Anne was surprised how good she felt. For the first time since Gordon had entered the nursing home without her, she whistled down Main Street.

A number of high school students were referred to Jennifer by the school counselor. Many of the kids suffered from anxiety and depression. It was common across the world, not just the Midwest.

It was on her tenth day in Amicable when Mr. Carson called Jennifer about a sensitive matter in the elementary school. It seemed that a young boy was being constantly harassed by his classmates. The boy, J.T., was struggling socially and academically. Mr. Carson had not been able to make any headway with J.T. so he referred the boy to her.

After hanging up the phone, Jennifer scratched her head with her index finger. That would be an interesting conversation with Leo and Rhonda. Noticing that it was three o'clock on a Friday afternoon, she studied the list of places that Butcher had set up to understand what Amicable was all about:

Bowling Alley/Greedy Pecker
X-Er-Size studio
Peterson's Butchery
Human Beans Café
Newly reconstructed grain elevator
Amicable Community High School
Nuestra Casa Spanish Restaurant
St. Clements Sunday worship service.

When Jennifer questioned Leo about attending church, his reply, although enigmatic, was that she would have a better understanding of the communal psyche of the people. When she stated that 'church had never been her thing,' Leo smiled and said, 'well, normal hair color never was your thing either, but look at you now.'

In the first week she had checked off Human Beans. Amazingly, the coffee was better than expected. The Spanish restaurant was even more surprising.

As the list shrank, she took a personal inventory about how she was feeling being isolated and alone. Sensing an acute awareness to the *distance from everything*, she made a mental note to drive to Omaha or Des Moines to escape. She did not want to fall into the mistake of becoming the same kind of 'fungus or flower' of which she had accused Leo.

Jennifer placed her journal into the cupboard, locked it and smiled at Hossein, the receptionist, who nodded uncomfortably. Hossein was, perhaps, the only person in Amicable who hadn't warmed quickly to Jennifer.

"Have a good weekend," Jennifer waved to the receptionist.

"Salaam."

With winter setting in, Jennifer wondered how she would cope with the cold. Boston was chilly, but she had heard the Midwest was something entirely different. As she put her on coat and wrapped a scarf around her neck, she prepared herself for the chattering wind that rattled windows and fogged up glasses. Though only early December, she was already shivering.

Exiting the Chop Shop, she turned left and walked towards Main Street. A few pickups were parked on the streets. Christmas decorations were up already. Entwined around the poles were fake greenery and the bases of the poles were an assortment of stars, bells, balls and even a manger scene. These Christmas decorations (not 'holiday decorations' as the *Progressives* wanted to call them) were reminders of the coming long darkness. Wandering down Main Street, she paused to take in the festive feel and she astonishingly, felt something different. Something palpable about Amicableans and how they greeted each other pleasantly as if it truly *was* the most wonderful time of the year.

Her thoughts turned to Leo. Their shared proximity in the office had been interesting to say the least. The air crackled with electricity. She felt him watching her, probably reading her at the same time. The tingling sensation travelled up and down her spine. Somewhere in the near future they would have to confront that particular white elephant in the Chop Shop.

During their shared lunchtimes, they spoke very little of the past. Sometimes they discussed cases, or issues that were beyond Leo's understanding. Because he had only done his counseling course online, he wasn't adept at diagnosis. But he was a master at helping people see a positive future and move towards it.

Butcher had purchased a small table and chairs to put in the corner of the room where they could eat lunch together. On the coldest days, the light shone through the window casting a reflected glow off the table and illuminating the two people who sat across from each other.

"You eat like a woman who hasn't seen food in a week."

She smiled and wiped her mouth with the back of her hand. "These things are to die for." She held up a burrito.

"Yeah, my tuna sandwich… I'd trade at least one kidney for it. I'd throw in my spleen if necessary."

Jennifer swallowed and sat back in her chair. "This is still pretty weird."

"What is?" He took another bite.

"This," she pointed at the table and their plates. "All of this. Having lunch together. In the middle of Iowa of all places. Both of us working in the same place, same job, and you," she motioned towards him, "the same, but not quite."

Butcher's hands paused in mid-lift. They trembled slightly which annoyed him, so he set the sandwich back on the plate and put his hands in his lap. "What are you getting at?"

"You're different. It feels like as much as you want to be happy, you're not – just covering it well."

Butcher frowned. "I'm happy."

"Okay, then," Jennifer said leaning forward. "Tell me what happiness is."

"What kind of a question is that? It's like asking someone to describe the color green. You can't. But you know what it is and you can point to it, right?"

"Chicken," she needled.

"Whatever."

She cleared her throat theatrically, sat up straight, placed a hand on her heart and recited: "We hold these truths to be self-evident that all people are created equally, that they are all endowed by their Creator with certain unalienable rights, namely, Life, Liberty and the Pursuit of Happiness."

Butcher smirked at the small woman. "You're quoting the Constitution?"

"Close – Declaration of Independence."

"Why?"

"Because these are the conversations that all people should be having, not about football teams or the weather, although it is dreadfully important in Amicable." He nodded in agreement. "But how often do we talk about the important things like the unalienable rights – Life, Liberty and the Pursuit of Happiness."

"But you started with happiness. Do you think this is an unalienable right?"

Jennifer wagged a finger at him. "First, Leo, we need to define happiness and then we can figure out if the right is unalienable or simply a luxury."

"All right," Butcher said, as he wiped his own mouth on a napkin. "You define it."

Jennifer's lips pressed together in mock frustration. "Why are you avoiding the question?"

"Because I can't answer it!"

"Yes, you can! You're not even trying. I didn't realize you were a quitter."

Jennifer saw that she had pressed the right button.

"All right, already! Just off the top of my head, I'd say that happiness is the state in which everything you want and dream of is lined up conveniently for you. Your family is healthy, your financial affairs are in order and maybe you've fallen in love... or... or..." he stumbled, trying to get back on track, "your marriage is vibrant, your kids are far above average and life seems enormous." He raised his eyebrows and lifted his hands. "How's that?"

"Is that everything that you want? Where do you find meaning?"

"Meaning? Does everything have to have meaning?"

"Of course!" Jennifer stood up and began to pace, marking off her points with her fingers. "If the things we do and say and believe don't have meaning, then are we actually living or just taking up space?"

Watching her, Butcher was taken in by her graceful movements and poise. "So are you saying that the Declaration of Independence was crafted so that we could experience meaning?"

"Yes! Instead of slavery to an old regime and an outdated way of life, class systems, inane tax distributions, fealty to country without respect. Think about it," Jennifer said, as she tapped her head, "What is life without reflection? Didn't Plato say, 'The unexamined life is not worth living?'"

"Socrates, I think," Butcher responded.

"Whatever. Is liberty without thought empty? And what of happiness? Not just what makes you happy, but *who*. If all we think about is *what* makes us happy, we die of shallowness." Jennifer's eyes glowed with intensity.

"Why would they add happiness to the Declaration if it's shallow?"

Jennifer grabbed the sides of her head. "I think they made a mistake."

Butcher laughed out loud. "The founding fathers made a mistake. That's rich."

"Why? Do you think that the founding fathers were perfect?"

"No, but…" He looked out the window. "So what should they have said then?"

Jennifer stood behind him and whispered near his ear. "It should have said, 'Life, Liberty and the pursuit of Beauty."

Leo shivered in spite of himself. "Explain."

For the first time since her arrival, Jennifer touched Leo. She put her hands on his shoulders. Professionally and morally she knew that she had crossed a line, a Rubicon. An irrevocable step had been taken from which she could not return. Jennifer felt the solid muscles of his shoulders, the strength and the heat emanating from him. He tensed, and then relaxed. This was something he hadn't thought about wanting, at least not consciously, but now that it had happened, it was okay – they were friends. Just friends and colleagues. Friends and colleagues touched each other. Right?

"I don't necessarily need happiness in my life," Jennifer started in a low voice, and then removed her hands. "Although, happiness is enjoyable, it is not a goal. It's something that happens along the way to encountering beauty."

"I don't know what you mean," Leo responded almost breathlessly.

"What I've found," Jennifer said, as she ran her hand through her hair, "is that in everything, if I find beauty, it's there that I'll find happiness."

"Even in pain? Sorrow? Anxiety?"

"Absolutely, Leo. When I find beauty, I find meaning. When I'm in pain, I think about the beauty of health. Sorrow? I find beauty in sharing my grief with others. It's a universal connection point. Anxiety?" She moved back around to stand in front of him. "How else can we confront our death unless we experience the intersection of loss and love?"

"Wow, you've really put a lot of thought into this."

"It's part of the reason I came here. How can we counsel others unless we fully understand how to help them get better, to find meaning in their pain and questions?"

"Jeesh, I never thought of it that way. Did you learn that in your psychology classes?"

Jennifer laughed and looked down. "No. Ecclesiastes."

"I thought you said you weren't religious."

Shrugging, Jennifer sat back down in her chair. "You can find a great deal of wisdom in religious literature that isn't available in the secular. But just like everything else, you can't believe everything that you read."

Leo smiled at the double entendre of her statement. He was wondering if he had read her correctly in the first place.

The bank door opened. A wreath with tiny silver bells tinkled and a youngish man, mid-thirties walked out stuffing his wallet in his back pocket. He looked both ways as he exited and adjusted his collar before noticing the petite stranger standing on the corner looking up at the sign.

"Hello," he called out.

Jennifer smiled and nodded which was enough of an encouragement for the man to approach her. Noticing the difference between big city and small town, Jennifer smirked that this moment would never occur in Boston or New York without the woman producing a canister of mace just in case.

"I'm Stedman," he said.

"Excuse me?" Jennifer's eyebrows raised.

"My name is Stedman. Stedman Boswell."

Jennifer was sure she had heard that name before. "Stedman? That's not a typical Midwestern name." She laughed. "I've met a lot of Davids, Thomases, Johns, Steves and Brians – maybe a Chad here and there – but you're the first Stedman."

He shrugged and spread his hands, then shoved them into his pants pockets.

Jennifer's head tilted. "How long have you been here?"

"Two years almost."

"Where did you come from?"

Stedman sniffed and looked towards the southwest almost wistfully. "Kansas City."

"Why Amicable?"

Stedman paused then spoke deliberately. "I was sent here as part of an insurance investigation for the elevator – you knew about the explosion, right?" She nodded and they both turned towards the hulking edifice behind them. "When the investigation finished, I decided to stay."

Finally, the information clicked. Jennifer snapped her fingers. "Aah, yes! I remember reading about you. The insurance adjustor with a conscience. The headline in the Boston Globe said, 'Blessed Insurer.'"

"I hadn't heard that one," he laughed.

"It was a good article. You came out well."

Stedman flapped his elbows, embarrassed. "Well, sometimes you make good decisions after bad ones."

"So why did you stay?"

"Sometimes you find the unexpected unexpectedly beautiful."

Nodding but not convinced, Jennifer blew on her hands. "What do you find beautiful about this place?"

"You mean besides the weather and the scenery?" He said sarcastically. "I don't know. It's hard to put a finger on it. Mostly, it feels like a sanctuary from the big, bad world. People here care about you, you know what I mean? You see folks bringing a fresh pie to their neighbor and then stopping to chat. If you look closely, you'll find a heart of gold in this town."

"A regular Garden of Eden, then?"

His eyes narrowed. "You've got an awful lot of questions."

"Sorry," Jennifer extended her hand. "I should have introduced myself. Jennifer Adams. I'm a friend of Leo's."

Stedman shook it, feeling her frigid fingers in his own. "Leo? Oh, Butcher. Man, that guy knows everybody."

"You would think…"

"So… not to be forward, but why are *you* here in Amicable? I'm sure it's not *just* to visit a small town butcher."

"You probably could say 'former' small town butcher." Jennifer watched his reaction to see if he and Leo were friends. The tensing jaw muscles gave it away. Definitely friends.

"Yes, well, I suppose you could say that, but I wouldn't. It wouldn't be the first time a butcher lost a finger and went back to work."

"I didn't mean to offend you."

"It's okay." He looked around as if ready to move on. "So anyway, are you in Amicable for a while?"

"I've taken a leave of absence from work to come and help out."

It was Stedman's turn to raise his eyebrows. "Really?"

"Butcher hired me to work as a co-counselor in the Chop Shop."

"That's you! I'd heard rumors, but I've been in Kansas City all week. Summer had been talking to Rhonda and Tracey and…" he noticed the faraway look in her eyes as she melted at the names, "… never mind about who, but they said a new shri… er, psychologist was in town."

Jennifer's eyes sparkled. "That's me."

"How's business?"

She held his gaze. "People need to talk. I've got deep ears."

Stedman's smile faded. "I see." He took his first step away from Jennifer, then stopped and turned back. "Just be careful with all the secrets," he said. "Amicable is still… tender."

Chapter 12.

As Jennifer watched him go, she noticed the first snowflake of winter as it floated delicately downwards unable to support its weight in the sky.

It wouldn't be long before it melted.

Chapter 13.

The Deakins family always looked forward to the pensive, deceleration as Christmas and New Year approached. For John, the season was an opportunity to ponder both blessings and curses that occur to him personally, and the community. In the last two years, Amicable had substantially recovered from the destruction of their fiscal temple, the elevator, and reverted back to placid sailing. Whether or not this was a good thing was yet unknown. Interestingly, as the elevator rebuild neared its reconstructed completion, the less people came to worship. People need people in tragedy; people desire independence in the non-tragic.

Checking his appearance in the vestry mirror, John surveyed his shape. In the last months Leslie had 'encouraged' him (this was the polite way to say, 'John, your pants are getting a workout from holding in your front and backsides') to exercise and *maybe lay off the after-church-doughnuts*. He turned his head sideways and frowned at the new patch of grey hair at his temples. Why couldn't people just grow older, do the things they always loved and then, when their time was up, go to sleep and wake up somewhere else doing exactly the same things they enjoyed while alive?

John picked up his Bible, exited the vestry and walked out into the altar area noticing the visual changes in the sanctuary for Advent. Twin Christmas trees, decorated with gold and silver ornaments, bookended the altar while wreaths were positioned on the walls. Joanne Benson had wanted to place a mistletoe at the rear entrance, but John had firmly, yet nicely, indicated that the 'holy kiss' had nothing to do with worship services.

Turning away from the altar, John spotted a few extra decorations placed by some plucky Confirmation students. A Santa bobblehead was placed underneath the pulpit and eight tiny reindeer were sitting underneath his chair next to it. Shaking his head, he sighed and smiled. *It could be worse,* he thought. *They could have put Elves on Shelves in charge of protecting the offering plates.*

The congregation was gathering. A low rumbling was heard just below the mournful playing of Jim-the-Postman/Organist's prelude. Jim sat at the organ bench, head leaned backwards so he could peer through his bifocals at the sheet music in front of him.

John noticed Dick and Linda halfway back on the left side of the church in their normal seats. Surrounding them were the typical cast of characters. They might have been gossiping about Jennifer Adams, the new counselor. John had met her only once when he had walked out of the Chop Shop for some fresh air and a coffee. Briefly, they had introduced themselves, but John was taken aback by her friendliness.

Continuing his sanctuary scan, John saw the Jensen family arriving at their normal ten-seconds-before-the-service time, but the parents looked eminently frustrated. Georgie was crying and clinging to her mother while Butcher stared at his hands. The knees of his jeans looked dirty. J.T. stood impassively to the side.

As the Jensen family positioned themselves in the pew, Rhonda placing service bags containing coloring books and crayons for the children into their laps, Jim the Organist finished the mournful prelude. He took a deep breath and spotted the pastor who gave him a surreptitious thumbs up.

"Good morning," John greeted the congregation. "Welcome. Christmas is on the way, but now we wait."

At the word Christmas, most of the elementary aged children looked up from their brown, red and green nativity scribblings, but when the pastor took up the word 'Advent' again, they started to fill in the picture again.

"Advent means the 'coming of something big.' For most of us who think about the holiday season, we may already be pondering the advent of gifts, or meals or family gatherings. Some of these may be positive and others…" he waggled his hand, which brought polite laugh from the gathering. "Not very often do we talk about Advent as a time of preparation for suffering. We avoid those kinds of discussions because Christmas is supposed to be 'the most wonderful time of the year,' 'happy holidays,' and 'dreams of white Christmases.' But what about the beginning of suffering, or the middle of suffering like the Virgin Mary? She, and her country, who had been suffering for centuries, desperately wanted and needed someone to save them. When the angel arrived, don't you think it's fascinating that his message is not only one of great joy, but also a precursor to Mary's own personal suffering?"

"Some of you, right now," he glanced at Linda and Dick, "might be in the center of suffering's hurricane. In the midst of the storm, where do you find hope? And more importantly, if the suffering isn't eased, what is the point of faith then?"

Nods all around.

"So, today we look at Mary's advent of simultaneous joy and suffering." John smiled at his turn of phrase, but then a figure appeared in the back door.

Jennifer Adams.

The worship service was in disarray from that moment onwards. The congregation, always aware of visitors, tittered noisily. The handful of women surrounding Linda Harmsen immediately pressed into a football huddle whispering animatedly peering over their shoulders towards the tiny woman in the back entrance. Jennifer, noticing that she had caused a stir, quickly took a seat near the rear of the church. The Dozer family shuffled sideways to create space for Jennifer to sit by herself.

Feeling uncomfortable, Jennifer spotted the Jensens ten pews ahead of her. Leo's wife, Rhonda, seemed to be either annoyed or worried. Strangely, in the fifteen seconds that she watched him, Leo studied his hands three times.

During the pastor's speech, she kept her eyes from rolling when he spoke about the virginity of Jesus' mother. Her 'overshadowing' by God (or the Holy Spirit, or something like that) was most certainly not a blessed thing. She had personally met dozens of women who had been overshadowed by powerful men. It was not something she'd want for her worst enemy.

Jennifer felt fortunate to be part of a church service where they played lots of Christmas music that she had heard of. It was irrelevant whether she believed the words or not; there was something distinctly comforting about a little town called Bethlehem and a mournful song begging someone called Emmanuel to come.

As the last notes of the postlude echoed into rafters, the priest took his position at the front and invited the congregation to meet downstairs after the service to have a cup of coffee and some homemade delicacies. This was, of course, the only reason she had come to church. She waited for the people to file past and lead the way to wherever the 'basement' was.

The Dozers politely excused themselves past Jennifer's knees. The smallest child had two identical streams of liquid boogers running down her philtrum. Without thinking, Jennifer brought her hand to her nose but dropped it quickly. The father, carrying the older child, nodded cordially to Jennifer as he squeezed past, but as for a warm, Midwestern welcome, that was left to the gaggle of women, all of whom had come to the office last week.

Carley, effervescent in a pink sweater, dark blue slacks and wrap around shawl, stood impatiently across the aisle dancing in anticipation. Carley waved a flat-handed wiggle under her chin while grinning, and then pushed through the coffee-crowd surge towards Jennifer. Jennifer had wanted to catch up with Leo first, but once in Carley's grips, she was pulled inexorably through the same surge to the other side of the church where Linda, Leona, Jeannie, and Angela circled. They had left two spaces open for Jennifer and Carley to dock.

"Good morning, Dr. Adams," they all said, almost simultaneously.

"Good morning. Please, when we're not in the office, call me Jennifer."

Carley looked around at the others and giggled into her hand. "Okay, Jenny."

"I would prefer 'Jennifer.'".

"Will you come sit with us?" Jeannie asked expectantly.

Glancing over her shoulder, she saw the Jensen family move out of the sanctuary. Leo tilted his head back in greeting and a mirthful smile played across his lips. Rhonda followed his gaze and politely nodded also. Surrounding the Jensen family were various other families and couples.

"Well, yes, I suppose," Jennifer responded.

The circle of women moved like an amoeba out into the aisle, down the carpeted stairs in the narthex, and then to the basement. As they stood in the coffee line, the women chattering animatedly about five different topics at once.

Jennifer noticed that many of the young families had rushed out the door, to head home and release their children from the bondage of both Sunday clothes and church restrictions. A few, though, stayed and allowed their children to move around the basement at will, supervised not just by their parents, but by the community at large. In the far right corner away from everyone else, a table of high school teens morosely sipped coffee and ate the largest of the doughnuts.

At the kitchen window, Jennifer received a cup of percolated black coffee from a matronly woman with blue hair. The woman smiled, greeted Jennifer and pointed quickly to the seats so as not to engage her in conversation. Her task was simple and pre-scripted: serve the coffee, dish the cake and keep 'em moving. Too many people in line waiting for coffee would not be nice.

"So, Dr... um... Jennifer," Leona started. "Tell us a little bit about yourself."

"Well," she kept one eye on Leo and his family, who were now separated across tables, men at one, women at the other, "I was born in Massachusetts."

"Oooh, that's exotic," Carley looked agog.

"I wouldn't go that far," Jennifer had never heard anyone call Boston 'exotic' before, "but it was an interesting place to grow up. A lot of history. A lot of conflict. But, overall, it suited my tastes."

The women leaned into the table, chins in hand, listening intently.

"I have two brothers and parents."

"Tell us more," Linda said.

"My entire life, I've been small. When I was born, supposedly the doctor made a joke, something like, 'Well, Mrs. Adams, you won't have to worry about this one being a basketball player.' I did everything in my power to do the opposite of what anyone expected."

The others nodded, even though they couldn't sympathize. Most of them had always done what others expected of them.

"When I was seven, while everyone else was in swimming lessons, I volunteered to be part of the fire department." Jennifer laughed. "They treated me like a mascot, so I quit. At age ten, when everyone else my age and size began to play sports, I decided to take up the tuba. Even though the stupid thing was bigger than I was, I was bound and determined to show everyone else that my size would not limit me."

"Good for you, Jen," Leona encouraged, but the statement caused her to frown.

"There are two things I can't stand: people who try to mother me and people who try to pick me up. I'm not a toy, or a doll, or a puppy. The last guy that tried to pick me up, I kicked him in the balls."

A collective gasp arose from the pious Amicablean table. They looked around the basement to see if anyone else heard.

Their reaction was just what Jennifer wanted to see. They were listening, and she was hoping that no one would attempt either of the two things she hated most.

"Now," Jennifer continued, "when I reached high school, most of the people my age were mixed up in the endless hamster wheel of popularity, educational success, athletic prowess and the perpetual race of needing to be beautiful. So, I did the opposite. I was voted least popular, I passed most of my classes with a sparkling straight C plus average, my athletic prowess was limited not by ability, but by anti-popularity snobbishness. Most of all, I tried to look different. My hair was always a strange color; my clothes never really matched and God forbid I'd ever wear jeans and a t-shirt."

The ladies all looked around at each other. Each one of them wore jeans and a t-shirt on a daily basis. Except Sundays.

"So what you're saying is that you don't want to be like anyone else." Jeannie wanted to make sure she said it in a way that was neither motherly nor kick-in-the-balls-worthy.

"How did you end up looking so... normal and... and..." Jeannie motioned with both of her hands at Jennifer, who grinned over her cup of coffee before taking a sip.

"Sooner or later, I think, we all figure out that people are important, and I was missing out on almost every chance to connect with them." She snuck a glance at Butcher who was engaged in conversation with the twin butchers, the reverend and the youngish man that she had met on the street – the one with the funny name: Stegman, or something like that.

Butcher was unaware that Jennifer was watching him. Holding the coffee cup gently between his hands, he opened them and looked at his palms. They were scratched and raw. Rhonda scolded him for being clumsy; he had almost knocked Georgie over when he fell on the way into the church, but Georgie was more frightened of seeing her father fall then stumbling herself.

"So what happened?" Nash asked. "Were you looking at the new psychologist?" He grinned and stared at Jennifer, who guiltily looked away as if she had been caught doing something wrong. "She's kind of a hottie in a midgety kind of way."

Butcher frowned and tried to respond, but as had happened that week, his mind produced the words but his mouth couldn't seem to translate them into intelligible language.

As he stumbled over the simplest of responses, John raised his eyes and tilted his head slightly. "Are you all right?"

"I'm fine," Butcher said, finally engaging his mouth. Truth be told, he had wondered if he'd suffered a small stroke a week or two back, not only because of the speech issue, but his right leg seemed to be less responsive. And the numb fingers… "I tripped over a piece of sidewalk outside the school and fell over. Scraped my hands and my ego."

"It's a long way to fall," John said.

"Tell me about it."

Derek leaned into the table. "What do you know about this psychologist. Stedman says that you were friends a long time ago." He nodded towards Stedman, who crossed his arms and leaned back in his chair.

Butcher shrugged and began to speak, but he didn't look up. If any of them were able to read non-verbal signals like he could, they would know that he was withholding parts of the truth. "We were friends when I lived in New England. She'd buy her meat at the grocery store where I worked."

"Huh," Derek grunted.

"Yes," Butcher responded, with a wry grin, "we went out a couple of times, but it never would have worked."

Derek nodded his head sagely. "You're right, giants and elves should never mix."

Nash laughed and pretended to take a swipe at him.

"Anyway," John interrupted them, bringing the conversation back to task. "It seems like an amazing reconnection. A coincidence, really. She is a psychologist; you are a psych-something. You used to date and now you're sharing an office. What does Rhonda think about that?"

Butcher watched Rhonda who was deep in conversation with Naida, Shania, Tracey and Leslie. Even as she grew older, Butcher understood the depth of her beauty. But in the weeks that Jennifer had come to Amicable, the stirring inside Butcher had been tremulous. The strangeness of what it was like to fall... he wouldn't go so far as to believe or think that it was love, but something akin to amorous intrigue, if there was such a thing.

"Rhonda is fine with it. We're mature adults, aren't we? Jennifer and I, even though we share a brief, common past, are professionals – colleagues. She is an excellent fit." He motioned to the table with Jennifer. "The town seems to be welcoming her nicely."

Stedman cleared his throat. "Just be careful, Butcher. Rhonda is the best thing that ever happened to you."

Frowning, Butcher pondered Stedman. Knowing that the younger man previously had feelings for Rhonda, Butcher read him. It was a noble gesture to prod Butcher to remain pure, but Butcher wondered if there was something else going on with him.

"Stedman's right," John said. "The past has a way of sneaking up on us when we least expect it and stabbing us in the back."

Butcher studied the gazes of his concerned friends and looked back down at his injured hands. "Don't worry about it," he said. "Nothing is going to happen." He noticed Rhonda's profile and the tired, worried expression in her eyes.

Rhonda lifted the cup to her lips. Naida, Christmas glee already glowing on her cheeks, was ebullient about the fact that the Yule was only a few weeks away *and* a wedding was about to occur. Almost everyone in town was talking about Connie's engagement to Carl. Weddings had been a scarce event but now, in the midst of the decline of rural America, a deluge of four weddings in the last five years had given Amicable many reasons to celebrate. Connie and Carl sat at the same table with a group of older women. Carl, the doting beau and Connie, the debutante glowing in the light of their love and excitement, sat side-by-side holding court. Naida smiled delightedly and pushed in towards Rhonda.

"I think it's just beautiful that old people are getting married, too."

Rhonda shivered. It wasn't that she didn't like Carl, she just didn't like the *idea of Carl*. In her mind, she constantly flitted over her mother's insecurities and needs. What if this was just another guy who would rip out what was left of her heart?

It hadn't entered her mind that Rhonda was jealous of her mother's newfound love – not Carl, of course, but the *feelings*. The quickened pulse, uncontrolled thoughts, visions of... she shook her head. That was not what she wanted to think about her mother doing with Carl.

"Yes, it's very nice."

"Changing subjects here," Tracey interjected, "but it seems like Dr. Adams has created quite a stir in metropolitan Amicable." Tactlessly, all but Rhonda looked towards the other table.

"She seems very nice," Leslie nodded.

Tracey smiled. "And a welcome addition to the community. Do you think we should try to invite her into our circle here before she is... how shall we say... corrupted by the current table?" Leona reinforced the idea by pressing a finger into the table in front of her.

All eyes turned toward Rhonda. Without knowing why, the rest knew that the decision would be hers alone. "I think that would be a good idea." It wasn't jealously that motivated Rhonda, but something much more clinical. A few more eyes on this *interloper* would be a good thing. Rhonda knew that her friends would be honest with her. She looked back towards Butcher who stretched his long arms above his head. She saw the cuts on his hands and nine fingers.

"Then it's settled," Naida said, rubbing her hands together. "Should we all have a cup of coffee together tomorrow afternoon?"

"It's a date," Rhonda responded, hesitantly.

Chapter 14.

Linda Harmsen leaned back in the chair in Butcher's old office, which, at this moment was Dr. Adam's office. "What are you feeling today?" Jennifer asked as Linda closed her eyes and adjusted the scarf which was wrapped around her head.

"I'm feeling grateful."

"Say more about that." Jennifer took a sip of tea.

"I'm alive. Each breath seems different. I don't know how to explain it, really, but when Dr. Neale told me about my diagnosis, something inside me changed. It was very weird."

Jennifer waited for her to go on.

"I feel..." Linda grasped for words, "... I feel reconditioned, repurposed. Do you know what I mean?"

"Kind of. Give me more."

"I have this sense that most people kind of wander through life like we're all dry erase markers." She laughed at her joke. "Sooner or later, we're all wiped off the board to make room for others."

Jennifer smiled and nodded.

"So when I saw the eraser coming for me, I've reflected on the words I've written during my life, and to be honest, I wasn't really enjoying what I was reading."

"That's an amazing way of putting it," Jennifer encouraged. "Tell me what words you read."

Linda took a deep breath and blew the air out her nose slowly. "I've been self-absorbed, difficult and..." she paused, "... shallow. Is there anything worse than being shallow?"

"You tell me."

Linda squeezed her eyes closed. "We waste so much time talking about meaningless things," her laugh sounded almost like a hiccup. "We talk about other people that threaten our happiness.

We start to think that our happiness is buying and keeping things and we forget." She tapped her head and opened her eyes. "We forget that we were created to love and receive love."

Jennifer's eyes strayed towards the picture of Butcher and his family. "What else have you remembered?"

"The other day, Dick and I went for a walk. It was early in the morning, cold – biting cold – but neither one of us wanted to stay inside. The sun was just coming up; it had snowed in the middle of the night. Six inches unmarked by footprints, human ones at least. I remember seeing my breath, and something tweaked inside of me. This thing that I'd taken for granted, breath, reminded me how much I loved life."

Linda smiled at the memory. "At that moment, the first rays of sun appeared over the trees. Orange and pink and the snow became a whiteboard and I remember thinking, 'Someday, all of us will have to face the fact that our footprints will be gone and this world will just go on without us.'"

"How did that make you feel?"

"At first, I was scared. I suppose we all get scared at the thought of dying. But then, I felt joyful. At that moment I realized that I have been given an unknown, yet significant, amount of time to appreciate life."

"What did you do next?"

"I grabbed my husband's hand. Even though we were wearing gloves, I could feel the heat from his fingers. I leaned my head into his shoulder and as we watched the sun come up. Dick leaned his head onto the top of mine and told me he loved me."

"That's very nice," Jennifer said.

"Of course it's nice! Amicablean men tell their wives that they love them just before they get married, on their wedding day and then there's radio silence. It's like, 'I'll let you know if anything changes.'"

"Dick isn't forthright in sharing his emotions?"

Linda snickered. "Let's just say that there is a sieve through which all of his feelings have to pass."

"Okay, so he said he loved you. What does that mean?"

Touching the side of her face with her hand, she smiled as she blushed. "It wasn't a cursory 'I love you,' like you might say when you finish the dishes and he appreciates that. It was one of those proclamations that you hold on to. It was like he told me he loved me because he didn't know how long he'd be able to tell me that."

"And...?"

"We finished our walk and then went home. We made love. He treated my body as if it was a temple. All of its imperfections seemed to have been transformed into perfectness for him."

"Wonderful," Jennifer encouraged. "So you are feeling...?"

"Like a new woman. I might have cancer, but now I also have purpose."

"And what is that?"

"I want everyone to feel what I have. I want people to see their breath."

Setting her tea down on the desk, Jennifer smiled. "You've made some significant progress today, Linda, I haven't found many people who are able to elucidate their mortality quite as well as you."

Linda felt pleased with herself. "Thank you."

Glancing at the clock, Jennifer was aware of her next appointment. Coffee. She had been invited to join Leo's wife, Rhonda, and a circle of friends from the community, at Human Beans.

Linda sighed. "Well, thank you for your time, Dr. Adams. I really appreciate it."

You've done all the work, Linda. I'm just an asker of questions."

"Thank you anyway." Linda walked toward the coatrack where she had hung her large, down-filled jacket. "Can I see you next week at the same time?"

"I'll pencil you in."

The two exited the office. Hossein looked up from his desk where he was biting on the cap of a pen. Smiling politely, he nodded and stood. "Have a good day, Mrs. Harmsen."

"You too," Linda replied.

Peering outside the window into the icy street, tire-rutted, frozen into the dirty road like ancient, fossilized dinosaur tracks, Jennifer wondered if she would be able to make it through an entire Midwestern winter. She had already driven to Clancy to purchase warmer clothes, better gloves and a woollen stocking cap. Unprepared for the harshness of the interminable winter, Jennifer could appreciate those who knew how to do it.

Leo's body filled the front window. She watched him look up and wave at someone across the street, and then take another few steps. He was limping.

Pushing open the front door, Hossein and Jennifer braced themselves for the wind and winced as Butcher slammed the door behind him. Stamping his feet and clapping his hands, Leo greeted them. "Good morning," he said happily. "How are we doing today?"

"Just fine, thank you," Hossein responded.

Butcher turned his attention to Jennifer. "And you, Doctor?"

"Very funny."

"Did you bring your lunch today?"

"No," she raised an eyebrow. "I'm being treated to lunch by your wife and some of her friends."

"Really?"

"They're taking me to Human Beans."

Butcher took off his coat and moved into his office. She could smell his cologne. Her face only reached his chest. She was once again aware of his largeness, his significance.

"What time will you be back?"

Jennifer shrugged. "I don't think I will be back this afternoon. Enjoy your meetings." She reached up for her own coat, like the passing of a baton, and moved towards the front door. Enjoying the fact that she knew Butcher was watching her, she smiled slightly and saw that Hossein's eyes were also following her. He, on the other hand, was not smiling at all. After nodding at him, Jennifer moved out the front door and into the frigid midday air.

Human Beans was brightly lit with colorful Christmas decorations and an artificial tree which took up most of the front window. The warmth of the café, along with the mouth-watering smell of coffee and lunch, made her sigh contentedly. Jennifer smiled at the buzz, conversations above the Christmas music playing lightly in the background. As she entered, she unbuttoned her coat, removed her stocking cap and gloves, and looked around. The women who had invited her were seated near the Christmas tree. She knew Rhonda, of course, and the other one was the preacher's wife, Desley, or something like that. One waved at her cheerily. Jennifer smiled and waved back. As she moved between the tables, a few other coffee drinkers watched with curiosity at the stranger in their midst.

"Hi!" Carley exclaimed, her face beaming.

"Hello," Jennifer responded, casually. "Is this space for me?"

"Yes! Of course! We're so glad you're here! I'm Carley. I run the studio across the street." She motioned out the window. "This is Shania Peterson, she's married to Nash Peterson who works at the Butchery." Shania nodded.

"So, you work in the Butchery?" Since moving to Amicable in the last couple of weeks, Jennifer noticed that she was beginning to start a majority of her sentences with the word 'so.'

"No," Shania said, "Nash works there. I work at the Greedy Pecker. I'm one of the bartenders there."

"She practically runs the whole thing," Carley blurted out nervously.

Shania smirked but didn't respond.

"And this is Tracey Thomas, soon to be Tracey Peterson." Carley's grin broadened and she clapped her hands daintily. "These two are going to be sisters-in-law."

"It would be a fascinating thing to talk to the wives of identical twins and compare stories."

"Oh, don't you worry," Carley jabbered uncontrollably, "they already started sharing secrets."

"Nice to meet you," Tracey said.

"Tracey was just voted in as mayor of Amicable."

"Congratulations. A young woman mayor. How very progressive."

Tracey's eyes narrowed. "That's what most people on the outside say."

"Please, don't be offended."

"Most people don't mean offense, but they can't help it. I'm tired of being judged."

"Tell me about it," Jennifer laughed. "Most people want to pick me up and give me a good squeeze just because I'm small. I hate that."

"Sounds like you and Amicable are made for each other."

"So anyway," Carley interrupted, "this is Leslie Deakins, Reverend John Deakins' wife. I think you heard him yesterday at church."

Leslie, Jennifer thought. *I was so close.*

"Lastly, you already know your boss's wife, Rhonda. She also is on the town council."

"Nice to meet you again," Rhonda remained seated. Rhonda was almost the same height as Jennifer, even sitting.

"Now, what can we get you to eat and drink?"

"I'll take a chai latte, almond milk and whatever you suggest to eat. But if they have any reubens, I would like that."

Carley giggled. "Whatever a chailatay is, we'll find out."

"Thank you."

When Carley left to order Jennifer's food and drink, Rhonda broke the awkward silence. "It seems strange that someone with such... how shall we say... big cityness, should end up in Amicable. I guess we're all kind of wondering what your intentions are... or why you're here..." The veiled threat surprised the others.

Jennifer was not intimidated. "It's all good, I can assure you."

Rhonda gritted her teeth and faked a smile, but her cheek muscles twitched under the strain.

"Look," Jennifer tried to mollify her counterpart, "I really did see Amicable's story in the newspaper in Boston. It intrigued me. When I saw Leo in the background, I wondered if I couldn't put my skills to use and see an old friend at the same time."

"How do you know him? Where did you meet? How long are you planning to stay?"

The other women glanced nervously at Rhonda.

Jennifer paused before speaking. She chose her words carefully. "I'm sorry if my presence is threatening to you. I'm simply here to assist the town in its recovery. I can leave tomorrow if that would make you more comfortable." Jennifer had no intention of leaving Amicable yet, but she knew that her deprecatory manner would work with these women.

"No, no," Tracey said, placing a hand on Rhonda's arm. "That won't be necessary. It's just been a trying time for Rhonda since Butcher's accident and... other things."

Leslie nodded and agreed with the mayor. "Tracey's right." She looked at Rhonda. "Right?"

Rhonda took a deep breath and noticed that her friends seemed to be holding their breaths. "Yes, yes, I'm sorry. Please forgive me."

Jennifer cleared her throat. "Do you think Rhonda and I could have some privacy for a few moments? I have something sensitive that I'd like to discuss with her."

The other three women appeared shocked, but being the nice women that they were, none resisted. Pushing back their chairs, the women moved just out of ear's reach toward the café bar, where they perched themselves on dark stained oak stools.

Rhonda surveyed the diminutive woman who sat across from her. Her large, expressive eyes seemed inquisitive; her pert hair curled slightly at the ends framing her face, elfin, a non-threat.

Jennifer spoke first, "Amicable seems like an amazing town."

That was not what Rhonda was expecting. "Yes."

"Everyone I have met seems to be very... nice."

"That's the word that most outsiders have for it."

"I'm an outsider?"

"Look, Jennifer, I'm not sure what you needed to talk to me about, and surely it isn't to ease your mind about fitting in here. It seems that you've done pretty well on your own already."

Jennifer touched her cheek. "You don't like me."

Rhonda's eyes held Jennifer's and she leaned towards her. "Put yourself in my place. After a couple of hellish years and a slightly underwhelming last few months, my husband, a butcher, has lost a finger, my mother, who has had serious mental health issues is getting married in a couple of weeks and now my husband's friend – I can only imagine what that means and the kind of history that you two have actually shared – shows up in *my* hometown and takes up residence in *his* office. You tell me, is this a recipe for happiness?"

Spreading her hands, Jennifer smiled. "When you put it that way, sounds like a recipe for disaster."

"You'll have to pardon me if I don't throw out the welcome mat."

Jennifer laughed. "Fair enough, but I don't think Amicable has a monopoly on lack of trust. It seems pretty much like a universal human trait."

"What did you really want to talk to me about?"

The smile faded from Jennifer's face. "The guidance counselor at school called me on Friday and asked if I would get your permission to meet with J.T."

"What's wrong? What happened? Is he being bullied again?"

Jennifer shook her head. "No, not bullying. She said that she had talked to you before about J.T.'s unwillingness to join with the rest of the class in many activities.

"Yes," Rhonda said, defensively, "he is probably a little shy and introverted."

Jennifer's eyes exuded empathy. "Has J.T. suffered any traumas that may have caused him to pull back? Physical, emotional?"

"Aside from the trauma that everyone else has endured, the elevator explosion and all the strain from that, I would say probably not."

"Deaths? Struggles?"

Rhonda's jaw tightened. "Do you mean domestic issues at home?"

"No, that's not what I meant. Struggles with other relationships – grandparents, siblings, other friends."

"Our next door neighbor died. That was traumatic." Rhonda's heart was still racing. "But what are you suggesting?"

The way that the teacher describes J.T. is that he might be on the spectrum."

"On the spectrum? What, you mean the autism spectrum?" Rhonda's back was up. "Just because J.T. is a little standoffish and has difficulties making friends doesn't mean he's one of those kind of kids. He doesn't rock back and forth and do mathematics in his head; he's a kind little boy who is figuring out life."

The café patrons turned a few degrees to follow the confidential conversation.

Jennifer quietly spoke again. "Everyone is on the spectrum somewhere. It's just that when people think of autism, they generally think Rainman. Autism, though, is certainly not a disease and it is not a mental issue."

"Then what are you saying?"

"Autism Spectrum Disorder is a brain disordering which inhibits a person's abilities to filter sights, sounds, thoughts into order. This usually causes that person to have difficulties creating and sustaining relationships. Generally, people who have a more severe case of ASD have problems with communication and tend to create routines to help them deal with the dis-order of their lives."

Momentarily, Rhonda flashed through J.T.'s personality. Sure, there were times when he seemed withdrawn and certainly, he was intelligent. The more she thought about it, the more she could possibly see that point of view. But J.T. was far too normal to be labelled on the stupid spectrum. "My son does *not* have autism."

"Of course, of course, but the counselor asked me to see if you would at least let me talk to him."

Locked eyes, a showdown. Whoever would blink first would lose.

"I'll have to talk to Butcher about it. I'm sure he'll be thrilled to know that his son is being stereotyped by a significant segment of Amicable."

Jennifer shook her head. "That's not the way it is, Rhonda."

"It is now."

Chapter 15.

Leo's office was changing.

As Jennifer's inexorable will pushed farther and farther into Butcher's consciousness (and unconsciousness), he wasn't even aware that she had begun to make adjustments to the décor in the Chop Shop. Although Jennifer hated the name, she had not yet begun to suggest alternatives. 'Chop Shop' sounded decidedly irreverent, and even though she realised that the name had more to do with his other profession, she'd heard enough negativity about 'shrinks' to believe that this name might actually be doing more damage.

Some of the taxidermy, specifically the pheasant, had been allocated to the front office with Hossein. Helping Leo to understand that patients staring at dead animals, with their cold and expressionless eyes, might symbolically and subconsciously push patients to think that they, too, were stuffed and emotionless, was important. Thus, Jennifer had driven to Omaha one afternoon to purchase some decorations which might allow for a more vibrant expression of life in their office. Much to Hossein's chagrin, Jennifer had already begun to think and talk about the office that way. *Their* office. *Their* clients. *Their* business. He still was wary of her.

Initially, Butcher was resistant to what he considered the 'feminization of his office,' but the joy that it brought her overwhelmed his resistance and he gave in. Now that there was a softer cushioned sofa, a wooden table with four matching chairs, books on the shelf that he might actually read, Leo noticed that lamentably Jennifer was right.

Jennifer and Leo began to act like an old married couple.

Glancing at her watch, Jennifer sighed. December 21st was the shortest day of the year, and today, the heavily falling snow depressed her even more. Her patient sat quietly across from. He studied her, and for a brief moment she felt like shivering, as if he was looking inside of her rather than at her.

Unable to hold his gaze, Jennifer peered out the office window.

"What are you thinking about, J.T.?"

J.T. stared at the woman. Conflicting emotions, unrecognizable – feelings he couldn't quite put names to but knew that they were… different. His mother and father wanted him to 'see' this woman. She wanted him to call her 'Jennifer,' even though his mother told him to call her 'Doctor Adams.' When he had been told he had to 'see' the school counselor, he had been confused. Why did he have to go talk to someone else? Especially that weirdo?

Now that J.T. was 'seeing' Dr. Adams, a woman with tiny hands and subtle movements, the antithesis of the school guidance counselor, he felt less confused and more intrigued. Who was this woman? His father appeared genuinely excited for him to interact with Dr. Adams. His mother was not.

"J.T.?" Dr. Adams brought him back from his reverie.

The young boy sniffed, wiped his nose with the back of his hand and readjusted himself in his father's large armchair. His legs were not yet long enough to reach the ground and he did not swing them like many children did. "I'm wondering why my dad's office and pictures have been changed."

Jennifer glanced behind her. "Which one has been changed?"

"Four have been changed."

Obviously, he had an acute sense of organization. "Okay, which ones have been changed."

"Me and Mom and Georgie on the swings. Dad's fishing photo with Derek and Nash; a picture of Georgie and me, and Dad sitting on the front porch with Unca George."

161

"Who is George? Is he your grandfather?"

"I called him 'Unca George, not Grandpa." J.T. crossed his arms. "I don't have any grandpas."

"I'm sorry," she made a quick note in her book. "Tell me about him."

"He was our neighbor and my best friend. Sometimes he would take care of me and Georgie when Mom and Dad needed to have some time to theirselves." Jennifer imagined what the small boy was talking about and it made her frown. "He died."

"Is your sister named after him?"

J.T. shrugged. "I don't know. I don't know what that means."

"You have a pretty good memory," she said, changing the subject. Jennifer reached to the lampstand table beside her and noticed the winter storm brewing outside. The snow was really coming down. From the drawer of the table, she pulled out a children's picture book. Immediately, she could see that J.T. was interested. He had leaned forward slightly and was looking over her hands to the front cover.

"Do you like books?"

He nodded.

"Well, this book is a special kind of book. It's not just one you read, but it's kind of a game. A memory game."

J.T. shifted in his seat. He liked both games and books, but he didn't really like books without words. That was for babies. He leaned farther forward in his chair. His little hands rested on the nobs of the armrests.

Jennifer opened the book to the first page and read the directions to him. "There are lots of pictures in this book. Some of them are just one big picture with lots of stuff in it and others have a series of pictures. I want you to take as long as you need to try to remember everything on the page and then I'll ask you some questions." She paused to see if he understood, which he did. "If, at any point you start to feel anxious, just let me know and we'll stop."

J.T.'s head tilted his head to the side. "What's wrong with feeling anxious? Why would we have to stop?"

"I just don't want you to feel uncomfortable."

"What's wrong with feeling uncomfortable?" J.T.'s eyes followed hers.

"I... well... never mind." She opened the book. "If you can't answer a question, just answer, 'I don't know.'"

The young boy sniffed. "Duh. If you don't know the answer, why would you make something up?"

Jennifer laughed. "That's what adults do."

"Why?"

She shrugged and looked down at the book. "I don't know, really. Maybe adults are more afraid of looking stupid than kids are."

J.T. stared at the doctor. She seemed to be hiding things from him which made him nervous, but now it seemed like she was relaxing.

Jennifer pulled a chair closer to J.T. "Shall we start?" He nodded. "On the first page is one large picture."

"And I memorize it and then you ask questions."

"Right."

J.T. received the open book with open hands. It was a picture of a rustic farm scene. An old red barn with peeling paint was the focal point and it listed slightly to the left. The hay mow door was open and a handful of grey and white pigeons were contentedly perched in the opening. A russet-colored horse stuck its head out of the lower wooden window. There were ducks and chickens, pigs and cows; a squirrel sat on a fencepost caught in mid-chew. Behind the barn, the sun shone through a shadowed weathervane. The rooster indicated the direction of the wind to be from the east.

After perusing the picture for thirty seconds, J.T. looked up.

"Are you ready?"

"Yes."

Jennifer leaned forward slightly. "Are you sure you've had enough time. The questions will be…"

"Yes."

"You can have more time if you need it."

"No."

"Can you tell me three kinds of animals in the picture?"

"Yes."

She waited, and then realized that she had only asked a yes/no question. Mentally, she made a note that J.T. was exhibiting some stereotypical autistic tendencies. "What would they be?"

"That's easy," he said, as he closed his eyes. "There are pigeons, ducks and pigs."

"Any other kinds?"

He shrugged. "Yes. You only asked for three."

"What are the others?"

J.T.'s eyes remained closed as if he had painted the picture on the back of his eyelids. Jennifer held the book open in front of her as he reeled off the names. He named the animals from left to right on the page.

"Squirrel, chicken, horse, spider, cows and a cat."

Jennifer lifted the book to her face and then back towards the little boy who had his eyes closed. "I don't see a spider or a cat."

Slits appeared in his eyes. "The spider is in the upper left corner of the open barn door." She rubbed at what looked like a white spot, but then realized that it was indeed a spider in a small web. "Huh. I missed that one. What about the cat? I don't think there is a cat in the picture."

Chapter 15.

J.T. opened his eyes and looked out the window at the gathering snow and the small flakes which flicked against the window. "On the other side of the pigeons, if you look really close, there is a cat face in the shadows." He smirked. "The cat looks like he's about to have pigeon for breakfast."

The shadowy image of a Cheshire-like cat seemed to emerge. She had never before seen the dim, grinning face with malevolently squinting eyes, crouched near the ground, crawling across the dusty floor towards its avian meal.

Jennifer looked up sharply at J.T. "You saw all this in thirty seconds?"

"Yes." If, at that moment, Jennifer would have asked him how many boards were visible in the barn's face, he would have quickly counted them in his head. His teacher had been very impressed with his ability to count to a hundred. J.T. was positive that he could count higher than that, but the opportunity to do so in first grade had not yet arisen.

Paging further into the book, Jennifer found a set of block photos, all different pieces of a puzzle. Most adults could see the order to complete the picture by rearranging them, but children, especially those as young as J.T., found this difficult. "Can you organize these puzzle pieces and put them by number into an order that creates a larger puzzle? Do you understand?"

Before she had finished the questions, J.T. was already doing the task. Within ten seconds, the numbers had appeared in his head.

Jennifer handed him a piece of paper. "Can you write them down, please?"

Amazed, Jennifer watched him write in the careful scrawl of a six-year-old boy. After he finished, Jennifer felt a sneaking suspicion that J.T. was definitely not an ordinary child. She had come across only one other child savant, a boy with Asperger's, who had an acute ability for mathematics. That boy, unlike J.T., was unable to interact in social settings, but J.T. seemed to be able to see things – rearrange, memorize and order – the same gift as his father?

Turning to the second to last page, Jennifer chose the hardest memorization puzzle. She'd never met an adult who could see all seven differences, much less a child. It would be a telling challenge.

"Okay, J.T., this one should be a little tougher for you." She held her finger in the page of the book to mark it. "On this page," she moved her hand over the picture, "is a jumbled mess of people from a long time ago." In the picture, there were peasants and nobility, drab clothes and colorful outfits; there was a clown and a firebreather, drunks and horses; a pod of prostitutes were lecherously laughing at a few boys who had crept closer to get a look at their wares. In the center of the picture was a makeshift throne being carried by four, bare-chested servants. They wore brightly striped pants and had golden hoops through their noses. On the throne was an obese monarch gazing forlornly out over the stinking mass of humanity. He was gesticulating with his hand, bored with his surroundings and wanting to go home.

"Now," she continued, as she turned the page, "this is the exact same painting but with a few small differences. Your job is to see if you can locate them in five minutes. Do you want to give it a try?"

"Yes." J.T. looked at the second page. This one was more difficult for him, but only in the same way that a bird might find flying up rather than down.

"I'm starting the timer now. If you need to write anything down…" she paused. J.T. may not know how to write many words yet. "Never mind. I'll just ask you questions."

"Go."

For thirty seconds, J.T. examined and re-examined both pages. Now that he had them memorized, he had already picked up on all the differences, but he just liked looking at the pictures. The details of the pictures captivated him. Within the time, he found the seven differences and put them in his memories. They were: different colored juggling balls, the gate on the castle had one extra spiky thing… all the differences seemed to jump out to him, even the last two, which were very subtle. Just as he entered the last minute of memorization, the lights in the office flickered. Dismayed, Jennifer hoped that they wouldn't lose power, but flickering lights usually meant that a powerline was dangerously close to snapping, and when that happened…

The lights in the room blinked off and the office was bathed in darkness.

"Oh dear," Jennifer mumbled. "I'm so sorry, J.T. Are you scared of the dark?"

J.T. was silent. Jennifer worried that he had been paralyzed by fright, but a second later, she heard a page turning.

"J.T." Jennifer stood, and bumped her way to the desk to find her phone, "is everything okay?"

Page turn. "Yes."

Page turn. "What are you doing?"

Page turn. "You said I had five minutes to figure out the differences."

The sound of the turning pages was magnified by the darkness. Back and forth. Back and forth. Jennifer searched for his face and found the outline. "The lights are out. It's too dark to see."

His next words brought a chill up her spine to the base of her skull. "I can see everything," he said, quietly.

"But it's dark," she responded, trying to locate her phone.

Silence.

Turn.

"What is 'dark?'" he asked.

Jennifer paused. "I don't understand the question."

167

"You asked if I was afraid of the dark. My mom sometimes asks me that, but I never know what she's talking about."

"You mean the room is not black for you? The lights are off. I can barely see anything."

"That's weird," J.T. said, as he looked up from his book. It seemed as if his eyes were glowing.

"Are you telling me, J.T., that you can see everything right now?"

He nodded. Turn. Flip. Snick. He giggled at the picture of a dog sniffing the butt of another.

"What are you laughing at?"

He pointed to the photo.

"J.T.?" she whispered.

"Yes?"

"Can you see the picture in front of you right now?"

"Yes."

"What is it?"

He giggled again. "Two dogs. They are…" he smiled up at her, "introducing themselves, or that's what dad says."

"What is the name written on the collar of the black dog?"

J.T.'s eyes focussed on the picture and then he frowned. "There are no black dogs, only two tan ones."

A cold chill gripped her. Was it actually possible that he could see in the dark? "And the name of the dog in front?"

"It says," J.T. sounded out the name slowly. "C…a…r…l… o…s Carlos!" he shouted proudly.

Jennifer swallowed hard. "How many fingers am I holding up."

He shook his head. "Duh. Three."

Jennifer slowly put her hand down. "Oh my God, J.T. You've got a gift."

"Don't you want me to tell you the differences in the pictures?"

She had completely forgotten about the test. "Yes, of course." While he watched, she went to the windows and closed the curtains. The room was utterly dark (for her) now.

He cleared his throat and set the book aside. "Different colored balls, the gate has an extra sharp thing, the clown is missing a shoe, there are fifteen trees in the first and fourteen on the next page." He rattled them all off. "The last one was harder for me." She swallowed again. "One of the people in the crowd has a word written on the bottom of his shoe. I don't know that word."

"Spell it."

"M…u…e…r…t…e." He attempted to sound it out, but it came out like he was chewing on cheese.

"Muerte," she responded softly. "It's a Spanish word."

"I don't know what that means. I only know a few words in Spanish. I know how to count, and some of the colors. What does that word mean?"

It means death, she said inside her head, but she did not speak it out loud. "I don't know either," she lied.

J.T. squinted, and his eyes narrowed on hers. "You're lying," he said softly.

"How do you know?" she asked fearfully.

"I can see everything, even that beat in your throat. It just got faster."

It can get a lot faster than that, she thought.

Chapter 16.

Randall Simpkins was a very white man. Randall was not an albino, and the moniker offended him quite deeply, which he explained to his bullies every time, but his skin was very light.

Wanting to be different, Randall insisted that people call him Ran-dall (pronounced Ran-DAHL). For the most part, the accent change worked. People in the art world appreciated oddness. But those from his hometown in Liberal, Kansas (the most oxymoronically named town in the United States), they still accented the first syllable. This was part of the reason he never went home.

After graduating from high school, Ran-DAHL Simpkins moved to Wichita State University where he studied art. His parents were less than impressed by his choice of major, but Randall was willing to prove them wrong. *Never mind,* his father said, *a few good cuffs around the ego will change his mind.*

At Wichita State, Randall had the good fortune of rooming with Ken Bailey. Although Ken was much more socially adept than the carrot-colored Simpkins, they had many things in common, not the least of which was that they were both art majors. For four years, the two were inseparable. As the years progressed, they had less and less classes together. Ken majored in the Master's, his favorite, Degas. Randall chose Modern Art. Randall's father thought he'd have more chance making money planting a citrus orchard in Kansas than making a career out of 'finger painters' as he called them.

After graduation, the two parted ways. Randall had awkwardly hugged Ken goodbye, then they drifted into memory. Ken took up a teaching position at Mid-America University while Randall was hired as an assistant curator at a small art gallery in

Omaha. Even though the drive was less than two hours, they never bridged the distance.

Randall often wandered through the gallery (or 'museum' as his father annoyingly called it) pausing to ponder the stark lines and oblique patterns which defined Modern Art. The first time his parents entered the gallery, his father pushed back his baseball cap, took a deep breath and exclaimed, 'Did you get all these paintings from a kindergarten?" His mother was much more accommodating, but she, too, had no idea the breadth and depth of Modern Art. Fifteen minutes after entering the gallery, they were waiting patiently in the foyer chatting amiably with Diane, the receptionist, about the weather.

At Mid-America University, Ken was the entire art department, and even though he often felt overworked, he enjoyed his role immensely. Every year seemed to pose new and wonderful weirdness in understanding the newest generations, the tiresome battles between self-discipline and self-absorption. Some of the students had gone on to modest careers in art, but none of them approached the feats of his greatest student. Ken marvelled at (and honestly envied) the skill and artistry of Demetrius Chandler. The gigantic young man was so shockingly good that often Ken wondered if Demetrius should be teaching the class.

At the end of the semester, Demetrius had produced what Ken had believed to be 'the most beautiful and significant piece of art' he had ever seen. Titled *Sebastian's Death,* a tongue-in-cheek reference to the small crustacean from a Disney movie, Chandler created a masterpiece of sculpture.

At Mid-America University.

When Demetrius had shown him *Sebastian's Death,* the battle between good and evil, life and death, medicine and disease and the surrounding light of the supportive community, Ken openly wept. Demetrius was frightened that he had offended his professor. It was just the opposite. Both of Ken's parents had succumbed to the disease in the last five years, and he had yet to recover from their deaths. Every time Ken saw it, the piece of art took his breath away.

"What will you do with the piece?" Ken asked Demetrius one afternoon early in December.

Demetrius shrugged. "I don't know. I hadn't really thought about it. I guess it's an assignment at this point."

Bailey waggled his finger in Demetrius' face. "Don't ever say that again. This is not an assignment. This is a Mona Lisa."

"Aw, come on, KB, I'm just a kid."

Ken moved in closer to the young man who towered over him. "Michelangelo, Mozart, Chopin – all younger than you. This," he motioned towards *Sebastian's Death*, "could put you with them."

Demetrius' heart pounded. "But I was going to give it to…"

"Promise me one thing, Chandler, before you give it away, let me call a friend of mine, a curator of a small gallery, and get his opinion. Then, you can do with it as you wish."

So it was that Ran-Dahl Simpkins drove to Montage, Iowa, the home of the Fightin' Ferns of Mid-America University, to lay his eyes on what his former roommate called 'the best artwork he'd ever seen.' As he drove, Randall hunched over the wheel and imagined what this candelabra, or whatever it was, would look like. Not much for sculpture, Randall was sceptical, but he was surprised how much he wanted to see Ken again. He hadn't thought about him in years.

Randall attempted to smile into the rearview mirror. His teeth were very much like his skin. He had them professionally cleaned and each one of them sparkled like a freshly minted TicTac. His red hair, thin and wavy, receding back from his temples giving him a vampirish look, still had the indented marks from his boater hat, Randall's trademark in the industry.

His blue eyes, magnified by the skin, radiated an intensity that matched his passion for Modern Art. More than once, Randall greeted a patron in the gallery but had subsequently frightened them away because of his spectre-like appearance.

As Randall's Saab sedan approached the Mid-America Campus Administration Building, Randall peered through his fogged windows in an attempt to find a place to park. Because most of the students had finished their exams and had migrated to their parents' homes for Christmas, there were plenty of spaces just outside the building.

Killing the engine, Randall opened the car's door and shivered as he put his foot outside the cozy, warm cocoon. The snow crunched under his shoe as he pulled his small body out of the driver's seat and then reached into the back for his black coat. Wrapping himself in it, he grabbed his boater's hat and walked quickly, hurrying over the snow-covered sidewalks to the administration building.

Before he got to the door, Ken Bailey walked out of the building in nothing but a pair of shorts, a flannel long-sleeved shirt with woollen socks and Birkenstock sandals. Randall's momentum was arrested as he took in his former roommate who looked much like the young man he'd roomed with all those years ago. Ken had put on a lot of weight and his eyes were ringed with thick glasses. His thinning brown hair shrouded his head like a dirty halo. In spite of the cold, actually, in denial of the cold, Ken approached Randall and gripped his shoulders.

"Hello, Randy."

Randall grimaced. "Ken."

Ken stepped back a pace. "You look well – you haven't changed. I tried to find you on social media, but you're like a ghost."

Randall sniffed. "I find social media to be unfulfilling."

Ken laughed, turned and slapped him on the back, pushing the smaller man towards the admin building. "Kind of like Modern Art in general."

"Well, I don't…" Randall's back was up.

"I'm just kidding, Ran-DAHL," Ken responded good-naturedly as he opened the door. "It's good to see you."

Randall nodded and walked through the door. As he entered, he took off his hat and then his coat and looked around for a place to hang them.

"Just hold on to them for a little while. I've got a cupboard in my office."

Randall was sure that Ken's 'cupboard' looked more like a chair than anything else. Judging by Ken's appearance, he hadn't really moved on from the droll, shabbiness of the '90's. Who wore sandals and socks in winter? Shorts? Randall was certain that he hadn't seen anyone wearing a long-sleeved flannel shirt since college.

As the odd duo walked the halls and covered areas of Mid-America, they chatted amicably about the last thirty years of separated history. Randall spoke reverently of his work; Ken described the students who had moved through his sphere of influence at MAU.

When they reached the art building, Randall paused. "So you have a modern day Michelangelo, is that right?"

Ken smirked. "Michelangelo couldn't tie his sandals."

"Oh please," Randall's mouth pinched in derision, "there are no prodigies anymore."

Shrugging, Ken smiled and moved through the long corridor. Panels of glass lining the hallway oozed cold air from outdoors. Outside, the winter had created a world of modern art: snow had been pushed into heaps as the sidewalks had been cleared. Dirt and salt, twig and branch lay in contrast with the blue sky above. A few unfortunate souls who were still working four days before Christmas moved briskly from car to building clapping their hands to build warmth inside their mittens.

Ken opened the door at the end of the hallway. "Now, I want you to set aside any preconceptions you might have about sculpture. All the classes you took at Wichita State, delete for just a moment and approach this opportunity as one who enters your gallery for the first time."

"I can't do that," Randall said sharply.

"Just try, Randall. Just try." Ken moved through another hallway lined with the students' artwork. Some of them had the temerity to sign their own art. This drove Randall crazy. He hated it when artists destroyed their own artwork by etching their ego into it. If anything, they should lightly inscribe their initials, or first name, perhaps, on the back or underside.

"If this art is any indication of what I'm about to experience, I think I should have stayed in Omaha."

Ken opened another door that had his nameplate positioned centrally at eye level. Randall waited, taking in the mess that was Ken's office. "Is there anything in your office that is going to eat either me or my belongings?"

"That's the ticket, Randy! Now, let's get to the studio. I want to introduce you to Chandler."

"Are you telling me that the young man who has created this priceless candelabra has the last name of Chandler? One who actually makes candles?"

"Ironic, isn't it?" Ken tugged on Randall's arm. "Now, I just want you to know that the artist does not look like a stereotypical artist."

"What's that supposed to mean?" Randall's grimaced, as he perused an example of Modern Art by one of the students. *Hideous.*

Ken wrung his hands "You know how when we were younger and someone said 'artist' and immediately you thought of some strange hippie, Andy Warhol, or Jackson Pollock, and you wondered, 'why do they have to be so weird,' but then you recognized that abstract is only weird, and then..."

"Ken, you're rambling. What do I need to know about this Chandler?"

Smiling, Ken pushed open the studio door.

Demetrius Chandler stood nervously in the back of the art room. Although selling artwork had been a dream of his, he had never had a curator come to visit him. Ola said he should feel like an athlete working out for a team. At his side, Kelly was cradling her right arm in her left and chewing nervously on her fingernails. Demetrius nudged her. "You know, this doesn't really mean anything. From what Mr. Bailey said, the guy is more into Modern Abstract."

"I know," Kelly didn't look at him, "but that doesn't mean it doesn't 'mean' anything. What if he does like it? I mean, how could you not?" She briefly paused her nail munching to gesture towards the candle mounting. Professor Bailey had positioned the sculpture in the middle of a tablecloth covered desk. He had lit the sculpture from above giving it a shadowy, yet glowing, appearance.

Demetrius shrugged. She was right. Any person with any sense of beauty could see that Chandler's creation was perfect.

The door opened and they jumped. Demetrius saw Mr. Bailey and his guest behind him. The man was one of the strangest looking white people Demetrius had ever seen. Not quite five and a half feet tall, he was dressed immaculately from head to toe in white. Shoes, suit, tie. The only thing that stood out was his flowing red hair. For a moment, Demetrius thought that Mr. Bailey was playing a practical joke on him. This guy looked like Colonel Sanders.

Meanwhile, Randall Simpkins thought the same thing about the student. This had to be a practical joke. The young man who stood before him looked like a professional football player. Positioned next to him was a stunning young woman whose eyes were wide – frightened, as if they had been waiting for the bogeyman to walk through the door.

Instead, it was Caspar the Not-So-Friendly Ghost.

The man whispered something to Professor Bailey who smiled and held out a hand allowing Colonel Sanders to enter.

"Randall Simpkins, I'd like you to meet Demetrius Chandler. His colleague is Kelly McMurtry."

Demetrius moved forward. "Nice to meet you,"

"Likewise," Randall responded, somewhat overwhelmed by the young man's mass. "So, you're the artist Ken has been touting as the next Michelangelo."

"Professor Bailey is very good at hyperbole."

Randall raised his eyebrows. "Yes, well, he was…" At that moment Simpkins' eyes fell on the lit sculpture and his breath was taken away. Unable to speak, Randall was drawn by an irresistible gravity towards the candelabra. The dull glimmer of the pewter against the white light caused his eyes to quiver. The setting and the subject matter demanded silence. After a few awkward moments, his hands itched to touch it. He looked up towards Demetrius again, the unasked question posed by his eyes instead of voice. Demetrius nodded. With trembling hands, Randall lifted the candelabra and brought it nearer his eyes. Its heft was a thing of purpose; its meaning, weighty, heavier than life itself. The faceless forms all seemed to be focused on the figure at the center, a woman of indeterminate age, hunched over in a voiceless prayer, cry and scream.

Licking his lips, Randall turned the figure around to see that the supporting cast were joined together. No creases, no etching or molding. They were made from the same material to stand beside the suffering woman and to protect her while the crustacean at her feet was slain.

For five minutes, the curator turned Demetrius' work of art over and over. While he studied the pewter, his mind turned in the same way, faster and faster. This was the Pearl of Great Price. Randall knew that he did not have an unlimited budget, but with this piece, his gallery would attain notoriety, even in a relatively non-notable place like Omaha, Nebraska.

Randall licked his lips and asked the inevitable question about price. "What are you hoping to get for it?"

Demetrius put his hands in his pockets and looked down at Kelly who smiled back at him. "I was hoping for at least an A minus."

Randall frowned. "What?"

Ken moved forward slightly and put a hand on his former roommate's shoulder. "This is his semester project. It's for his art class."

Eyes quickly moving back and forth between Ken and Demetrius, the information finally sank in. "You're joking, right?"

"Nope," Demetrius said. "I really would like an A, if possible."

"That's the most ridiculous thing I've ever heard. One doesn't give a grade to something like this! One puts it on a pedestal and shows it to the world." He paused and lowered his voice. "How much money would it take for me to purchase this from you?"

At that moment, the art room door opened again, and to Randall's immense amazement, another monstrous black man walked into the room. Stopping quickly, as if finding who he was looking for, the young man moved to stand by Demetrius and Kelly. "Yo, Meat, I've been looking for you."

Demetrius shook his head slightly.

Randall's attention diverted, he wondered if Mid-America University was a college for giant African American people.

"What's going on?" Ola asked, as he entered the room.

"Ola, this is Mr. Simpkins from an art gallery in Omaha. He was looking at my semester assignment..."

"Stop calling it that," Randall sniped.

Ola moved closer and looked over Randall's head. "It's pretty good, isn't it? Meat's like a modern-day Bernini." Ola pronounced the sculptor's name 'Berninny,' which just about threw Randall into an apoplectic fit.

"It's *Ber-nee-nee*," he responded tightly, as if speaking to a four-year-old. "Bernini. Now, if you'll excuse us, sir, the young man and I are negotiating a price for this work of art, and unless you are his agent, I'd appreciate some space, thank you." He looked over his shoulder derisively, not directly up at Ola.

Ola saw the expression and he gritted his teeth. "Listen, man..."

Demetrius moved forward. "It's okay, Ola." He shifted his gaze to Randall who now had two enormous and mobile mountains made out of basalt standing like the twin pillars of Gibraltar on either side of him. "I'm sorry, Mr. Simpkins, but the art isn't for sale. It really is my semester piece, you know what I'm saying? And after that, I've already promised it to this lady." Demetrius pointed to the focal character in the candelabra. "Her name is Linda."

Randall attempted to look down his nose at the boys while staring up at them. "Preposterous. Everything is for sale."

"Not everything," Demetrius responded.

Mr. Bailey stepped in. "Let's just relax, everyone. I've asked Randall here to give his opinion on your art. I think you can at least read from his interest that he believes *Sebastian* deserves an A. Now, as for the value of the piece, why don't you just hear him out and then decide what to do?"

Demetrius nodded. "Agreed."

Randall, relieved, calculated in his head how much money it would take. He needed to have the artwork but his budget dollars were almost spent. With only $7,500 left, he knew that he'd have to be creative, but he was convinced that the owner of the gallery would approve some excess funds if he showed him what was at stake.

Clearing his throat, Randall put the candelabra back on the table. "If you had to sell it," he said with clarity, "what amount of money would move you to let me purchase it?" He stepped back from between to the two young men, adjusted his white tie and smoothed down the lapels of his white jacket.

"What are you thinking?" Demetrius had no idea what his art might be worth. A few of his paintings had sold for a few hundred dollars, but as for *his own* sculpture, he wasn't sure.

"It's a nice piece," Randall said simply. "I'm sure that one day the gallery could fetch three or four thousand dollars for it. I'll give you... two."

Demetrius' jaw dropped. He hadn't expected that much. For a moment, Randall's heart leapt with excitement. *The boy was going to go for it!* If he did jump at it, Randall would purchase it himself and bypass the gallery altogether. There was a chance, with the right connections, that he could sell it for twenty times that amount, maybe even twenty-five.

"I..." Demetrius was about to respond when Kelly interrupted.

"Excuse me, Demetrius, but you promised this to Linda. Don't you think you should talk to her first?"

"No," Randall's voice echoed with nervousness, "the boy and I are negotiating the price."

Ola sidled next to Kelly creating a wall of solidarity. "As his agent," he jerked a thumb towards Demetrius, "and as one who is comfortable discussing works of art by Rodin, Donatello and Brancusi," Ola paused to allow his previous faux-ignorance to set in, "I think we'll be asking for a *wee* bit more than what you were hoping to lowball Demetrius with."

Demetrius flashed him a look of surprise. *So he had been listening in Art History!* But how could Ola possibly know how much to ask for? Ken Bailey watched bemusedly, as Randall got taken to task for his arrogance.

"Here are the facts." Ola began to check them off on his fingers. "Firstly: Mr. Bailey called you to drive from Omaha four days before Christmas, so Mr. Bailey's assessment, even as generous as an A plus, is probably a giveaway that Demetrius' art is valuable. Secondly: Demetrius doesn't really need to sell the piece. In fact, he was going to give it away, which means that he has all the bargaining power in the world. If we don't sell it for the right price, this woman will treasure it." Demetrius began to laugh at Ola's change of pronoun, from 'he' to 'we.' "Thirdly, as if my client," now Demetrius and Kelly did snort out loud, "needed any more leverage, it would suffice to say, that in contacting the afflicted woman, perhaps we could negotiate a price that would take into account her suffering and, should we say, split the proceeds, half to Linda, forty percent to Demetrius, and I'll take my agent's cut of ten."

Randall ground his teeth. "This doesn't make sense. You're just college students for crying out loud."

"I think the bidding will begin at seventy-five." Ola looked at his friends who nodded.

Randall breathed a sigh of relief. That was the upper end of his budget and he was quite sure he could whittle them down to five. "I'll give you four," he said.

Ola's eyes narrowed. He had answered too quickly. "I meant seventy-five *thousand*, not hundred."

Randall's eyes widened. For one of the few times in his life, he had completely underestimated his opponent.

"Ola, that's a little…" Demetrius tried to butt in, but if Ola was reading the man correctly, he was closer to the mark than Randall was wont to like.

Ola held up his hand. "What do you say, Mr. Simpkins?"

"I think that you have overestimated your friend's talents," he responded. Unfortunately, the small quake in his voice gave him away.

"I think that you want this piece of artwork way more than you would like to let on."

"Well done, sir," Randall said simply, acquiescing to Ola's astute ability to read him. "I do think that this piece has incredible potential, and I do think that I could probably sell it for fifty thousand."

The numerical amount caused an intake of breath from the rest of the room, but Ola and Randall were locked in on each other.

"How about this," Randall continued after a moment, "I'll give you twenty-five, and if that's acceptable to his friend, we'll shake hands and you can have your ten percent broker's fee." He stuck out his hand in hopes that Ola would shake it.

"I'm not the one who's going to shake off on this thing, it's him." He pointed to Demetrius. "And we already know, I'm not taking a cent for it. His art is going to make him famous, and I just want to end up in his autobiography." Randall switched his focus and hand towards Demetrius.

Hesitantly, Demetrius looked at Ola who shook his head slightly.

"What? What is it now!" Randall threw up both hands exasperatedly. Already, he'd be shelling out a good deal of his own money on this acquisition. Fortunately, he had a nice nest egg stashed for sunny days.

"If you said you could sell it for fifty, my guess is that we could get eighty at an auction or open sale."

Guiltily, and frustratedly, Randall averted his eyes. *This boy was amazing!*

"Forty thousand and I think we can call it a deal."

Chapter 16.

Knowing that he had been defeated, and by a college student nonetheless, Randall extended his hand one more time to Demetrius who recognized the look of victory from his roommate. Demetrius smiled broadly in triumph and grasped the small man's hand in a vice-like grip. "It's a deal. I'll call Mrs. Harmsen on the way home to Amicable and let her know that she has forty thousand dollars to spend on her recovery."

Randall held on to his hand. "Forty thousand? I thought you were keeping half?"

Demetrius smiled. "That's what he said," motioning with his head towards Ola. "I never wanted any money for it. Remember, I was giving it away."

Randall finally smiled. His eyes rested once more on the sculpture, the face of the sufferer and the connectedness of the community. "I'll transfer the money once you send me her details."

"One more thing," Demetrius said when the clapping died down. "If possible, we'll let Linda name the piece of art, is that okay?"

Randall thought for a moment and then his own eyes gleamed. "I tell you what, I'll agree to it with one caveat."

"What's that?"

Looking up at Ola, he took one step towards him. "During your spring break," he pointed towards Ola's chest, "I want you to travel with me to be *my* agent. I'll have a budget of over a hundred thousand dollars, and I could use your talents."

Ola's eyes registered shock. "But, I was going to go to Florida!"

Randall's eyes reflected bemusedly. "How about we start there? You can hang out with your friends in the afternoons and evenings, and you can talk down galleries and artists for me during the day. We'd be a formidable team…"

Ola, looked down at his complete opposite – a diminutive white man, wearing an entirely white outfit, his head topped by carrot-colored hair, who seemed to have no sense of social settings – and then at Demetrius and Kelly, who were smiling at him.

"All right, Randy. I'll do it." He shook the small man's hand.

Randall's irritation expressed itself on his lips. "Don't call me Randy."

Ola lifted Randall's hand and smacked his own against it. "All right Ran-Dahl. You can call me Ronald – that's my real name."

The entire room exploded with laughter again. A white man wanting a black name, and a black man having a white name. It seemed like life was turning up roses.

Chapter 17.

Beyond the lights and the tinsel, Christmas trees and 'Merry Christmas!' well-wishes, well past the warbling crooners and their dulcet tones of being home for the holidays, Amicablean families began to itch with anticipation, not just of what would be opened under the Christmas tree, but what would be opened in the new year. The future was as murky as the celestial sky, and in the Jensen household, Rhonda couldn't conceive of why she felt so... so... nervous. The children, as well as her mother and Carl, were excitedly dancing around the house singing along with the carols and furtively eyeing the ever-growing mound of presents. But Rhonda felt as if something was missing. Subconsciously, she should have felt how Butcher's *oddness* was affecting her. Certainly, the former flame's arrival wasn't helping matters. Rhonda, too, was noticing things happening with her body. Thus, her own preoccupation with shaping it. This took a toll on the family, but she couldn't help it. She needed her own escape.

While Rhonda went out for her morning run, she noticed that Butcher was already outside shoveling the snow from the driveway. Both J.T. and Georgie were 'helping' him. J.T. attempted to scoop small amounts of snow onto the same pile that his father was creating, while Georgie's version of assisting was leaping onto the top of the heap causing the snow to cascade back onto the driveway. While Butcher thought this amusing, J.T. was less than impressed and he told her so.

"I'm going for a jog," Rhonda shouted to the rest of her family. Butcher paused to glance up.

"Okay, I'll see you whenever."

This was Butcher's subtle way of expressing displeasure. Rhonda knew that it irked him when she went running every morning, but this was *her* time and *her* need. He should *know* how much this helped her soul. For Cripes' sake, he could read everyone else. To Rhonda, he seemed to be getting a little more selfish – always wanting extra sympathy about his finger.

Rhonda shoved the headphones into her ears and started her playlist.

A few Amicableans were expending varying degrees of energy in freeing their sidewalks of snow. Most of them, when they spotted Rhonda jogging past, were quite happy to lean on the handles of their shovels, or stop their snowblowers, and wave at her. Politely, she lifted a hand and kept running.

Jogging towards the west side of town, she turned left on Sixth Street and made her way past the nursing home and into the winter wonderland of Winslow Park. In the center of the park was a small, frozen pond, which was covered with snow. Some high school students had already been by, presumably somewhere in the middle of the night, to sign the wintery white work of art with their urine. As her feet crunched onto the mostly cleared path, she began to reflect on the state of the union in her own household.

Last night after she had picked up J.T. from Butcher's office, (it still grated on her nerves that his ex-flame was sharing office space) J.T. had been noticeably quiet and the woman had a strange expression on her face. Neither J.T. nor Dr. Adams said anything about the session, so Rhonda assumed everything was fine. But it was disconcerting to watch Dr. Adams kneel in front of J.T. and adjust his coat collar. A non-verbal look passed between them which had caused Rhonda to frown.

Continuing her ruminations, she reflected on her daughter. Georgie was effervescent in her excitement, and even though the rest of the family was feeling varying amounts of stress, the little girl only had eyes for all-things-Christmas.

Connie Redman's own excitement grew exponentially day-by-day. Rhonda was sure that she had never seen her mother this happy before. Rhonda wanted to feel that way again – to be electrified by love and the excitement of the future.

The preparations for the wedding were finished and it was just one week until the big day. One week. The ceremony, which John had reluctantly agreed to perform, would occur at St. Clements with the reception following at the Traveler's Choice. Rhonda had tried to pare down the invitation list, but Connie was dead-set on inviting as many people as possible to celebrate with them.

As Rhonda passed the far side of the park for the fifth time, she felt a renewed vigor and wanted to finish strong. Her thoughts moved back to the upcoming wedding. Not only had she organized most of the wedding and reception, her mother had also asked her to be the Matron of Honor. Still not entirely comfortable with Carl as a father-in-law, Rhonda had hoped that her mother would come to her senses. But she was smitten, and there was nothing that Rhonda could do about it. Unfortunately, her suggestion of one of the exercise ladies as a decent substitute for Matron of Honor fell on deaf ears. Connie wanted Rhonda to be right next to her on her day of joy.

As this last thought echoed in her mind, Rhonda made her way back home. Guiltily, she was relieved to see that the car was gone from the garage. Butcher must have taken the kids somewhere. With another twinge of guilt, she recognized that not only had Butcher cleaned the entire driveway, shovelled the deck and swept it, but he had also finished cleaning up the kitchen from breakfast.

A note on the table read:

I've taken the kids with me to go to my follow up doctor's appointment. I hope you had a good run. See you whenever.
Love,
Leo.

Rhonda laid the page back onto the table with a huff, and shook out her hair as she walked down the hallway. Ever since that woman got back into his life, she found he was calling himself 'Leo' more and more often.

She'd really have to keep an eye on that witch.

Leo waited patiently for Dr. Ditmore to finish typing information into his computer. J.T. and Georgie were leafing through children's books in the corner of Dr. Ditmore's office. J.T. read a Beverly Cleary novel about a mouse who rode a motorcycle, and Georgie was perusing a book about a monkey named George (which made her giggle every time J.T. leaned across to read a page for her).

Finally, Dr. Ditmore looked up from his computer, removed his glasses and smiled. He had tired circles around his eyes. It seemed that every person, and their dog, wanted to get a last check-up in before the holidays.

"Hi, Leo. I see we've got an appointment to check your finger."

"Or what's left of it," he said, as he held up the missing digit.

He smiled. "Let me take a look."

Dr. Ditmore came out from behind the desk and took a chair to sit beside the tall man. He had noticed a difference about Butcher – subtle, but still apparent. He seemed to be favoring his left side and, concerningly, his speech was slightly slurred.

After checking his finger, he sat back in his chair. "Everything seems to be healing nicely with your finger, Leo, but do you mind if I ask you a question?"

He shrugged. "Sure."

"I'm noticing some shortening of your trap muscles," he pointed to his own shoulders. "What's going on there?"

Unconsciously, Butcher reached up to touch his left one. "Not sure. Maybe a little stress and I'm just compensating a little bit."

He cleared his throat. "And the... slurring of words?"

Now uncomfortable, Butcher looked down. "Is it that noticeable?"

"It's not bad. Just a few words, like your esses. I hadn't heard that before."

"I thought it was just the cold." Butcher's voice rose slightly, which caused J.T. to look up from his book. He caught the tension in his father's voice and noticed the pulse in his throat racing, but he didn't say anything.

Dr. Ditmore paused, folded his hands, and then leaned forward. "Any issues with tripping or stumbling?"

"Yes. It seems like my left foot keeps dragging slightly. It's like my leg is always tired. Do you think I'm having a stroke?"

The doctor held up his hands to calm him. "No, no, I don't think it's a stroke. You're pretty young for that, and there are no prominent residual difficulties that seem to happen with strokes, no sagging muscles, your face seems quite intact."

"That's a relief," he said, half-heartedly.

He was quiet for a moment. "Do you mind if we try a little test while you're here?"

"Sure." He looked over his shoulder where Georgie was still enrapt by her monkey and J.T. was tracing his finger over the orange front cover of his mouse book.

"I'll be back in just a moment." Dr. Ditmore left Butcher to sit with his nervous thoughts.

It seems like people always know, way down deep inside, when something is really wrong. He'd been watching Dr. Ditmore's face to read anything from him, but as of yet, it seemed that his

189

concern had stayed at a relatively surface level. He would, of course, know if something was deeply wrong by the way his face would move.

Dr. Ditmore came back inside the room with what appeared to be a medieval torture device. It looked like a shock machine with small black and red alligator clamps. He sat down again next to Butcher. "This is a SEMG – a surface electromyograph. Basically, this car battery looking thing tests to see how the electricity is moving between muscles." He took the pads out of a small box and asked him to pull up his left pant leg and take off his shoe. "I'm going to place these electrodes on your calf and foot muscles. These dials will read how the electricity travels." He saw the look on Butcher's face. "Don't worry, this is not a painful test."

J.T., intrigued by the machine, had put down his book and was standing next to his father, hand on his arm.

"Now," he said, "when I tell you, I want you to flex your calf muscles and then the muscles in your feet." He adjusted the SEMG and then nodded.

Alternating between calf and foot, he checked multiple times. Writing down a few notes, he nodded and then ripped the pads from his skin, which hurt only for a second. Then, without speaking, he moved back behind his desk and wrote into the computer.

"What are you writing?" Butcher asked.

"Just some preliminary thoughts on the test." The screen glowed against his glasses, but as he looked back to Leo, Butcher could see it written all over his face.

Oh, shit. Everything about Dr. Ditmore's demeanour had changed. His jaw muscles had tightened, his pulse had quickened and worst of all, he couldn't hold Butcher's gaze. *It's bad.*

"Dad," J.T. said, "what's ALS?"

Both Butcher's and Dr. Ditmore's eyes shifted quickly to the young boy. "Why… How did you know to ask that question?"

J.T. shrugged and pointed at the doctor's face. "I can see a reflection in your glasses. It was backwards, but I'm good at reading things backwards, right, Dad?"

Without thinking, Dr. Ditmore removed his glasses and looked at Butcher. "Leo… I… it's just one test. We need to get a biopsy of your muscles. It could be lots of things…"

But Butcher was already lost in another world.

ALS.

Amyotrophic Lateral Sclerosis.

Lou Gehrig's Disease.

John Thomas Deakins was just finishing up his Christmas Eve sermon when he saw Butcher's car driving slowly up the street towards his house. Checking his watch, Deakins noticed that it was about noon, and for some reason, the number 11:17 on 12/22 would be permanently etched into his memory. This was the moment that his best friend showed up on his doorstep to let him know that he was dying.

Slowly and surely, the tall man explained, he was about to melt from the world and there was nothing anyone could do about it.

And after the two of them sat, face to face, despair to desolation, in silence and shock, John Thomas stood slowly, ran a hand through his hair and moved to the front window where he stared out at the indelicate unfairness of both the natural and spiritual worlds.

"Have you told Rhonda yet?"

Butcher's hands were trembling. "No, and I think I'll wait until after the wedding. There's no sense in upsetting all of Connie's plans."

"But Rhonda would want to know…"

"It's not as if the news will change in five days."

Deakins turned around, frustrated. "There have to be more tests, more options. Surely the doctor could not have known anything from looking at a little computer screen."

"You don't think I know that? Look, he took a muscle sample. Supposedly, that will tell him if it's genetic. I mean, I don't even know what my own father died from. My mom never talked about him."

Deakins couldn't focus. "This can't be right. You're healthy. You don't smoke. You don't drink that much. This kind of thing happens to old people. People far away. People who… who… deserve it. Not you, Butcher. Not you." Tears began to well up in his eyes.

"Bad people like Lou Gehrig, right?" Butcher stood and took a deep breath. "How about this, Amigo. You and I head over to the Pecker and toss back a few suds. We'll pretend, just for a few more days, that this was just a bad dream and I'll wake up somewhere else, somewhere far, far away."

Deakins nodded, but still couldn't look back at his tall friend. Then, Butcher put his hand on Deakins shoulder.

"It'll be all right."

"Sure," Deakins lied.

Nothing would ever be all right again.

The wedding came at an inopportune time. Although Christmas had been somewhat joyful, or at least from Connie's perspective who fawned over Carl with sickening displays of affection, Rhonda continued to be somewhat cross with Butcher. Something was eating at him. Something she couldn't quite put her finger on. Of course, she had noticed a profound difference in his attitude since he'd been to the doctor, but he had made some kind of excuse about a slight irritation near the scar which was causing him discomfort. This didn't make up for his and John Deakins' incredible display of drunkenness a few nights before Christmas. They'd all gone to the bowling alley, but after a couple of games of tenpin, the men left the children with the wives and two hours later, when Leslie and Rhonda were ready to take the kids home, they were intoxicated. When Leslie and Rhonda had entered the bar, Shania had flashed them a look of apology. She didn't think they'd drunk that much.

Leslie and Rhonda mirrored each other in pulling their husbands from their bar stools. Deakins looked like he'd been crying for a while, and when pressed about the reasons, he said that he was still in mourning regarding the elevator deaths. The women pulled the men from their seats and helped them to the door. Waving weakly over their shoulders towards Shania, they laughed to each other and thanked her for her service.

Georgie inquired about her father's impaired state, which was met by a finger pressed to his lips and a slurred, shushing sound, which really pissed off Rhonda. Why in the world had they done it? What were they trying to do? It's not as if John did not have a reputation to protect.

After Rhonda had extricated Butcher from the car and led him up the stairs to the house, he stumbled on the deck and went down face first into the snow. Laughter turned to crying and then laughter again.

"What in the world is wrong with you?" she asked, angrily.

"You'll have to get used to my little stumbles here and there," he said enigmatically.

"Get up, Butcher! You're scaring the kids." She pulled him to his knees and finally to his feet where he leaned against the wall waiting for Rhonda to open the door.

"Mommy, what's wrong with Daddy? Did the doctor give him funny pills?"

J.T. looked sharply towards his sister. Although he didn't know what those three letters meant, he, too, noticed the look of fear on the doctor's face.

On the wedding day, the sanctuary looked beautiful. Candles, glittering in the late afternoon darkness, sparkled like fireflies. The lights above had been dimmed, leaving the room bathed in a warm, fairy tale glow. Beside Rhonda, Carley giggled nervously at things that weren't funny and laughed uproariously at everything else. It had been a long time since Carley had been a bridesmaid. She considered herself 'second in command,' right after Rhonda. Anne, alternatively, yawned loudly. The last time Anne had donned a floral bridesmaid's dress was sixty years ago, and even then, she didn't really enjoy the pageantry of it. Because Connie had been adamant, Anne gave in. Frowning all the way to the front of the sanctuary, Anne pouted because she could read people's lips: *Isn't that sooooo cute. Look at the little old lady in the pink dress and the walker!*

Rhonda walked in and noticed her groomsman husband. Despite being peeved at him, she noticed how handsome he still was. His immense height dwarfed Carl's son and grandson, and his tuxedo seemed to accentuate his power. Glancing down as she always did, she noticed his missing finger, but she was getting used to it.

John Deakins asked Carl's son, Lazlo, for the rings, which he produced after feeling in the wrong lapel pocket. "With this ring," Carl said with emotion, "I pledge my faithfulness and love all the days of my life." He slid the ring onto Connie's finger.

"With this ring," Connie repeated, "I pledge every day from this one till the end to be yours and yours alone." A stream of tears leaked from her eyes and down her cheeks and clung to her happy smile.

As the couple kissed, which was far too long for almost everyone, and certainly much too long for Anne Johnson who whispered loudly, "Get this over with, you two. My sciatica is acting up," Rhonda looked past the groom to Butcher who was staring intently at her. Something passed between them. She noticed in his eyes a quiet and unspoken repentance for the last time of neglect and she, begging for forgiveness for consistently making him out to be the fall guy for her own insecurities.

They both smiled.

Still, there was something wrong. In spite of his smile, he seemed worried. She would have to ask him about it later. He would have to tell her the truth.

After the ceremony, after the reception, after the line of well-wishers had exited the premises of St. Clements Church, even after the bride and groom had boarded the 'country limousine,' a Ford F350 pickup driven by none other than her new step-brother Lazlo, Rhonda and Butcher stayed back to help Leslie and John clean up. Butcher had taken off his tuxedo jacket and Rhonda had removed her shoes. The dance at the Treveler's Choice had been short-lived as most of the crowd did not enjoy dancing and most of them were usually in bed by nine o'clock. At 11:17, the Choke clean and ready for its next use, John had gone home to the parsonage to retrieve a truly special gift.

Four glasses and a bottle of wine.

When Butcher saw what it was, his eyes looked up sharply.

"You know what this is, don't you?" John asked him.

Butcher nodded and swallowed. "Grange, 1971."

"I take it that's a good one," Rhonda said, as she rubbed her feet. The label looked comically insignificant – red lettering on white paper wrapped around a green bottle.

Leslie tilted her head. "I've never seen that before."

John Thomas set the four wine glasses down, one in front of each of them, and then meticulously pulled the cork on the bottle. It made a satisfying popping sound. He closed his eyes as he smelled the wine. "I think by the time I tell *my* story, it will be ready to share *its* story." He passed the bottle around to Leslie who sniffed it also. Although not a wine aficionado, she could tell the difference from a good bottle to a great one.

"I never showed it to you, because it was going to be a surprise – on our silver anniversary, if we ever made it that far." Leslie noticed a tear forming in his right eye.

"What's going on?"

John looked at Butcher who put his head down.

He cleared his throat. "In 1974, just before I was born, my father went to Australia on a business trip. My father, heavily involved in electronics, connected with some people regarding new technology. My father, one of the first computer programmers, worked for Texas Instruments and the Aussies brought him out to pick his brain and show him a good time. Dad, quite socially adept, charmed the Aussies with his wit and his weirdness, and by the time he was about to leave, he gifted them the inside scoop on some up-and-coming tech." John reached for the bottle again. "To show their appreciation, the company gave him six of these bottles. Penfold's Grange is one of the most expensive bottles of wine in the world and the mere fact that they gave him six, well, I suppose that speaks to the kind of information he gave them."

Deakins poured out a little in each glass. Slowly and deliberately, John allowed the wine to cascade over the lip of each glass obscuring it in a blood-like curtain. Butcher took his glass with his right hand and raised it to his face. He relished the thought of its taste. Although he had experienced many fine wines in his life, Butcher knew that this might exceed the others.

"How much is this bottle worth?" Leslie asked.

John smiled not taking his eyes off of Butcher. "This bottle of wine is probably worth somewhere over three thousand dollars on the open market."

The women gasped. "For one bottle! That's ridiculous," Leslie said, and carefully set her glass back on the table. "Why didn't you sell it? We could have used the money for other things?"

Looking at his wife with great love, he tasted the aroma again with his nose. Almost ready. "One of the disciples once said that to Jesus about a jar of perfume, but Jesus was quite insistent that the woman's sacrifice was fitting for his upcoming…" he couldn't quite finish the word before the first of the tears spilled from his eyes.

"John," Leslie reached for him. "What's wrong? You have to tell me! Are you dying?"

He shook his head. There was silence.

"No, Leslie," Butcher's voice echoed in the room. Leslie and Rhonda's eyes turned towards him. "John's not dying." He took a deep breath and let it come out in a quick, quivering sigh.

"I am."

Chapter 18.

Jennifer Adams lazed on her brown lounge suite. With her glasses positioned securely on the bridge of her nose, she gazed at the glass of red wine. In her other hand she had an open book, the newest romance novel. It was a strangely weird pleasure for her and one that was completely counter to her personality. Jennifer Adams was as tough as nails and despite her diminutive form, there was nothing soft about her personality. Jennifer Adams knew what she wanted, and she would do anything to get it. Many years ago she had what she wanted and let him go. But now, all these years later, she realized he was once again within her reach.

Somewhat irritated that she hadn't been invited to the town wedding, Jennifer had positioned herself in her chair just before four o'clock in the afternoon. Because she had a free weekend, she had thought about driving to Omaha, or even Des Moines, to take in a show, but the weather the night before had knocked out those plans.

Jennifer yawned loudly and placed the book on the table beside her. Stretching her arms above her head, she looked around the room and noticed what was *not* there. Absent were any signs of the religious aspect of Christmas. The quaint and often cloying depiction of the childish Savior and his holier-than-thou parents had always given Jennifer a queasy feeling in her stomach. Those that still clung to the idea of a god, or even the ideals of any religion, were, as Freud posited, caught in an infantile need to feel secure. But the truth of the matter was, in her professional opinion, that God's manifestation in the lives of humans was a desperate need for people to connect with their parents, especially after they were gone. All those weekly trips to church and Sunday school held a desperate kind of mesmerization over the faithful few. Thankfully, across the United States and world, the new humanity was beginning to discover the fairy tale nature of all religions. And certainly, that was good for her business. When people gave up hope in favor of reality, their psyches needed to be dealt with.

When she had attended St. Clements, she had held her tongue and her patience. If she had to sit through that meaningless play and pretend that faith was important to her life, she would do it, if it meant that the reward was Leopold Jensen.

During the time she had been apart from Leo, she had always looked back on the moment of their separation as one of necessity. She needed to grow and he needed to shrink. But something happened to her when she saw his picture in the newspaper. Something stirred. Something which had been missing...

Jennifer looked at the wall clock and noticed it was approaching ten o'clock. The sun had set almost six hours ago and the darkness seemed like a comforting blanket. Standing, she moved to the window to peer out into the deep, white snow glittering like a galaxy of stars in the cold streetlight. A few cars careened around the icy streets. Obviously they were heading home after the wedding reception. If the town police officer had felt any sense of danger, she could have booked quite a few Amicableans for reckless driving. Jennifer was sure that the police officer attended the wedding, too.

Small towns.

When Leo was hers, they would return to New England where she would remind him of the good life he had left behind. He could slowly erase this little hiccup from his life and get on with living. They could explore the world together. They could sail the seven seas even if they had to bring his kids along. Eventually, they might settle down somewhere in the south of France, or if fortune favored, they might emigrate to the South Seas, build a little castle and settle down for the rest of their lives. She had played out the scenarios in her mind many times.

Already, she had Butcher's attention.

Already, Jennifer had positioned herself between Rhonda and her friends.

Already, Jennifer was needling her way into J.T.'s life.

The pastor's wife.

The daughter.

The mother.

And then, Leo Jensen would be hers.

"Stop it, Butcher. Not funny at all." Rhonda ground her teeth.

Leslie, mortified, paled. "What's happening?" Her eyes searched Butcher's and saw that he had a wild, despairing look in his eyes. He kept sniffing his glass. Sniffing and swirling, but he didn't seem to ever take a drink. Sniff. Swirl. Sniff. Swirl.

Finally, after an eternity, Butcher raised the glass once to his lips. He closed his eyes. Always, he had wondered what it would taste like, to drink something pure and unadulterated, properly aged and aired out. He assumed this is what life, at its very core, was supposed to be like – pure, unadulterated, liquid joy swirling and mixing with the air around it. Age would bring about a deeper sense of purpose and longing, and when he was finally old enough to take a sip, he would savor and enjoy it like nothing else.

Tilting the glass, he opened his mouth to let the rich, velvety red liquid pass his lips. An avalanche of flavors overwhelmed his tastebuds. Nothing could have prepared him for that moment, especially with the knowledge of his future. Swirling the wine in his mouth, he tasted and retasted it.

"I… went to the… doctor and he said that I have a particularly nasty disease." His halting speech was in direct proportion to the emotion coming out. "She said that they'd do some more tests, but the symptoms and the EMG were conclusive enough."

"I don't understand," Rhonda said, breathlessly. "What is it? How long have you known? What is the diagnosis?" Questions, like a tidal wave, crashed against her reality, cracking it. What seemed a sturdy future was now crumbling beneath them.

Butcher opened his eyes. The intense brown was magnified by the calmness he now felt. The wine had brought him back from the ledge and now he could discuss that which he had rarely contemplated.

"Amyotrophic Lateral Sclerosis."

"What is that?" Leslie asked.

Butcher took another drink and relished it. How bittersweet this night was.

"Lou Gehrig's Disease. Motor Neuron Disease. Nerve deterioration. Lots of names, same prognosis. There is no cure. My nerves will slowly begin to shrivel; then my muscles will atrophy. Eventually, I'll stop talking, walking, swallowing and, ultimately…" his voice faded out, "… breathing."

Rhonda's shocked mind couldn't quite take it in. "How long have you known? Is this why you keep tripping?"

Butcher glanced at John whose eyes were as red as the wine he had started to taste. "One week. Dr. Ditmore told me last week. And yes, this is why I keep tripping and certainly why my finger is now missing from my hand."

"Oh, Butcher," Leslie said, as she reached out to him.

"There aren't many worse ways to die, methinks." Butcher reached for the bottle of Grange and filled up his glass.

Rhonda's chair fell over as she stood up. Covering her mouth with a hand, she began to run the new narrative of her

201

melting future. She would be watching the children grow up by herself. Their graduation parties would be absent of their father. Georgie would need a surrogate arm on which to cling to on her wedding day. They would never visit the places they wanted to, nor would they grow old together.

"THIS IS NOT FAIR! THIS CAN'T BE RIGHT!" She began to move towards the door unaware that she was leaving her husband behind. "We'll get a second opinion. He probably misdiagnosed it. Who knows, you might just have a minor infection."

"Come back and sit with us, my love," Butcher said quietly and reached out to her.

With fury in her eyes, she strode back to the table and grabbed the wineglass. Hurling it with rage, the glass shattered against the wall into brilliant, sparkling pieces. Wine dripped in small rivulets down the white paint. The wall seemed to be bleeding. "I'm going home. I can't... I can't..." she threw her arms in the air.

If she would have looked behind her, she would have seen that Butcher had closed his eyes and held the cup of blessing and death close to his mouth.

The Finish Line

My dearest Reader,

To chronicle the death of a close friend is not for the faint-hearted, and I would not suggest the attempt if it can be avoided. To grapple with endless emotions, reflecting on a life lived and life that could have been, leaves one null and void, like the vast emptiness of pre-Creation. Floating over the limitless cosmic sea in both darkness and silence is the spirit of fear that this infinite and undefeatable foe – Death – will someday rap softly on the door of my own house, and not just for me, but for all the people I love who deserve to be immortal.

Death is never a stranger. It wears the clothes of an unmistakable friend. We encounter it every day, we see its footsteps and fingerprints on the television. We hear its voice calling to us in the rage and malice of our contemporary world and yet we are free to ignore and deny its power and presence, to our great loss. When introduced to the grimmest of reapers, even from afar, the shape of time becomes beautiful and each precious second reminds us that the smile of a loved one, or the embrace of a lover, is a beautiful speck of dust in the hourglass of eternity.

For me, as I put pen to paper, as I hear the stories of Leopold Jensen's closest friends and family, I see Death, or more importantly, I hear his call and it reminds me to put down the pen so that I can read the pages of my own life. For some, when Death approaches home's stoop, it does not pause but comes in uninvited and unwelcome. As it makes itself comfortable in what was a happy life, its grinning is always tinged with a hue of sadness. For even Death knows that in the beginning it was a figment of the Creator's unlimited imagination, but the birth of Death allowed the pain and sorrow of life to be silenced, even for a little while.

For others, the approach of Death is a whisper on the westerly winds, a phantom song lilting and carried aloft on the updrafts of previous decisions and unfortunate circumstances. The hearer tilts his or her ear into the breeze *straining to hear what the strange melody is. Somewhere in his or her soul, the tune is well known but unplayed. So, he or she goes back to hoeing the garden, driving the car, watching the television or minding their own business, all the while, the song increases in volume.*

Butcher, after hearing Death's melody, found a strange and freeing pivot point in his life. As the pages of this missive continue and ultimately finish, you will find that he made choices that neither you nor I should judge, even if we do. Rhonda, God bless her soul, will react in unimaginable ways, some of which you might have already guessed, others might come as a shock — they were to me. In the unfathomable mystery of dying, the Jensen family was...

Well, I shouldn't give away the rest of the story because you've come this far and I need to tell it in its entirety.

I'm sorry that it has taken so long to relate how we came to the point of Butcher's knowledge of his tragic and horrific demise but consciously, or subconsciously, I needed the time to process, and time to delay the inevitable. In the time that it has taken to write their story, I have begun to understand the difficulty with which all people welcome the unwelcomed friend.

I hope that I do their story justice.

Sincerely,

Leslie Deakins

Chapter 1.

"Is this your wish?"

The face that stared at him was devoid of emotion. Eyes, black like anthracite, reflecting what little light there was in the night, seemed to absorb him and consume his hope leaving him destitute and despairing.

"I don't know what I should wish." His voice squeezed through his vocal cords. Checking his surroundings, he saw that they were again approaching another cave. The mouth, behind the boatman, yawned wide with darkened, jagged teeth. He tried to sit up but once again, there was a resistance. His heart raced. This was the way that it had been for some time. Trapped. The river journey had been frantic and frenetic. Somehow, the boatman had steered them through without incident. At times he thought capsizing was inevitable. Because of the slimness of the last cavern, claustrophobia hit him full force, not because of the cavern, but because the boatman was now leaning forward. In his hands he held a garment, or cloak – some kind of fabric.

"Then I will choose," the boatman said, his voice low and rumbling, like the sound of the river itself flowing ceaselessly beneath them.

"No! NO!" he shouted, *"I will choose! I want to go back! I want to return to the place where we've come from, back to the light and land."*

Sadly, the boatman shook his head and reached down with the fabric. Gently, the boatman lifted his feet and began to encircle them with the gauze. Trying to move his legs, he found that he was unable. Adrenaline pulsing, he screamed at the boatman to stop. If he couldn't move, he couldn't live. The boatman stopped and wiped his brow. With relief, he saw that the boatman had pulled back from his legs, but with horror, the boatman moved to his hands and bound them together. Eyes widened, he again pleaded with the boatman to take him back.

"Please," he begged, *"have mercy. I have a wife and children. They need me."*

The boatman sighed heavily. It was the same plea for everyone: at this point in the river, when the inevitable approached, they all attempted to play the boatman's keyboard of pity. The lyrics changed but the tune was always the same.

"Don't worry," the boatman whispered, "we will be there soon."

The boatman stood up and moved back to the tiller. Speaking an unrecognizable word, a word of meaning and power, the boat floated out into the current. Straining against the fabric, he tried to move, but the strength of his bonds was too much. With a shriek of horror, the boat entered the maw of the cave.

Silence and darkness swallowed his scream.

Butcher woke from his nightmare drenched with sweat. The recurrence of this particular dream, one that he had never spoken of, the symbolism of both Charon and his boat and the mystery and fear of the unknown waters of death, was easily recognizable. It didn't make it any easier to know what was coming, though.

He saw that Rhonda was still sleeping. In the revelation of his condition (that's what they'd been calling it, rather than a terminal disease) his marital relationship was set on edge. Rhonda, already worried about J.T. and his difficulties at school, was unable to vocalize the things that were happening to her. Butcher longed to talk about their time together. It was hard for him to say their time *left*.

As he rolled to his other side, he saw the streetlight shining through the edge of the curtain. The intense winter chill had strangled Amicable. Furnaces pushed their warm, steamy breaths into homes. As he lay there, Butcher was aware of all things, not just the warmth of the house and blankets, Rhonda's breath and heartbeat, but also the haunting sound of ice flecks tapping the window. To Butcher, this was the sound of the Unnamed Enemy tapping malevolently on the insides of his soul reminding him that all too soon he would have neither hope nor health.

Butcher brought his hand up to his face and held his fingers before his eyes. Gritting his teeth, he tried to move his fingers quickly. He did this dozens of times a day in the chance that somehow, his muscles and brain could overcome the diagnosis – he could be the first one to defeat ALS. But each successive day, he saw the unrelenting power of the disease as it took one nerve and muscle cell from him at a time.

Slowly, Butcher rolled out of bed. The cool air near the floor brought goosebumps up his calves and thighs, and he sucked in air. Attempting to not wake Rhonda he shuffled to the bathroom where he opened the door, which creaked slightly, and moved quietly to the toilet. Sitting down, he relieved himself and flexed his toes. His right foot still responded relatively well, but not the other. Frustrated, he wanted to curse his own body, but it was too late for that.

Finishing, he made his way back into the bedroom. He was cold.

"Are you okay?" Rhonda asked worriedly.

"I'm alright," he whispered as he hurried back to bed as quickly as he could. "Go back to sleep."

Her body followed him and his progress rolling toward him as he pulled back the covers and got into bed. Grabbing his hand, she pulled him close.

"Have you been sleeping?"

"A little," he said as he enjoyed the feeling of being pulled closer to her. Over the months, before his diagnosis, she had not offered much in the way of physical touch.

"Me too." Rhonda was still but then she rubbed his hand. "Can you feel this?"

"Yes."

Moving the hand to her cheek, she closed her eyes. "What about this?"

"Warm. You have a beautiful face."

Then, almost without thought, she moved his hand onto her breast.

Butcher cleared his throat. "I can feel that."

"That's good," Rhonda responded, quietly. Seconds later, she pulled his face towards hers and kissed him, hesitantly at first, then with a fevered fierceness, as if she was going to devour him.

It had been a very long time since they had kissed like that. He left himself be drawn into the feel of her lips and the smell of her hair, her heat and her warmth. The darkness seemed to magnify the moment and fleetingly, his mind was able to picture every minute detail of her body. Sadly, he had taken this for granted.

Hungrily, they consumed each other with their urgency. Their clothes became a hindrance. Pulling back, they shed them and then resumed their need for life and love. Butcher felt his wife's skin and remembered how this physical, intimate contact created a bond so deep that nothing could tear it asunder. Rhonda, for her part, attempted to set aside the fact that these moments would be incredibly rare in the next months. Ultimately, they would vanish.

Unfortunately, Rhonda could not halt the one, singular thought that wrecked the moment. *Will this be the last time?* Even as she kissed him, even as she felt his need for her, even as she desired this moment, her mind enslaved her body and she felt her will withdrawing. *No, no, no, no!* Leo kissed her face, but then stopped as tears broke the dam of her need for him.

Tenderly, he pulled back from her, but his hands, his almost useless hands, remained on her cheeks. "Hey," he said softly, "it's okay. It's okay."

Chapter 1.

Rhonda, unable to control her anguish, felt the waves of pain erupt. Her body convulsed and her shame in her inability to continue with their lovemaking was too great for her. How could Leo be the comforter? He was the one who was dying? He was the one who needed to be released from his fear? And she was the one contorting in torturous agony at the thought of making love to a dying man?

"I'm so sorry, Butcher."

Butcher sat up in the bed. For now, he was warm, and as he leaned back against the headboard, he drew her up onto his lap. Cradled like a small baby, he rested her head on his shoulder and pulled the covers up over her. He rocked her against his shoulder. Patting her hair and kissing her forehead, he did his best to hum a little song. Rhonda reached up with her left hand to grab his neck. She felt the taut muscles, the strength of his body and she marvelled at the power he still had.

"What are we going to do?"

Leaning his head back, Butcher looked to his right where the flakes of snow were still tap tap tapping away on the window. "I guess we'll just make the most of each day we have…"

He didn't say *left*.

Rhonda was fully aware, though, that this would be an impossibility. Her mind was already firmly entrenched in the cavernous valley of the shadow of death.

"Okay," she said quietly. "I'll do my best."

After a quiet minute, Butcher felt her breath lengthen. She had been listening to his heart, and maybe this is the way it would always be. He gently slid her down under the covers and pulled the blanket up over them both. He would try to sleep, too.

Jennifer Adams whistled as she opened the front door of the Chop Shop. Hossein was already at his desk typing notes into the computer.

"Good morning, Dr. Adams."

"Good morning, Hossein." Jennifer unwrapped the scarf from around her neck and hung it on the antique coat tree by the front door. "Nothing like Syria, is it?"

"Not in the least, but I don't miss it. Here in Iowa, only snowballs, not bombs."

Laughing, Jennifer shed her coat and placed it on the tree. "There's something to be said for that."

He motioned with his finger towards the office door. "The boss is already in."

"And to what do we owe the pleasure?"

"He said that he wanted to talk to you this morning."

Jennifer opened the door to find Leo sitting behind the desk, reading glasses on, looking through an old black and red notebook. The pages were tattered and yellowed.

She pulled the door shut behind her. "What are you pondering?"

"An old diary. Traveling around the country."

"What kinds of things were important back then?"

"Oh, prob..l.bb.y." He stopped. The effects of the disease on speech hadn't started in full force, but he knew it was coming. Swallowing, he pushed the chair back and moved Jennifer out of the way.

"Are you all right?"

He stood and grunted.

"Come on, what is it? What's going on?"

Moving to the sofas, Butcher was aware that his leg was dragging, but he attempted to hide it by holding on to the furniture. After sitting down, he motioned with his hand at the chair opposite him. His eyes were dull. "Do you remember what it was like to be young?"

Chapter 1.

She laughed and frowned at the same time. "I'm not sure what you mean. You're still young. Mid-forties, handsome and debonair. A man at the top of his game."

His look was indecipherable.

Jennifer crossed her legs demurely. "Are you talking about the things in your book?"

"I suppose so." Butcher rubbed his nose with the back of his hand. "Sometimes I wonder what it would be like to go back to the best parts of life, sit on an allegorical sofa, and replay those good times on the television. You know, pull out the popcorn and remember."

"Whoa, getting a little introspective in our *old* age, are we?" She tried to laugh, but his expression stopped her. "What's this all about? The book? The deep conversation?"

There were many things about Jennifer Adams that Butcher still found attractive. As he read through his diary that morning, he had landed, not coincidentally, on their time together. Some of the things he had put on paper were quite racy and the memory of them brought a smile. The smell of her hair, the curves of her hips, even the way she spoke when they were about to...

"Leo? Are you there?"

He reddened. "Sorry, I..." Butcher rolled his neck around, trying to jog the memory from his adulterous sprint through his past. "Okay, you caught me. I was thinking back to those years when we were together as partners, and not in the business sense."

It was Jennifer's turn to blush. "I see."

"I wasn't specifically thinking about that part, but the rest of it, in general, you know? I think the older we get and, maybe, the longer we are with someone, we tend to look back a little more often to when things were... different." Butcher reached for the lamp beside him and stroked the chain on the old-fashioned lampstand.

211

"I think about them sometimes, too," she said. "But what do you think about? What comes to mind?"

He didn't look at her but at the cord. "When you're young and unattached, or at least loosely attached, nights didn't begin until eleven o'clock and mornings didn't start until ten; you spent money on excitement and nightlife and everything you wanted was at your fingertips." He held up his left hand, examined it and quickly put it down.

"The people you surround yourself with were exciting and unpredictable and your job was just a way to earn money so that you could continue do unpredictable and exciting things. Remember the time we went to the Catskills and it was so cold we decided to go looking for wood so that we could burn it in the little cabin we rented and..."

"And!" Jennifer interjected, finishing the memory for him, "you lost your footing, slid down the slope and onto the ice almost taking out some ice fisherman. They looked at us as if we were aliens, all wrapped up in fake fur coats and bell bottoms."

Butcher slapped his leg. "And one of them said, 'Stupid ass city slickers.'" When the laughter lessened, he stroked the chain again. "It just seemed so much easier back then."

"I know what you mean."

Jennifer leaned forward. "Do you have any alcohol here? Wine or spirits?"

Butcher snorted. "It's nine in the morning and I've got clients at ten!"

"Call them. Tell them that you have a staff meeting today."

"But I don't have enough staff for a staff meeting." Butcher was intrigued by the idea of doing something spontaneous.

"It doesn't matter. Tell Hossein that he can have the morning off. It's not like *he* doesn't deserve it. The man works really hard."

Chapter 1.

To be honest, Butcher really wanted to avoid all commitments for the day. He made a snap decision. "Okay," he said as he rubbed his hands together. "Put Hossein on speakerphone for me, will you?"

Jennifer hopped up quickly before the mood was lost. Touching the button on the phone, it rang once, echoing, then Hossein's voice answered. "Yes, boss?"

"Hossein," Butcher spoke from the sofa, "I want you to take the rest of the day off. Go home. Spend some time with your family?"

"Boss?"

"Don't worry, Hossein. Think of it is as a paid vacation day."

Silence. "Boss?"

"Don't worry, Hossein."

"Boss?"

"Hossein."

"Yes?"

"Go home."

"But I don't want to. I have a lot of work to do."

Butcher rolled his eyes. "Would you like to spend some extra time with Anala today?"

"Boss?"

"Hossein, honestly, just go home. Surprise Anala. Bring her some flowers, or chocolate."

Pause. "Can I go home in an hour?"

Sighing, Butcher laughed. "You're incorrigible, Hossein. Yes, you can go home in an hour, but cancel Dr. Adams' and my appointments for the day."

"Okay, Boss, thank you?"

Jennifer disconnected the line. "Now, where were we?"

"I have a bottle of merlot in the back cupboard. It seems like a good time as any to share it with someone."

Turning to the cupboard underneath the bookshelf, Jennifer stooped and opened the door. Behind some notepads and pens was the bottle. "Any glasses?"

"I think there are a few glasses out in the entry, but they aren't wine glasses."

Jennifer retrieved the bottle and brought it to the desk. "Glass is glass. Now, do you have a bottle opener?"

Nodding, Butcher leaned to the side and took out his keys. His fingers fumbled with the chain, but he tossed them to her. Missing them, the keys dropped onto the floor, but she picked them up and located a small corkscrew. After unwrapping the foil, she expertly twisted and popped the cork. "That was satisfying."

"Hmm." Butcher was glad that he didn't need to use the corkscrew.

As Jennifer retrieved the glasses, Butcher reflected on what was transpiring. Guiltily, he thought back to his interaction with Rhonda the night before and the beauty of the moment. At the same time, Butcher wanted to take advantage of all that life had left for him. It's not like he would do anything untoward to jeopardize his marriage and family, would he? He and Jennifer were just old friends having a couple of drinks and a few laughs. There was nothing wrong with that.

Jennifer re-entered the room carrying two glasses of water. Turning around to Hossein, she thanked him for helping her, then shut the door with her foot. Walking over to the potted plants, placed precariously by the freezing window, she dumped the water into them. "I had to get the glasses without arousing suspicion," she said.

"Good thinking."

Walking back to the desk, Jennifer poured the wine. She handed him one, which he carefully accepted with both hands.

"Now," she said, "where were we?"

Chapter 1.

After sitting on the opposing sofa, Jennifer casually took off her shoes and pulled her feet up under her. Butcher watched her situate herself and smiled. "So," he said slowly, "now that you've been in Amicable for a while, what do you think? Are you on the brink of purchasing some farmland or acreage for a life of retirement?"

"I wouldn't say Amicable would be an exotic destination by any means, but it has its... how should I say, comforts, I suppose."

"Such as?"

Without thought, Jennifer moved her right index finger around the rim of the 'wine' glass.

"The land prices." When she laughed it seemed natural. "I saw that the Johnson's house on the west side of town was up for sale. They're looking to get a good seventy-five thousand for it."

"Listen to you," Butcher smelled his wine. The aroma brought back a memory of a date with Rhonda. They had been sitting in a chalet on the eastern edge of the Rocky Mountains. The sun was rising below them, which was a strange sensation, and they laughed because they were drinking wine at five o'clock in the morning.

"You're getting to know the citizens; you've started using cardinal directions when telling people how to get somewhere. Even the phrase, 'looking to get,' good Lord, we'd better check your driver's license in case you've already emigrated."

As of yet, neither of them had taken a drink. Perhaps both of them subconsciously knew the symbolism of partaking of a forbidden fruit, that if either of them took a sip, a threshold would be crossed.

She shook her head and covered her eyes. "Yes, I suppose I've attempted to fit in. It seemed like a good idea. I joined the exercise group the other day. The women were quite happy to have someone my age join. They fussed over me like mother hens."

"I suppose it's been a while since a chick has been under their wings. Did you enjoy that?"

"As much as I could."

Butcher waited for her to continue.

"They… struggle with… personal space. Maybe that's my own bugaboo," Jennifer said as she ran a hand through her hair. "My size brings out that kind of reaction in people, especially women."

"And mine has the opposite effect."

"I don't think it's the size of your body," she said, "but probably your abilities that holds people at a distance."

He nodded. "You'd think after all the time that I've been here they would have torn down the walls of suspicion by now."

"You would think so." Jennifer's eyes searched his.

"What about you, Leo? What do you like about Amicable? You've been here for a long time. It's pretty surprising knowing the history with your mother."

Butcher set his glass on the side table. "Yes," he said quietly, "I suppose it is a little surprising."

"You've been all over the States, to exotic international locales, and somehow you end up in the state of Iowa of all places. I mean, what's keeping you here? What am I missing beside the housing market?"

What was it about Amicable that had sunk its talons into him? His personal Amicablean history appeared; faces and phrases, incidents and laughter. These people, not the location, were the reason he had stuck. Whether George Hendriks, the Peterson twins, Louise, or Linda, or Naida, or… he could continue with the names of almost all three hundred plus citizens who lived in idyllic slowness – not laziness by any means – but a true understanding of pace. These people had taught him how to grow roots – to grow deeper, not taller. When the grain elevator had exploded, Amicable circled its metaphorical wagons and had taken care of itself. When the moment came to let the next generation lead, the leading men and women of the town encouraged it. The school, now copied in various *cities* across the United States, not just other small towns, was a source of inspiration and joy. In the last few years as he and Rhonda withstood difficult issues, he had felt an uprooting that threatened to pull him away from this place he called home.

"You're a psychologist. You know what people are like," Butcher leaned forward and folded his hands on his thighs. "You're around people who need to share things, to tell you things because that's your job and they feel better by telling you and you feel better for listening. But do you know what it's like to love an entire community?"

Jennifer frowned cupping her wine in her hand. "What do you mean?"

"Living in Boston, or any big city, when was the last time that you walked across town to help someone who wasn't your neighbor? When was the last time you went to a high school basketball game knowing that your team was going to get pummelled by at least thirty points? But you went because it was senior day and some of your good friends have high school kids playing their last game?"

Jennifer shrugged.

"When was the last time you went to church, or any religious community service, not because faith was particularly important at that time, but because you didn't want to miss out on seeing people, because face to face interactions were still one of the most important pieces of entertainment in your life?"

Feeling a shallow shame, Jennifer gazed out the window at the frigid street as hardy Amicableans moved quickly, but carefully, over snow and ice encrusted sidewalks.

"Since I've lived in Amicable, my mind has been completely transformed by these people." She rolled her eyes and he held up a hand. "I was a stranger in a strange land, and now, I have a home." The words he spoke took him by surprise, and even more surprisingly, a tear came to his eye. Without warning, gratitude and sadness for these people bullrushed him and he dared not look her in the eye. "As strange as it sounds and as strange as it has come to be, Amicable is a beautiful and magical place."

"You mean like Oz."

"You mock what you don't understand."

"I'm sorry. I didn't mean to offend you."

Shrugging, Butcher picked up his glass of wine again, but still did not drink. "I'm not offended, or at least not in the way that you think. These are great people." Butcher felt his defensive goodwill for Amicable snowballing down the mountain of metropolitan ignorance.

"Jeez, Butcher, take it easy."

He took a deep breath. "Sorry, I've got a few things on my mind."

"It's okay."

Butcher leaned back in the sofa. "And yet," Butcher continued *sotto voce*, "there is a part of me that wants to…"

"…Escape?" Jennifer filled in the blank.

He looked into her eyes. Knowing that his condition allowed him no escape from anything, no open door to travel, or to experience, even create. He was locked into a short future that barred him from happiness. *Unless…* he could make it himself.

"I suppose 'escape' would be an appropriate word."

"What is holding you back?"

"Domestic responsibilities." He swallowed knowing the way he said it sounded critical. "Don't get me wrong, I love my family, but…"

"You and Rhonda are having problems?" Jennifer's question escaped her lips before she could retrieve it.

"I'm not sure that's an appropriate question."

Silence. Then, she spoke. "What's going on, here, Leo?"

Their connection pulsed. Although the wording of her question was vague, both knew what she meant. As the conversation swirled deeper and deeper into the miasma of faithfulness, Butcher to his family and Jennifer to her profession, both knew that eventually this topic had to be broached.

"Look, Jennifer, there are so many things about me that you don't know. We had our chance…" his words trailed off. He had been reading her, the pulse in her throat, the nervous twitch of her hands, the way she was licking her lips in preparation to have a sip of wine. It was obvious that she was stirred up and shaken, an emotional martini, but she did not seem to care that he could read it all. It seemed like she was encouraging it.

"Then tell me what I don't know." Her voice was husky.

"I…"

For a moment the inclination to tell her everything, especially about the disease, surfaced. But he didn't want her pitying him. God, that would be awful. "I love my wife and my kids and my town, but seeing you, it's brought back some disturbing thoughts."

Her pulse quickened. Like an angler playing with a fish, she reeled him in, then set the drag so she could wear down his defences. "What thoughts?"

"I know what you're doing, and frankly, I don't like it." He stopped and then murmured under his breath. "But I can't stop what I'm feeling either. I love that you're interested in me and that you've been wondering when I'm going to take a sip of wine, come over to sit by you, ease into the seat, ease into the way things used to be to just *test* the waters. Just a sip, mind you, to remind me of what falling in love was like. Those first, tender, electric and painful moments." He couldn't look at her.

"Tell me what else I'm thinking." Her voice resonated with desire, temptation, or something like it. The forbidden fruit placed just within reach. But it was forbidden for a reason.

"Don't, Jennifer," Butcher begged, but he found his words were hollow and the intractable situation made his pulse race.

"I can stop if you want, but you know that I don't want to."

Feeling her gravitational force, the power of her will and her small, lithe body reeling him in, he began to stagger to his feet. As he pulled himself to his full height, he looked down at the rose petal on his sofa. She had set her wine glass on the ground, unsipped. She stood. The distance between their faces was vast. Jennifer reached up to touch his stomach. Then, her hands moved to his chest and finally, she touched his cheek. Her touch was like the silky caress of a butterfly. Groaning, his unrelieved need from the night before, blended with the erotic feel of a woman's hand who was not his wife, Butcher allowed his face to be drawn downwards ever so slowly to a woman he used to adore.

"Please," he whispered, "don't make me do this."

Jennifer's smile was serpentine. "You can stop any time you want to, Leo, but one kiss. Just one to remember me by. Nothing bad will come of it. Just think of it as a gift." Butcher's eyes were wide, his pupils were dilated and his Adam's apple was bouncing. His mind shouted NO!, but his body was very much the opposite. Her lips were so soft and full, tender and ripe, like delicate berries. They looked enticingly sweet, just as he remembered them. Cheeks flushed, eyes suggestive, an open book to the delights which she promised.

Just one kiss. No one would know.

Then, a knock at the door.

Hossein.

"Boss? I go?"

The moment broken, magic bubble popped, Butcher stopped suddenly. "Yes, yes, Hossein. Of course. Have a fantastic afternoon."

"Okay, Boss. Your appointments are cancelled. Have a fine day."

Butcher stepped back from Jennifer. This happened for a reason. Interruptions were not coincidences. In the movies, when a couple was nearing unfaithfulness, there is always a phone call from the wife, or a child's voice, or any number of things where the viewer thinks to himself or herself, *See! I knew that he would stay strong! That was a close one, though.*

Even as Jennifer fumed, Butcher was relieved.

But then he turned around.

Jennifer had taken things to a different level. And the glass she'd picked up from the floor was now half empty.

Chapter 2.

Stedman stared morosely at his computer. It seemed like this was his life now, endless insurance issues. When he had accepted the proposal to work on Amicable's insurance claim for the elevator, Stedman was quite sure that his future was indecorously splattered on the front windshield of a four-wheel-drive called Irony. Instead of working on cases of arson, theft, or negligence, he was dealing with the tragic circumstances of two pickup trucks denting each other on slippery roads, or maybe the exciting prospect of working through the specs of a grain silo fan that caught fire.

Either way, this cold, overcast day offered nothing new in excitement. His girlfriend, Summer, had driven to Kansas City for a week of meetings with clients for her advertising business. Most of her work was done out of a home office in Amicable. "Sometimes," she told Stedman, as she motored southwestwards, "I really need to sit with my clients." Stedman rolled his eyes and asked if there was anything that he could do, anything at all, even if it was to drive her there, but on this occasion, Summer had kissed him on the cheek and said she needed a girl's weekend away. She was meeting a few friends and they were going out for drinks at a swanky, up-market club. Stedman pleaded with his eyes but she turned away with a laugh. "This is your hometown now, Studman," she used the moniker that made him grind his teeth. "Your people *need* you."

"They're your people, too," he said under his breath, but she ignored him.

Perched on an imitation leather chair in a building on the north end of Main Street in Amicable, Iowa, poring over Dennis Lipton's claim that a rock had been thrown up by the snow blower and broken one of his office bay windows, Stedman sighed.

Leaning on his desk, he gazed out his front window. Where was the adventure in life? Was he going to be cooped up in this small town for the rest of his life?

Just as he was about to reread the file, a figure emerged on the east side of Main Street.

Rhonda.

Striding with purpose, her collar turned up to her cheeks and her white stocking hat crammed down to her eyebrows, Rhonda turned into the alcove of Human Beans. She stamped her feet to free her Ugg boots of excess snow and opened the coffee shop door where Stedman could see a few of the regulars huddled over their drinks.

Stedman pondered the silent movie across the street. He couldn't imagine what they were talking about, but he knew what was going on inside his own head. Over the last eight months, Stedman hadn't been able to shake the niggling thought in his mind about Rhonda who had been such a distraction for him when he first arrived in Amicable. It's not that he wasn't happy in his relationship, but old desires were almost impossible to erase from the emotional hard drive.

Sometimes when he saw Rhonda, an ache came over him, like an old, scarred wound. When she smiled at him, or laughed at something he said, he felt a warm glow.

Stedman sniffed. Making a snap decision, he shut down his computer. Pulling a luxurious, warm black coat over his ironed long sleeve shirt and designer tie, he turned up the collar and put his leather gloves on. Some of the residents had tried to change his mind about wearing hunting mittens. But Stedman smiled and politely refused. *No thank you. I probably won't be out hunting anything this winter.*

Opening the front door of his office, he felt the icy winter wind bite at his face. Sucking in a breath, Stedman instantly realized his mistake, and he coughed as the painful wind eviscerated his alveoli. Looking both directions before crossing the street (an old habit which died hard in Amicable, especially since his office was on the one-way Main Street) he hustled across the slippery road. His expensive shoes were not designed for the ice and he almost slipped before catching himself with waving arms. Making his way to Human Beans, he encountered Carley, Linda, Leona sitting in the front window laughing. Linda's smile was broadest. She had a new lease on life as well as a new scarf that covered her chemically induced baldness.

The smell of coffee and good tidings wafted from the front door. Stedman noticed that his entrance, as always, caused a stir, but he knew that the same stir would be applicable to anyone who walked through the door. Raising a hand to wave a general greeting, Stedman pretended not to notice Rhonda's gaze (was he imagining that it lingered on him?) and moved towards the counter.

"Hello, Mr. Boswell. What can I get you?" Corinne's teeth were almost straight, and if she would have had her choice, she would have gotten braces a few years ago, but her parents couldn't afford orthodontics.

"I'll have a double shot mocha with almond milk."

Corinne shook her head. "Very funny, Mr. Boswell. You'll have the regular then? Bottomless black coffee?"

Stedman sighed. He really would have liked to have had a mocha with almond milk, not because that was his favorite drink, but because he wanted something *different*, not just bottomless. "Yes, that will be fine, Corinne," he sighed. Corinne gave his two dollars and fifty cents change, which he placed in the tip jar. Corinne thanked him for his generosity.

Surveying the café, Stedman's eyes rested on Rhonda again who was in deep conversation with Naida and Leslie. Not wanting to interrupt, he moved to a table by himself which had the Amicable Tribune open on it. He scanned the news. Grain prices were rising steadily. There was a blow-by-blow account of Elvin Pilgrim's cow giving birth to twin calves two weeks before. The proud farmer stood next to the recently birthed animals while mother cow looked on with doleful eyes.

"Do you mind if I join you?"

Stedman looked up to see Rhonda standing beside him. He motioned for the seat across from him.

"The others have to go but I'm not quite ready to head back outside."

"I'm happy." Stedman finished off his first cup and motioned for Corinne to bring him another.

"How's business?" she asked.

Shrugging, he pursed his lips and waggled his hand. "It's winter. The older folks fly south and the young ones don't think about insurance that much." When he saw the look on her face, he stopped talking.

"I'm sorry. Did I say something wrong?"

Rhonda covered her mouth.

"What's wrong?"

"Nothing," she said shortly. "It's nothing." Butcher had told her insistently that she shouldn't tell anyone yet. This frustrated her. Rhonda needed people to share it with, to talk it over, to see how people could support them.

And she felt ashamed after what had happened the night before. Sooner, or later, she would have to muster the courage to go through with it in spite of its difficulty.

"You can talk to me, you know."

She nodded. "I know. I know. Lots of people tell me that."

"Is this about Dr. Adams?"

Rhonda looked up sharply. "Why? What do you know?"

Frowning, Stedman pushed his hands down. "Take it easy. She's helping Butcher get the business back up. That's a good thing, right?"

"I suppose."

"There's something about her though, isn't there? It's like trying to look directly at a star at night, but the only way you can really see it is to avert your eyes a little. That's the only way you can kind of see who she really is."

Rhonda lowered her voice. "But who is she, really? I mean, Butcher intimated that she was an old fling, but after all these years, she shows up in Amicable? That seems a little too far-fetched to be coincidence."

"She's made quite an impression on the town." Stedman attempted to read her demeanor. It was obvious that she was hiding something from him. Was Butcher cheating on her? What an idiot! Butcher had the most beautiful and wonderful wife in the tri-county area. How could he even think about cheating on her?

"Like what?"

Clearing his head, Stedman returned to the present. He motioned with his head toward the front window where Carley, Linda and Leona were sitting together. "I heard she's joined the morning exercise group and they love her."

It was Rhonda's turn to frown. "That's strange. Mom hasn't said anything to me about it."

"The kids at the school think she's fantastic. It's probably because she's their size."

Rhonda laughed at the suggestion.

"You know what's funny, I heard that Josh Thompson plucked up the courage to ask her out."

Rhonda gasped. "He didn't! What did she say?"

"Well, if the rumors are true, she politely turned him down because she didn't want to mix business and pleasure in Amicable, but if he could wait a few months until her convalescence in Amicable was finished, she would think about his proposal."

"Interesting."

Stedman nodded. "Josh was so confused that he kind of dumbly nodded and hoped that convalescence was not some kind of disease."

"Why does she have that effect on people?"

"You don't know?"

"No. Tell me."

Leaning forward, he circled his cup with his hands. "Most people have a tendency to trust beautiful people, or tall people, or strong people. If you look at our politicians, how many of them are ugly? Or short? What about movie stars? Why do we pay attention to celebrities regarding climate change, human sexuality or abortion? Is it because they are more attuned to the debate, or more intelligent?"

She waited for him to finish.

"Nope. It's because they look good on camera, and good looking people bring out the hopefulness in us average looking people." He lowered his eyes unable to look at her.

"Are you saying the people of Amicable trust this woman because she's good looking?"

"Why not?" he responded. "They trusted Butcher because he's tall and good looking even before they trusted him for his kindness and common sense. They trust you because you are tall and beautiful..." He let the words trail off.

"But they know I won't hurt them."

"*I* know that and *you* know that, but the people of Amicable assume that there is nothing untoward about Jennifer Adams because she is tiny and cute, like a kitten. They go to her for counseling not just because she's got some extra letters behind her name, but because she makes them feel like they can take care of her. Haven't you watched the ladies behind us? They treat her like a doll."

"This makes me ill," Rhonda said.

"And you've got to put up with the fact that Butcher used to date her. Do you trust Butcher?"

"Of course I trust him. This is Butcher we're talking about, not..." She stopped her sentence. *Not you.*

Stedman paused, reading her thoughts, hurt. "Yes, well, I'm different now."

"Oh, Stedman, you know I didn't mean you. You are very different and completely smitten with Summer. We're talking about Butcher and there's certainly no way that in the time that he's got..." She suddenly stopped and clapped a hand over her mouth.

Stedman's eyes opened. "What were you going to say?"

"Never mind. Never mind." She looked at a non-existent watch on her wrist. "I've got to get going, Stedman. Thanks for the chat. We'll catch up sometime soon." Rhonda pushed back her chair and it almost fell over. Grabbing her coat, Rhonda opened the door and moved into the unforgiving, bitter world, without bothering to zip up.

What in the world...? Was there something wrong with Rhonda? He gulped. *Was there something wrong with Butcher?*

Chapter 3.

Demetrius Chandler bounced back and forth, foot to foot, frustration to frustration. His workload seemed overwhelming. Although his mother gave him a good talking to on 'the self-absorbed perception of youth,' he was pretty sure this was not that. The talking to, had occurred on New Year's Day. Demetrius began to unload his issues.

"So, Mom, I've been sponsored to create a few more sculptures for this dude in Nebraska."

"That's nice, Sweetheart."

Demetrius smiled down at his mother, the top of her head bobbing furiously in the work of her hands. "They're going to pay me ten thousand dollars each."

"We're very proud of you, Demetrius."

"Think of the things that we could do with the money. We could get you both anything you wanted. Dad could have a new truck; we could buy you a new sewing machine."

"I don't need a new sewing machine and dad's truck still works pretty well."

"Come on, Mom. These things would make you happy."

Angela Chandler rested her hands on the edge of the sink then grabbed the dish towel from Demetrius' hands and wiped them. When she looked at him this way, he always felt small. No matter how tall he got, she could bring him down to size with one look.

"Those *things*," she said the word as if spitting out a seed, "won't make us happy. They would be nice and useful, but what will make us *happy*, is that *you* find happiness in what you do. Sooner or later you'll find that the money people pay you to make sculptory kinds of things will be more frustrating for you because it locks you up. They'll lord it over you, mark my words." She shook a finger at him and then moved to the table to bring more dishes to the sink.

"I thought you'd be happy for me, Mom."

"You're not listening." She grabbed his arms and squeezed them. Her hands were remarkably strong for such a small woman. "What will make you, and us, happy is if you surround yourself with people like Kelly. I could care less if these ritzy rich farts want to hire you to put up some fancy artwork that nobody understands but you and the dog next door. Does that make sense?"

His mother's words were surprisingly prophetic. He wasn't enjoying the work of producing something specifically for someone else. For some reason, the commissioned projects, although emotive, didn't capture his attention as much as when he was purposefully creating something he'd like. When Demetrius told Linda and Dick what he had done with her artwork, she pulled his head down to hers and kissed him on both cheeks. Her tears were cold on his cheeks, and as he was released from her hold, he saw that Dick, too, was wiping his eyes. That was the kind of art that inspired him.

One of the projects for which he had been paid in advance, a piece for a watch making company in Colorado, had troubled him. The idea was there, but the actual ability to bring it about was stuck behind sculptor's block. He had needed to go home.

Two hours later, after packing the car and driving to Amicable, Demetrius turned down the familiar, tired old farm lane. Although his parents lived on a recently paved blacktop, their own driveway, almost a quarter mile long, was pitted with potholes. Putting on his blinker and slowing down, he turned into the family farm and the warm feeling of *home*. His heart felt bigger.

As he drove down the driveway, Sir Barkwell, the family dog, came running down to stand in the middle of the driveway to play chicken with the oncoming car. Demetrius yelled playfully at the dog. Just as Demetrius was about to lay on the horn, Sir Barkwell's head jerked around at a sound behind him. Demetrius could see his father standing on the front step, coat wrapped tightly around him, head reflecting the farm light. Barkwell ran alongside the car, shouting happily at his best friend who had returned home to see him specifically.

After driving over the crunchy snow in front of the garage, Demetrius saw the top of his mother's head in the kitchen window. Obviously, she was preparing dinner. Demetrius sat in the car enjoying the nostalgic view of returning home. He noticed the trees in the backyard were taller and rounder than ever. Even though they had lost their leaves, he felt their *solidness*. Had they watched him grow up also?

Demetrius stared up at the hulking farmhouse, squat and solid against the backdrop of the darkening sky. Shingles were sticking up on the backside of the house. Demetrius would ask his father if he needed help roofing this summer. His father would smile and nod his head, proud that his son was now old enough to help and assist him in the farm work. Through the second floor window, he saw his room. He knew that his mother would not have touched a thing; his bed would have the same bedspread and warm blankets would be tucked in under the mattress. The posters on his wall would still be hung, tattered and yellowing. In his closet, clothes that he hadn't worn for years would still be hanging from hangers. The smell of mothballs would be as strong as the dust in the room. He would be transported to the past as a ten-year-old.

His father, David, was still shivering for him on the stoop. Hands under his arms, bouncing from foot to foot, just like Demetrius had been doing hours before, David waved to him with one hand and then put it back under his arm.

The explosion of cold air shocked Demetrius, but after pulling himself from his vehicle, he put on his winter coat and gloves, opened the back door and retrieved his school bag emblazoned with the Mid-America mascot.

"Dad," he shouted, as he pulled his head from the backseat, "get inside the house. It's miserable out here." Sir Barkwell barked spastically at Demetrius while jumping up on him. Demetrius stopped to scratch him behind his ears but it was far too cold to linger.

"I know," David said, "but I like to be out here when you arrive. It's good for the soul." Demetrius was glad they liked to wait for him also.

David opened the door for his son.

Demetrius smiled at his mother. "It smells good, Mom."

"Go unpack your things. Throw your dirty laundry in the bathroom and I'll take care of it. You're staying for the weekend?"

"If that's all right?" Demetrius smiled.

"I guess a silly answer for a silly question." She smirked. "Are you going out tonight? Or tomorrow?"

"I was thinking about heading uptown tomorrow night. See if I can find anyone. Maybe to the bowling alley for a little while. Am I still young enough for free bowling?"

"Not likely."

As Demetrius moved up the stairs, he thought to himself, *If only we could always return home when we needed it most.*

Chapter 4.

Butcher's eyes widened with shock. Instead of diffusing the situation, Hossein's knock at the door had increased the tension. Behind the desk, Jennifer Adams stood, wine glass in hand, and shirt unbuttoned. Not just one button. All the buttons. A lacy black bra was exposed. Nestled in the cleavage was a circular necklace depicting the yin/yang symbol.

"What... who... what... are you doing?" Butcher's voice was an octave higher than normal.

"This is where we were heading slowly before your receptionists knock on the door. Unfortunately, one never knows when another knock will come, so I am offering you an opportunity."

Butcher swallowed and glanced at the unshaded window. Only a few brave souls were outside at eleven o'clock, but any of them could see into his office and see exactly what kind of session was taking place.

"Are you crazy?" Butcher moved quickly to the curtains and drew them shut. In pulling them closed, though, he was subconsciously acquiescing to what she was proposing. "If anyone saw you... us, I can safely say that my practice, not to mention my marriage, would be over."

"Maybe I'm a little crazy," she replied, suggestively. Moving slowly around the desk, Butcher now noticed that she had unzipped her skirt and it slid slowly to the ground revealing her short, but beautifully formed legs. White, creamy skin, toned muscles. This time, Butcher could not keep himself from looking.

"Jennifer, there is no way this can happen. No way. You don't understand. Please don't do this?" he begged her.

Shrugging, she smiled suggestively.

"No, Jennifer, put your clothes back on. Please. Please. I can't. I love my wife too much. This would destroy her and I don't have that kind of ti…" He stopped himself short.

"You don't have that kind of what? Resistance?" Jennifer paused two steps in front of him, shrugged off one sleeve of her shirt.

Butcher groaned. He wanted to run away. He wanted to stay. He wanted to cry out, call for Rhonda. He wanted to take Jennifer in his arms, crush her to himself – what he missed out on last night. The thought brought a flush of shame to his face. Even as he tried to pull his gaze away from Jennifer, he knew somewhere deep down inside himself that she was the one holding the keys to turn the engine off.

"Leo," her voice was husky, "this is your Rubicon."

Butcher's voice trembled. "I don't know what that means."

Casually, Jennifer ran a few fingers across her collarbone. "In the days before Julius Caesar's reign, the man who would be emperor had been practicing the art of conquering, training far outside of Rome near the Alps," she touched the tops of her breasts, "until he came to a river nestled inside a valley." Her fingers moved past the necklace to the place where the lace connected. Butcher could see there was a pink flower positioned delicately at the juncture. His eyes followed dutifully while his brain was partially engaged by the story.

"There was a law that said any person who entered the sacred territory with an army," her eyes held his own, "would be considered an enemy against the sacred city, the Eternal City, and thus, would be treated as such." Jennifer shrugged off her shirt and now she stood, vulnerable yet completely in control.

She moved another step closer. "This was the Rubicon River, and according to legend, once Caesar crossed the Rubicon, there was no going back. The choice was difficult, but once made, it could not be unmade." Instead of moving directly to him,

Jennifer walked behind him where her fingers touched his shirt. She could feel his heat. Out of his sight, her voice lowered. Seductively, she moved in next to his back, her breasts barely reaching above his buttocks.

"This your chance, Leopold Jensen. This is your Rubicon with me. All the delights we used to know, the way we connected, the things that I can do… they are all yours. You only have to cross."

Memories, sights, sounds, smells, heat, all coursed through Butcher's brain. It seemed as if the machinery to make decisions was short-circuiting. Once the machine failed, the entire business would come crashing down.

"I know that you have a beautiful wife, two wonderful children, the town loves you, people respect you, you have the best of everything, but you can have me too. No one will ever find out. I will never tell a soul. But I want you to know that I am willing to do whatever it takes to give you what you need to be the happiest man alive." Her hands reached around to his stomach.

Playing the world's most difficult game of tug-of-war, Butcher's conscience strained with bulging veins and muscles while his desire pulled unyieldingly on the other side. The flag over the Rubicon was not moving, but very soon, one side would tire.

"I can tell that you're wrestling with your emotions," Jennifer began to move around to his front again. "But this… is… what… I… *want*. And I like to get what I want."

"Nif," his voice was swallowed up in the room. All the air had been sucked out and a vacuum of static electricity remained. Just one small shock would send the office up in flames.

"Yes?"

"I can't. I just can't. You have to let me go. Someday it will all become clear."

Sensing his resistance, Jennifer stepped back. "Okay," she said slowly, "if you really want me to stop, then leave my glass of wine on your desk, but if you want to have one afternoon delight to overcome the monotony of your miserable, small-town existence, just lift the glass to your lips, and wet them."

He groaned and shut his eyes. "No games. I have to go. You get dressed." His words rang false. His will power was fading.

Jennifer pretended to pout. "Maybe you didn't get to see enough of the Rubicon." Jennifer's eyes lowered and raised again. Slowly she reached behind her back and unclipped her bra. Like a professional dancer, she turned and showed him her naked back while still covering her front.

"I'm all yours," she encouraged, "if you just take... one... little...sip." With each word she dropped her bra a little farther. Butcher's eyes lowered from the skin of her back to the outlines of her matching black, lacy underwear.

Without any control over his body and hand, Butcher reached slowly for the glass of wine on his desk. As he brought it closer to his face, his eyes were drawn momentarily to the shimmering crimson liquid. Red for passion. Red for excitement. Red for stop.

The glass rose closer and closer. Jennifer's smile broadened.

"Come and conquer me," she said.

Butcher made a decision that he knew he might regret for the rest of his life.

Rhonda heard the front door of the house open at five o'clock. Frustrated, she had been trying to contact Butcher all afternoon, but he hadn't answered his phone. Along with picking up the kids, doing the shopping, laundry and everything else, Rhonda had prepared for a town council meeting. She needed Butcher to come home so that she could get everything together by seven o'clock. Normally, she would have called her mother to fill in, but her mother was incapacitated at the moment. She and Carl were still honeymooning throughout the south-west United States. They were due back sometime near the end of February, but Rhonda needed her mother to help with the kids. Because of this, she felt neglected and alone.

Adding insult to injury, Rhonda still felt guilty about the night before, but, there was nothing that she could do about it. Her body and mind just weren't in sync. She just couldn't get it out of her head that each time they made love could be the very last time.

"Hello?" she called out from the kitchen. "Butcher, is that you? It's about time. I've been trying to call you all aftern…" She heard the thump before she saw it. Butcher was leaning against John Deakins, his clothes were wet, as if he had been lying in a puddle of water.

"Rhonda," John said tensely, "run a bath quickly. I think he's starting to get hypothermia."

Rhonda gasped and moved first towards Butcher but then followed John's advice and ran to the bathroom.

"Mommy?" Georgie's voice called out from her bedroom. She had an iPad in her hand.

"Just stay in your room for a little bit. Watch your show."

Georgie looked at her father who was stumbling down the hallway. "What's wrong with Daddy? Unca John, why are you carrying Daddy like that?"

"Don't you worry yourself, Pumpkin," John grunted, as he half carried/half dragged her father into the narrow bathroom. "Your dad just needs to have a bath. He got a little dirty."

"Oh, okay," Georgie turned her attention back to her iPad and returned the bedroom. On the other hand, J.T. stood spectre-like in the hallway. He said nothing while he watched both John and his dad struggle to make it to the tub. His dad's teeth were chattering and his lips were blue.

John sat Butcher on the toilet and spoke to Rhonda. "Get him into the tub. Don't make the water too hot yet, just lukewarm. I'll call the doctor to see if there is anything else that we should do."

Rhonda nodded but then grabbed his arm. "Wait. What happened? Where has he been?"

"He hasn't really told me. Hold on, I'll come back, okay?"

After the phone call, John returned to find Butcher sitting in the bath with the shower running over him. He was still shivering even though Rhonda had turned up the heat. "The doctor said the best thing we can do, once he stops shaking, is to dry him off and put him in bed. Get him under the covers. If you can lay with him and warm him up, he said try that."

Rhonda followed his directions. After a few more minutes of rubbing his arms and legs, massaging the blood back into his extremities, they towel dried him. He was still shivering and his skin looked like a ripe tomato. At least his teeth had stopped chattering. After maneuvring him into the bedroom, Rhonda pulled back the covers and they laid Butcher down. Unfortunately, the sight of him covered up like that brought the very real horror of his coffin-encased body. Rhonda's eyes filled with tears. Without thinking, she began to shed her clothes and Reverend Deakins took his leave.

"I'll watch the kids while you warm him up."

Rhonda did not apologize and quickly joined Butcher in bed. As he shivered, Rhonda pressed her warm flesh next to his skin. He was freezing and his cold made her cold. She clung to him desperately, praying and wishing for him to be all right, even just for a little while longer. Rhonda stroked his hair and kissed his forehead. She tried not to feel guilty about being frustrated with him. She didn't want to imagine what it was like for him – the stress and the fear, the isolation and the inability to do anything but dread the upcoming months.

Chapter 4.

As she snuggled in next to him, she smelled alcohol on his breath. Butcher never drank this early in the day. Could this be his new coping mechanism?

Butcher fell into an agonized stupor. Once she felt him sink into a restless tranquillity, Rhonda slipped from the bed and put her clothes back on. She was cold, but it didn't matter.

She needed to get some answers.

John was on the sofa reading to the children. J.T. was to his right and Georgie on his lap. The story about an adventurous button was one of the children's favorites. John gently placed it into J.T.'s lap when he saw Rhonda emerge from the darkened hallway. J.T. received the book gravely, as if the Bible itself. After John stood, he sat Georgie on the sofa beside her brother. She scooted in close to him, her blanket nestled securely in the crook of her arm and waited for him to continue reading.

He did, yet he kept one eye and two ears open to the whispering adults in the kitchen.

"What's going on?" Rhonda's head leaned in towards John.

"I don't know the whole story, but about 4:30, two high school kids called me on my cell phone. They'd been walking by the football field and saw someone lying in the middle of it. They said that they tried calling Louise, but she didn't answer. So, they approached the 'body' thankful it was still alive. Butcher was incoherent."

Rhonda nodded gravely.

"They recognized Butcher immediately, but they said he had a crazy look in his eyes. He was talking about a boat and a bony old man steering it. Obviously, he was delirious." John looked over at the children who were still reading. He lowered his voice again.

"The three of us picked him up and brought him to my car. I thanked the kids and asked them not to tell anyone. I could see in their eyes that they'd probably already done it, so be prepared for the fallout."

"On the way home, he kept repeating a few words that I could understand."

"What was he saying?" Rhonda asked.

Shamefully, John looked down. "It was garbled, but he kept saying, 'I'm sorry. I'm sorry. Rhonda. Rhonda.'"

"What was he sorry about?"

"I tried to ask him what he'd been doing, but it sounded like he'd taken a bottle of wine and had drunk the entire thing by himself. It could have been two bottles, who knows. He'll probably have a large headache when he wakes up."

Rhonda leaned her head back. Her brown hair hung limply.

"Is this going to be the norm?" her voice dropped to a whisper.

"I don't know," said John honestly, "but we'll have to keep a close eye on him."

"Where did he get the booze? Was he at the Pecker?"

John shook his head. "I already checked there. They don't open until four o'clock, and there's no way he could have drunk enough in an hour to be like this." He paused, hesitant about bringing up the next subject. "He didn't have any alcohol at the office, did he? Any wine?"

Rhonda's face hardened and her cheek muscles clenched. "Are you saying *she* might be involved?"

Lowering his eyes, John glanced towards the children. J.T. was studying his face intently while Georgie traced the pictures in the book with her finger. "I could be wrong, but when his first words are 'I'm sorry and Rhonda,' well, filling in blank spaces..."

Her mind wandered back to the night before. Her thoughts flooded with shame, Rhonda instantly filled with outrage and fury at this woman who was trying to wedge into their happy life. Her jaw twitched and she spoke through clenched teeth. "I'm going to go find her and beat the living daylights out of her." Rhonda pushed away from the sink and stalked to the door. John caught her before she got far.

"Easy. Think. If you go stomping out of here and confront her without knowing what happened, you might find yourself away from Butcher a lot longer than you imagine."

Taking a deep breath, Rhonda exhaled slowly. Much of what she felt was anger with herself. Why hadn't she paid more attention to him? Why hadn't she been more emotionally available? What was wrong with her?

John raised his eyebrows. *What are you going to do? What's your choice?*

Slowly, Rhonda stepped back from the ledge. Anger defeated, she turned from John and moved to her children. "Thank you, John, for being our friend."

"A pleasure." John looked over her shoulder at J.T. and waved. With a sadness beyond his years, J.T. lifted his hand and leaned his head back on the cushion of the sofa.

Chapter 5.

As he approached the north end of Main Street, Jennifer Adams ran into Stedman Boswell. The force was so great he almost fell to the ground. As he glanced up, Stedman saw that he was holding her coat, not wearing it. Her hair was mussed and her cheeks were red as if she was overheated. Eyes unfocused, she looked through him or around him as if he were simply a glass wall. With tears in her eyes, she seemed to be undecided about the direction to which she should go.

"Are you okay?"

Jennifer mumbled something under her breath and then Stedman noticed that she was carrying something in her hand.

A bra.

What in the hell...? Jennifer ran quickly across Main Street to her car. Stedman tried stop her, but his voice caught in his throat. His eyes turned to the Chop Shop where the curtains in the window moved. Stedman was sure that he had caught a glimpse of Butcher's ghostly face retreating into the darkness.

Stedman was stuck at the crossroads of what to do next. His first instinct was to continue towards Jennifer's car to see if she needed assistance, but he couldn't put his body in gear. *Did I just see what I think I saw? Did Jennifer just leave Butcher's office without her bra on?*

Although Jennifer had started the car, as of yet, she had not driven away. Jennifer stared straight ahead, thoughts idling like the vehicle. Wiping her eyes, she reached to her side and shifted the car into reverse. It took three or four attempts to maneuver out into the street, but eventually made it.

Stedman skipped the Chop Shop and entered Peterson's Butchery. Climbing the two stairs, he opened the glass door. Derek was standing behind the counter engaged in conversation with an elderly woman who was arguing with herself about what kind of roast that she and Ted would be having for the night. Derek smirked over Delores' head and nodded to Stedman.

"I'll be right with you."

Stedman shrugged, removed his gloves and waited. Delores chose the pork loin, which was on sale, instead of the beef shoulder.

When she had left the store, Derek turned and yelled back to Nash who was hauling meat from the freezer. As he came out to the front, Nash wiped his hands on the butcher's apron smeared.

"Hey Stud, what's happening?"

Stedman moved closer and lowered his voice. "Have you noticed anything weird with Butcher lately?"

"No more than normal for a nine-fingered man."

"I... I... was just walking by the Chop Shop and..." Stedman looked over his shoulder checking to see if anyone else was listening.

"Spit it out, Buttswill."

"I don't know, maybe I'm being paranoid, but there's something going on with the guy, like he's hiding something."

Nash shrugged. "This is Amicable. Everybody is hiding something."

"No, something serious. Something he wouldn't tell even us."

"What are you talking about, Stedman? Do you think he's having an affair?"

Stedman's face registered shock.

"No way!" Derek exclaimed as he pulled up the barrier in the counter. "You're serious! Butcher?"

"I don't know. He's just been acting so strange and then as I was walking down the street just now..." Stedman paused, unsure of how much to share.

"You gotta tell us now, man. It's like making it to the front of the rollercoaster line and then closing it for repairs."

"Okay," Stedman once more glanced out the window, "I was just coming to find you guys when I see..." Just as he was about to retell what just happened, Butcher appeared on the street outside the butchery. All conversation stopped as they stared at Butcher staggering down the sidewalk. He was wearing his coat. His face looked haggard and worn. The weight of the world draped on his shoulders.

"Why is he walking like that?" Nash asked no one in particular.

"Yeah," Derek agreed as he moved towards the window, "it's like he's dragging his foot."

Nash ran to the door, opened it and yelled into the street. "Hey! Hey, Butcher! You okay? Where are you going?" The cold air blasted Nash's bare arms, but what worried him more was that Butcher did not respond.

"Butcher!" Nash wanted to go after him but it was too cold. "Do you think we should follow him?"

"Yes," Derek said but Stedman stopped them.

"No. He's probably feeling guilty already."

"But who is it? The doctor lady?" Derek's face scrunched up. "She's cute... in a purely non-sexual way."

"I just saw her leave his office. She looked pretty dishevelled."

"That doesn't mean anything," Nash countered. "A lot of people who leave that office look dishevelled. When you reveal your darkest secrets..."

"Yes," said Stedman impatiently, "but most people are not carrying their bra in their hand when they leave the office."

"What?" Nash responded incredulously. "She was holding her bra?"

"Did she look like..." Derek's eyes were wide.

"Like what?" Stedman asked.

"Like she just, you know..."

Stedman rolled his eyes. "No, she looked like she was shocked. She wasn't even wearing her coat."

"I think we should go after him," Nash said.

Stedman shook his head. "I'll follow him and see if I can figure out what's going on."

"Come back," Derek said, "and let us know what happened."

Stedman exited the shop. Just as he was about to turn to follow Butcher, his cell phone rang.

Summer.

The decision to talk to his girlfriend instead of following his friend would have drastic consequences.

Meanwhile, while Stedman Boswell argued animatedly with Summer outside of Peterson's Butchery, Jennifer Adams drove aimlessly northwards towards the edge of Amicable. Her mind roiled with embarrassment over the events of the last few hours. Burning desire had transformed into burning humiliation. Just as she and Butcher were about to consummate their present by re-enacting the past, just as Butcher raised the wine glass to his lips, something happened.

"What are you doing? Why are you stopping?" Jennifer's naked body was pressed close to his.

The glass paused an inch before Butcher's lips. "I... I... don't know."

"This is what we both want," she said, as she rubbed his stomach.

"I know. I know. I can't believe how much I want you." He looked down at her. "You're desirable and every part of me wants to go back to the past - except my heart. But now that we are at the precipice, I don't think I can go through with it."

"It's because of her, isn't it?"

"Yes," he said quietly. It would always be her.

In her ultimate vulnerability, Jennifer knew that the moment had passed, but she didn't want to give up. "I'm just letting you know, Leo, that this moment is a onetime offer."

He nodded. He wished there was another universe, somewhere else where he could try out this life too.

She retreated even further, crestfallen. Reaching for her clothes, she quickly began to put them back on. Butcher turned away conscious of the irony of this movement. When she had finished, she walked to the door of their office.

"I'm going to have to leave Amicable, you know? It would be too difficult for the two of us to..." she motioned with her hand, "...share."

"I understand."

"You'll have to let the clients know that I'm moving on."

"Yes."

Emotions battled within her, but the overriding one was of regret, not just that they had not gone through with the act, but that they couldn't go back. Ironically, a Rubicon had been crossed, but not the one she wanted. Gently, Jennifer Adams shut the door behind her. In a fog, she ran into that insurance agent.

Jennifer drove north, away from Amicable and away from everything she thought would make her happy.

Loneliness had been a constant throughout her life. Wanting to be different and unique carried with it the inevitable singularity of lifestyle. Rarely had she let people in, and even rarer still, had she allowed herself to be vulnerable. Her career allowed her the opportunity to be professionally aloof, but there was never a moment in her life where she could let down all of her defences to be loved. Leopold Jensen had come the closest many years ago, but no one since had stirred that need. Now that he had rejected her a second time, she had a few options: she could run and hide, or she could stay and fight. As she drove north, running seemed the best course of action. The miles passed unceremoniously which cooled her humiliation. Checking her appearance in the rearview mirror, Jennifer Adams felt her previous iteration resurrected and she felt a stirring in her soul. *Even if he won't go back, I will.*

At the next crossroads, a country gravel road, she made a U-turn. She smiled grimly, malevolently.

Leopold Jensen was going to rue his decision.

Rhonda went back into the bedroom. Butcher was lying on his back. His mouth was open and he was snoring. His face had regained some of its color.

Why was he drunk? Why was he in the middle of the football field? Was he trying to commit suicide?

Rhonda sat beside him on the bed and touched his face with the back of her fingers. He felt febrile, but she hoped that was because of returned blood flow rather than sickness. He stirred but made no sound.

J.T. appeared at the bedroom door. "Mom, someone's here."

Taking one more look at Butcher, Rhonda went to the door. J.T. followed where she encountered a shivering Stedman Boswell.

"Hi. Do you mind if I come in?"

Without answering, she stepped aside. Stedman was unnerved by the unwavering gaze of the small boy. J.T. seemed to be reading him just like Butcher used to. Rhonda closed the door behind Stedman who wiped his feet on the rug and moved into the living area.

"What can I do for you, Stedman?" Rhonda asked.

"Is Butcher here?"

Rhonda looked nervously over her shoulder. "He's indisposed."

"Is he okay?"

Crossing her arms, Rhonda peered down at J.T. "Yes, he's fine."

"I was wondering..." J.T.'s eyes were watching him. "Is there somewhere private that we could talk?"

Rhonda frowned. "J.T., go read to your sister again, please." They sat at the table.

"Why are you here, Stedman? Is it because of what happened this afternoon?"

"What did happen?"

She put her chin into her hands. "No one really knows. He either had a bottle of wine with him, or he bought one. Somewhere in the middle of the afternoon he must have decided that he wanted to keep going."

"Do you know what set him off?"

She shook her head. "Do you?"

Stedman's pause was enough to raise Rhonda's eyebrows. "I don't know. I saw him leaving his office, and then when I was in the butchery with the twins, he slogged by."

"Did he look upset?"

Stedman leaned closer to her. "How well have you gotten to know Dr. Adams?"

"Why?"

"I just wonder if she's having an *effect* on him."

"What do you mean?" She knew exactly what he meant, but she wanted to hear it from his mouth.

"Since she arrived in town, things have been changing. People are kind of drawn to her like flies on... you know..."

"I know. I have been feeling the same way."

"And then this afternoon, they both left the office at the same time. Who knows what they were doing – er, I mean, talking about."

"Stedman, you have to tell me what you saw."

"Nothing. I mean, I don't know. Just a feeling…"

"She's an outsider with a history. That means she's dangerous."

Stedman sighed. "I think we should keep an eye on her."

"I agree," Rhonda said.

"Can I help?" J.T. asked, from his perch on the sofa. He was standing on the cushions looking over the back.

"J.T." Rhonda chastized, "you shouldn't be listening in on the conversation."

"I can't help it, Mom."

"No, you can't help. This is for adults to figure out."

J.T. sank back down on the sofa.

"I just want you to know, Rhonda, that I'm always here for you."

Rhonda reached across the table to touch his hand. It was cold, but the touch sent a surge of electricity between the two of them. Stedman covered her hand with his.

At three o'clock in the morning, Butcher woke up with a train rolling through his head. As Butcher put a hand to his temples feeling vaguely nauseous at the same time, he reflected on his own version of events the afternoon before. In spurning Jennifer's advances, he was aware that he had cost himself a moment of happiness. He was not sure of how many of those he had left. A selfish part of him believed that at the end of life, anything and everything should be permissible. Rhonda would respect that, wouldn't she? And yet, in the deciding moment, he had fallen back on the vows he had spoken on their wedding day.

He had promised to take her as his wife to the exclusion of all others. This included Jennifer.

Butcher was unable to sit up. He had to go to the bathroom. In order to do this, he would have to wake Rhonda. That would not be pleasant.

Rolling to his side, he pondered her dimly lit face and the outline of her cheek. Beautiful even in the silhouette, he knew that he had chosen wisely. Even though his mind had betrayed him, his body had passed the test.

Butcher tried to speak but the words would not come. Something was happening with his tongue and his voice box seemed frozen. Fear gripped him. Was this the beginning of the end? Dr. Ditmore had said that slowly he would lose his ability to speak. Gradually he would pull back into himself. It was natural, he said, to want to build walls and distance loved ones from the inevitable, but he cautioned him about keeping them out.

He tried again, resisting the urge to scream. His chest heaved. His voice was stuck. Face contorted, he attempted to pull himself upright, but his elbow was as far as he got. His feet were caught in the folds of the blanket. Fear gripped him. Like a mummy, he was wrapped in dread.

"Can I help you?" A whisper from the doorway. J.T.

Butcher couldn't respond.

"It's okay, Dad, I can see you."

Butcher shook his head. It was far too dark in the room.

Without speaking, J.T. wound his way through the clothes on the floor, the furniture, even stepping past a stacked pile of National Geographic magazines. Though Butcher could not see him fully, he could hear him approach. His tiny feet, though big for his age, seemed to settle, rather than shuffle, across the floor.

"Don't worry, Dad, I can help you." J.T. reached out for his father's arm and pulled him into a sitting position. Butcher's head pounded and throbbed. Finally, a groan escaped his lips.

A wave a nausea crashed over him and left him breathless. Only a desperate strength kept him from retching. In the darkness, he tried to discern his son's face, but he could only make out the shadowy outline of his head. J.T. tugged on his father's arm and with great difficulty, he was able to pull him upright. Butcher, still somewhat drunk, reeled but was steadied by his son's arm. Without turning on the lights, J.T. navigated his father through the chaos to the bathroom where, with great gentleness, he guided his father to the toilet. Thankful, Butcher patted his son's head. He was still unable to speak.

J.T. stood in front of his father as he sat down to urinate. "Are you okay now, Dad?"

Butcher nodded.

"That's good."

Frowning, Butcher wanted to ask him how he could respond, as if he had seen him, but the words…

"I'll help you back to the bed."

Reaching out, he patted J.T. on the shoulder and pushed him towards his own bedroom.

"I'm going to stay with you Dad, until you're ready to go."

Pondering those words and the multilayered truth under them, the hidden and unmistakeable truth that he needed and wanted his family to be with him until the end, Butcher felt a tear appear in his eye.

"You don't have to cry. Everything is going to be okay."

Butcher looked up sharply and the tear reabsorbed. He attempted to ask J.T. about it, but the words didn't come. Something was breaking the impulses between his brain and his mouth and this frustrated him.

J.T. nodded. "Yes, I can see."

Butcher made a circle around the room indicating the darkness.

"Dr. Adams asked me the same question when the lights went off in the office. You and Mom always talk about turning off the lights when you go to sleep, but I never knew what you meant until Dr. Adams explained it."

He pointed at the fingers on his right hand.

"You're holding up two fingers. Three. Five."

Butcher's pounding head spun. Was it possible that J.T. had a gift also? Butcher pulled his pants up quickly and then took his son's hand. Leaving the bathroom, they made their way down the hallway to the kitchen. Butcher turned on the light for himself and blinked with pain as the brightness seared his vision.

J.T., who was not affected by the light, neither squinted nor scrunched up his face, Butcher turned on the coffee pot. Then, as it gurgled and bubbled, Butcher went back to the table and pulled out a pen and paper.

I'm going to write. You answer with your voice, okay?

J.T. took a moment to read what he had written and then nodded.

Do you have any other superpowers?

The little boy's face scrunched up and he shrugged. For the boy, his gift was neither super nor powerful. It just was.

If I turn out the lights, does it make any difference to you?

J.T. shook his head. If his father couldn't speak, neither would he.

Turn off the lights and I'm going to draw a picture on the paper and you're going to tell me what it is, okay?

After jumping down from his seat, J.T. went to the light switch on the wall and killed the light. For a moment, Butcher was thankful for the darkness. He could hear the coffee drip into the waiting pot below. The cuckoo clock continued to click, tick tock, tick tock, endlessly and relentlessly. Time stopped for no one. Butcher could smell the dust. It had been a while since the house had been cleaned.

Butcher's fingers were clumsy and his brain had difficulties enforcing its will on them, but eventually he fashioned a crude boat onto the pad of paper and held it up.

"Boat."

Again.

"Chicken, or bird of some sort."

Three times more.

"Cross. Football. Mountains."

Turn the light back on.

J.T. returned to the light and turned it on.

Wow. You've got a great talent. And you could see my pictures from all the way over there.

"Is that a long ways?"

Butcher nodded.

"I can see from farther than that."

Head cocked to the side, Butcher got up slowly and pulled a coffee cup from the cupboard. After filling it, he turned around and held up the coffee cup and pointed to the small lettering on the side. It read: *Currently unable to engage in conversation.* J.T. was almost ten feet away. He read it slowly as they were big words.

That's very impressive. You've got good eyes.

"Yes, Dad."

How far away can you see things?

J.T.'s eyes strayed outside. "I think I could probably read that mug from over there." He pointed outside.

On the porch?

"No, at the school."

Butcher's blood froze and as he took a sip from his coffee, he was aware in a distant part of his brain that he had burned his lips, but it didn't matter.

Don't tease me.

"I'm not. I can show you."

Let's wait until tomorrow. Does anyone else know about this?

"Only Dr. Adams."

Why didn't she tell us?

"I don't know, Dad. But she seemed excited."

Butcher thought about Jennifer and a pang of guilt, shame and regret washed over him. She deserved so much more...

I don't think you'll be able to see her any more, J.T.

"Why?"

Butcher looked outside the window into the darkness. All he could see was himself. Somehow, the reflection seemed to be fading.

Chapter 6.

Rhonda took Butcher to see Dr. Ditmore a few days after the fateful day on the football field. He tried to convince him to share what happened, but each time Rhonda brought it up, he turned to stare out the window.

Jennifer Adams had gone away. No one knew where she was. He seemed depressed and he treated his family desultorily, more formality than love. Rhonda was frustrated with him, but she swallowed it.

Dr. Ditmore sat behind his desk, a file open in front of him. He didn't need to look at it. Already Leo was showing signs as the disease advanced.

Dr. Ditmore removed his glasses. "Obviously, the inability to speak must be discouraging for you." Butcher didn't look at him, but at a spot in the distance, outside where the trees seemed to be shivering in the cold sunlight.

"Yes," Rhonda replied for both of them, "that has been distressing."

Dr. Ditmore tapped his desk with his fingers. "Rhonda, you said there'd been an… accident. Can we talk about that?"

"He won't talk about it. Something happened last week which set him off and he got drunk and ended up in the snow."

Butcher blinked slowly. Embarrassed by the memory and annoyed that Rhonda was speaking as if he was not present in the room, he grabbed his iPad and began to type.

I made a mistake. Okay?

He did not watch her read it, but he knew that she'd be hurt by the response. She wasn't sure what the mistake was, but she hoped the mistake was simply getting drunk.

"You've got some frostbite, Leo," Dr. Ditmore said.

I can't feel it anyway. My fingers are... Butcher wanted to write a much more profane word, but he chose to refrain.

"What can we expect from here, Dr. Ditmore?" Rhonda asked.

"It's such a hard disease to put a timeline on. Some people go quickly, others hold on for years – Stephen Hawking, for instance, lived for decades."

"What is the average?" Rhonda asked, quietly.

Shifting uncomfortably in his chair, Dr. Ditmore leaned on his desk. "A better question, if I may say so, is how do we help your family enjoy the time you have left."

"No more pulling punches," Rhonda said, the edge of her voice sharp. "Just give it to us."

Butcher typed into his iPad. *I'd rather he pull punches.*

"But we need to know the process. Maybe there are some treatments that haven't been tried yet? Maybe we can do some exercises or try something..." Rhonda's hands flopped through the air as if she couldn't control them.

Dr. Ditmore waited. "I'm sorry, Rhonda. The disease will run its own course. At some point, Leo won't be able to walk. His arms will begin to curl in and his ability to write will stop also. We will organize a communication device run by eye movements. Your insurance company will provide Leo with a motorized wheelchair."

They were quiet as they pondered the finality of the words. Butcher wondered what his last sight would be.

"I am going to recommend that you both take advantage of counseling. It would be helpful as the disease progresses that you would have people to talk to – professional people – who would be able to help you."

Butcher snorted at the thought of visiting a 'professional.'

Rhonda clenched her jaw. The thought of visiting someone like Jennifer Adams turned her stomach. "Thank you for the advice, but Butcher and I are quite good at communicating, even if just through the iPad."

Although she and Butcher had, in the beginning of their marriage, been expressive in sharing their thoughts and ideas, it had been a while since they had opened up. Because the beginning of their relationship had been so abnormal, replicating that kind of openness would be impossible. Butcher would need to *remember* what it was like to be in love with her. He needed to trust Rhonda and in the midst of trusting her, she would have to be his companion to the grave.

Till death do us part...

As they rode home from Dr. Ditmore's office, the road thrummed beneath them, the car's tires threatened to lose their traction every quarter mile or so. The trip was an appropriate metaphor for their life: unseen slippery spots, black ice over a previously easy stretch of road. They had to slow down.

"What are you thinking?" Rhonda asked, as she drummed her fingers on the steering wheel.

Butcher switched the iPad to voice reader, allowing Rhonda to keep her eyes on the road. The digital voice, so completely foreign and odd, seemed out of place, but his words were distinctly Butcheresque.

I don't know. Everything is kind of surreal, like I've stepped to the edge of a cliff while sightseeing. It's a black hole – the end of the world kind of stuff.

"What do you see at the end of the world?" Rhonda asked, quietly.

Butcher turned to his left to look at his wife's face. A few days back, they had lain in bed wondering some of these same questions. It was there that the downward spiral began. He remembered holding her in his arms but then unbidden, the vision of Jennifer standing unclothed in his office appeared. For some reason he tried to hold both images simultaneously in his mind. It was one or the other – or neither, but not both.

I always thought that I would die of old age. Perched between a couple of cushions at home, in our bed, staring at photographs of my kids, grandkids, great grandkids and my heart would just stop. Like the shutter closing on a camera. Like George.

"That sounds beautiful."

Right now, though, each day is about losing something new.

A tear ran down Rhonda's cheek.

The unfairness of this disease. Listen to the voice that's coming from the iPad. I want to punch it in the face.

Rhonda choked out a laugh and then wiped the tear from her cheek. Briefly, she dared a look at him. He was beautiful. "Butcher," she said quietly, and waited for him to turn back towards her, "what happened the other day?"

I don't want to talk about it.

"But I do."

The irony of her words, the wedding promise, hurt his ears. Before he spoke, he wondered if these would be the last words his voice ever uttered to his wife.

"I can't."

"Butcher…"

Maybe someday, but not now. Not now.

They were quiet for a few miles. But then, just as they were approaching Amicable, a question formed in Rhonda's mind, one that she had kept at bay for a while. Her heart desperately wanted to hear just a few more phrases, terms of endearment, maybe even sorrow and forgiveness. Gifts given and gifts received. Not only was she beginning to understand what was happening, but the town, also, would need to know. They would need to understand how their beloved butcher was now going to fade from their midst.

"How are we going to tell the town?"

He shrugged and stared out the window. They passed Swenson's farm. Johnson's. Gilbertson's. The Mexican restaurant and finally, as they entered the Amicable city limits, Butcher turned back to her again and typed into his iPad.

I don't want to tell them. I just want to be normal.

"I know, but it can't be normal."

Butcher wanted to write, 'tell me about it,' but did not.

"How would you feel about after the service on Sunday when everyone is gathered together?"

Butcher did not say anything.

"I'll talk to John and Leslie. I'm sure it will be fine. Then, people can start talking with us about this."

Silence.

"I need to talk to people. It will help me."

Butcher's teeth ground. *Help you?* He thought.

"That's settled then. Thank you, Butcher." Passing the school, children were playing outside at recess. They were oblivious to the cold. Hearts beating healthily, hard, pumping blood through their toes and fingers, they packed snow into hard balls and tossed them at unsuspecting classmates. Eventually, minor scuffles would ensue, mostly verbal, but then back to playing. Back to life without any thought of the end of the world.

"I'm going to get you inside and then go for a run, if you don't mind." She said this apologetically as if wondering whether it was an appropriate thing to ask. Butcher sighed knowing that the sound of it would bring about a deeper sense of guilt for her, but he took a strange pleasure in it knowing that he could affect her.

"I don't have to go. We could go for a walk together." Butcher snorted at her sentence.

"Sorry," she said, as they pulled into the driveway, "we could have a cup of coffee together and then maybe watch a movie or something…"

No, he typed, *you go for your run. Enjoy yourself.*

The robotic computer couldn't express sarcasm, but Rhonda inferred it from the words and from Butcher's tug on the handle of the door to let himself outside.

Rhonda stared at his back and shook her head. Thankfully, she was going for a run.

Butcher was not that upset with Rhonda. It gave him a chance to explore the extent of his son's visual acuity. As they had driven past the school, he had noticed that J.T. was standing by himself next to the ladder of the slide. He looked like a saddened and wizened little old man contemplating the universal difficulties of climbing to the top of the world and the reason for doing so. Watching, endlessly watching, J.T. scanned his schoolmates wondering what they were like and how he could approach them without feeling self-conscious.

J.T. saw his parents pull into the driveway of their house. When his dad exited the car, he raised a hand. Although he was two hundred yards away, J.T. could see the twin chevrons of his father's frowning eyebrows. He knew that his dad was frustrated by something.

Ten minutes later, he saw his mother leave the house in her running gear and begin sprinting away, far, far away, from everything. Thirty seconds after her departure, his father appeared at the doorway and shuffled out in his winter jacket. Knowing that J.T. was watching, Butcher motioned for J.T. to come to the fence on the far side of the playground. J.T. smiled and began to sprint across the snow-covered playground to his dad. His father needed him. He ran faster, his arms and legs awkward because of the growth spurt. Once, J.T.'s feet caught on a small molehill of snow almost sending him to the ground, but he recovered.

When J.T. stuck his mittened fingers into the chain-link fence, it seemed like they were separated by a prison fence. As

Butcher and his son stood on opposite sides, the father looking from above at the son below, there was a casual intimacy and frustration at the same time. Together but separated. Butcher held up his iPad to J.T. who read it.

Go stand where you were and I'm going to hold up some words. I want to test how good your sight is.

It took J.T. a few moments to figure out all the words, but eventually he made it and nodded at his father. He smiled and raised his hand to the fence. Like family members and prison inmates separated by glass, Butcher touched his son's.

J.T. ran back to his position by the slide and Butcher sidled slowly backwards ten steps to the street where he held up the word, 'monkey' written in forty-point font. Then, the next, 'mouse,' in twenty-eight. Lastly, the word 'peanut' in twelve-point font. Butcher had a tough time reading it even from a close distance. He knew that there should be no way J.T. could read the words from the distance, but a little part of him held out hope.

After he had held them up, he raised a thumb and signalled for J.T. to come back to him. When he was halfway there, the school bell rang, signaling that he needed to go back to the classroom. Caught between the rules and his father's insistence that he continue the path to the fence, J.T. made a snap decision and ran to the fence. He heard the on-duty teacher blowing the whistle and shouting his name to come back.

Butcher's face, raised eyebrows and open mouth, signalled a question: *Well?*

J.T. smiled and put both his hands on the fence.

"Easy," he said with a smile. "Monkey, mouse and peanut." J.T. looked over his shoulder at the teacher, who was not happy about having to stomp across the playground to capture one of the escapees. "I have to go, Dad." He retracted his fingers from the fence and began the awkward sprint back across the playground toward the teacher who had stopped and crossed her arms. J.T. avoided her and finished the journey well ahead of the cold educator who stared with frustration at Butcher.

Butcher was smiling and crying at the same time.

Chapter 7.

Instead of returning to Amicable, Jennifer Adams, drove all the way to Sioux City.

Splurging on accommodation, she enjoyed an entire week of non-wood panelled walls, no shag carpet, no ancient garage sale furniture, and, for goodness sake, no Cornell crockery. The sound of the plates clattering together made her shiver.

She luxuriated in the deep, soft bed with down comforter and thick curtains over the windows. Her living area was tastefully decorated with contemporary art wall hangings. Room service was heavenly. Jennifer even splurged on a hundred dollar spa.

Every time she looked in the mirror, she felt shame. Jennifer had changed everything to fit into the little town: she cut her hair shorter, her dangling earrings were replaced by small hoops. Stupid blue jeans. After telling Leo that she would not be returning, Jennifer was confident she would be faithful to that vow. Even though she left her meagre belongings in the little house on the edge of the town, she thought, *Good riddance to good rubbish.*

Jennifer Adams, though, had never been a quitter.

It took two days of convalescence away from Amicable before Jennifer felt human again. She wasn't sure how many times she had looked into the mirror and grimaced, wondering how she was going to wipe the little town from her psyche. Amicable felt like a booger on her face.

On the last day, Jennifer cut her hair. The stylist created sharp edges and layers. Then, on a whim, she decided to have her hair tinted. Perusing the spectrum of dyes, she chose the one that would stick out most prominently in Amicable, one that would certainly cause the ladies to shake their heads and stare, tsk tsk and smile without smiling.

Green.

After her hair styling, she decided to get tattooed. Each one of the tattoos depicted something that would probably be offensive to Amicableans: A naked female dancer with a 'co-exist' symbol across her chest and a five-pointed marijuana leaf. She didn't smoke marijuana, but the symbolism of freedom was important.

Surveying her new Leprechaunish look, the brightly mascaraed eyes tinted purple with glitter, her shapely neck now scarred with the tattoo, Jennifer nodded and smiled. The transformation to the past was complete.

Back to work.

Angela Chandler knocked on her son's bedroom door.

"Yes," he grumbled. She could tell he was rolling over to look at his phone.

"Seven-thirty, Sweetheart. We've got church in a couple of hours." She heard him roll over again.

An hour later, Demetrius showed up in the kitchen ready for church.

"Good morning."

His father didn't look up from the iPad but smiled and repeated the phrase.

"Good morning, Sunshine," his mother chirped happily as she sprinkled various spices on top of the beef roast and surrounding vegetables. "How did you sleep?"

"Like the dead."

"That's nice."

"What's for breakfast?"

"Scrambled eggs and some toast in the toaster. I made some strawberry jam last summer, so you can have some of that."

Demetrius rubbed his hands together and moved towards the food. As he busied himself with breakfast, his father lowered the iPad. "What did you do last night?"

After licking the butter knife smeared with strawberry jam, he spoke without looking at his father. "I went to the bowling alley. Had a couple of drinks with the fellas."

"Is it good to be back?" His father asked.

"Yeah, it's nice. Cold. Interesting, too."

"What do you mean?" His mother lifted the roasting dish and carried it to the oven where she put the heat on low. By the time they left for church, the aroma would have begun to waft through the house.

Demetrius took a large bite of the toast. He gestured with the half-eaten bread as he turned towards his father to sit at the table. "Supposedly something happened with Butcher last week. Do you know what it was?"

Angela put the roast in the oven and closed the door with her foot. "I heard something about that – just a rumor."

Demetrius rolled his eyes. "Me too. I heard that something happened between him and that psychologist, what's her name?"

"Dr. Adams. Jennifer Adams. She's lovely," Angela said.

"According to Shania, Butcher came into the Pecker kind of stumbling and mumbling. She thought he was drunk already, but he shook his head. After he had a couple of drinks, she said he kind of stared at himself in the bar mirror for a while. She asked him a few questions, but he wouldn't respond. Eventually he just left by himself."

"Maybe he just needed to let off some steam," his father posited.

"Maybe."

Angela started to speak and then lifted an index finger to her lips. Remembering something, she turned to the fridge, but continued to keep up her commentary.

"Carley was saying something yesterday about how he's been really distracted and then," she returned from the fridge with a Jell-O mold, "he and Rhonda have been spending a lot of time in Clancy. Nobody seems to know why, but some people seem to think it's…" she lowered her voice, "…marriage counseling."

Demetrius finished the last bites of his food and used his finger to wipe up any excess strawberry jam that he'd missed. He licked his finger. "They could be shopping."

"Oh, I know, I know," his mother dolloped a healthy scoop of whipped cream on top of the orange mold with bits of pineapple and carrot embedded in it, "but I'm getting worried about them."

"Maybe you should try talking to them?"

"I could never do that," his mother responded as she blew a strand of hair out of her face. "They'd think I was prying."

"Yes, it's much better that you discuss it with your friends, irrespective of the actual facts."

Angela looked hurt.

"I'm not picking on you, Mom, but maybe you should see how they're doing rather than just watching what they're doing?"

"Thank you, Demetrius," his mother responded tetchily.

"You're welcome."

Jennifer Adams was late for church, but when she showed up, she definitely made an appearance. As she stepped through the back doors, all heads turned towards her one pew at a time. Instead of sitting in the back row, Jennifer walked to the front. The singing quieted the further she entered. The congregation could not sing while staring at her green hair, her newly minted 'co-exist' tattoo on her neck, which was still red and puffy, and the fact that she was wearing a floral print knee-length dress with red woollen tights underneath. Her appearance was such a distraction that even Jim the Organist fumbled. Jennifer took a seat in the front row on the right side at least fifteen pews in front of everyone else.

When John Deakins turned to face the congregation from his place at the front, he wondered what had caused the disturbance. It took milliseconds for his attention to be drawn to the fluorescent green head-cap sitting in the front row. Jennifer smiled at him. He glanced over at Butcher and Rhonda who were both staring at Jennifer. Rhonda's eyes, full of jealous fury, drilled holes in the woman, while Butcher's widened with surprise. She told him that she would not be returning. But the true shock was not that she had returned to Amicable but the manner in which it had happened. For Butcher, this was a significant moment of déjà vu. From this position, in a church, in a small town, a universe and fifteen years from the last time he saw her like this, he was stunned.

When the service finished with a confused fanfare by a perplexed organist, the congregation did not immediately move. J.T. looked up at his father, at Dr. Adams, then to his mother and finally resting on Unca John. Something was about to happen; something distinctly unpleasant.

"Well," John said, "we're going to have coffee downstairs, whoever wants to join." He paused, but no one moved. "Is everyone okay?"

"I have something that needs to be said," Rhonda said softly.

"Did you want to use a microphone?"

She shook her head and made her way to the center aisle. John had no idea how she was going to explain what was going on in their lives. Rhonda took a deep breath.

"Many of you are aware of what happened last week with Butcher." Guiltily, most of the congregation shifted their eyes.

"But you don't know the entire story. You see…" a pause, along with the fidgeting of her hands, manic, nervous energy, "there is something going on with Butcher."

"Why isn't Butcher telling us?" Derek Peterson called from near the back.

"Because he can't," Rhonda said quickly.

A murmur ran through the gathering. Even Jennifer frowned.

"What does that mean?"

Rhonda's hands stopped as she composed herself. Her eyes rested on Demetrius Chandler. He tilted his head sideways wondering what Rhonda was trying to say.

"Slowly, my husband is losing the ability to speak." Gasps.

Georgie moved in next to her father and grabbed his arm. "What is Mommy talking about, Daddy? Why can't you talk?"

He touched her face and turned his attention back to Rhonda.

"Butcher has Amyotrophic Lateral Sclerosis. Motor Neuron Disease. Lou Gehrig's Disease." A collective moan arose. One hundred people racked their brains trying to remember what Lou Gehrig's disease was. Many of the kids were wondering, 'Who is Lou Gehrig?'

"In the last months, we've been meeting with doctors and specialists trying to understand how to fight this." Rhonda glanced at Jennifer's face and felt a guilty pleasure that she seemed destroyed by the news. "In the next months, the doctors don't know how long, Butcher will lose muscle function. Already, the disease has taken much of his speech."

Derek and Nash passed a non-verbal, instinctive message between themselves while Stedman Boswell rose out of his seat for a moment. He, like everyone else, seemed stuck – immobile – reflections of Butcher: no speech, no swallowing, no movement and eventually, no breath.

"Although Butcher won't be able to speak, he can still communicate. Nothing will happen to his brain or his intellect. His senses stay intact so please continue to make contact with him. ALS is not a transmittable disease. You cannot catch it. Unfortunately, there is no cure. It sounds clinical and sterile how I'm saying it, but I'm just trying to hold it together." Her voice quivered, but she got control of it.

She was about to sit down, when a voice rose from the back. It was a nameless voice. It could have been anyone, or everyone at the same time. It trembled. "How long does he have to live?"

Rhonda's head sagged slightly. Butcher's head was bowed. John Deakins was deep in prayer; Jennifer Adams was uncomfortable now to be in such an obvious place.

"It's different for everyone... We'll be closing the Chop Shop in the next couple of weeks..."

Another voice from the back. "Could Dr. Adams take over for a little while – maybe just until... you know... a little later?"

Jennifer did not look around at the speaker but she was pleased that someone in the small town appreciated what she brought. "No, I don't think that's a good idea," Rhonda didn't look at her. "We'll thank Dr. Adams for her work to this point and allow her to go back to wherever she came from." Rhonda's words seemed a bit rude.

"Just for a little while," the voice pleaded.

Rhonda looked at Butcher who did not answer positively or negatively.

"We'll talk about it."

With a sense of finality, the questions stopped. Each member of the congregation seemed to fall, or sag back into their seats, heavy of heart and thought.

Demetrius Chandler watched Rhonda Jensen ease back to her seat, and without thinking, she placed a hand on Butcher's back. Somewhere in his mind, Demetrius was aware of the significance of the hand that rested between his shoulder blades, and already a picture was forming in his mind. It seemed as if disease was bringing out the most creative parts of his brain.

He had an idea.

Chapter 8.

Butcher and Rhonda circled each other like human satellites each with different trajectories and orbits. Neither was quite able to enter the gravitational field of the other to understand what they were thinking. There was enough gravity pulling them to the ground, pulling them apart, pulling them to pieces. Rhonda did her best to take care of Butcher's needs, but she also felt guilty about her sense of abandonment. This sense of guilt drove her to jog longer each day, drowning in the air, gasping for a sense of joy and realizing that it would be quite a while before she surfaced beyond the nightmarish reality.

Unconsciously, Butcher slowly began to resent his wife. He resented her for her health and for her movement, the way that she could hold the kids, tickle them, walk uninhibited with them down the street without wondering which small crack in the cement might cause her to fall. He resented her for her ability to sleep at night. He resented her for her continued ability to be an active part of the community while he lost the centrifugal battle and was sent to the edges of communal life.

In turn, he began to resent Amicable and its unconscious attempts to act as if everything would eventually return to normal, that he would move back into the Chop Shop or the butchery. He would spend his Saturday nights at the Greedy Pecker and his Sunday mornings at St. Clements. The perpetuation of this myth, that life would always *be*, was omnipresent on his mind and the empty conversations that had brought such joy to him about the weather, about the high school football team, seemed just that: empty.

He wanted someone to discuss the important things. He wanted someone to scoop out all the pity from their faces (well-intended, yes) and dump it, so they could get into the nitty gritty of life and figure out how to live in the midst of dying.

One morning, Butcher made his way past the playground southwards towards the Deakins' residence. John and Leslie were sitting just inside the porch window in the living room. Their faces were framed by the window and they seemed content. Leslie was sipping from a cup while John was reading a book. He was desperate for someone to talk to. Although Dr. Ditmore had said he'd need professional counseling, he just needed amateur counseling by a friend: someone who knew him, who could commiserate and communicate in a way that didn't leave him sorrier than before.

Climbing the steps with effort, Butcher struggled to the front door where he knocked instead of ringing the bell. His fingers could not quite curl up into a ball anymore, so the open fingered knock lacked force.

John smiled as he opened the door. "We were just thinking about coming to see you."

Butcher raised a hand in greeting.

"Hi Butcher. Do you want to come in for a while? I'll make you some tea," Leslie asked.

Butcher nodded and pulled his right leg up and over the threshold. John's eyes followed his friend's sloping shoulders.

Butcher flopped down into a chair knowing that the effort to unfold himself from it would be difficult, but he wanted to retain this normalcy as long as possible.

John studied Butcher. His hair was mussed and he hadn't shaved for a few days. He wore long grey sweatpants so he didn't have to manipulate buttons, zippers or belt buckles. Butcher looked like a vagrant. Butcher let John help him with his coat. After a short silence, Leslie entered with two steaming hot teas.

"How are you doing?" John asked. "Or is that the stupidest question in the world?"

Butcher haltingly took a sip of his tea, burned his lips and grimaced, but he was thankful that neither Leslie nor John attempted to take it from him.

Retrieving his iPad, Butcher typed a response. *It's actually the question no one ever asks.*

"Really?" John answered.

Nodding, Butcher took a deep breath as if he was going to speak. *People will talk about the normal stuff, the weather, you know, but nobody asks me how I am. Or if they do, they kind of cover their mouths as if they've said a swear word.* He paused. *Does that make sense?*

John nodded.

It's weird, Butcher wrote, *I can't tell if people don't actually want to know how I'm doing or if they just can't handle it if I tell them that it sucks. I feel like most people are beginning to pull back already.*

"I'm sorry," John nodded.

It feels like everything in my life is breaking. My health, my hands, my heart – but worst of all, it feels like my soul is actually splitting in half. I can't understand what is going on. I'm angry. I'm upset. I want to go out and throw snowballs with Georgie. I want to run down the street with J.T. I want to make love to my wife, but it's all broken. He looked up at his friends who were staring at Butcher's fingers. *I resent almost everyone. On television, I watch happy people doing happy things and I resent them for their happiness. I'm resentful of Connie because she's found love and I'm losing it. I'm resentful of Linda Harmsen because she's 'only' got cancer and she's getting better. I feel guilty about being resentful and I feel like I'm just sitting in a bathtub and all the water's going down slowly. I should have a lot more years of living, of sitting in the bath.*

"That's an amazing metaphor, Butcher," Leslie said. "You don't have to feel guilty. It's perfectly natural."

But what do I do? How do I enjoy anything when I could die any time? It's the only thing that I can think about.

John bit his lip. "How honest do you want me to be?"

273

Butcher snorted. *What are you going to say that could make things any worse?*

"Fair enough," John responded as he leaned forward in his chair and tented his fingers before him. "Sooner or later you're going to have to make a decision. Do you want to spend the rest of your life being bitter, knowing it isn't going to get better, or do you want to spend the rest of your time pleasantly surprised by the ways that you have made an impact on the lives of other people? Sulking is okay for a while, but eventually..."

That's easy for you to say...

John nodded. "That's the piece that needs to be laid to rest, and that pun is intended." John swallowed. "If you wallow in your resentment, you will push everyone out of your life that you want in it. Let the devil have the disease but *you* have the joy. We should all be living in this way."

Butcher heard and understood John, but it frustrated him that he would confront him on his attitude. He should be feeling sorry for him, praying for a miracle, or something like that. That's what preachers do.

That's a nice platitude.

"What do you want me to say, Butcher? Do you want me to say that if you just stay positive, everything's going to turn out roses? Do you want a 'Buck up little camper' and a tap on the shoulder and a shove out the door, 'Hope you feel better tomorrow?' Or do you want the truth that we waste a lot of time, all of us, by distracting ourselves from conversations like these?"

Butcher's eyes were wide.

"Okay, so now you've got me riled because your disease, your damn Lou Gehrig's Disease, is eviscerating me because my best friend is disappearing before my eyes." The tap on his tears and words opened. "You stopped today, God knows why, but I lied to you before: I didn't want to stop and see you today because it's painful for *me*. This pain of watching you suffer and wage a battle in which I cannot help you, is killing *me* too." John's voice hitched and his lips quivered.

"All my life, Butcher, I've been avoiding relationships for fear of this very thing. That they'd break down, or somehow the other person would disappoint me, and I would put on my clerical collar and pretend – that's a good word (without being pretentious) - that I was too spiritual to feel what the 'lay person' would feel, because I had some kind of deeper connection with God. But that's bullshit, Butcher. It's all bullshit. You're dying, and I don't have the will to find another best friend."

Butcher watched his best friend begin to cry. Leslie moved over to him and placed an arm around his shoulders. John's shoulders shook and Butcher wished with all the might in his body that he could get up, to move closer, but the disease...

Butcher typed into his iPad.

I need to hug you.

John looked up, his eyes red, still weeping and fell from his chair and crawled to Butcher's feet. There at the foot of his weak friend, his frailness on full display, John pulled himself up and positioned his head on Butcher's knees. The sobs came in starts and stops. Leslie knelt beside him while Butcher leaned over and laid his hands and head on John's back.

Butcher drew in a steadying breath and then leaned in very close to John's ear forcing the words from his ruined mouth. "My friend," he slurred, "I love you. I'm going to miss you."

New spasms of grief washed over them. For the next minutes the pastor and his wife, along with the treasured friend who had brought them together, floated on an infinite sea of sorrow. No human in existence is ever prepared for this kind of suffering. When it happens, the only hope is to have someone to hold onto.

When John finally sat up, Butcher's lap was wet with tears. He laughed and his nose was running.

Butcher smiled also. *You got my iPad wet.*

"I feel like Mary Magdalene washing your feet with my tears."

Don't even think about it. I haven't washed my feet for weeks.

As Leslie went into the kitchen to retrieve some tissues, John pulled up a chair next to Butcher. "I'm going to be in this position a lot in the upcoming months, and I don't want you to push me away."

Butcher held up three fingers like a Boy Scout as a promise.

John looked up at Leslie. "Now, we need to talk about you and Rhonda." Then he added. "And you and Dr. Adams."

Here we go.

As Rhonda walked down the last aisle towards the cash register, she paused to pick up a magazine. Something to distract her for a few moments. As she was scanning the pictures of shiny, happy people, she felt a pressure on her elbow.

Stedman.

"Hi," she said lightly, replacing the magazine. "Fancy seeing you here."

"It's a good day to go shopping."

"Shouldn't you be working? It's Monday morning."

He sighed. "I suppose, but I'm tired of sitting in my office."

"So you're having a good day?" Rhonda asked, sarcastically.

He smiled. "How about you?"

"I'm fine."

Stedman moved in front of her cart. "I need to talk to you."

"What is it?"

"In private," he whispered.

Chapter 8.

Stedman waited impatiently at the other end as the bagger took her time. When she was done and the groceries were paid for, Stedman helped carry them to the car.

"Just get into the car and come to my house. I'll make you some coffee and we can talk about it."

"Okay." Stedman hopped into the minivan.

Back at the Jensen house, Rhonda was embarrassed by the disarray. Rhonda cleared some space and they placed the bags of groceries on the table. She turned on the electric coffee pot and once the coffee had percolated, she brought him a mug.

"All right, Stedman, what's going on?"

He fidgeted. "Ever since your announcement at church, there's just something that I needed to tell you. Something... well... it seems like it would be important for you to know."

"Sounds serious."

"You know that day when Butcher was on the football field?"

"How could I forget?"

"I saw something that day that I haven't told anybody." Stedman sucked in a deep breath and held it. Then, he spoke. "I was walking down the street to visit the Petersons when I neared the corner of the Chop Shop and literally ran into Jennifer Adams."

"So?"

"She looked really upset, like something had happened."

"How could you tell? Was she crying?"

"I think so. But she wasn't wearing her coat, no hat – just bustling out into the frigid winter street without winter clothes."

"Maybe she was hot."

Stedman looked into the eyes of this woman who had been such an infatuation for him a few years before. And now that his girlfriend wasn't around much, and Butcher wasn't going to be around… The thought made him flush with shame, but *feelings were real no matter what, right? It was only if you acted on them.*

"She was so warm that she was holding her bra in her hands."

"What? What are you talking about?"

"When we ran into each other, she was not wearing any underclothes."

"But that's ridiculous! Why would she be carrying them? Unless…" Rhonda's mind took an incredible leap. "No, there's no way."

"I'm only telling you what I saw."

"But… but… he wouldn't rape her, would he? I mean, Butcher is not that kind of person. And certainly, with their history, he wouldn't have to resort to…" Rhonda's horror magnified, recalling her own difficult past with Gus.

"I don't think so. But she didn't look happy."

"I can't believe this, Stedman. And why are you telling me this? What do you have to gain by it?"

"Nothing!" He held up his hands. "Honestly, I'm just trying to protect you. I just don't trust Dr. Adams. She's got a lot of people in town convinced that she's legitimate. Your mom's friends, they all think the sun shines out of her. Some of the residents quite openly proclaim that this town has needed a professional counselor for years, never mind the fact that Butcher has done an incredible job helping people. The people are indebted to him."

"Damn right they are."

"But this little midget shows up strutting her stuff and the fact that she and Butcher were an item all those years ago and suddenly they're sharing an office and now who knows what else…"

"Did you talk to Butcher?"

"I tried. After Jennifer got into her car and disappeared, I walked by the shop and noticed a 'closed for staff meeting' sign on the door. I thought it was unusual since Hossein and Jennifer are the only staff there."

A few pieces of a dark puzzle came together in their minds.

"So, I went into Petersons and as we were talking, Butcher staggers by. And I mean that he was staggering, like he was drunk. Now that I think back, it seemed like he had a bulge in his coat pocket which could have been a bottle of something."

"Did you try to stop him?"

"I did. I ran out the door and called his name but he kept going. He must have just gone to the bowling alley to keep loading up and then eventually John found him." Stedman paused. "Has he talked to you about that afternoon?"

Rhonda ground her teeth. "No."

"Look, I'm sorry for bringing it up, but with Jennifer back in town, even if she does look like dwarfish cotton candy, you never know what kind of ideas might be running through his mind."

Rhonda could imagine a few ideas. *How could he? After all she had done for him. AND he was sick. That was sick!*

"What are you thinking, Rhonda? What's going on?"

"Nothing. Maybe it's time you left, Stedman. I need to do some thinking about this."

Stedman stared at his untouched coffee. "Okay, but let me know if you need anything. Anything at all."

Rhonda didn't answer.

Before he stood, Stedman paused, fighting with both conscience and emotions.

"Rhonda," Stedman said softly, "I need to tell you something else."

Rhonda looked up.

"You know," he stuttered slowly, "that when I first came to Amicable, my intentions were unprofessional... and yet, well, I've been doing some thinking lately, that I needed to tell you..."

"Just spit it out, Stedman," Rhonda said, irritably.

He took a deep breath. "I love you."

Rhonda's jaw dropped. "Excuse me?"

Stedman blew out the breath that he'd been holding. "I know this sounds crazy, and I know this probably isn't the best time to tell you this, but I've been holding it inside for a long time."

"I... don't know what to say..." Of course she had known of his desire when he first moved to Amicable, but he and Summer seemed so happy.

"Look, Rhonda, there has always been a piece of me, a large piece, really, that has always been attracted to you. I know that you and Butcher have always had a happy marriage and until recently, I would have guessed..." his voice trailed off.

"Let me get this straight, Stedman. You have kept these feelings for me hidden by dating Summer? Does she know about this?"

"Of course not, and to be totally honest, I'm not sure why I just revealed it to you. Maybe I just wanted to get it off my chest."

"Or," Rhonda ground her teeth, "you thought with Butcher's impending departure, you might be able to somehow fill in the gaps."

Stedman realized what he had said and flushed with shame. "Oh, Rhonda, I'm so sorry. That's not the way I meant it. I didn't even think about it. I just blurted out what I'd been feeling."

"Stedman..."

"I should go." He pushed back his chair and almost knocked it over in his haste.

"Wait, just a second."

"No, I think I've done enough talking."

As he moved, Rhonda caught his arm and pulled him towards her. Unintended, he fell into her, and without thinking he kissed her. He had dreamed of what kissing her would be like, and as his lips connected with hers, something exploded inside of him. Rhonda, caught off guard, could not react quickly enough to stop him. Surprised, the kiss lingered and without thinking, she let it happen. It had been such a long time since the flutter of unique, illicit feelings had occurred. She felt shocked. After a moment, she found that he was holding her cheeks in his hands.

"Oh," she said softly, and pulled back. "That was not what I was expecting."

Stedman's face was flushed. "I'm... not... sorry." He pulled his hands from her face but she caught them in her own on the way down.

"We can't do this."

"I know," he attempted to pull away.

"Not now."

Stedman's eyes widened. "Not now? What does that mean?"

"It just... I don't know; I'm confused. I'm terrified by the future. And this," she squeezed his hands, "just adds another level of complexity that I'm not quite prepared for."

His eyes widened and he took a small step closer. "So you're saying I should wait..."

Silence ensued and an unspoken and unknown response passed between them. Time seemed to stop until, at the worst moment, the front door opened.

It was hard for Jennifer Adams to look at herself in the mirror. In the maelstrom and aftermath of Leo's revelation, Jennifer found herself pondering over and over and over how to best re-insert herself back into his life. Yes, the rejection had been painful, but even more painful would be watching him waste the remaining time of his life in that cesspool of a town. His wife, though well-meaning, was not equipped to handle a man of his magnitude. She couldn't appreciate him and his giftedness. He was like a priceless opal unearthed, swirling in a multitude of colors, but Rhonda did not know how to polish him, to bring out those lights. When Jennifer looked at him, she saw him as he could be, as he was all those years ago, with his vivacity and kindness. Now that he only had a short time to live, Jennifer wanted to extract him from this sucking, festering bog.

Ethically, she knew what she was plotting was wrong – very wrong. In fact, she had already stepped to the other side of that river, the bridge burned after her, so there was no turning back. Dr. Jennifer Adams knew, though, that Leo Jensen was the only good and pure thing that had ever happened to her life and she would give it all for one more shot.

Jennifer studied her reflection in the mirror. The week before, Jennifer entered Harmsen's Hair and Beauty and changed her hair color from green to a gentle shade of lilac with silver ends. She needed more subtlety, but not traditionality. Midwestern brown would not catch his eye, but lilac would cause him to look again. Checking her clothes, she smoothed down her dress. Even though it was still cold in Amicable, she needed him to be watching. Her stockings were black which seemed to elongate her short legs, and her high boots – pirate boots as he used to call them – came up to her knees which added an extra inch to her height.

After putting the finishing touches on her makeup, Jennifer made kissing noises with her lips. The bright red lipstick stood in contrast to her black dress.

Walking into the living room of her rental house, she sighed. The table was stacked with paperwork. Letters from her practice back East were threatening to become an avalanche. Her boss was demanding a quick return or 'she could begin looking for other career opportunities.' The first time she read those words she felt an icy dread grip her, but the more she thought about it, she wondered why she was scared to start over. Why shouldn't she and Leo go somewhere, maybe west? to live out the rest of his life, she could take care of him, let him enjoy the months before...

She shook her head.

Grabbing her coat and keys, Jennifer stepped out the door. It was 8:55 a.m. and she had an appointment at school.

After Demetrius returned to college, Kelly asked him about his trip, but he had difficulty explaining what had happened. Even before he returned to the dorm room, he drove his car to park outside the art room. Almost jogging to his workspace, Demetrius threw open the door so that he didn't lose the picture in his head. As he burst into the room, Ken saw him and attempted to greet him, but Demetrius didn't stop. There was only room for one voice in his head, and it belonged to Butcher.

For two weeks, Demetrius drew, scrunched up, trashed, drew, scrunched up and trashed. This was a project that demanded perfection of the aesthetic, composition, detail and meaning. Life was perfect – perfectly messy and beautifully tragic and wonderful. Thus, the project required a different eye for movement and emotion in a static sculpture. To create and portray the imperfectly perfect life and its transformation to the perfectly imperfect life would be to imagine a true sense of tragic drama.

Demetrius grew frustrated – more frustrated than he had ever been – but for the first time in a long time, the frustration was a source of motivation. Because the artwork was motivated by altruism and artistry, rather than for a grade, or financial reward, Demetrius felt encouraged.

Ola entered the art room. He saw Demetrius hovering behind a small model. It remained just beyond his creative vision. An itch in the middle of his back and no hands to scratch it.

"Yo, Meat, it's time."

At first, Demetrius did not respond. Finally, he looked up. A scraggly beard, patches of fuzz on his cheeks and neck had appeared. Ripe plums seemed to have been stuffed beneath his eyes.

"Time for what?"

"It's time to go out. Kelly's waiting for us."

"I don't have time."

"Come on, man, you've been staring at that lump for a couple of weeks ever since you got back from Whiteville. Whatever it is, it's got control over you. And I got to say, nobody's real happy about it. Kelly's about to kick your ass."

Demetrius sighed. "I'm so close. I just can't quite solve the problem."

Ola was now a half a dozen steps from his roommate. "Look, if you're anything like me, you can't solve a problem by staring at it. You kind of got to look at it sideways, from another perspective, like when you're trying to see a small star in the night sky. You just move your eyes a little and the thing lights up as if you were staring at it all along."

Demetrius put his hands on the table surrounding the design. "If I can just..."

"You can just stand up and walk out of here. I'm not averse to dragging you out. I'm a lot stronger than you."

"All right," Demetrius responded, as he held up his hands in surrender. "I'll meet you back at the room in fifteen minutes. I have to get this cleaned up."

Ola shook his head. "No way. These are your options: I will help you clean up and you will come with me. Or, you will leave everything where it is, and you will come with me. I know you, bro. I'll leave and you'll lose track of those fifteen minutes and I'll end up going on a date with *your* girlfriend."

Demetrius laughed and made a sudden move at his roommate as if he was going to attack him, but then grabbed Ola around the shoulders. They walked to the door and Demetrius flipped off the lights. Like a photographic plate, the image of the lump was super-imposed on his eyesight, just for a second – light coming from it, shining – and then it faded.

The bar, Joseph's Night Eagle, a strategically placed college bar situated on the corner of the main street and two blocks from the college, was famous for its tap beer and unusually short-tempered bouncers. Affixed to the walls were ancient, yet very retro, neon lights indicating various kinds of cheap beers served on tap. As Demetrius pondered them, it was as if he could feel the presence of former collegiate ghosts, smoking cigarettes and trying to steal things. Those ghostly alumni seemed to fill the space with their long since spoken words, thoughts on the Vietnam War, a round of drinks as the Berlin Wall came crashing down, Kurt Cobain's newest lyrical gem, Y2K and all the hoopla and so on and so forth. Demetrius wondered, ever so briefly, if these ghostly apparitions sat in neon-haloed judgement on the vapid and empty discussions decades later. Demetrius noticed contemporary faces front lit by glowing cell phones each taking photos of what was most important in their life: themselves. There was something incredibly depressing about living in an age which focussed almost exclusively on self-deception and self-promotion. Where was beauty and honesty in the world?

After they had ordered their drinks and pushed into a round booth in a dimly lit corner of the college bar, they noticed some of the other collegians gyrating weakly, almost spasmodically, ineptly and drunkenly convincing the other side of the gender pool to swim their way.

Ola shook his head. "They look like they've got epilepsy."

Demetrius laughed and took a sip of his beer. "It's not them. It's the music. Got no soul, no heart. It's vasectomy music."

"What in the world does that mean?"

"Some good feeling, but no life is gonna arise from that."

Ola almost spit out his drink. "Oh, man, that's funny. I'm gonna write that down."

Kelly rolled her eyes. "Is that why you never want to dance with me?"

"I'll dance with you someday. Don't worry."

"Should I go get some more drinks?" Ola said.

"Yes!" Kelly and Demetrius said, simultaneously. Ola never volunteered to pay for drinks.

"You said something about having a problem figuring out this piece of art." Kelly's eyes were focused on the dance floor, on the neon blue and green lights which gave an eerie glow to the dancers caught in an endless loop of thumping music. "Tell me about it."

Demetrius glanced at Kelly and then saw Ola arriving with a pitcher of beer, most likely the cheapest kind on tap, and a lit candle.

"What are you doing with the candle, Ola?" Kelly asked.

He set the pitcher of beer between them and then the candle in the center of the table. The glass surrounding it was red and rough. The light glittered and spread out bathing the vicinity in a warm sparkling blanket of rose-colored water.

"The bartender said that he forgot to put candles on the tables. He saw us over here and thought that we might like one. Romance and such…"

Kelly laughed. "Such romance surrounded by all of this." She gesticulated to the area of congregated people, all smushed together, all shouting and laughing. Life was such a dream.

"What were you guys talking about?"

"Kelly just asked me about the creative problem."

"Okay…" Ola said as he swallowed a mouthful of beer and wiped his mouth.

"The piece won't be going up in a gallery. In fact, it won't be going up indoors at all."

"What is it, a statue?"

"Yes, but I don't know what material to make it out of."

"Marble," Ola said, as he slapped the table. "Done."

Demetrius shook his head. "Okay, let me break it down." He looked at the candle in the middle of the table and took a deep breath. "When I was in high school, this guy moved into Amicable. His name is Leopold Jensen, and he's as tall as I am." The other two raised their eyes. "He's got the weirdest ability to look at people and see everything – like not just notice stuff, but *know* stuff. If he met you both, within seconds he could see things about you and your past that you had not told anyone and were trying really hard to hide."

"Sounds like a fun guy. Party tricks." Ola smiled.

"Anyway," Demetrius continued, "Leo is a world class butcher and he took a job at the local butchery. He married one of the most popular citizens, Rhonda, and now they have a couple of kids."

"That's a white person dream."

"You're not helping me."

"How can I help you? You haven't told me what the problem is?"

Sighing, Demetrius continued, mesmerized by the flame. "A few weeks ago, when I was at church, Rhonda stood up and told everyone that Butcher has Lou Gehrig's Disease."

Kelly's eyes looked up at Demetrius. "That's terrible."

"I know. He's young – mid-forties.

"What's Lou Gehrig's Disease?" Ola asked.

"It's a disease that affects your nervous system," Kelly answered. "Nobody knows how you get it and there's no cure for it yet. It destroys the connections between muscles and nerves. Pretty much anyone who gets it kind of just spends the last years of their life wasting away. Can't move. Can't swallow. Can't breathe. It's horrible."

Demetrius looked at her. "How did you know all that?"

"I had a family friend who contracted it later in life. We used to visit him in the nursing home. It was horrible. He was all curled up and couldn't talk, but the doctor said that his mental faculties never failed. So the entire time he was perfectly aware of what was happening to him, but there was nothing he could do to stop it."

"I think I'd just kill myself," Ola said, with finality.

"Most people want to."

"So, that's where I'm up to," Demetrius rubbed at a spot on the table. The red glow of the light behind them reflected and mixed with the glow from the candle. "I want to do something special for them and the community."

"What are you thinking?" Kelly asked.

A wisp of smoke arose from the candle and framed Demetrius' face. "Do you know the *Pieta,* Michelangelo's masterpiece sculpture?"

"Is that the one of Mary holding Jesus right after he died?"

Demetrius nodded. "It's one of the greatest works of art ever. From a solid piece of marble…"

"See…?" Ola said and spread his hands.

Demetrius ignored him. "From a purely artistic standpoint, it's not entirely realistic. The dimensions are not perfect and Mary is made to be a young woman rather than someone old enough to have a thirty-three-year old son. That doesn't matter. What does matter, is that I want to replicate this in some way."

"I think that's wonderful," Kelly's eyes lit up with pride.

"So what's the problem, Meat?"

"It's going to be an outdoor piece, so the natural thing would be to make it out of stone, but there's something missing..."

Ola nodded. "You're looking right at it."

"What?" Demetrius frowned.

"Remember, if you want to see something as it is, you can't look right at it. You have to look to the side. Then it will become clear."

"Wise words, bro, but I have no idea what you're talking about now."

Ola reached forward. "Take this candle, for instance, hold the flame up and people see. The essence of the candle is not just the light that it emits, though, but its truth – that when you burn it, it begins to melt and create a pool of wax that reflects the light from above."

Kelly's jaw dropped. "Wow, that's awesome."

Demetrius stared at his friend. "Holy smoke, Ola, you've solved the problem."

He looked surprised and confused but pleased. "What? I don't... I was just making shit up."

Leaning over to Kelly, Demetrius kissed her squarely on the cheek. Standing and almost upsetting the beer glasses, which Ola rescued from tipping over, Demetrius clapped him on the shoulder.

"Thanks. Don't wait up!" He opened his wallet and threw a twenty-dollar bill on the table. Both Kelly and Ola stared at him.

"But..." Kelly said too slowly.

Ola picked up the money. "Guess we'll have a few drinks and our own dance tonight."

Kelly plunked her chin down in her hand, frustrated.

The morning, like many early Iowa winter mornings, lingered with an ache-in-the-bones kind of chill. J.T. asked what they were doing but Jennifer told him that she wanted to take a walk with him. This pleased J.T. who ran ahead of her down the school hallway to retrieve his small jacket, mittens and stocking cap. As he brought them back to her to help him put them on, she felt a tug at her soul, and an unravelling of her professional ethos. When she had first arrived in Amicable, Jennifer had never imagined that she would be using a little boy to ruin his own family but she justified it in her own mind: saving the forest by cutting down one tree.

He sprinted ahead to the doors. Looking back, he smiled at her. She sighed and waved back. As she approached, he waved his hand for her to hurry up. He held the door for her and they exited into the cold wintery air.

Moving to the sidewalk, J.T. unconsciously reached for her hand. Jennifer flinched. She needed to remain impassive. This was the best thing for Leo.

Stopping on the cement, he looked up at her. Despite their age difference, they were not far apart in height. "Why is your hair purple?"

Shrugging, she looked down the street. "People do strange things sometimes."

"Why did you do it?"

"I guess I like to be noticed for something other than my stature."

"What is your 'stature?'"

"I'm a small person," she responded.

"I'm a small person, too," he said, standing on his tiptoes.

"Yes," she said, "but not for long. Both your parents are very tall. Someday, they will be very proud to see you as a fully-grown, tall man.

A cloud passed over his face. "I don't think my dad will see me."

Jennifer cursed herself. *You idiot.* "Yes, well, that's something we can talk about today if you like."

"Why are we outside?"

Glancing around, she put her hands in her armpits. "I wanted to test your vision."

"I like tests."

"I know you do, and this one will be really cool." She leaned forward and tugged on his collar, then ruffled his stocking cap which fell over his eyes. He pushed it up. "Here's what we're going to do." She waved her arm around her. "I've put some signs on trees. Some of them are pictures, some of them are numbers or letters, some are colors. I want you to tell me how many you see, where they are and what is on them."

"Easy," he said, confidently. He scanned his surroundings and then nodded.

"Do you want to start now?" she asked.

He frowned and tilted his head. "I'm already done."

Jennifer pressed her lips together. "Listen, just take your time."

"But I know where they all are..."

"Okay, prove it. How many are there?"

"Seventeen. I counted. I'm good at counting."

She swallowed and her eyes widened. "All right," her voice quivered slightly, and not from the cold. "Where are they and what are they?"

For the next minute, J.T. systematically pointed out the trees and stated what was on each of them. Astounded, Jennifer checked them against her list. As he continued, she watched his eyes. There was something eerie about them as they adjusted, focused and adjusted again.

Finally, they came to the real point of the test. "Do you think you can see as far away as your house?"

J.T. scoffed. "That's easy. So easy." He turned his attention to his home.

"Can you see what's happening in the house?"

"Yeah, Mom is with someone."

"Who is it?"

His eyes refocused. "Stedman."

Jennifer's heart pounded. "Stedman? Is that normal? Does he spend a lot of time at your house?"

He shrugged. "I don't know."

"What are they doing now?"

"They're just talking."

"And, can you read lips? What is she saying?"

"I'm not very good at that."

Frustrated, Jennifer tried another tack. "Just tell me when they move and where they go."

J.T. looked up at Jennifer, distrustful. "Why do you want me to watch them?"

"I'm just seeing if you can do it. Scientific stuff."

This satisfied him, so turned back towards the house again. "Okay, I think they're still in the kitchen."

There was a sound behind them and they both turned. J.T.'s face lit up and he ran to the father.

"Dad!" he cried out and threw his arms around his dad's legs.

Butcher looked over him at Jennifer who stood embarrassedly.

Butcher raised his hand in greeting.

"Hello, Leo."

Pulling out his iPad, he typed, *What are you doing?*

Jennifer cleared her throat, but J.T. offered the first alibi. "We were doing some visual games. It was really fun!"

Butcher raised his eyebrows and Jennifer fumbled for words. "It's just a thing I was doing with him to bring him out of his shell."

"Yeah, she knows, Dad, just like you."

Jennifer drew in a breath of air. "You know?"

He tilted his head in question. His eyebrows pinched.

"I thought I was the only one," she stammered, "Er… it's not as if I was… trying to hide anything from you, but I thought… well, it would be good to surprise you – to show you his gift – but it sounds like you've already seen it."

Butcher nodded.

"J.T.," Jennifer said, "how about we get you back inside so you don't catch a cold?"

J.T. protested. "But I want to be outside and do more games with you. Maybe we can see what Mo…"

"No!" Jennifer interrupted quickly. "Leo, would you like to come inside with us? Maybe come to my school office. We can have a cup of coffee and talk. There's something I want to tell you."

Butcher's eyes narrowed and he searched her eyes. The disease had slowed his ability to read people, but he could certainly tell something untoward was happening.

Butcher made a circle with his thumb and forefinger. *Okay.* Jennifer turned back towards the school.

After J.T. hugged his father, he moved towards his first-grade classroom. Jennifer turned around to see Butcher following his son's departure, a proud father taking in the details of his young offspring, knowing that there weren't many days that he'd be able to watch. She felt another stab of guilt.

As Butcher approached her, his left foot dragged. He held onto the wall for support. Both Butcher and Jennifer were aware of the sound of his shuffle: step, *shuffle*, step, *shuffle*. He tried to keep his eyes on her, but he also needed to concentrate on the unevenness of the bricks. The beads of sweat on his forehead were created by concentration and overheating because of their winter gear. By the time they had reached Jennifer's office Butcher's face was dripping.

Jennifer waited for him to enter and then shut the door behind him. Amicable High School had fashioned an office out of an old storage room. Her room, the size of a prison cell, had a small school desk crammed into a corner beneath a dusty window. There were no personal identifications: no pictures, books, posters or drawings. Everything was clinical and tidy.

"Have a seat," she said to Butcher, pointing to a cushioned chair opposite her own desk chair.

Butcher reverted back to his iPad.

Thank you.

She nodded and waited for him to finish typing.

You said you had something to tell me. I read from your expression that it must be relatively serious.

"Such an amazing gift."

He shrugged. *It's not as strong anymore.* She could see that he was trying to work his mouth into word shapes.

"The disease?"

He shook his head. *No. Actually, a gift from Amicable.*

"What do you mean?"

He rubbed his nose with a finger. *My ability never allowed me to ever get really close to people. I was always wary that people were lying to me. When I found Amicable, though, I finally realized that much of my problem connecting with people had to do with me and my trust – or, distrust, I guess.*

"That's not exactly a rare human trait."

No, but to the extent that I distrust, bordered on psychotic.

Jennifer laughed. "I would guess we're paddling the same boat."

Chapter 8.

Butcher smiled. *Something changed inside of me, maybe it was Rhonda, maybe it was the town itself. But I escaped the fear. And once I was able to trust people, my gift kept shrinking. Still does.*

Jennifer clapped her hands twice in amusement. "So you can only interpret the same amount of non-verbal signals as the rest of us?"

He nodded. *With people I trust.* The double entendre was not lost on her. *They're proud people, but beautiful. I wouldn't be where I am today without their help.* He took a deep breath and spoke. "Especially Rhonda."

"Leo…" Jennifer started.

He held up a hand to stop her. He frowned and typed. *I don't need a supernatural ability to read you now. I realize that we have a history together. I might have made a physical mistake in not taking you up on your offer the other day.*

"It wasn't an offer. It was a gift. Not just to you, but to me. You have to understand, after all these years of being apart, when I saw your picture in the newspaper, something shifted inside me and I remembered all of the good things we shared all those years ago. I needed to see you. I needed to feel that way again."

I'm married.

"Leo, I need to tell you something." He tried to interrupt her, but she held up a hand. "I need to tell you this first before we go any further." Butcher's mouth hung open slightly. "About Rhonda." Jennifer felt an odd sense of guilty excitement.

His eyes widened. Suddenly, Butcher could read exactly what she was going to tell him. He had just told her that when he trusted people, his gift diminished, but if he could read her…

I can't believe you saw that. Rhonda?

"What? What did you read from me?"

You saw her with someone else. Someone I trust. Jennifer's eyes shifted. She tried to control them.

"How…? But…"

Butcher's teeth clenched as he stared at the small woman across from him. The purple hair hung limply; her large glasses drew attention to her pupils which were dilated with nervous excitement. Her finger tapped unconsciously on her leg. Her pulse quickened and throbbed in her neck. The skin on her cheeks had turned a bright rosy red.

He should have been outraged. He should have been shocked and horrified. He should have felt anger. Butcher saw in her eyes what she had seen, but he saw slightly more. He saw that her vision had been interrupted, or at least it was incomplete. Butcher found himself not outraged by Rhonda, but angry at Jennifer. How could he have not seen this when she first arrived? Why had he been so easily deceived? What had he done?

"Leo, I saw her with him."

Butcher looked away, over her head and out the lonely window into the frigid winter. Frosty patterns appeared in the corners of the panes, intricate patterns never again repeated, created by once-in-a-lifetime updrafts of heat and swirling air which came into contact with the icy cold air kept outside by the thin pane of glass. His eyes admired the design and marveled how much that pattern was similar to his own life, unrepeatable and beautiful. His story caught as a snapshot in time by heat and wind and cold.

Butcher looked down to his iPad and began to type. *It doesn't matter. I forgive you.*

"But Leo, Rhonda is the one who has been indiscreet. I saw her in the house with Stedman. They were in there a while…" Moving to Leo, she placed a hand on his leg. There was still an electric pulse between them, but she could feel it ebbing, fading. Desperately, she tried to reach out, to let him feel the way he used to feel.

You didn't see her.

"Yes! Leo, I saw her and him. They were in your house."

Chapter 8.

No, you used my son. Butcher's jaw clenched. His distrust of her was growing by the second.

"No," Jennifer responded, "that's not how it happened. You see…"

You can't lie to me anymore. As much as I want to trust you, I can't.

"Leo," she pleaded, "she cheated on you. I know it. You know it."

"STOP!" he yelled. His voice rang out with a clarity not heard in weeks. "I cheated on her! I let myself be drawn in."

Jennifer got down on her knees in front of him. "Leo, you don't understand. There is still life for us. I can get the best doctors in the world to work on your case. We can slow it down. We can finish out life… together… content. I realize that this town has come kind of hold over…"

Jennifer, I remember the day I left you. He gently pushed her hands away from his legs and all of his frustration and anger towards her melted away; he saw her as she really was: a lonely and frightened woman who couldn't find hope. A strange light filled his eyes as he leaned forward. Then, he worked his iPad. *We were different back then. Life was beautiful and tragic. You were so young and hard. Everyone assumed you'd be soft, but you had thorns and they got me too. I wish I could go back to that moment when I left you. I wish I would have turned back just one more time and opened the door of our home. I wish I would have memorized how you looked and how you smelled, the taste of your lips and the sound of your voice.*

I should have stopped running and said, 'I love you.' We should be doing this every day of our lives, reminding people, the ones that matter; we should be touching their faces, their hands, their souls and say, 'I love you because you are part of my story.' Nobody knows how long they get. We don't know…

"We don't know…" Tears filled Butcher's eyes. He let them fall over his cheeks and down onto the sides of his chin.

Jennifer felt her own tears start and wondered when the last time was that she cried. She reached out for him, wanting to pull him back, return him to the place when they were together in the past. "Leo, I still love you. I want to spend the rest of your life with you. We can make it work…"

Butcher shook his head and took her hands and placed them on his cheeks. He put his hands on her face, the tears wetting his fingers. For an intense moment, they travelled back through time, young man and woman tumbling through life, excitement and passion and commitment-less life. Jennifer saw herself reflected in Butcher's eyes, a desperate woman afraid to move forward.

He typed again as she held his cheeks. *I should have told you that I loved you just before we separated, not to keep us together, but to send us on our way, two ships leaving dock.* Their eyes were locked together.

That's what I should have done, but now, I'm going to let you go for good. We can't go back.

"You have to go," he whispered. He struggled to look at her.

Jennifer pleaded with him. "Leo, please. Please don't say that."

Butcher leaned forward his face inches away from hers. His voice and words were painfully slow, but the message was clear. "Jennifer Adams, I loved you. I want you to remember that. I will take a piece of you with me. Thank you." Closing the distance, Butcher kissed her lightly and gently, their lips connected and tears mingled. The intimacy was infinitely more powerful than their rushed and pseudo-sexual encounter in his office. Time swirled, and as they closed their eyes, each of them felt a powerful incandescent glow.

As Butcher began to pull away, the past ripped away like Velcro, Jennifer tried to keep him there. "No, no, no, Leo." Her

Chapter 8.

tears began again in earnest. He dragged her hands away from his face.

The sudden loss, the amputation of her sense of touch, left Jennifer unable to stand. Now that she had been cut adrift from what she thought could have been at last a stopgap in her life, she was laid low by grief.

Without a word, Butcher picked up his coat, his hat and his iPad. He put his large hand on the doorknob and walked out of Jennifer Adams' life.

The snow glistened brightly as Butcher left the school. Even after wiping his eyes of remaining tears, he realized his spirits were strangely high. It was as if he had shed a great weight. It felt like his gait seemed quicker, his foot lighter and less oppressive. Instead of dragging through the snow on the sidewalk, it tapped like a telegraph, a Morse Code of relief.

Making his way down the frozen sidewalk, he passed the frozen landscape of the elementary school playground. Ghosts, kicking their feet in despairing expectation, caused the swings to move. The yellow plastic slide emitted an ominous moan as the wind echoed in its empty throat. Haunted, the playground populated the spectres of yesteryear, each successive generation of children imprinting their laughter, hopes and fears into the landscape. Butcher paused to contemplate this thought and his own less-than-desirable memories of childhood. Grasping the chain link fence in his fingers, he stared at the seesaw, the monkey bars and the vast field of safety tarmac covered by packed snow and ice.

It was time to go home. It was time they had the discussion about the future.

Finishing the journey, his right hand, stronger than his left, grasped the doorknob and pushed the front door open.

His eyes widened with surprise as Stedman and Rhonda were standing just outside the front foyer. They were facing each other holding hands. Even without his full gift, there was no way Stedman could hide the guilt that was written all over his face. As soon as they saw him, they dropped hands.

For a moment, neither of them could speak. Rhonda took a step towards Butcher. "This is not what it looks like, Butcher."

Stedman covered his mouth, his face reddened with embarrassment. "Butcher, I just came over to talk to Rhonda and we were just…"

Butcher held up his hand and stopped him. The future flashed before Butcher's eyes. He hadn't had a vision like this for years, not since George's death. Not only did Stedman desire his wife, he desired his life. Stedman wanted children and he wanted simplicity. He wanted a family and a future that was not shrouded in resentment and rejection. For the years that he had known Rhonda, Stedman had watched how she treated Butcher with steadfast, unshakeable love. He wanted that, envied that in Butcher. Now that Leopold Jensen had one foot out the door, Stedman was willing to take one step in.

For a moment, Butcher wanted to let his unbridled self-righteousness run roughshod over what had happened: both wife and adulterer were guilty of hastening his death. The indecency of what he read in Stedman caused Butcher to almost lose his emotional footing. The moorings of his faith in his wife were shaking loose. Like a conductor, his hand was raised asking for silence. Butcher moved past them to the table where two cups of coffee were still steaming. Rhonda and Stedman were frozen in place, unsure of what Butcher was about to do.

Butcher sat and invited them with his hand to each take a seat. They shared a glance and moved warily to their places behind coffee mugs. Sitting at the foot of the table, Rhonda on his right and Stedman on his left, Butcher pulled his iPad from the pocket of his winter coat. He pondered what was going on in his mind, but just before he touched the screen with his capable right pointer finger, he stopped and a narrative ran through his mind:

How could you?

Is this truly how you wanted to spend the last months of my life?

Stedman, I thought we were friends?

Rhonda, I thought it was 'til death do us part, not 'til almost dead?'

Just as he was about to type the last thought first, something in his consciousness flickered, an image of Jennifer Adams in his office, naked before him. This was his own battle to do the right thing or to squeeze the last drops of joy out of this lemon of life that he'd been given. He wanted to be angry. He wanted to vent his fury at them, but hypocrisy struck him with physical force. Instead of writing what he wanted, he flexed his fingers and changed his mind.

I'm sorry.

I haven't been a good husband and friend.

I have lied, covered up lies and put you both in an awkward place.

Stupefied, Rhonda reached out to his arm, but did not touch him. "What are you talking about, Butcher?"

His fingers typed slowly, deliberately, as if searching for a digital word that would express how he was feeling and needing. *I can read you, Stedman.*

Stedman swallowed, worried.

You saw me – us, Jennifer and me. Rhonda's heart quickened. Was Stedman right? Had Butcher cheated on her?

I'll use your words… It was not what it looked like, although it was close.

"I… c'mon Butcher, I didn't see…"

DON'T LIE TO ME! I CAN READ YOU! Butcher ground his teeth and held the screen up to Stedman. Setting the iPad down, Butcher's face glowed maniacally. Sweat appeared on his brow. The eerie voice spoke again.

301

That day when you saw Jennifer leave my office, I almost gave in. He looked up at Rhonda tears glistening. *Jennifer never gave up on trying to make a life together.* Rhonda's jaw tightened. *I would guess it's the same feeling that you have for Rhonda. Sometimes we just can't give up the past.*

"Yes," Stedman admitted, hanging his head in shame.

I don't blame you. She is perfection. Rhonda raised a trembling hand to her mouth. *I don't blame either one of you. I blame myself. I made a mess with Jennifer and you also.*

"Butcher, this is not all your fault. We..." Butcher shook his head and held up a hand again.

When we give in, we do stupid things. He looked at Stedman. *What you saw was like not reading the last page of a book. She professed her love for me.* Stedman's eyes flicked to Rhonda and back to Butcher. *Then, she did what I unconsciously wanted and probably encouraged. She tried to seduce me. Not just away from Rhonda, but away from Amicable and its people. She doesn't understand.*

Stedman and Rhonda's eyes remained fixed on Butcher's fingers which were trying desperately to keep up with his thoughts.

Fortunately, I stopped at the last moment. I thought of you, Rhonda, my most beautiful wife, and my precious kids. Her eyes moistened. *But I thought of you, too, Stedman, and the twins, and the exercise ladies, and Demetrius and the high school kids and all of Amicable. You are all priceless.*

When Jennifer left my office, she was upset; so was I. I wondered if I'd done the right thing. To be honest, I regretted letting her go. So, I left my office with a bottle of wine and headed to the bowling alley to load up. I felt guilty. In my mind, I'd cheated on you, Rhonda, but I'd also cheated on everyone.

We're all complicit in this. He motioned with his hand around the circle. *You, me, Amicable. There is a darkness in our humanity. We're all sick. I have a physical disease which is killing me. Rhonda, yours emotional, and its eating you alive. Stedman, yours is psychological – you've been betrayed and abandoned your whole life. You cling to whomever will give you instant attention.*

"Now what?" Stedman asked quietly.

Amicable will go back to the way it used to be: forgotten, forgetful and forsaken.

"This isn't about Amicable, Butcher," Rhonda's eyes radiated a furious light. "This is about you and me."

It is and it isn't. In the next months before I die, it will be, but then, when I am gone, it will be about you, and the kids and the town.

"Butcher, can we talk about this some other time…"

Butcher looked into his wife's eyes. Stedman faded into the background. He shifted uncomfortably and then reached for his coffee but remained silent.

I came from Jennifer's office at school.

"What?" Rhonda emotions were being yanked like a tug of war. "What the hell were you doing with her?"

Butcher's face remained impassive and then he typed. *I told her it was time for her to go. And then,* he paused, and wondered how to write the next part. *I told her I loved her. Notice how I said it. "I loved her." I did, I loved her fifteen years ago. I loved that time of life and who we were. I wanted to tell Jennifer that I would always love who we were because it shaped who I am today; and it was far better for her to have my last words to her be of love than of rejection. It is a transformative thing for me, telling people I love them. And now, I feel like that's how I want to spend the last months of my life. Loving people.*

"But you've always done that, Butcher. You've loved people just as they are." Rhonda pulled her chair closer to his and grabbed his hands. She saw the sweat on his head and reached to remove his jacket. As she unzipped it, a draft of superheated air escaped from his chest. Her cool hands found his neck and remained there until she began to remove his coat. With tenderness, Rhonda pulled the coat from his shoulders and then helped with his arms. He was passive and allowed her to help him. In this act of intimacy, Stedman pushed his chair back.

"I'm going to go." He stood and looked down into the eyes of one of his closest friends. "I'm sorry, Butcher. I was a fool. Please forgive me."

As Rhonda freed his arms at last, he took a deep, hitching breath and began to cry. *I forgive you, Stedman. Will you forgive me?*

Stedman's face imploded. "Ah, Butcher." Stedman moved forward to join Rhonda at Butcher's side and bent down to hug his friend.

Eventually, Stedman pulled away and wiped the tears from his eyes. "Goodbye, Butcher."

Butcher worked his mouth. "I love you too."

Rhonda laughed through her tears. "That's not what he said, Butcher."

Butcher tapped on his iPad. *I know. But that's how I want to say farewell to everyone. I'd rather tell them that I love them. Those are the last words I want to speak to everyone.*

And that's exactly what Butcher did.

Chapter 9.

Hossein greeted the patient with a smile. She looked tired, worn out. Even though the winter was mostly finished, (it tended to obstinately cling to the spring months) March was still cold. Taking off her coat, she hung it on the tree near Hossein's desk.

"How are you feeling today, Mrs. Harmsen?"

"Oh, not too bad." She smiled and adjusted her head wrap. Although her hair was now coming back, she didn't have enough to keep her head warm.

"That's good. Butcher will be with you in a moment." Hossein nodded and went back to typing.

Linda perused the entry of the Chop Shop. A stuffed pheasant was positioned on top of an old filing cabinet. Its dead eyes were turned towards the ceiling, focused high above the trivialities of the human condition.

Facing away from Hossein were photos of his family, beautiful dark children with black hair and glittering onyx eyes. Linda smiled at their faces remembering her own children at that age. Standing straight, hand on cane, a necessity since her back surgery, she walked to the window. Outside, Amicable was waking up from the long, dark freeze. Beneath the window, from under the snow, tulip leaves were beginning to peak through the snow.

Across the street, four farmers stood in a square talking and watching the traffic. This constancy, this impatient waiting, was a beautiful thing. These men and their families were anxiously excited to get back into the earth, to do what they were made to do. To grow things, both plants and relationships. At them, too, she smiled.

The phone buzzed, but no voice.

"Okay, Boss."

Hossein nodded to Linda. "He's ready for you."

"Are you sure?"

Smiling, Hossein spread his hands. "We've been together long enough now, I know. Please." He motioned to the door.

Butcher's wheelchair was positioned in the center of the room across from a cushioned chair in the glow of the window overlooking Main Street. Opaque curtains gave some privacy, but they also allowed light to filter through.

His head listed to the side, but Butcher was smiling. His eyes went to the computer screen. *Welcome.*

Still unused to seeing him like this, Linda looked down and touched her heart.

You don't have to be nervous.

"I know," she said. "But it's not often that the doctor makes an appointment with *you*."

He snorted. *I'm not a doctor.*

"Close enough."

Do you want a cup of coffee? Water?

"No, thank you."

Please, have a seat.

Linda moved past him noticing that his hair had thinned. His face, cheeks gaunt, was pale and his muscles seemed to be dripping. Where once there had been a muscular man was now a skin-covered skeleton.

Once she sat down, Butcher wheeled his chair to face her. *Thank you for coming. I appreciate it.*

"Don't mention it." She studied his eyes. "But why…?"

Why are you here? Well, I thought we could have a chat. I need to ask you a favor.

"From me?"

Yes.

"What is it?"

I need you to not feel guilty.

She frowned. "I don't…"

Even though I trust you, I can still read you.

"Butcher, I think that maybe you might be reading something that's not..."

Linda.

She stopped.

Don't feel guilty because you survived and I'm not going to. Her eyes moved. He had read correctly. *Survivor's guilt is a real thing and it can be very unhelpful.*

"What do you mean?"

It diminishes happiness. Butcher glanced up from his screen to read her eyes again. *You don't have to be sorry that you are living.*

"But I'm not. I'm grateful. It's just..."

It's just not fair?

She nodded silently.

Butcher took a deep breath. *I know it's not fair. It's not fair that I've had the most amazing life. I've been all over the world. I've seen so many things and known so many people and I ended up in this incredible town with amazing people. It's not fair that everyone else can't have a life that I've had.*

"You know what I mean." Linda felt her tears start.

I know what you mean, and yet as I think back over my life, would I be willing to live longer but be less happy? Would I trade another couple of struggling years with less happiness?

In a word, 'No.'

Some people live a long time and they get tired of everything. Those are people who haven't come face to face with death. But you and I have. And because of it, we know — beyond a shadow of a doubt — that every day is more precious than gold. So we live, and we love, and then we die. And that's okay.

"But people aren't supposed to die young."

What is young? Ten? Forty? Eighty? People aren't supposed to die unhappy.

"What are you saying, Butcher?"

In spite of what happened to me – to spite my tragic end – laugh and smile with your family, go on holidays, go to church, gossip…

Linda laughed through her tears.

But I have one more favor to ask.

"Anything."

Take care of my family.

"Butcher…" Linda's voice broke and she began to cry. "I can't. I don't know if…"

My family is your family. George is gone. Connie and Carl have their own lives. They're going to move away – they just haven't told us yet – to live near his family.

"But…"

Before you answer, I want you to know something about Amicable. It's something that I've been reading about the community. He paused and looked out the window where Nash and Shania were walking together to go to lunch. *Amicable is dying, too. It's not fair. This way of life, these people and the way they hold on to the past, their love for one another – so rare in this world. If we (even without me) don't continue to love each other, the town may last a few more years, but every disease, every virus, every cancer will eat away at it until it stops. We can't let that happen.*

"But I have cancer."

So? You have life and you're breathing. That's what you were made to do. To love. So do it. With my family, and the family next door. John and Leslie will need some support. Now that you're in remission, just enjoy loving Amicable.

"It sounds so easy."

And yet…?

"It's not. These people can be so frustrating and stubborn."

And lovable.

"And lovable."

What do you say? Can you take care of my family?

"Which one? Yours or Amicable?"

Same thing.

Linda Harmsen sighed and leaned back in her chair. Crossing her arms across her fake chest, she blinked rapidly clearing the tears from her eyes.

One last thing.

"Good God, you're going to kill me, Butcher," she laughed at the ceiling.

Don't forget to tell people you love them.

She leaned forward to ponder his face. Even though his body had been ravaged by a disease, he looked angelic. Something had changed in his demeanor. He was content. The shriveling muscles had somehow released him from part of the anxiety all humans feel about living. After wrestling with death, he had come out victorious.

"Can do."

Okay, he smiled. *Now, get to work.*

"Does that mean our session is finished?"

You tell me.

"Okay, I'll tell you. We love you, Butcher."

Now you're getting the idea.

In the next months, Butcher kept the Chop Shop open as long as he was able. Although it was not easy to counsel others, his ability to listen was a precious treasure. Some came in to talk about their past; some wanted to talk about life and love, others about the prospect of dying. Through all of this, Butcher opened his heart even if he couldn't open his mouth. As each person left his office, he told them that he loved them – his last words to them. Eventually, his mouth was unable to pronounce the words, but whatever sound that he made, everyone in Amicable knew that he was saying, 'I love you.'

It took a while for Amicableans to get past their discomfort of hearing someone not related to them tell them that they were loved. Butcher's last gift to them was to teach them that love was not wrapped up in sexuality. It was the lifeblood of relationships and it took different forms. When Butcher said 'I love you,' he meant that he honored and respected them despite their failings and quirks. Because Amicableans knew and felt love, they were able to change and adapt. And they started treating each other differently. For a while, the respite from hopelessness felt like a break in the clouds.

Derek and Tracey moved their wedding forward so that Butcher could attend and be part of the wedding party. On Memorial Day weekend, the town gathered to witness the wedding vows of two of Amicable's young leading citizens. Resplendent in white lace dripping with pearls, the mayor of Amicable looked stunning as she walked towards her beloved, who fidgeted nervously, bouncing from foot to foot on the verge of fainting.

Waiting at the front of the sanctuary, Rhonda, a bridesmaid, and Butcher, a groomsman, smiled at each other. Life was certainly going to be different and she would miss him terribly.

When at last bride reached groom, Derek ceased bouncing and his mouth was agape at his bride's transcendent beauty.

"Derek," Tracey whispered, "close your mouth."

"But… you're so beautiful," he stammered.

"Thank you," she responded. "You don't look so bad yourself."

Derek looked down at his tuxedo. "What, this old thing?"

Behind them, a voice cleared. "Do you mind if we get this show on the road?" John Deakins said with a laugh.

Nash clapped his hands. "How's about we start with the 'dearly beloved' part. Butcher's getting thirsty." The bridal party's eyes snapped towards Butcher who grunted.

"Dearly beloved," John intoned into his microphone from the front. "We are gathered here today to celebrate..."

Thankfully, the wedding ceremony went without a hitch unlike the explosion at Nash and Shania's wedding. After the ceremony, the reception was held at the Greedy Pecker. There was a perpetual stream of well-wishers for Derek and Tracey, and a similar stream of people who wanted to share a drink with Butcher. Rhonda and the kids sat with him at a table. The kids played games on his iPad while he eyed-in responses on his computer. The noise was so loud in the room, though, that eventually, Georgie and J.T. left with Grandma Connie and Grandpa Carl.

As the reception continued, Amicableans forgot that Butcher was teetering on the edge of life and death. His goodbye had turned into goodness.

As Amicableans danced, reservedly before alcohol, (most willing to wait until the Chicken Dance, the Electric Slide or the Macarena) and with abandon after alcohol, twisting and turning, jumping and falling – a dance of light, darkness, life and death, they understood that these precious moments of celebration were far too few. The time to live was now. The time to mourn was later.

Throughout the night, Butcher looked around at the people he loved. His heart moved even if his head could not. By the front door, Louise Nelson, the town police officer, was speaking with a group of early twenty-somethings, wayward boys who had painted on the water tower once. By the bar, roaring with belly-aching laughter were Dick and Linda Harmsen. Dick's arm was around his wife's waist. She leaned her head on his shoulder as they conversed with Leona, Carley, Angela, and Anne Johnson. John and Leslie were on the dance floor, faces aglow, vibrant that they, along with everyone else, could let their hair down. A few times, John raised his glass in silent toast towards Butcher, who smiled in recognition.

311

Stedman and Summer were deputized bartenders. Shania and Nash, as members of the bridal party, did not want to work. Even though Stedman and Summer were busy, they were able to be part of the celebration too. It was a night to slow the pace of life and remember.

Rarely did Rhonda remove her hand from her husband's arm. In this small, intimate gesture, both realized that nothing, not even death, could separate them entirely. Every few minutes, Rhonda would turn, almost instinctually, to lift a spoon of wine into his mouth. When it dribbled down his chin, she wiped it up.

After the party finished in the wee hours of the morning, Rhonda helped Stedman, Summer, John and Leslie clean up the bar. The rest of the bridal party were driven to Lake Ikmakota. Derek and Tracey outlawed Amicableans from staying anywhere near their cabin. Thus, everyone else had rented cabins on the other side of the lake.

Butcher, Rhonda and the kids rented the cabin with wheelchair access. J.T. and Georgie were already in bed, as were Connie and Carl when Rhonda opened the door for Butcher to enter, but he stopped her.

"What's wrong?" she asked.

Nothing. I just want to be outside for a little while. It's a beautiful night.

"Do you want me to wait with you? I don't mind."

No, you go to bed. I'll be there in a little bit. Even though my body is tired, my brain is wide awake.

Butcher's eyes floated out over the lake, the reflected moonlight created shards of glittering, moving glass across the water's surface.

"Okay." She bent down to kiss him. "I love you," she said.

Butcher's ears trapped the words, the ones spoken every night for the last two months and often in between. Whenever they woke up, whenever they left, whenever they felt like it, they said it.

Hearing his wife, Butcher desperately wanted to look up at her. From his curled-up position in the chair, he wanted to call her back, to see her face in the subtle and pale light of the moon. He wanted to memorize this moment of beauty, this night of love. Almost as if sensing his distress, Rhonda went back and knelt in front of him.

"What's wrong? Are you sure you're okay?"

I'm okay. I just wanted to stare at you again. You're quite attractive.

She laughed. A tear formed quickly, but she was unashamed. "You're not so bad yourself."

Liar.

"I stopped doing that with you years ago," she whispered.

Thanks.

"For what."

For being the love of my life.

"My Sweet," she said, as she began to cry softly, "I'm the love of your eternity too."

Butcher made a sound from his throat. They both knew what he meant. *I love you.*

Now, go get some rest. Tomorrow will be a big day.

Rhonda kissed him on the cheek. They both felt their tears mingle and then she turned to leave. With a last glance, Rhonda looked at her husband in his wheelchair. As she left the door ajar behind her so that he could enter later, she noticed that the darkness seemed to swallow him. Later, she would remember that the moonlight was greater than the darkness.

Charon no longer seemed frightening. In fact, the opposite; his face radiated tenderness and care. On this last voyage, he had come across many who had deserved the trip. The arrogant and relentlessly prideful, the soul scavengers feeding on both the life and livelihood of others — they went kicking and screaming. But this man, this tall man felled by an unreasonable disease, would be afforded the greatest care on the final journey from death into life.

Butcher looked up at him knowingly. His hood had been thrown back and Charon's eyes moved back and forth between him and the darkened shore ahead.

"It's almost time, isn't it?" Butcher asked. In his dreamland, Butcher was pleased that his voice still worked.

"It is," Charon said simply. He adjusted his oar and the subtle sound of moving water hit the watercraft.

"What is it like? What's on the other side?"

Charon remained silent. But then, without looking at Butcher, he spoke into the darkness. "Like you imagine, I suppose."

Butcher lay still in the bottom of the boat. His inability to move had now translated to his dreams. His body had forgotten what it was like to twist and turn and sit up on its own accord, but this was no longer a source of fear.

"I imagine it to be somewhat like I've heard in church, golden streets, jewel covered paths and such." The boat driver smiled knowingly. "I've also been told that there is nothing on the other side — just a void. nothingness, of non-existence."

Charon's face went grim. "I suppose some imagine it that way."

"Will I see them all again, my family and friends? You know I love them, by the way, so it seems only natural that death is not the final word."

"Love does have a way."

"But will I see them again?"

The boatman looked down. His long, drawn face, previously shrouded by a hood was not covered by a shadowed darkness. His eyes, twin onyxes embedded in granite, were as black as the night.

"Will I see them again?" Butcher asked for a third time, suddenly fearful that love was not powerful enough.

"Yes," he nodded gravely, "but not in the way that you remember them, only the way you imagine them."

"What do you mean?"

314

"It's no use trying to keep your idea of people in the past as the ideal for the future. They will change; you will not."

Butcher asked the question that suddenly became the most important. *"But will they remember?"*

Charon's voice grew quiet. *"Most assuredly, I imagine."*

The water underneath the boat was flowing faster. The course of the river was pushing them onwards, downward to a distinct, yet unknown, imagined destination.

"I feel the weight," Butcher said, *"it's on my chest. Every day it gets heavier. I find it harder to breathe – even here in my dream."*

Charon's eyes turned again to him. *"Do you think this is your dream? Why couldn't it be the other?"*

"Because that's not the way it works. No matter how many times you row the boat, life is most decidedly not *a dream."*

Smirking, Charon checked the boat and ducked his head. A low hanging stalactite, one that he'd passed thousands of times before, attempted to throw him from his perch.

"Then what is it?"

Butcher's breath caught once and then twice. Something was definitely not right. He tried to take a breath, but it only came shallowly. Charon watched him and noticed his turmoil.

"You're almost there," the boatman whispered, and pointed to a place that Butcher could not see, but from the faint glow in the distance, he felt warmed to know that in the place beyond, light still overcame the darkness.

"Thank God," Butcher said automatically.

Charon grinned again. *"Get ready to do just that."*

Butcher woke with a start. He was sitting on the front deck of the cabin. On the far side of the deck, Butcher could see a well-used grill. Wooden benches were attached to the railing where healthy people sat. To the right of the grill was a large pane of glass which reflected the serene lake water. Between the cabin and the lake, maple, oak and pine trees stood in repose. Evergreens waved their branches in the early morning breeze. The moon, floating just inches above the western horizon, seemed large and overbearing, a white eye into the night of man's soul. Watching him with an unblinking gaze, the moon seemed to understand man's distress.

On the lake, a few ducks interrupted the serenity of the shimmering surface. Butcher sniffed lightly sensing an almost dormant campfire still emitting the remains of its firewood. He loved that smell. He loved everything about life.

With a small sigh, Butcher cast his thoughts to the cabin behind him. Inside were the three most important people in his life, and someday, they would forgive him, but this is the way it must be. For the last weeks, Butcher had been planning the best way to let go, and this seemed to be the one way which allowed him to do it under his own power. Moving his wheelchair forward, he motored down the ramp across the stony, bumpy path. He hoped that no one in the cabin slept lightly enough to be disturbed by the hum of the motor. Slightly jolted, Butcher was thankful for the chest straps which kept him upright and stable.

Fortunately, the wheelchair stayed true. With a clickety-clack across the decrepit boards, he maneuvered it to the end of the dock. This had been one of his favorite places in the world – especially at night. Butcher closed his eyes and listened carefully to the voices of the past, his wife, his children and even his mother, a set of twins and a beautiful pastor and his wife. For a few minutes he soaked in the glorious moments that had been embedded in his life.

And he was thankful.

The disease had taken almost everything from him: his mobility, his ability to take care of himself, and at times his self-respect. What it couldn't take from him, though, was his ability to love and receive it. Heart swelling with gratitude, Butcher sealed these memories in an envelope inside his heart and wrote, *Don't open till you're all together again.* Then, he opened his eyes.

He gasped. On the eastern horizon he caught the glow of Amicable's night lights. Their twinkling was a beacon of courage for him. Amicable had been the home that he imagined, and if Charon's words came true, he could imagine what the 'other side' was like. It would contain the streets of Amicable somewhere in the city of God. In the middle of heaven there would be an enormous grain elevator holding the goodness of God's riches; on the edge of the city, there was a table prepared for Butcher with all the good things that he hadn't been able to eat. A heavenly Traveler's Choice. Heaven's water tower, tall and bold, a pinnacle rivalled by nothing else, would have the word *Amicable* scrawled across the side. Heaven itself was the nicest place in all of creation. Across the street with bright neon lights, the bowling alley, resplendent with new paint and a new sign, the sounds of cracking ten pins busting against the back of the lane. Every person could have a drink at the Greedy Pecker, although in heaven, Butcher was quite certain they'd have to rename it. That, or else God would continue to have an impeccable sense of humor.

And somewhere on the other edge of town, a place prepared just for him and Rhonda, right next door to George and Mabel; a perpetual late afternoon glow, lightning bugs polishing their bulbs for their pre-nocturnal flight. Crickets would be singing loudly causing the sky to echo with Utopian glee. And the Jensen's would sit, lean back and enjoy, laugh and love.

Amicable.

As he pondered the glow to the east, he smiled.

And grunted.

I love you, Amicable.

The wind shifted and pushed the hair poking just above the top of his chair.

317

It was time.

Without a second thought, Butcher put his wheelchair into motion. Even though the wheels caught once on the decking, the power was greater, and with a splash, Butcher and his machine fell into Lake Ikmakota.

The chair turned over quickly and sank. For the first time, Butcher was fearful that he'd made a mistake. Silently he wished he could take it back. Maybe they'd find a cure in the next months – a way to reverse the dreadful disease. But then a voice, somewhere subsonic, a scratchy and breathless voice, unfrightening arose from the depths.

You're almost there, Leopold Jensen. You're almost there.

As Butcher's chair sank three feet below the surface of the water, the moonlight was still visible and his left hand floated up with a mind of its own. His four fingers floated in front of his vision, a final wave to the world and the moon, his guide to the other side.

Butcher's chest began to heave and the pressure he felt caused his adrenaline to pulse through his veins.

Good job, Butcher.

You're there.

The pain was only momentary. When the light appeared, drawing him closer, he was quite sure, positive, actually, that his imagination had been severely lacking.

Chapter 10.

Leopold Jensen's funeral was the most widely attended event in the history of Amicable. Anyone who had known Butcher in any way arrived to pay their last respects. Knowing that St. Clements would not be large enough to hold the mourning crowd, Amicable High School opened up its gym doors and filled it with chairs. Even this space, which sat over two thousand people, was not big enough. Closed circuit televisions were set up in some of the classrooms so that everyone could see and hear.

In his instructions for the ceremony, Butcher asked that no one wear black. He asked that most wear orange or blue, the color of sky and sun, but greens or yellows would do also. As per his wishes, anyone who wanted to say something had to keep it to less than two minutes.

No one followed his wishes.

People could not say enough about the man they called Butcher. Everyone called him friend. Each ended their memory saying, 'I love you.'

The last person to speak was the youngest. Most people stayed just for this moment. J.T., decked out in a sky blue suit, strolled to the front. John Thomas Deakins, his godfather, unashamedly weeping as the little man came forward, set a footstool behind the podium so that J.T. could see over. Everyone noticed how tall this young boy was going to be. Most of them thought he was already nine or ten years old, but when he spoke, his small voice resonated with the innocence of youth.

John put his hand on J.T.'s shoulder who smiled up at John. "It's okay, Unca John. I'll be all right," he said bravely.

J.T. looked out over the crowd. From his position, he could see the lines around the eyes of Amicableans. He could see their

319

heartbeats in their throats. He could sense even the pulse in the wind, for this was his father's gift and he would share it with them.

His dad had written the eulogy which of course, J.T. had memorized. He took a deep breath and confidently pulled down the microphone to his mouth.

"My name is J.T. Jensen. My dad died. But he said not to cry, if you can help it." This brought a slight laughter through the tears. "When my dad was getting sicker near the end, he asked if I would say this for him."

"So, it's all in here." He tapped his head. "'But even more importantly,' my dad told me, 'is that it's all in here.'" He tapped his chest. "This is what he wanted to say." J.T. looked to his right where his father's coffin was stretched out. It was an extra-long coffin, or at least that's what the funeral director said, and it was draped with various kinds of plants and pictures. His dad's face, a picture of him in full laughter, his hands thrown in the air, was positioned right in the middle. J.T. like that picture best.

"I love you. You are my family and my friends, my neighbors and my colleagues, my closest human connections. A while ago, I stopped saying goodbye because it doesn't mean anything, and I started speaking words of love. It transformed me. It works. You should try it."

Despite the sadness, faces were smiling.

J.T. took a deep breath focusing on the upcoming words. "Nobody teaches you how to die. There's no class in high school or college, no exam or paper, that prepares you for the practical test. In some places, lots of people try to tell you how you should live; if you buy a certain product or drive a certain car – Studman." J.T. had been practicing how to say Stedman's name just like his dad, which used to make Butcher laugh uproariously, "or drink a certain number of beers, Peterson twins…"

"Or even waste enough time pretending that sports or art or any other diversion is more important than spending time with people you love. If you want my opinion, that's the slowest and most painful way of death. That's a strangulation of the soul. My disease, ALS, was kind in comparison to that." J.T. pounded his small hand on the podium just like his dad had taught him. This made many in the crowd jump.

"Now that we've got that cleared up," J.T. continued, "I think it's important for you to know the truth. Dying is not fun, but each of us is slowly dying every day – we all know it. The clock is ticking down, the sand is rushing through the hourglass, whatever meta…" He paused. "Unca John, what's that word again?"

"Metaphor," John whispered.

"Oh, yeah, mephator." Laughter.

"However, you see time running past you, don't keep your eyes on the clock, but keep them on your family and your friends, your neighbors and yourself, too. In this, you will find that time ceases to matter. When you feel scared, visit your friends. When you feel hopeless, visit your church. When you feel joyful, walk across the street and knock on your neighbor's door and say, 'I just had to tell you this!' Share your happiness even more than your sorrow and then," J.T. put up a finger like his dad said, "you win at life."

"I've never been a person with a lot of words – not like a few of you in town, Linda, Leona, Carley…" The three women tittered delightedly at being mentioned in the eulogy.

J.T. took a breath and stepped down off his stepstool and asked John to hand him the microphone so that he could stand and finish. They had practiced this. J.T. moved to the center of the dais.

"My dad told me to speak from my perspective to finish. My dad said that he loved being a husband, a father, a friend, a colleague and a butcher, but what he loved most at the end?"

Silence, rapt and attentive for the last word.

"He loved being from Amicable." J.T. smiled, just like his dad told him, and placed the microphone softly on the floor beside his leg.

Almost on impulse, the entire town of Amicable arose from their seated positions in the gymnasium and began to clap and whistle and cry and shout and sob and unroll every emotion that life had and laid it on the casket of one of their beloved.

Butcher.

At the graveside, a hollow, elongated hole had been dug for the final resting place for Leopold Jensen's remains. A small tent had been erected just beyond the grave where the mourners, still wearing their bright colors, sat preparing for the internment. John Deakins, no tears left to cry, spoke the words without feeling but full of meaning. A small headstone sat in front of the grave with Butcher's name, date of birth and date of death, but nobody noticed. What did attract their attention, though, was a life-sized sculpture behind the grave. Demetrius Chandler had created what would be called one of art's greatest masterpieces. As a re-enactment of Michelangelo's Pieta, Rhonda was holding the limp form of her beloved on her lap. Rhonda's face full of sorrow yet somehow tinged with hope (Demetrius had done a miraculous job making it so lifelike) stared down at the irenic face of her husband who lay across her lap. His large form, too large for her lap, was made from wax. As a symbol of Butcher's disease, Demetrius had carved his body to melt and drip to the ground as the years went by.

What Rhonda didn't know was that as Demetrius had carved the memorial, he had placed her hands underneath Butcher's heart, where he had left a gift – a secret.

When Butcher's form finally faded from sight, where his heart had been, was a small box of soil and in the soil was a seed –

a dormant Indian lotus seed.

After all was said and done, new life would spring from the heart of the old.

The End.

www.ingramcontent.com/pod-product-compliance
Lightning Source LLC
Chambersburg PA
CBHW070059120726
47909CB00002B/440